The Oakhu

B

Alex R Carver

THE OAKHURST MURDERS DUOLOGY

First edition. August 5, 2018.

ISBN: 978-1386783312

Written by Alex R Carver.

WRITTEN IN BLOOD: THE OAKHURST MURDERS #1

Prologue

"**I** said stop!" Georgina was as surprised as He when she slapped him, it was completely out of character.

She sat there for several long moments, too stunned by what she had done to move, while He pulled back, the hand he had been sliding up her leg now at his cheek. It was only when he reached for her again, this time with something other than lust in his eyes, that Georgina found the impetus to move.

She fumbled with the door next to her and tumbled from the Land Rover when she got it open, hitting the ground with a wet splat.

Under other circumstances she would have been concerned about getting her dress muddy, and what her mother would have to say; just then, though, she had other things to worry about, most important of which was the groping and grasping fingers of the person she had thought she knew.

Scrambling to her feet she looked around wildly for a means of escape. To her right was the farmhouse the yard they were in belonged to - there was no help to be had there, the house was a burned-out ruin that had been unoccupied for years. To her left was the drive, at the end of it was the road to the centre of Oakhurst - going that way would mean going past the Land Rover, and Him, which she was too afraid to do. The third option open to her was the overgrown field in front of her, on the far side of which was some woods - there was no help to be had in that direction, if anything it led further away from help rather than towards it, but it led away from the person she now feared, and that was more important.

All of that flashed through her mind in a fraction of a second, too quickly for her to be aware of it, and then she was off. She wasn't the fastest runner she knew, but she was faster than her pursuer; she reached the fence, climbed it, and was ten yards into the field before he was even halfway to the fence.

"Get back here, you bitch!"

The shout – harsh, cruel and loud – was so unexpected that Georgina couldn't help slowing to look back over her shoulder. The look of insane rage on His face was a shock, she had never seen anything like it. She had thought she was scared when she scrambled from the Land Rover, now she knew what it was to be terrified.

His footsteps pounded and echoed in her ears, the sound made her heart beat so fiercely she thought it was going to burst from her chest, while beneath the mud that coated her hands she could feel her palms sweating.

She was so intent on what was behind her that she wasn't aware of what was in front and she stumbled on the uneven ground. Terror and shock made her want to scream, but before she could she hit the ground, burying her face in the mud and grass, which left her unable to utter so much as a syllable.

Georgina was almost on her feet when He caught up to her, crashing into her like a rugby player desperate to keep the opposition from scoring. He knocked the air from her lungs and crushed her to the ground with his body. The weight disappeared after a moment as He lifted himself, so he could roll her onto her back, but before she could refill her lungs he had a hand at her throat, choking her.

"You fucking bitch! Look what you've made me do," He snarled, screaming the words even though his face was barely a foot from hers. "I was just copping a feel; why'd you have to overreact?"

Georgina was a passive person usually, but when He began pawing at her, as he had back in the Land Rover, she found the courage and the strength to fight.

She clawed at the hand that groped at her breasts and tore at her dress, and then at the hand that was squeezing her throat. When she failed to stop him that way, she reached up to his face, searching for either his throat or his eyes, the two areas she knew instinctively were his most vulnerable.

He continued to tear at her dress and grope at her with one hand, while he took the other from her throat to keep her hands from his own. Once, twice, three times he pushed her groping hands away, until finally he got angry – angrier – balled his hand into a fist and punched her.

"Lie still, you little bitch," He ordered. His blow rocked her head to the side, so that she was no longer staring up at him. "If you don't fight, this won't hurt." He immediately gave the lie to his words by hitting her a second time, splitting her lip and drawing blood.

Georgina was afraid of what he was now capable of doing, and that fear, and the adrenaline it flooded her system with, gave her the strength to throw him off her with a sudden heave. It came as such a surprise when his weight disappeared that she almost didn't react in time to free herself.

It was a second or so before she realised she could move, and once she did she scrambled out from under him, hitting him in the groin in the process. His face twisted into a grimace of agony, while his mouth hung open, though no sound escaped him, and his hands clasped at his balls.

Her chest heaving, Georgina rolled onto her front and, with an enormous effort, pushed herself to her feet. She glanced quickly in the direction of her attacker but saw no sign of movement, which was a small comfort to her, and then set off across the field towards the trees.

Her face hurt from the blows she had been struck, her throat felt as though his fingers were still around it, squeezing, and her lungs ached from the effort of trying to get air into them while he was strangling her; she couldn't move quickly so she half walked, half jogged, her eyes fixed on the trees at the far edge of the field.

She would have been better off circling around and returning to the yard, from there she could reach the village in about five minutes. Even if He used his car, there was little chance of him catching her, let alone stopping her, before she reached safety. None of that occurred to her, however, her thoughts were fixed on reaching safety, and she had already decided that safety lay within the trees she was heading for.

"Get back here, you bitch!"

Her fear, which had been beginning to subside, returned at that, and Georgina felt a fresh burst of adrenaline flood her system. She spared a brief glance over her shoulder and saw that He was on his feet again. The sight of him pursuing her spurred her on and she covered the final twenty or so yards in under five seconds, slipping between the trunks and into the darkness of the woods when she got there.

Despite having reached what her mind thought of as safety, she didn't stop, not until she had gone another thirty or so yards into the trees and felt certain he couldn't find her.

Georgina rested with her back against the trunk of a large oak and took deep breaths to calm herself. It was hard for her to achieve any measure of calm, for every slight rustling noise she heard made her heart thump a little more rapidly in her chest as she imagined Him creeping up on her.

"Where are you, Georgie? Come on, where are you? I'm sorry, I didn't mean to hurt you. Come on, I'll take you home. I promise I won't hurt you again."

Georgina heard Him crashing through the woods as he searched for her and remained frozen where she was, determined not to give herself away. It was only when the sounds of his approach grew nearer, and she felt certain He must find her at any moment, that she moved. Frightened, she slipped away through the trees as quietly and as quickly as she could, heading, she hoped, towards the far side of the woods, and the river that would lead her back to the village.

Leaves, twigs, and branches all slapped and caught at her as she fled, but she made no effort to defend herself from them. Instead of fending off the foliage she clutched the torn fabric of her dress to her chest in a vain effort to protect her modesty and searched the belt at her waist for her mobile phone; dismay joined with her fear as she realised she had lost it.

How long it took her to make it through the woods to the far side, she didn't know, but the relief she felt when she did was incredible. That relief disappeared as quickly as it had appeared when she realised she could see no sign of the village.

Her eyes darted rapidly left and right as she tried to figure out where she was, and, more importantly, where the village was; she should have been able to see the steeple of the church, but not even that was visible. The only evidence of human habitation she could see were the ruins of an ancient stone building atop a hill a short distance to her right.

Georgina turned to her left, so she could follow the river, which was bound to lead her to the village, eventually, but had only taken half a dozen steps when He came crashing out of the woods. His chest was heaving, and his hair and clothes were a mess of leaves and twigs, which gave him the appearance of a crazed woodsman from a horror movie – the sight magnified her fear to even greater heights.

"There you are, Georgie, I've been looking all over for you."

Georgina felt like a rabbit in the headlights of an oncoming car; her brain screamed at her to run, the direction didn't matter so long as it was away from Him, but her body wouldn't cooperate. She was glued to the spot, and could only watch as he approached, one slow step at a time.

1

The nervousness that had afflicted Lucy Goulding since she left her parents' house seemed to grow with every step. She had set out with just a single butterfly fluttering about her stomach, but now she was almost at her destination her stomach roiled and churned with what seemed like thousands.

Her nervousness was made all the worse by her lack of familiarity with the feeling. She was the only daughter of the richest family in Oakhurst, was worth more than anyone she went to school with, and was one of the most attractive people she knew; because of that she had never encountered a situation where she couldn't do or have what she wanted, so she had been given little cause to experience nerves during her young life.

A loud tut made Lucy forget, momentarily, about her butterflies. She looked around without slowing and saw Constance Hawkins in her front garden; the elderly woman was shaking her head disapprovingly, and when she saw where Constance's gaze was fixed, on the point where her micro mini-skirt stopped, Lucy grinned. It amused her to think that she was probably showing more leg publicly than Constance had ever shown in private, the thought buoyed her and made some of her nervousness disappear; if her outfit was disapproved of by Constance Hawkins then she had chosen the right one.

"Afternoon, Mrs Hawkins," Lucy called out cheerfully, before the overgrown hedge that surrounded the house next door cut off her view of the old woman.

ZACK WILD'S ATTENTION was diverted from his laptop by a sudden flash of colour, which he saw out the corner of his eye, but when he lifted his head to look out the window he saw nothing. He had just decided that it must have been a bird when the doorbell rang.

He cursed the interruption, and was tempted to ignore it, he was on a roll with his writing and didn't want to lose his momentum. The courtesy his parents had drilled into him wouldn't let him do so, however. It might have been easier for him to ignore the doorbell if he was still living in Southampton, where the person at the door was as likely to be someone from a charity, pestering for a donation, or a political canvasser, as a genuine visitor. Here in Oakhurst, though, the odds of the person at his door being a genuine visitor were much higher, and he didn't have enough visitors that he could afford to ignore any.

With an unhappy sigh, Zack pushed his chair back from the desk and got to his feet.

The greeting that rose to his lips died there when he caught sight of the person on his doorstep. The first thing he saw was a pair of tanned legs, followed by a red micro mini-skirt that was only a little bigger than a belt, then a red top, cut low to show off the cleavage and so skin-tight he couldn't help thinking that it must be at least one size too small. From the skirt and top his eyes took in the rest of the figure, which he liked very much – he could not remember the last time he saw someone in such a revealing outfit, at least not in person - before moving up to the face.

He quickly cut off his thoughts when he saw how young his visitor was. She had the body of a woman, but it was clear from her face that she was a teen, no older than sixteen. He couldn't think why such a provocatively-dressed teen would be on his doorstep at any time, let alone at a quarter past two on a Friday afternoon, when he was sure she should be at school, and for a few moments he just stood there, staring.

"Hello," he finally managed to say.

"You're Zack Wild," Lucy said excitedly, the last of her nerves gone now that she was there and she saw how he looked at her – the same way almost every other male did, regardless of their age.

"That's right," Zack agreed. He was still getting used to people reacting to him in that fashion, though he didn't think he would ever become truly comfortable with the semi-fame that came with being a best-selling author. "And you are?"

"Lucy, Lucy Goulding, I'm a huge fan," she declared breathlessly. Her nervousness might be gone, chased away by her usual confidence, but she wasn't yet in complete control of herself – she was as attracted to Zack Wild as she suspected he was to her, and his looks were having an effect on her.

"Hello, Lucy," Zack shook her hand briefly. "I wouldn't have thought my books were the sort of thing a girl like you would read," he said. He was not interested in such things, but his agent had provided him with a breakdown of his reading audience, which told him that it was mostly twenty to forty-five-year olds that read his books.

"Oh, I absolutely love them," Lucy enthused. "I love them all. I've read everything you've written. I borrowed the first one from my dad, and just had to get the rest. Your true crime books are great, but I prefer your Inspector Deakins books. Would you sign them; I've brought them all with me."

Zack watched in amusement as Lucy took the rucksack from her shoulder and knelt to open it. He saw that she wasn't lying, she had brought copies of all seven of his books, in hardback no less.

"Will you sign them?" Lucy asked, looking up at Zack from her kneeling position, her most winsome expression on her face.

The question drew Zack's attention away from the books in the bag, though before it reached her face it came to rest on her cleavage. Her cleavage was not as large as his ex-wife's, but it was generously displayed by her revealing top, and he felt distinctly uncomfortable when he remembered that she was a teen and he shouldn't be looking. Despite that, he couldn't seem to drag his eyes away.

"Mr Wild?"

Zack flushed and wrenched his gaze from the view he knew he shouldn't be enjoying. When he found her face, he was surprised to see that she didn't appear to be bothered by his ogling, to the contrary, there was a hint of a smile playing about her lips; that suggested to him that she was amused rather than annoyed or upset.

"Sure, I'd be happy to sign them," he said once he recovered his composure. "Let me get a pen."

"Can't I come in?" Lucy asked. "I didn't just come for your autograph, though I do really want that."

"What is it you want?" Zack asked, his hand on the door as he prepared to close it at the first sign of the trouble he now sensed was in the air.

"I want to be an author, like you," Lucy said. "I'm writing a book. I was hoping you could give me some tips, and maybe some advice on getting it published. Please, it's the only thing I've ever wanted to do; when I heard you'd moved to the village, I thought it must be a sign."

If there was one thing Zack had learned over the years, it was how to tell when someone was lying, and he didn't get the feeling Lucy was. "You'd better come in then," he said, opening the door wide.

He was closing the door when he glimpsed movement through one of the bare patches in his hedge. He frowned. He liked Constance Hawkins, she was generally a pleasant and friendly person, but she was curious about the limited comings and goings of her neighbours, and not all that discreet in her curiosity. He couldn't make up his mind whether to be concerned, or amused, by what Constance Hawkins was likely to make of him inviting a barely-dressed teen into his house; one thing he was certain of, was that news of his visitor was likely to be all around the village in next to no time, whether he cared or not.

He put his overly inquisitive neighbour from his mind as he closed the door and followed his visitor into the living room. He arrived in time to have his eye caught by something bright orange on the sofa - it was a moment before he realised that it was his guest's underwear, being revealed by her too short skirt.

A half-smile, a duplicate of the one he had seen when Lucy knelt on his doorstep, made Zack realise the flash was deliberate, that she wanted him to look. She had said she wanted his help, and from what he had seen so far, she was prepared to offer herself to get it, or at least to suggest that that was what she was willing to do. If it wasn't for all that he had seen during his former career, he would have had a hard time believing anyone capable of acting in such a way.

"Would you like a drink?" he asked from the doorway, doing his best to ignore the orange that peeked out again as Lucy shifted position. He hoped she did, he wanted a chance to recover his equilibrium, and to do something about his parched throat.

2

Lucy was pleased with how her visit with Zack Wild had gone; he had not come right out with a declaration of interest, but she knew when someone was attracted to her, and was sure that attraction would get her what she wanted. He had already agreed to her returning with her manuscript, so he could look it over – she was not vain enough to think that her, as yet unfinished, novel was perfect, it needed work, and that was where Wild came in - and help her make it better. More importantly, he had agreed to get his agent to read it when it was done.

With her mind occupied by her successful visit with Zack Wild, it was no surprise that she was unaware of the Land Rover until it skidded to a halt, practically on her heels, as she took a short-cut home. It startled her out of her thoughts and made her jump; when she came down she spun around to see what had caused the noise – it was a green Land Rover, identical to the one she had just passed in Zack Wild's drive, though she couldn't tell if it was the author behind the wheel for the sun was reflecting glaringly off the windscreen.

Lucy remained blinded as the driver's door opened, and so had no idea who it was that shouted at her.

"Whore! Cock-teasing whore!"

There was such anger and hatred in the voice that it was impossible for her to be sure who it belonged to. Her inability to tell who was speaking, she could tell that it was a man but that was it, combined with the anger and hatred to make her concerned, even a little afraid.

"What's your problem?" she demanded as she moved around the Land Rover, so she could start back the way she had come – it occurred to her that leaving the road to cut across the field was not such a good idea, and that returning to it was probably the best thing she could do.

"You. You think people don't see what a cock-teasing whore you are, but they do." The anger in the voice increased. "You dress like a tart; you act like one as well. You make everyone think they can have a piece of you, if they do what you want. You buy your grades with your body, you buy everything with your body, and you don't care who you buy it from. You'd fuck Sir Virgil if it'd get you something you want."

The verbal attack, especially the suggestion that she would sleep with her own great-uncle, struck Lucy like a physical blow and left her reeling. She wanted to say something, anything, to defend herself, but no words would come.

"It's time you learned what happens to cock-teasing bitches."

Lucy wanted to break into a run, she was a good runner, and was sure she could outpace whoever the Land Rover belonged to, but she realised she should conserve her energy until she needed it. She also realised that running would put her in danger of tripping on the uneven ground - she had seen enough horror films to know what happened to pretty, young girls when they were chased by a maniac.

"You're just like Georgie."

Lucy felt a ball of cold dread settle heavily into her stomach at that; Georgina had been missing for a week, and now she had the unpleasant feeling she was going to find out what had happened to her fellow teen. That knowledge didn't help her, though it did intensify her desire to get away before she suffered the same fate.

It was just as well she had one eye over her shoulder, for He suddenly rushed around the Land Rover and lunged towards her. She reacted the moment she saw him get close; pivoting, she slid her bag off her shoulder and swung it with all her strength. Her timing could not have been more perfect, the bag crashed into her would-be attacker just before he reached her, throwing him into the side of his vehicle, from there he fell to the ground at the edge of the waist-high golden corn.

Dropping the bag, Lucy ran for the gate. She couldn't be sure if she was being pursued, she didn't dare risk looking back in case she lost her footing, but she believed she was. The thought spurred her on until, after she had covered about a third of the distance to the gate, what she had feared would happen did, she stumbled and fell, her momentum sending her sprawling along the dirt path.

Winded more than hurt, she scrambled to her feet, where she discovered she had sprained her ankle. She was reduced to a hobble after that, and over her own, too slow, footsteps she could hear Him getting closer. She thought about calling for help, but decided she was better off saving her breath for her flight; the only person who might hear her was Constance Hawkins, and that was doubtful given how far away her house was.

She made it about half-way to the gate before being caught. One moment she was moving at a fast hobble, the next she felt a sharp pain as she was yanked off her feet by her hair. She landed on her back and was then spun around to face Him, before being pinned to the ground as he sat on her.

"Think it's funny d'ya, hitting someone with a bag of books?" The question was snarled in a voice that remained unrecognisable, though there was something familiar about it that time. "How 'bout this?" He smashed his fist into the side of her jaw. "Think that's funny? How 'bout this?" He hit her again, and then reached down to grab her skimpy top, which tore as he gave it a quick yank.

Lucy was dazed by the two blows, but she was a fighter. She couldn't see clearly enough to be sure of where she was aiming, but that didn't stop her lashing out. She bucked and heaved, writhed and twisted, but most of all she struck out again and again with her fists as she sought to make Him either get off her or shift his weight, so she could get away.

When her efforts failed to get Him to move, or even to stop his painful groping of her breasts, Lucy changed tactics. Instead of lashing out blindly, landing blows that had barely any strength, she sought to use the only weapon she had that might do some damage – her nails.

Lucy had only a moment to enjoy drawing blood and a quick curse, for her defiance inflamed his anger. He hit her again and again, until he succeeded in knocking out two of her teeth, one of which she managed to spit out before it went down her throat, the other she didn't. She was unconscious before her jaw broke with a sharp crack, which was a blessing since it meant she couldn't see the lust-filled expression on His face as he finished tearing her top in two, and then ripped from her the scrap of bright orange that protected the last vestiges of her dignity.

3

Michael Black was elbow deep in soapsuds when the front door banged open. Since the weather was pleasant, he could only conclude that someone had entered the station, an angry someone since calm people didn't bang doors.

Knowing that angry people didn't like to be kept waiting, he pulled his hands from the sink and grabbed a tea-towel to dry off with as he made for the reception counter.

"Good evening, Mrs Goulding, how can I help you?" he asked when he saw who was waiting for him.

Theresa Goulding fixed the constable with her sternest look. "There's nothing good about this evening," she said stiffly. "My daughter is missing; I want you to find her."

"Your daughter – Lucy?" Black queried.

"Of course, Lucy, who you did think I was talking about? I have only the one daughter, as you should know."

Black flushed at that but didn't respond, instead he said, "When did you last see Lucy?"

"What difference does that make?" Theresa demanded. "She's missing, and I want you to find her, that's all that matters."

"It's not as simple as that, Mrs Goulding," Black said, wishing that he were not the one stuck dealing with this problem. "Lucy is sixteen..."

Theresa flared up again. "I know how old Lucy is, what difference does her age make to her being missing?"

"A lot. Being sixteen, Lucy cannot be reported missing until she has been gone for at least a day, unless you have cause for concern. Given her history, and her habit of doing whatever she wishes, I think it likely the inspector will insist that we wait until Lucy has been out of contact for forty-eight hours to make a search. There's every chance she's off with friends, probably in town. She'll turn up when she's finished having fun."

"Forty-eight hours! You want me to wait two days before you'll consider looking for Lucy? How can you even suggest such a thing? Especially when poor Georgina Ryder is still missing after a week, and you have no clue what's happened to her. Don't try and deny it," Theresa said sharply when Black opened his mouth to respond. "Did you even look for her after the first day?"

"We searched for her," Black said defensively. "We searched the entire village, and we spoke to just about everyone; no-one saw her after she headed up the road to the Wright Farm, though. We've searched again and again, throughout the week, but there's been no sign of her.

"You can't compare the two situations, though," he told her. "Georgina Ryder has never been in trouble, and she's always told her parents exactly where she was going, what she was doing, who she was meeting, and when she would be home. The same can't be said for Lucy; Lucy has a long history of bunking off school, staying out all night, getting into trouble, and associating with people she would be better off avoiding."

"I am well aware of my daughter's history, more so than you, I imagine. It is irrelevant on this occasion, however," Theresa said. "No matter what she might have done in the past, or how she may have acted, I can assure you, Lucy is missing on this occasion."

"Can you tell me what makes you so certain the circumstances are different this time?" Black asked, curious to know why Theresa, who had never been concerned about her daughter before, was concerned now.

The look on Theresa's face suggested she thought the question rude in the extreme, nonetheless she answered him. "I'm certain Lucy is missing because she was supposed to meet her father, myself, and her great-uncle, Sir Virgil, for dinner at The Oaks. She was supposed to be there early to greet Sir Virgil, he comes to stay every couple of months, when his work permits – The Oaks was his first hotel and he has always been especially fond of it, and when he visits he expects to be met by Lucy. She wasn't there, nor did she show up for dinner."

"Perhaps, on this occasion, Lucy decided she didn't want to have dinner with her great-uncle," Black suggested. "Maybe there was something she preferred to do, and that's where she is now." He braced himself for an explosion that didn't come.

"Under other circumstances, Lucy might well have decided not to do what her father and I wished; when it comes to her great-uncle, however, she's a different person to the girl you know. She's polite, punctual, respectful, considerate, everything you could want of a daughter."

Black tried to reconcile that description with the Lucy Goulding he knew and found it difficult. "Okay, so you have reason for concern," he conceded. "But there could be any number of reasons why Lucy wasn't at the hotel to greet Sir Virgil, or at the family dinner. She could have gotten involved in something and lost track of the time, she could have missed the bus, or been unable to get a lift back to the village."

"If that had been the case, she would have called either me or her father, or Anna. Sir Virgil is a stickler for punctuality, Lucy would have called if she was going to be late, so we could give her apologies. I was put in the most uncomfortable position of having to lie to Sir Virgil; I told him that Lucy was at home, ill. I can only hope he never discovers I lied to him, he hates liars, even more than he hates people who aren't punctual." Her unhappiness was clear. "Something has happened to Lucy, that's the only possible answer, and I want you and your colleagues to find her, without your usual bungling and bumbling."

Black ignored that comment; instead of reacting to it he chose to act as though Theresa Goulding had a case to be dealt with. "When and where did you last see Lucy?" he asked, pen poised.

"What on earth difference does that make?" Theresa wanted to know. "She isn't a set of keys, to be found in the vicinity of wherever she was last seen."

"Of course not, Mrs Goulding, I'm sorry if that's how it sounded, but to find Lucy I need to know where and when she was last seen, what she was wearing, who she was with, and, if possible, where she was heading."

Theresa scowled at the constable before sighing. "I last saw Lucy this morning before she left for school, Anna will be able to tell you what time that was; she was wearing her uniform, so I assume she was intending to go to school. That's as much as I can tell you," she said. "Anna may be able to tell you something more."

"And she hasn't been seen since then?"

"Since lunchtime."

"Who saw her then?"

After taking all the details Theresa could provide, Black promised to look around the village, and to make sure that both the inspector and the officer on duty in the morning knew Lucy was believed to be missing.

As soon as she was gone, slamming the door to make it clear how dissatisfied she was, he locked up the station and completed the end of shift chores he had been in the middle of when Theresa arrived.

He was about to get into his car, so he could do as promised and drive around the village looking for Lucy, when he thought better of it. Instead of getting into his car, he wandered down the road, stopping at a house a short distance from the station, a house rented by a trio of troublemakers, one of whom was the person Lucy Goulding was supposedly dating. If Lucy was in the village, he thought it most likely that she would be there with Ollie Ryder.

The house being quiet and dark, he doubted anyone was home, but he thought it best to knock before making a tour of the village, just in case. He didn't want Theresa to be able to say he hadn't done everything he could to find her daughter.

4

Lucy Goulding stirred at the sound of an approaching vehicle. Her chin lifted from her chest, so she could search the darkness that surrounded her; the movement was minimal, but enough to reawaken the pain caused by her arms being tied above her head so that she was suspended from something, she didn't know what, the pain that had earlier made her decide it best to stay as still as possible.

She wanted to scream but didn't, she knew it would be pointless; not only was her jaw broken, a gag had been stuffed into her mouth while she was unconscious. Even if she could make a noise, it wouldn't go anywhere.

It was a minute or so after she first heard the approaching vehicle that it came to a stop, and the sound of a door opening and then slamming reached her. A few moments later a door was opened across from her and light flooded in, revealing her prison; she had been hung, naked – she had no idea where her clothes were – from a beam in an old barn. She had suspected she was in an abandoned building of some kind from the smell, which she now knew was that of rotting straw, but had no idea where.

There was no time for her to look around and see any more than that, her attention was caught by the figure that entered the barn. For a moment there was nothing but a black silhouette, then He moved closer and she was able to see him more clearly. She couldn't believe who had attacked her; she was so astonished that He reached her naked figure before she could recover from the surprise.

"Let me go."

"What was that, I couldn't make it out. You're mumbling." He reached up to remove the gag.

"Let me go," she said again, trying to make something more than a barely audible, unintelligible noise.

He cocked his head to one side, as though he was trying to listen more closely, and then he shook it. "Nope, can't make out a thing, you're still mumbling." He reached a hand up, as though to caress her cheek, and grabbed her jaw, sending fresh pain shooting through her as he waggled it back and forth. "You need to move your lips if you want people to understand what you're saying."

The comment amused him, and he laughed at his own wit. His laughter died quickly when Lucy lashed out with her feet; her left foot struck him in the arm, which he ignored, but her right caught him in the groin. His eyes widened, and his face went white with pained shock as he doubled up.

Lucy was pleased she had hurt him but couldn't help wishing she had hurt him more seriously.

"Think that was funny, do you?" He demanded when he recovered. "You've obviously learned nothing about behaving. I guess you need a lesson."

The pleasure Lucy felt at having hurt Him disappeared when she saw him pull his belt off and fold it in half. She felt a cold shiver of fear run up and down her spine. She couldn't take her eyes off him as he smacked the belt emphatically into the palm of his other hand; the sound it made spoke eloquently of pain.

"My dad used to take a belt to me when I did something wrong, or he thought I had," He said, staring up into her face in a way that made her wish he would pay more attention to her naked body. "Let's see if it's as good at making you behave as it was me."

Lucy anticipated what was to come and prepared herself as best she could; despite that, the pain that came with the first lash of the belt was still a shock. Again and again he whipped her with the belt, making her body jerk and twitch. She would have screamed if she could; not only did the blows hurt, but the way her body moved in response to them made her shoulders howl in protest.

How long the assault continued for, she had no idea. All she was sure of was that by the time it ended, she couldn't tell where the pain was coming from, it seemed to be originating from every nerve in her body.

"That's the lesson out of the way," He said, his voice ragged from the exertion of whipping Lucy, as he tossed the belt aside. "I hope you've learned to behave, because it's time for playtime." He took a large lock-knife from his pocket and cut her down, letting her fall to the floor, while he began stripping the clothes from his sweat-soaked body.

Even before He unbuttoned his jeans to reveal his arousal, Lucy knew what he had in mind for her, and what he must have done with Georgina. She hoped her fellow teen had fought him, she didn't like to think that Georgina had simply given up and let him do what he wanted; there was no way she was going to do that. She hurt, worse than she would have believed possible, but she still intended fighting with every last ounce of energy she possessed.

5

"**M**itchell," he said groggily when his groping hand found the ringing phone and brought it to his ear.

"Sorry to wake you, sergeant."

"What's up?" Mitchell asked, recognising the voice of Constable Pritchard. "Has something happened?" He could think of no other reason for him to be called before seven a.m. on a Saturday, as the clock on the bedside cabinet told him the time was.

"There's been a report of a body being found."

Mitchell instantly became wide awake, though it was a moment or two before he could speak. "Did you say a body's?" he asked when he found his voice.

"That's right. The call came in just a few moments ago; that new guy, Wild, said he's found the body of a girl along the river near that old watchtower. He said she's dead – murdered."

"Murdered!" The word escaped his lips before Mitchell could stop it and he looked quickly over at his wife, who was still asleep. "Are you sure about that?" he asked as he slipped from the bed.

"I've not seen the body, so I can only go on what Mr Wild said, but he sounded pretty definite about it," Pritchard said. "I can't imagine why he'd lie about something like that."

"Me neither, you can never tell with some people, though, and it's not like we know Mr Wild well enough to tell what he might do."

"Do you think it could be Georgina Ryder?" Pritchard asked.

Mitchell went cold at that. The notion that the girl he and his officers had spent the week looking for was dead was not one he liked – the possibility that she had been murdered was worse – but he couldn't think who else the body could be, the village had only the one missing girl as far as he was aware. "Unless you know of any other Oakhurst girls that have gone missing, I think it has to be Georgina," he said, feeling no satisfaction at the thought of her having been found.

Pritchard hesitated for a moment and then said, "I wasn't going to mention it 'til you came in, I didn't think it was important, I mean, she's never home..."

"Are you going to get to the point?" Mitchell asked, pressing the phone to his ear with his shoulder while he struggled into his uniform.

"Mike left a note, Theresa Goulding came in last night to report Lucy missing."

"Damn," Mitchell swore, abandoning his efforts at getting dressed. It amazed him how quickly a situation could go from bad to worse. "Okay, here's what I want you to do; call Doc Kelly and Mel, tell them both I'll be by shortly to pick them up, then call the inspector. Chances are, Wild's wrong about the girl being dead, but just in case, the inspector is going to want to know what's going on."

"Wouldn't it be better to call Mike or Adrian?" Pritchard asked. "Mel's never dealt with a dead body before, perhaps now's probably not the best time for her first."

"No, I want Mel, she's got to deal with this kind of thing sooner or later. Besides, if I have to go and see the Ryders afterwards, Melissa will be more help than either Mike or Adrian. You'd better make those calls, Paul, I'll be at Doc Kelly's in a few minutes, tell him he'll need his bag."

MELISSA TURNER LOOKED down the bank at the rapidly moving river, and then over at her superior. It made her shudder just to think about what he wanted her to do.

"Wouldn't we be better off going back and crossing at the bridge?" she asked. "That water looks bloody freezing. I don't fancy going in there, and I'm sure it's not a good idea for Doc Kelly."

"Don't you worry about me," Kelly said as he settled to the ground and began rolling up his trouser legs. "I've never been bothered by a bit of cold water. It's that far bank I'm concerned about, it looks a little steep for my liking."

Mitchell looked across the river at the far bank and then at the doctor, before finally down at himself. He wasn't as large at the waist as the doctor, but he was still far from slim; climbing the far bank was likely to be as much of a challenge for him as for the doctor, but there was nowhere better.

"It'll be a struggle," he admitted. "But we'll manage. If we go back, it'll cost us three quarters of an hour, maybe more, and there's a dead-fall on that side, near the bridge, that's been threatening to drop for a year. I'd rather not be under it, if it finally decides to go."

Melissa thought that a bit of a weak argument – if the tree hadn't fallen in a year, it was unlikely to fall while they passed it. She suspected Mitchell had not even thought about crossing the river after parking at the pub and was reluctant to correct his mistake.

"I'll go first," Mitchell said. "Doc, you come second, Mel, you bring up the rear. Once I've got to the top I can pull you up, Doc, while Mel gives you a shove from behind."

The river at the chosen spot was only about fifteen feet wide, but it still took the three of them almost five minutes to make it to the top of the far bank. Most of that time was spent climbing the bank on the other side, which Melissa had no difficulty with, but which proved a struggle for her companions.

"IS THAT MR WILD?" MELISSA asked when they had gone another half a mile or so.

"I can't imagine we're going to find two people this far out from the village so early on a Saturday. Thinking about it, you're not likely to find someone out here any day of the week, regardless of the time. I wonder what he was doing out here," Mitchell said suspiciously before striding ahead so he could reach the man who had disturbed his Saturday morning lie-in. "Mr Wild, Sergeant Mitchell."

"Hello, sergeant." Zack held out his hand. "I know who you are, doctor." He shook the older man's hand when the other two had caught up. "My neighbour, Constance Hawkins, pointed you out to me in case I should have need of your services. I've not seen you before, though, constable, and I'm sure I'd remember."

Melissa flushed as she shook his hand, having been taken by surprise by the compliment. "Mel, Melissa," she stammered before taking a deep breath to calm herself. "Constable Turner I mean." She couldn't believe how she was reacting to the compliment, or more accurately to him – in shorts and a t-shirt it was clear that he kept himself in good shape, without being overly muscular, which she didn't like in a man – and the touch of his hand. "Nice to meet you."

"If you're quite finished," Mitchell said sharply. "You told Constable Pritchard, when you called the station, that you found a body; what can you tell me about it, the person you found, I mean."

"Female, mid-teens at a guess, but it's hard to say for sure," Zack said as he led the two police officers and the doctor around the bend in the river on his way to where he had made his discovery. "One thing I can tell you for sure, she was murdered, and she's been out here for at least a couple of days, perhaps as long as a week."

"How can you be so certain the girl you found was murdered?" Mitchell asked; he couldn't say why, but he was suspicious of the way the stranger talked so casually about murder, and how long he thought the body had been there. "And how did you find her?" He had to lengthen his stride to keep up with the younger man. "This isn't the sort of place people come without a good reason. Even the local fishermen use the other side of the village. The last person I can recall that came out this way was an archaeologist we had in the village last autumn, and he only came out here because of the old watchtower." He gestured to the ruined structure, which stood on a hill a short distance away, where it would have commanded a view of the river and the surrounding lands. "He seemed to think it's Roman, reckoned there's an old fort around here somewhere."

"I was out jogging, that's how I found her," Zack said. "I was heading along the other bank from the pub, saw something out of place, got curious, and waded across. Wish I'd ignored it and gone on jogging, I wished that before I was even sure what I'd found; wading the river wasn't my brightest idea.

"As for how I know she was murdered, there she is." He indicated with a nod of his head. "You'll understand when you see her."

"Bloody hell!" The oath escaped Mitchell the moment he got within a dozen feet of the girl Zack Wild had stumbled on. There was no question about her being dead, or about her having been murdered. He swallowed convulsively against the urge to throw up. "You'd better stay back, Melissa, you don't need to see this," he said when he had himself under control.

The warning came too late.

"Oh god!" Melissa turned away from the body on the ground, disgusted by the sight of what had once been a teenage girl, dropped to her knees, and vomited. She threw-up until there was nothing left in her stomach. Only when she was finished did she realise that she had emptied her stomach all over the feet of the man she had so recently met. "Sorry," she apologised in a weak and miserable voice.

"Don't worry about it," Zack said unconcernedly. Kicking off his running shoes, he carried them the short distance to the river, so he could wash them and his feet off.

"No, I'm sorry, they must be ruined now. Let me know how much they cost, and I'll pay you back."

"There's no need to do that," Zack told her. "I was thinking about getting myself some new running shoes, now I've got the perfect excuse for doing so, I should be thanking you."

Mitchell ignored both Melissa and Zack Wild as he moved closer to the body on the ground. His first glimpse of the girl had been bad enough, the sight got worse as he drew closer, though. Her face was such a mess it was all but impossible to tell it was a girl, let alone who she was, but that was nothing compared to the rest of her. There wasn't an inch of her body that wasn't either bruised or covered in blood; if she hadn't been naked, he wasn't sure he would have been able to tell her sex.

As if the injuries done to the rest of her body weren't enough, the person who had killed her had taken a knife – he assumed it was a knife – and carved letters into her stomach.

It was the letters that made Mitchell feel as though he was going to empty his stomach, as Melissa had. He simply could not imagine why someone would have done that, it was an act of evil beyond his comprehension.

"Is it Georgina?" he asked of the doctor, who was at his elbow.

Kelly studied the face of the girl on the ground dispassionately for several long moments. He was not as affected by what he was seeing as the two police officers – he had seen plenty of horrible things during his career as a medical professional – but was not unaffected, though in his case he felt saddened rather than disgusted by the scene.

Finally, he shook his head. "At a guess, I'd say it's Georgina, but I wouldn't want to be held to that. It could be just about anyone, if I'm honest."

Mitchell frowned. "Why can't you be sure it's her? You've been treating Georgina since she was a baby, you must have some idea whether it's her or not."

"The face is too badly damaged to say for definite who it might be. Georgina has a mole in that position." Kelly indicated the growth near the girl's left armpit. "But I wouldn't want to base an identification on it. You're good friends with the family, you've probably seen more of Georgina over the years than me, can't you say if it's her?"

Reluctantly, Mitchell was forced to admit that he couldn't. "I don't think I could be certain, if I thought I was looking at my own daughter," he said unhappily. "Could it be Lucy Goulding, rather than Georgina Ryder?"

"My gut feeling," Kelly said. "Is that this is Georgina, but I think you're going to have to rely on blood tests or dental records to be certain. Sorry, I wish I could be more help."

Mitchell clapped the doctor on the shoulder. "No need for you to be sorry. If I can't be sure who she is, I can't expect you to be. Can you give me any idea how she was killed? Obviously, she was beaten, severely, but was that enough..." Before he could finish, the phone in his pocket began ringing. He quickly excused himself, so he could answer it, though he was sure he knew who was trying to get hold of him.

Kelly used the excuse of giving Mitchell privacy for his call to get away from the body. He moved to where Melissa was standing with the village's newcomer and found them in conversation.

"Why do you say I'll be lucky if I don't see more murders like this?"

Melissa's face was ashen, and her voice trembled in a way that made Kelly worry she was suffering from shock.

"Because a murder like this is often only a beginning," Zack told her. "It's usually the result of someone bottling up frustration and anger until something or someone pushes them over the edge and they explode. When that happens, they generally react in one of three ways: either they immediately commit suicide out of remorse, they hand themselves in to the police, or they go back to bottling things up until they explode again. If they do that then each explosion is likely to be worse than the one before. Not only that but there's a risk they'll have enjoyed killing the girl and will actively want to duplicate the thrill. If that's the case, you're in real trouble."

MITCHELL MOVED AWAY from the body on the ground as he took his phone from his pocket. He preferred not to look at the young girl any more than necessary, and he was going to have to pay enough attention to her while investigating what had happened. "Sir," he answered the phone. "I wondered how long it would be before you called."

"Paul said he received a phone call from our new resident, Wild, saying he found the body of a murdered girl, is that true?" Robert Stevens, who commanded Oakhurst's small police force asked in a concerned voice.

"Yes," Mitchell said. The bloody mess that had been made of the girl's stomach sickened him, but he couldn't keep his eyes from straying to it repeatedly, despite him dragging them away every time it happened. "I'm at the scene now. There's no doubt about it, I'm afraid...she's been murdered."

"Jesus!" Stevens swore. "Paul also said Lucy Goulding's been reported missing by her mother. Is it..." His voice faltered, and it was a moment before he regained it. "Is it Lucy or...or Georgina?"

"I can't say for sure," Mitchell admitted. "She's quite a mess, she's been worked over pretty badly. It's hard enough to tell she's a girl from the state her face is in, without trying to work out who she is. If you push me, I'd say it's Georgina; the girl has dark hair, and the last time I saw Lucy, which was only yesterday or the day before, she had blonde hair. Not only that but Lucy was only reported missing yesterday, and I'm pretty sure the – the body has been here for at least a couple of days, not that I'm an expert or anything."

"What's Kelly got to say?"

"He's as unsure as I am. There's a mole he recognises, but he doesn't want to hang an identification on that." He could hardly blame the doctor for that. "He said it's probably going to take a blood test or dental records to be sure if we've found Georgina, or someone else."

"What about her parents?" Stevens asked. "Can't John or Verity make an identification? Surely they're best suited to say one way or another if the girl you've found is Georgina."

"I don't think so," Mitchell said, thinking back to his last visit to the Ryders. "They're not coping with things very well, especially Verity, and the body isn't very recognisable. Georgina, if it is her, must have gone through hell; her killer - he left her bruised and battered all over by the looks of it, especially her face, and something was...something was carved into her stomach – words, I couldn't make out what because of all the blood. I don't think either John or Verity would have much luck identifying her, and even if I thought they could, I wouldn't want to put them through it.

"I'm sure it will be a simple enough job for the pathologist to identify her from dental records or medical records or something."

"Okay, that's your decision, Lewis." Stevens changed subjects then. "I know you haven't long got there, and this is your first time dealing with a murder, but have you got any idea who could be responsible?"

"I wish I had a clue," Mitchell said. "I don't, though. I can't believe anyone in the village, anyone we know, could be responsible for this, but that only leaves Mr Wild." He dropped his voice, not wanting to be overheard. "I've never met the guy before today, so I don't have a clue what he might be capable of; if I'm honest, though, I can't see why he'd tell us about the body if he's responsible for it. Especially since, if it is Georgina, she's been here for up to a week without being found.

"Chances are, she would have remained here almost indefinitely without us knowing she was here."

Stevens was silent for a few moments. "I know what you're going to say, it doesn't make sense," he said eventually. "But you do hear of people who commit crimes, and then almost dare the police to catch them. I can't say I understand why anyone would do that, but they do; like the parents who go on TV to make an appeal for the return of a missing child, when they're responsible for the child's disappearance. Maybe Mr Wild is one of those kinds of people." He sighed, unhappy with the thought that someone like that might have moved to Oakhurst. "There is another possibility," he said, his mind racing as he sought alternatives to the unpalatable thought that someone he knew was a murderer.

"What's that?" Mitchell asked. He couldn't think of anything, he was still trying to wrap his mind around the fact that there had been a murder in his quiet little village.

"Someone from outside the village could be responsible," Stevens said. "It might even be that the girl is neither Georgina nor Lucy but someone from town, or even elsewhere. I realise it's pretty unlikely, but it is something we have to consider."

"Yes, sir." Mitchell had his doubts but chose not to mention them. "While I've got you, I need you to arrange a few things for me. I need a forensics team, Mike to come out here and keep an eye on the body until they can get here, and I need to know if you're going to get a detective to come in and handle the investigation."

"I think that's something we should discuss when you get to the station."

"...DON'T YOU DRIVE THAT Aston Martin I've seen around the village?"

Zack had to laugh at the question from the young constable, though he quickly stopped when he remembered they were at the scene of a murder. "You mean, how can I afford such an expensive car on a detective inspector's salary, especially when I'm not one anymore."

Melissa flushed, but didn't deny that that was the question she really wanted to ask. Before she could get an answer, however, Mitchell interrupted.

"You're a detective inspector?" He was surprised, not just because Zack Wild looked too young to have reached inspector's rank, but also because, like Melissa, he couldn't work out how he could own a car that had to be worth more than many of the houses in the village.

"I was, now I'm an author," Zack said.

6

Barefoot, his soiled trainers in a carrier bag found in the boot of Mitchell's car, Zack followed the two police officers up the stairs and into the police station.

He felt eyes on him and looking around he found himself an object of interest for those villagers who were out and about. Based on the suspicion and anger in the looks, he could only conclude that news of his discovery had already made it around the village, and that he was being fitted for the role of murderer in the eyes of the villagers. He supposed he couldn't blame them, a village wasn't like a town or city, where it was rare for a person to know more than two or three of their neighbours; in Oakhurst, everyone was likely to be related to, or at least know, everyone else. The only person for whom that wasn't true was him, which meant if anyone was going to be suspected of a brutal crime, it was him.

The anger and suspicion of his fellow residents disappeared from Zack's mind the moment he entered the police station. His feet were knocked out from under him by an elderly woman who was energetically mopping the reception area.

"Sorry," she apologised unconvincingly.

"That's alright," Zack dismissed the apology, while thinking that perhaps he had been wrong, and angry looks were not all he could expect. He got quickly to his feet and bent to retrieve the carrier bag holding his trainers.

"Are you alright, Mr Wild?" Melissa asked, coming back to help him, though he was already back on his feet by the time she reached him.

"It's through here, Mr Wild," Mitchell said before the author could answer his colleague's question. He made no effort to conceal his dislike of the friendly air that seemed to be developing between Melissa and Zack Wild.

"Thank you, sergeant," Zack said, ignoring the obvious lack of concern over his tumble. "I'm fine," he said to Melissa. "It's nothing paying more attention to my surroundings won't help."

With an unpleasant wet feeling on his feet, Zack followed Sergeant Mitchell through to the station's sole interview room, which didn't look big enough for the four people it was supposed to accommodate.

"We'll begin the interview just as soon as I've taken care of a few things, Mr Wild," Mitchell said before disappearing from the doorway without giving his interviewee a chance to say anything.

"Can I get you a drink?" Melissa asked. Unlike Mitchell, she hadn't taken an instant dislike to Zack Wild – if anything, she had taken an instant liking to him, in part, mostly, because he was attractive.

Zack nodded. "Thanks, my water bottle's just about out."

"Tea, coffee?"

"Coffee, white, no sugar."

"Be right back."

"HOW BAD IS IT?" INSPECTOR Stevens asked the moment Mitchell entered his office.

Mitchell didn't answer straightaway, he waited until he had taken a seat across from his superior. "Bad," he said finally. "You remember how bad James Goode looked after his tractor rolled on him?"

Stevens nodded, it wasn't something he was likely to forget; it had surprised everyone at the scene that the farmer had survived the accident, let alone that he made an almost complete recovery.

"Worse than that. She looked like a victim from one of those horror movies you see on TV late at night. Whoever killed her, he must have really hated her, or been really angry with her, because he beat the hell out of her. I mean he just beat the hell out of her. She had cuts and bruises just about everywhere I could see: arms, legs, body, face. God knows how many of her bones must have been broken." Mitchell had to take a moment to try and force away the memory of what he had seen. "I'm no expert, and Kelly's out of his depth with this, but it looks as though she was kicked and punched repeatedly; her face...it's just unrecognisable. It's so badly damaged it's almost impossible to tell whether it's a girl or a boy. If she wasn't naked I think it would have taken me a while to figure it out.

"That's not even the worst of it...I told you something was carved into her stomach."

Stevens nodded.

"Well I was able to make it out before I left – whoever killed her, he carved 'Tease' into her." He shook his head at the memory of what he had seen.

Stevens could only stare at his subordinate. "She's naked?" he asked finally, focusing on something he found less troubling. He was inexperienced in investigations, of any kind, but especially murder investigations, just like Mitchell, but he did think that the nakedness of the girl they believed to be Georgina Ryder was more important than the fact that she had been beaten so badly.

"Yes," Mitchell said with a slow nod of his head that made plain he was thinking along the same lines as his superior. "Near as dammit anyway. She had on the remains of a dress – it looked like it had been all but torn from her – same for her bra, and we found her underpants a short distance away. If you ask me, it looked as though they were ripped off her and simply thrown aside."

"Was she...?" Stevens couldn't bring himself to finish the question, and it was several long moments before Mitchell could bring himself to answer it.

"That's something the pathologist is going to have to answer when the post-mortem is done," Mitchell said finally. "But if you're asking my opinion." He hesitated for a moment before nodding. "Yes, I think she was raped. I think he beat her unconscious, ripped her clothes off, and then – then he did what he wanted with her."

There was silence for several long moments, during which time Stevens pulled a bottle of whiskey from behind the files in the bottom drawer of his desk. Two glasses joined the bottle on the desk, both of which he filled half full. He said nothing until they had both finished what he liked to call a good stiffener. When he had drained his glass, and the fire in his throat had subsided, he asked, "How was she killed? Was it the beating?"

"I don't have anywhere near the experience to answer that," Mitchell admitted, his voice a little hoarse after the strong liquor. "I'm inclined to think it was the beating, and Kelly's of the same opinion – he couldn't see any obvious signs of anything else that might have led to her death, though he did admit that a post-mortem might pick up any number of things he couldn't see. Mr Wild, however..."

"That's our newest resident, the gentleman who found our murdered girl, isn't it?"

"Yes, sir. He claims he's a former detective inspector." Mitchell was pleased to see his own disbelief mirrored in his superior's face.

"Isn't he only about thirty?"

"Mid-thirties I think; all I know for sure is, he's a damned sight younger than you or me. Anyway, he claims he's a retired detective inspector, he also claims that marks around the girl's throat mean she was strangled."

"Beaten, raped, and strangled. My God!" Stevens couldn't help gasping. "How did we ever reach the point where something like this could happen in our village?"

"I've no idea." Mitchell was as much at a loss as his superior. "You read about this kind of thing in the papers, but I never thought we'd have to deal with it here."

There was another period of silence as the two long-serving police officers tried to come to terms with things.

"What are the chances Mr Wild is responsible for the murder?" Stevens asked.

"I won't know that until I've spoken to him. He's in the interview room, waiting to give his statement. He didn't seem all that bothered by having discovered a body, but I suppose if he is a former detective inspector, he must be used to that kind of thing. Any chance you can find out if he really is an ex-DI?"

Stevens nodded. "It's likely to take me a while, unless you know what force he's supposed to have worked for."

"Not yet, but I'll ask him."

"Good. While I'm checking that out, I'll see what else I can find out about him. If it's not Mr Wild, who could have killed Georgina, if that is who's been found?"

"I have no idea," Mitchell admitted. "Either it's someone from outside the village, which seems unlikely given how far we are from anywhere, or it's someone we know, and I can't think of a single person in the village who could have done what I saw. If I hadn't seen it myself, I wouldn't have believed it possible for someone to do that kind of damage to another person." He shook his head at the image that crept, unbidden, into his mind. "You should be glad you weren't there, it was enough to turn your stomach; it was all I could do not to throw up – Melissa wasn't so lucky, she threw up all over Mr Wild's feet."

"Okay, so you're going to interview Mr Wild, while I see what I can find out about him, Mike is out at the body, keeping an eye on it, and I've got forensics on their way. I take it you're going to see the Ryders after you've spoken to Mr Wild."

Mitchell nodded. "I'd rather not, not until I'm more certain the body is Georgina, but we both know how rumour and gossip goes around the village. It's probably too late, but I'd rather they hear about this morning's discovery from me, at least that way they'll get the facts, what few we have, rather than whatever Jean Frost has overheard and embellished."

"Are you still set against them making an identification?"

"I'll do my best to talk them out of it. Verity will never be able to handle a trip to the morgue, she's been a wreck since Georgina went missing; I don't think John'll handle it any better, especially given the mess she's in, and I don't see any point in putting him through the ordeal when he's unlikely to be able to make an identification."

"I'll leave that up to you. Do you need anything, other than what I've already organised?"

"Yes, I'm going to need a search party to comb the woods around where Georgina was found; as many officers from town as you can get."

Stevens frowned. "Officers from town? Surely we can get enough volunteers from the village, why do we need officers from town?"

"Two reasons," Mitchell said, having had the time to think about what he needed. "Firstly, the villagers won't have a clue what they'd be looking for, they're likely to stop the search for every little thing that looks out of place, which means it'll take forever for the search to get anywhere. We can't afford to waste that kind of time. Secondly, if the murderer is someone from the village, not Wild, I'd rather not give him a chance to destroy any evidence he might have left behind."

Reluctantly, Stevens accepted the logic of that. "That brings me to the next thing, the chief inspector, I called him this morning to get the forensics team and he offered me a detective to handle the case, but said we can handle it ourselves if we wish, it's my decision, for the time being. What do you think?"

Mitchell's first instinct, which he almost went with, was to accept the offer. He held back, though, to give himself time to think. Finally, he said, "A part of me wants to say, 'get the detective', let him handle this, he'll know what he's doing. Another part of me thinks it's a bad idea. The village is going to have a hard enough time dealing with what's happened, without having a stranger come in and poke and pry about – they'd have no idea about anyone and will only jump to all kinds of wrong conclusions."

"I have to admit, that is a concern that occurred to me," Stevens said. "I'll tell the chief inspector that we'll handle things ourselves for now. I think he'll be glad, I got the impression he was wondering where he'd be able to find a detective for us. If things change, though, he'll have to find us someone. Talking of things changing, what do you intend doing about Lucy Goulding?"

"I hadn't planned on doing anything. You know as well as I do that Lucy is almost certainly not missing, she'll turn up soon enough, having been at a party or something, just like she usually is, and Theresa will have made a fuss about nothing."

"You're probably right, but under the circumstances I don't think we can afford to ignore the possibility that she really is missing."

MITCHELL FOUND ZACK Wild and Melissa deep in conversation when he entered the interview room. He wasn't happy with how friendly Melissa seemed to be with the man he was about to question, he said nothing, however, since he didn't want to antagonise his witness and possible suspect.

"Sorry to have kept you waiting, Mr Wild," he apologised. "I see Constable Turner got you a drink, is there anything else you need before we get started with this interview?"

"Thank you, no," Zack said. "She makes a strong coffee, I'm going to be bouncing off the walls as it is, without having anything else. I'd rather just get on with the interview, I'm sure we all have stuff to get on with."

"Fair enough, perhaps you can start by telling me how you came to find the body," Mitchell said.

"Sure. I was out for a run, saw something on the opposite bank, called it in, then waited for you guys to arrive," Zack said succinctly.

Mitchell stared at the man on the other side of the table for several long moments, not quite able to believe that that was all he seemed to want to say. "Can you expand on that for me?" he asked. "For instance, why were you out for a run? Is it something you do regularly, or a one-off?"

"Regularly," Zack answered. "I go running most mornings, it's a good way to keep myself in shape."

"Do you run the same route every morning?"

Zack shrugged. "More or less. I try to do about five miles every day, keeping to the same route helps me know how far I've gone, and gives me some idea of whether I'm keeping to a regular pace."

"Five miles?" Melissa blurted. "You must be really fit if you do five miles a day." The moment the words escaped her she found herself blushing, she sounded like a schoolgirl with a crush.

A smile played about the corners of Zack's mouth. "I guess fit is a matter of perspective," he said. "The older I get, the more exercise I have to do just to keep my weight stable. Working used to keep me pretty fit, but now I'm stuck at a computer all day, I've got to work that much harder not to go to flab."

"If you run the same route every day," Mitchell said, far from pleased with the way the interview was going. "How is it you didn't see the body until this morning? I'm not an expert, but it looked to me as if the body – he found it easier to think of the body as simply that, rather than as a former person – had been there for a couple of days at least. Surely you should have seen it before now."

"I said more or less," Zack pointed out. "Usually I follow the road through the village and out towards town; it's nice, straightforward, and it's easy for me to know how far I've gone. The downside, though, is it's boring," he said with an exaggerated roll of his eyes. "Since the weather was so good this morning, compared to what it's been this past week, I thought I'd take a different route on my run; I do that every now and then. A change is as good as a rest, as they say. I only got as far as the pub before I decided not to bother with my usual route; I turned off the road, so I could head along the riverbank, and found the body after about a mile and a half, well, you saw where she was." Mitchell nodded. "If you left the road at the pub, how is it you saw the body?" he asked. "It was right at the edge of the trees, not easy to see from the East bank, especially with the grass about a foot tall, as it is there."

"I couldn't see it clearly," Zack admitted. "I caught a glimpse of something in the grass, that was all; unfortunately, I've had enough experience of dead bodies to be pretty sure of what I was seeing, even if I couldn't see it clearly. I didn't want to call you guys, and lady," he said with a nod towards Melissa Turner, "out there until I was positive, though, so I waded across to make sure my eyes weren't deceiving me. I wish they had been. I thought I left all that sort of thing behind when I left the force."

"Have you seen many bodies?" Melissa asked, curiosity getting the better of her desire not to annoy her superior.

"Too many," Zack said. "Of course, one is too many, as I'm sure you'll agree."

Melissa nodded. "I hope you're wrong about the body you found just being the first," she said. "Because I don't think I could ever get used to what I saw this morning."

"You never really get used to it," Zack told her. "At least most people don't. You sort of become inured to it, so you can keep going and do your job. It's when you become used to it, if you ever do, that you have to start thinking about whether it's time for you to stop and find something else to do."

"Is that why you stopped being a detective?" Melissa asked, realising too late that it might sound rude.

"If you don't mind," Mitchell said irritably. "What did you do after you were sure you had found a body?" he asked of Zack Wild.

"I called the police station to report it, then I went up to the bend in the river to wait for you guys to get there."

"You didn't check to see if she was alive or anything?" Mitchell asked. "Constable Pritchard said that when you called the station you said she was dead; did you check to be certain?"

Zack shook his head. "There was no need. I knew she was dead as soon as I saw her. It would have been a waste of time to check, and doing so would have put any evidence there might be at risk. My old boss would crucify me if I did something like that, being retired is no excuse."

Mitchell spent a few moments absorbing that before he posed his next question. "If you didn't get close enough to risk any evidence, why did you insist on your trainers being bagged up for the forensics team? Surely they won't find any trace of you on or around the body."

"No, they won't," Zack said confidently. "But if the forensics guys are at all thorough, they'll check the ground for some distance around the body for evidence, and take casts of every shoe print they find; once they've done that they'll want prints from the footwear all three of us were wearing this morning, so they can eliminate us from whatever they find." It had been some time since he last had to explain forensics procedures to anyone. "If they want to be really thorough, they'll even take our DNA and fingerprints."

"Had you ever seen the girl before this morning?" Mitchell asked, not at all happy to be having his job explained to him.

"That's hard to say," Zack told him. "Given how unrecognisable she was, I could have seen her every day and I wouldn't know it. Do you have any idea who she is?"

"We have reason to believe her name is Georgina Ryder, she's been missing for a week."

"The name's familiar; I heard around the village she was missing, but since I didn't have a face to put to the name, it meant nothing to me," Zack said.

"So, you can tell us nothing about her disappearance and murder?"

"Sorry, no," Zack answered, doing his best to ignore the accusatory note in the sergeant's voice.

7

Melissa stood at the police station door, watching Zack Wild as he walked off up the road, seemingly unconcerned that he was barefoot, having left his running shoes at the station for forensics.

She had been there for half a minute or so when she became aware of a presence at her elbow. Turning, she found that Mitchell was standing there, his eyes on the author, a look of distaste and annoyance on his face that Melissa found troubling.

"You think he had something to do with the murder, don't you," she said.

Mitchell shrugged, and said unconvincingly, "I don't know. He has an explanation for his discovery of the body, one that could be true, or could be completely made up. Right now, we have no reason for thinking he's lied to us, and a number of reasons for thinking he's telling the truth. If he's connected to the murder, why would he have led us to the body? And why would he tell us he didn't touch the body and voluntarily give us his trainers, that doesn't make any sense if he's the murderer."

"But you think he might be involved in the murder, so why didn't you question him about it more?" Melissa didn't believe Zack Wild was a murderer, though she realised she didn't know the man and so had no idea what he might be capable of; despite that she couldn't understand why the author had been allowed to leave without being questioned more thoroughly.

"Because I've got no evidence, and if he is the killer, I don't want him to know I'm on to him until I do," Mitchell told her. "The inspector is making inquiries into Mr Wild to find out if he really is a former DI, and whatever there is to know about him. Hopefully, when we know something of the man, we'll have some idea of whether he could be the murderer. If he isn't, we'll have to start looking elsewhere, at the rest of the village."

Melissa could tell Mitchell didn't like the thought of having to do that, it wasn't something she particularly liked either. "How long until the forensics team, and the detective who's going to handle the investigation, get here?" she asked.

"The forensics team should be here in another hour, hour and a half," Mitchell told her. "But there won't be a detective, at least not for the time being." He saw Melissa's surprise. "The inspector and I discussed having a detective and decided it would be better for the village if we try and solve this ourselves."

"What are we going to do to catch the killer then?" Melissa asked, wracking her brains to try and think how an investigation should be conducted.

"First things first," Mitchell said. "We need to go and see John and Verity to let them know about this morning's discovery, assuming they haven't already been told. After that we need to talk to everyone we spoke to last week, when Georgina first went missing, they may remember something now that they didn't at the time. We also need to speak to anyone who might have held a grudge against her. Then we need to speak to Theresa Goulding, her housekeeper, and anyone who may have seen Lucy yesterday, before she apparently went missing, so we can try and find out what's happened to her, assuming she hasn't already come home."

"HELLO, JOHN, CAN WE come in?" Mitchell asked when the front door opened.

The man who stood in the doorway looked, understandably, to be in the midst of a nightmare, Melissa thought as she took in his rumpled clothing, the stubble on his chin, and his generally unkempt appearance. She had never seen him look less like the accountant he was – he looked more like a homeless person.

"Ha-have you found Georgie?" John Ryder asked.

Mitchell inferred from that question that his friend had not heard from anyone in the village that morning. "We should talk inside," he told his friend, his voice neutral to avoid giving either hope or cause for alarm.

"You have, haven't you, you've found Georgie," John said in a stricken voice as he stepped back to let the two constables in.

"We may have," Mitchell said as he entered and made his way into the living room. "I'm sorry, but the body of a young girl was found first thing this morning, early indications are that it could be Georgina. We still need to confirm the identity of the girl," he hastened to say, "and that could take some time."

"What do you mean you need to confirm her identity?" John wanted to know. "You've known Georgie all her life, you're the closest thing to an uncle she's got, surely you can say if it's her or not."

"The outfit matches what you said Georgina was wearing when you saw her last, but there are complicating factors that make it hard to say for sure who the girl is; the length of time she's been out there, the weather during that time, and the fact that she was..." Mitchell hesitated for a moment and then went on. "There's no easy way to say this, John, but the girl found this morning was beaten – beaten to death, that's why it's hard for me to say that it's definitely Georgina."

"Georgina was murdered?"

The shocked question came from the doorway, not the sofa, and three pairs of eyes turned in time to see Verity Ryder collapse to the floor in a dead faint. John was on his feet in an instant, so he could hurry over to his wife, and with Mitchell's help he got her to the sofa, where he set about trying to revive her – it took a short while.

"Is Verity right?" John asked hesitantly once his wife was fully revived, and he had assured himself that she was going to be alright, or at least as alright as anyone could be under the circumstances. "Was Georgina – was she – murdered?"

Mitchell would have preferred not to be asked the question, but since it had been asked, he couldn't ignore it. "Based on what I saw this morning..." He nodded heavily, sadly. "Yes, the girl that was found this morning was murdered. But," he went on quickly to try and forestall a second collapse from Verity, "we don't yet know for sure that the body is Georgina."

"How can you not know something like that?" Verity snapped. Although she appeared frail, and overwhelmed by the strain of her daughter's disappearance, sitting there in the protective embrace of her husband, there was a strength to her voice. "You've known Georgie all her life, and honestly, how many missing girls can there be in the village?"

"As of Theresa Goulding's report last night, two," Mitchell told her. "Georgina and Lucy, and there's always the possibility that the girl that was found is someone from outside the village. A slim possibility, I know, but one that can't be ignored at the moment."

"If you're not sure it's Geor-Georgina," John said, his voice catching in his throat momentarily. "Why're you here? Can't you see what an effect this is having on Verity?" He tightened his arm around his wife's shoulder, pulling her closer, as if to comfort her, though she seemed less in need of comfort than he did.

"I appreciate that, John, Verity, and if I could have avoided this visit, I would have, especially while the identification is uncertain," Mitchell told his friends. "We all know how quickly gossip goes round the village, bad quicker than the good, though. Sooner or later, and more likely sooner, someone would have been in touch to tell you about the body that was found. Most likely they would have taken a small amount of information and embellished it out of all recognition. I thought, and Inspector Stevens agreed, that you would prefer to hear what was going on first-hand, from me, and to hear the facts, few as they are."

John digested that for a while before nodding. "You're right. There's a lot of people in the village who like spreading gossip, no matter how bad, and they're none too careful about getting things right when they tell people what they've heard. I wish, with all my heart, that we didn't have to hear this, that Georgie would come walking through that door like nothing's happened, and she's only been gone for a few hours, but I think we both knew, when she didn't come home that first night, that something had happened. She's such a good girl, she'd never stay away from home without contacting us, not even for a night, not unless something happened."

Mitchell was a little disturbed by the way his friend's attention wandered, and how it seemed as though he was talking to himself. He made no mention of his concerns, however, just then wasn't the time.

"Was Georgina really murdered?" Verity asked. "Could it have been an accident?"

"As I said, we don't know for sure the girl found this morning is Georgina, we still need to confirm her identity. As for whether she was murdered – I wish I could say otherwise, give you some comfort, but yes, I believe she was. It will be for the pathologist to say for certain, however, once he's completed the post-mortem."

"A post-mortem? Is that really necessary?"

Mitchell nodded. "I'm afraid so; apparently, it's a legal requirement under the circumstances. It'll establish how she died and help confirm whether it is Georgina."

John roused himself from the reverie he had fallen into. "Shouldn't I go to the morgue and see if I can identify Georgie?" he asked.

Mitchell's immediate thought was that it would do no good for John to go to the morgue, the odds of him being able to identify the girl were somewhere between slim and none. He didn't say as much, though, for he suspected that going to the morgue would provide John with a measure of closure he wouldn't otherwise get, despite the circumstances.

"One of you should," he said, after thinking about it. "I'm not sure how much success you'll have with making an identification," he admitted. "But if you can, even if you're only able to say that it isn't Georgina, it will provide us all with an answer, rather than waiting for the results of whatever tests the pathologist has to run."

"I'll go," John said decisively.

8

Mitchell was about to ring the doorbell for a second time when he heard approaching footsteps. He immediately dropped his finger and stepped back to wait.

Nigel Hunter wore an expression that could only be described as one of resignation when he saw who was on his doorstep. "What's Kelly done now?" he asked as he automatically stepped back to let Sergeant Mitchell and Constable Turner enter his home. "It's not her, you know, it's that Lucy Goulding," he said in a well-worn defence of his daughter. "I've lost track of how many times I've told Kelly to stay away from her – she just won't listen. It's only a matter of time before the pair of them get themselves in real trouble, and I just don't have the money the Gouldings do; they'll get Lucy off and Kelly will be left holding the can."

"Calm down, Nigel," Mitchell told the younger man as he passed him. "As far as I know, Kelly has done nothing wrong. I do need to speak to her, though, is she in?"

Nigel snorted. "In, she isn't even up yet. If she didn't have to be up for school, she'd never be up before midday."

"Would you mind getting her up? It's important that we talk to her."

"She won't like it," Nigel said, nonetheless he made his way up the stairs after closing the front door.

While Nigel headed upstairs, Mitchell and Melissa made their way into the living room, where they took seats on the sofa. Raised voices came from above them after a minute, and a short while after that heavy footsteps descended the stairs; it could not have been more obvious that the approaching person was a teen who was determined to make it clear that they were not happy about something. Mitchell was reminded of Harry Enfield's character from the 90's, Kevin the angry teenager.

"What d'you want?"

Mitchell bit back the urge to respond to the rudeness of the question; he should be used to it, he knew, but somehow it annoyed him afresh every time Kelly Hunter spoke to him like that.

"Good morning, Kelly, sorry to have woken you," he apologised. "But I need to ask you a few questions. Would you have a seat?"

"I ain't done nothing," Kelly said automatically as she entered the room and dropped gracelessly onto the sofa. "Neither's Lucy."

Mitchell's irritation increased as the teen pointedly ignored him. "I need to ask you about Georgina Ryder," he said, speaking loudly to be sure he was heard over the TV Kelly had turned on. "When did you last see her?"

Kelly scowled. "You already asked me that last week," she said without taking her eyes off the TV.

"I know I did." Mitchell was tempted to turn the TV off, but he didn't imagine that would encourage Kelly to pay attention to him, so he left it. "Things have changed since then, though, and I'd like to see if you've remembered anything new. So, when did you last see Georgina?"

"Last Friday." Kelly waited until the music video she was watching finished to answer the question. "At school," she expanded when pushed. "I saw her at the end of school; Lucy and me were on our way into town, we saw her at the bus station, she was waiting for the bus back here."

"And that's the last you saw of her?"

Kelly nodded, though her eyes never left the television.

"You're certain of that, you didn't see her at any point after you returned to the village?" Mitchell wanted to know.

"You've got to be kidding," Kelly said with a laugh. "I didn't get back to the village 'til well after Georgie's bedtime. Before you ask, I don't remember what time I got back, but I've heard Georgie say before that she's always in bed by eleven, even at the weekend, and it was way after that."

"I can vouch for that," Nigel spoke up from by the door. "It was around half-one when Kelly got home. I remember because I was up, waiting for her. I was worried when she wasn't back on the last bus, and spent hours wondering when she was going to get home, and how."

"I'm never on the last bus, you should know that by now; I'd have to be home before ten if I was." Kelly looked at her father as if he was crazy. "Nothing happens before ten, nothing worth doing anyway. I did the same as I always do, I got a lift home."

"And I hate to think who from. I can just imagine the kind of person who'd come so far out of their way to bring a teen girl home – nobody does that without being after something."

Kelly laughed again. "Most of the time it's Ollie who brings us home, and he's already getting what he wants."

"Ollie, Oliver Ryder?" Nigel moved round so he could see his daughter's face. "You're telling me you've been hanging around with Oliver Ryder, even though I've told you to stay away from him and his friends?"

Mitchell spoke up quickly to head off the argument he could see brewing. "This is something the two of you can talk about later, once we're finished. Can you think of anyone who might have wanted to hurt Georgina?" he asked of Kelly. "Someone with a grudge against her perhaps."

"Are you kidding, who'd want to hurt her? Georgie's a goody two-shoes pain in the ass that most of us want nothing to do with, but I can't think of anyone who'd hurt her. Even if someone did want to, who'd be crazy enough to do anything, we all know she's Ollie's cousin and he's crazy about her and would do anything for her. If anyone did dare do anything to Georgie, they'd have to deal with Ollie, and we all know how that would go." The bored expression she had affected dropped away and she turned her attention from the TV to the sergeant. "Something's happened to her, hasn't it."

Mitchell hesitated for a moment, reluctant to say anything. He realised there was no point in keeping what had happened from her, though, not when she would hear about it soon enough. "Yes," he said with a quick nod of his head. "This may not be easy for you to hear, but first thing this morning, the body of a girl was found in the village, we believe it's Georgina."

"Bloody hell!" Kelly swore, her face pale with shock.

Nigel went even whiter than his daughter. "Wh-what happened to her?" he asked in a voice that shook.

"Get a grip, dad, Jesus!" Kelly told him. Once over her initial shock the colour returned to her cheeks and she showed enough animation to ask, "How did she die? Was she killed? I bet she was killed, that's why you want to know if anyone would hurt her."

"Don't be morbid," Nigel told his daughter, even though he had only just expressed his own interest.

The look Kelly threw her father's way showed she knew how hypocritical he was being. She said nothing to him, though, instead she turned her attention back to Mitchell. "Come on, what happened to Georgie? I'm right aren't I, she was killed. How? When? Who by?"

"Behave," Nigel told his daughter, with more sharpness than either Mitchell or Melissa had ever heard him use before. "Whatever's happened to Georgina, you should show some respect, not act like it's something exciting to tell your friends about; she's a friend of yours as well."

"No, she's not," Kelly denied quickly. "We used to be friends, ages ago, but we haven't been friends since Mayfield's. I'm sorry she's dead, but I'm not gonna pretend to be sad when I'm not, and I'm not gonna pretend not to be curious about what happened when I am. So, come on, what happened to her? Was she killed?"

As distasteful as he found the teen's morbid curiosity, Mitchell couldn't help admiring her honesty. He nodded. "Yes, she was killed. Are you certain you can't think of anyone who'd want to hurt her?"

"There's no-one. Honestly, I don't think Georgie could have upset anyone enough to make them want to hurt her, not even if she tried, she just didn't have it in her."

"Clearly someone wanted to hurt her," Mitchell said before changing the subject. "When did you last see Lucy?"

Kelly reacted to the question as though she had been slapped. Her legs shot out from under her, she sat bolt upright, and an expression of anger settled over her face as she glared at Mitchell. "Lucy ain't done nothing," she said, leaping to the defence of her friend. "I don't know what you think she's done, but she didn't do it."

If looks could kill, Mitchell thought as the teen's glare struck him. "I never suggested she has," he said, annoyed by Kelly's reaction. "I simply asked when you last saw her."

"Why d'you want to know?" Kelly asked suspiciously. "If you're not after her for something, why d'you want to know when I saw her?"

"Because her mother has reported her missing." Mitchell saw the shock that overtook the anger on Kelly's face and went on quickly. "We don't have any reason for thinking anything has happened to her; given her history, there's every chance that she's simply gone off somewhere and hasn't come home yet. Theresa Goulding is concerned, though, and with this morning's discovery we're taking that seriously. Now, I understand you spoke to Mrs Goulding yesterday, and told her you hadn't seen Lucy since lunchtime, is that right?"

"Nope," Kelly said with a shake of her head.

"No, that isn't right?" Mitchell asked. He was annoyed when he received only a nod. "Which part? Did you not speak to Mrs Goulding yesterday, or yesterday lunchtime isn't the last time you saw Lucy?" He felt like he was trying to draw blood from a stone.

"I never spoke to Lucy's mum; it was Anna who called me."

"Okay, so it was Mrs Becker you spoke to, you did tell her you last saw Lucy at lunchtime, though, didn't you?"

"Uh huh." Kelly nodded, then volunteered. "At the bus station, she was coming back here."

"Back here, to Oakhurst, you mean? Do you know why?" Mitchell was not surprised to hear that Lucy Goulding had bunked off school.

"She said she was meeting someone. Don't ask me who, she never said."

"Could it have been Oliver Ryder she was coming back to see?" Melissa asked.

Kelly shook her head quickly and decisively. "Lucy would've told me if she was coming back to see Ollie; I'd've bunked off and come with her so I could spend the afternoon with Tom."

"Tom, Tom Bottle?" Nigel leapt angrily on what his daughter had said. "You're seeing that criminal? What have I..." He was interrupted by Mitchell before he could say anything more.

"If you don't mind, this is another conversation you can have another time. I appreciate that Lucy didn't tell you who she was coming back to see, but did she say anything that might have hinted at who it is?" he asked of Kelly.

A short while passed before Kelly answered. "She said she was coming back to see someone who could make all her dreams come true."

"Have you got any idea who that might be?" Mitchell asked. When Kelly shook her head, he tried another tack. "How about Lucy's dreams, do you know what they might be, what she might have been trying to get help with?" He couldn't imagine why Lucy would have needed to see anyone other than her great-uncle to make her dreams come true.

Kelly shrugged. "Get rich, get a fit guy, have an easy life. Aside from that, the only thing I've ever heard her talk about is writing."

"Writing? What sort of writing?" Melissa asked, a suspicion creeping into her mind. "Was Lucy interested in writing novels or something?"

"She says she is," Kelly said. "She's always scribbling in a notepad, or typing something into her phone, and she says she's writing a book, but she's never let me read any of it. Not that I'd want to, I'm not into reading. Can't think why she'd want to be a writer, but I can't think of anything else I'd call a dream for Lucy."

"Does Lucy know a Zack Wild?"

"Who?" Kelly asked. "Never heard of him. If she does, she's never told me. Wait," she said suddenly, "is that the new guy that moved into the village?"

Melissa nodded.

"Never knew his name."

"So, you don't know if Lucy knows Mr Wild," Mitchell said.

Kelly shook her head. "If she does, she's kept it a secret from me; can't think why she'd do that, though." After a moment, a thought occurred to her. "Is he hunky?" she asked.

"Pretty hunky," Melissa said, looking embarrassedly at Mitchell.

"Maybe she was keeping it from Ollie, not me," Kelly said, speaking more to herself than to the two officers. "He wouldn't be happy if he found out she was seeing someone else."

Mitchell didn't doubt that Oliver Ryder would be unhappy if Lucy were seeing someone else, and he wondered if that could be the reason she hadn't come home. It was something to consider, but not immediately helpful to them in finding Lucy.

9

Melissa couldn't see much, but that didn't stop her trying to watch the house in the wing mirror as Mitchell drove them back down the road towards the centre of Oakhurst. All there was to see was her grandmother, who was pottering around her front garden – of Zack Wild, who they had gone to see, there was no sign.

"D'you think he's actually out, or in and trying to avoid us?" she asked after finally abandoning the wing mirror and settling back in the passenger seat.

Mitchell shrugged. "That fancy sports car of his isn't in the drive, so I'd say he's out, but you never know. I can't think why he'd be avoiding us, though, not unless he's the killer; even then I can't see him avoiding us – he doesn't know that we know Lucy is apparently missing, or that we have reason for thinking she might have visited him.

"Hiding or just not in, we'll have to try again later. Right now, I want to speak to Oliver Ryder before we go and see the Gouldings."

Melissa didn't relish the thought of dealing with Oliver Ryder at that time of the morning, and she was slow to exit the car when they reached their destination. She knew from experience that Oliver and his friends were reluctant to talk to the police at the best of times, and it was usually best to wait until after noon to speak to them. Mitchell had no such concerns, however, and strode up to the front door, where he waited for Melissa to make her way around to the back door, as per his instructions.

When there was no response to the doorbell, he banged on the door, and then stepped back so he could shout, "Open up, it's the police," loud enough to be heard by Oliver and his friends even if they were still in bed.

The movement of the curtain in the front bedroom was minimal, no more than a quick twitch as someone peeked out, but Mitchell spotted it.

"We're not here to arrest you, we just need to talk," he called out, returning to the front door so he could ring the bell and bang his fist on it again, though he doubted his words would get anyone to the door any quicker.

MELISSA HEARD MITCHELL'S shout and listened for some indication that the house's occupants had too – it didn't take long. Within moments of Mitchell's second shout, she heard thunderous footsteps approach the back door. She tensed, one hand on her extendible baton, while she waited for the door she was standing at the side of to open; it did so with a bang and Melissa pushed away from the wall.

Tom Bottle and Simon Deacon got themselves jammed, momentarily, in the doorway, as they both tried to exit the house at the same time. When they freed themselves, they burst into the garden, straight into the leg that Melissa stuck out to trip them up; they went down in a tangled heap of arms and legs that made them look like some weird, many-limbed creature.

"Morning, boys," Melissa said cheerfully. "I guess you didn't hear Sergeant Mitchell. We only want to talk to you, so there's no reason for you to be running off anywhere."

"Since when have you guys ever only wanted to talk to us?" Tom Bottle wanted to know as he extricated himself from his friend. "You always think we've done summat. Well, we ain't done nowt, so you can bugger off and look elsewhere for whoever did whatever's been done."

"If you've done nothing wrong, why were you running?" Melissa asked, though she didn't give either of the two men a chance to respond. "Come on, on your feet and back inside. If you cooperate, and don't give us any hassle, you'll both be back in bed before you know it," she told them. "Where's Oliver?" she asked as she shepherded Simon and Tom back into the house. "He's normally the first one through the door."

"He's not here," Simon said.

"Where is he?"

"He's out."

"I gathered that, where?"

"What's it matter?"

Melissa didn't bother answering, instead she headed for the front door, after seeing Simon and Tom into the living room, so she could let Mitchell in.

"Good work, Melissa," Mitchell said when he saw the two in the living room. "But where's Oliver? Don't tell me you let him get away."

"There was no sign of him," Melissa said, a little offended by her superior's suggestion. "He didn't try and make a run for it, like these two."

"Where's Oliver?" Mitchell asked of Simon and Tom as he crossed to the stained armchair opposite the sofa they were on, where he reluctantly sat.

"Not here," Tom answered, with an abruptness that suggested it was all he was going to say.

Mitchell got the impression Tom was not about to reveal where his friend was, he had to ask though. "Okay, so, where is he?" As he did so he signalled to Melissa that she should make a search of the upstairs, in case Tom was lying, which was likely. "If he's not home, where is he?"

"Not here," Simon said in a frustrated voice. "Tom told you." He followed Melissa with his eyes as she left the room and started up the stairs.

"He didn't say where, though," Mitchell pointed out. "And don't try and tell me you don't know where he is, it won't wash."

Tom scowled at his friend, but it didn't stop Simon, who was the weaker of the pair, answering. "He's at work."

"Work? Do you take me for an idiot?" Mitchell asked. "Oliver hasn't done a day's work in his life, not honest work anyway. Where is he really? Somewhere he shouldn't be, I'll be bound."

"I told you, he's at..." Simon's insistent words were interrupted by the return of Melissa, who shook her head briefly to indicate that she had not found Oliver Ryder during her quick search of the three bedrooms and one bathroom. "Work," he finished. "See, if I was gonna make something up, don't you think I'd come up with something better?"

Mitchell could hardly deny that; Simon was not the most creative of liars, but he was capable of coming up with something more believable than Oliver being at work.

"If Oliver has a job now, where's he working, and what prompted him to turn away from a life of crime? Assuming he has. He's never showed the slightest inclination to do anything legit before."

Tom scowled at Simon again, but then went on to answer the question himself. "He's working at the golf course, training to be a gardener or something," he said. "Georgie talked him into it. You know what Ollie's like when it comes to Georgie, he'll do anything for her. She told him he needed to straighten up and get a job, then she saw the job at the golf course and got him to apply for it.

"What're you doing here anyway, we ain't done nothing."

Mitchell couldn't help but snort at that. "I'm sure that's a lie; if it's not, it'd be the first time in history. That's not why I'm here now, though. I need to speak to Oliver. Since he isn't here, I'll talk to the two of you. When's the last time either of you saw Georgina?"

"What the hell," Tom said angrily after his momentary surprise had passed. "You've dragged us out o' bed, she's tripped us up, and all because you wanna ask us 'bout Georgie. You already asked us 'bout her last week; you know when we last saw 'er."

"I know what you told me at the beginning of the week, but I'm hoping you'll have remembered something fresh that will help us, especially given this morning's discovery."

"What discovery?" Simon asked.

"I guess you two wouldn't know, since you've both been asleep," Mitchell remarked. "Not that I suppose anyone would have called you anyway, given that neither of you is all that popular. Early this morning, the body of a young girl was found by the river, it looks like it's Georgina." The reaction he got was just what he might have anticipated.

"Bloody hell! No way! You sure?" The exclamations and questions came tumbling from the lips of Tom and Simon in unison, falling over one another.

Mitchell waited until the two had calmed down and were no longer urgently denying any knowledge of the death, to say anything more. "We're as sure as we can be at this time," he told them. "Now, I need you both to tell me everything you can remember about the last time you saw Georgina. I don't believe either of you had anything to do with her death," he said loudly and quickly to make himself heard over the protestations of innocence.

"Sit down and shut up," Melissa finally shouted at the pair, who hovered somewhere between sitting and standing. "If you'd listen instead of making an unnecessary racket," she said when they fell silent, "you'd have heard that we don't think either of you had anything to do with what's happened to Georgina, but we do need to know whatever you can tell us, so we can figure out what did happen."

Mitchell was both surprised and pleased by the way Simon and Tom did exactly as Melissa told them. "Right, now you're ready to listen, when did you last see Georgina?" he asked.

It was Simon who answered first. "Georgie was here last Friday, as we told you before," he said. "Musta been 'bout six, half-six, when she got here. It were a flying visit on her way to see Kieran, she said; that pissed Ollie off and he told her she should dump him – he's always telling her to dump him. Georgie ignored him, like usual, and told him the house was a mess, that were normal as well. She washed the dishes in the sink, asked him 'bout his job, and told him she'd be 'round in the morning to clean up the house. She left after 'bout twenty minutes. That's the last I saw of her."

"What about you, Tom?" Mitchell asked.

Tom shrugged. "Same. Haven't seen her since then."

"Has Oliver?" Mitchell wasn't sure if either Tom or Simon would know whether their friend had seen or heard anything from his cousin, but he had to ask. "He's not mentioned hearing from her?" he asked when both men shook their heads. "And I take it Georgina didn't show up the next morning to clean the house." From the appearance of the living room, which he was sure was representative of the house, the place hadn't been cleaned in quite some time.

"No." Simon shook his head. "She didn't show up, and Ollie hasn't heard from her. I know he's tried calling and texting all week, but no luck. He's not gonna like it when he hears how she's been found."

Mitchell didn't need Simon to tell him that, he could easily imagine how Oliver was going to react – explosively would be understating it. It was just a question of who the explosion would be directed at, and that was something he didn't fancy taking bets on, especially when he was one of the possible targets.

"Okay, so you can't help us with Georgina; I assume you don't know of anyone who might have wanted to hurt her." He couldn't even bring himself to feign hopefulness as he waited for his answer. "When did you last see Lucy?"

"Lucy," Simon groaned, though it was unclear why the question should have prompted such a reaction. "Whatever she's done, we weren't involved in it," he said, hastening to distance himself from the teen's troubles.

Tom was quicker on the uptake than Simon, he realised almost immediately that there was a connection between the discovery of the body that might be Georgina and the question about Lucy. "What's happened to Lucy?" he asked, leaning forward to stare intently at Mitchell.

"We don't yet know that anything's happened to her," Mitchell said. "But her mother has reported her missing. She hasn't been home since she left for school yesterday morning." He quickly held up a hand to forestall the barrage of comments he could see coming. "I know it's far from unusual for Lucy to stay away from home for more than a day, and the chances are she's just been out having fun and will turn up soon; after this morning's discovery, though, I have to make enquiries. So, I'll ask again, when did you last see Lucy?"

"Thursday," Tom answered. "She was here Thursday night, with Ollie."

"So, you didn't see her yesterday?"

Both Tom and Simon shook their heads.

10

After leaving Oliver Ryder's house, Mitchell and Melissa drove out to the Goulding's house, which was on the edge of the village. Melissa wasn't sure what they were doing there, but didn't ask, she was sure she would find out soon enough without doing so.

"Sergeant, constable."

The strong, Germanic accent of Anna Becker, the Gouldings' housekeeper, could not entirely mask her concern at finding the two police officers on the doorstep. "Have you found Lucy? I've heard about poor Georgina; it's so terrible, her parents must be devastated. Nothing's happened to Lucy, has it?"

"Not as far as we know," Mitchell told her reassuringly. "We haven't found Lucy, but we don't have any reason for thinking anything has happened to her. We're here to talk to you and Mrs Goulding, she is home, isn't she?"

Anna Becker nodded. "She is. I'll ask if she will see you."

Mitchell was not happy to be left to wait on the doorstep, fortunately, he did not have to wait long.

"Mrs Goulding will see you," Anna said when she returned.

"Good mor..." Mitchell started to say when he was shown into the office, he cut himself off when he saw that Theresa Goulding was on the phone.

"Anna said you wish to speak to me," Theresa said once she had hung up the phone. "I assume, since you don't have her with you, that you haven't yet found Lucy."

"No, not yet," Mitchell admitted, not that he could pretend otherwise. "We're investigating, though, to try and work out where she could have gone."

"I hope you are having more success than you did when you investigated Georgina Ryder's disappearance." Theresa's voice betrayed her doubts. "I understand that if it was not for Mr Wild, you would still be in the dark as to the whereabouts of that poor girl, and that you have no idea who is responsible for attacking her."

Mitchell was not surprised that news of the morning's discovery had reached Theresa, he was sure everyone in the village had heard about it by now.

"Do you know Mr Wild?" he asked, thinking that if she did it would lend weight to the theory that Lucy had returned to the village the previous afternoon to see the author.

"No, we haven't met, yet," Theresa dashed his hopes. "Though I have written to him regarding the charity event I am organising for next month. I don't see that that has any relevance to Lucy's disappearance, however, unless there's something you need to tell me." She fixed Mitchell with a look that would have done an interrogator proud.

"At this stage, we have nothing definite," Mitchell told her. "But we have spoken to several people already about Lucy and her last known movements. Kelly told us she saw Lucy yesterday lunchtime, leaving school, and that she didn't return for the afternoon session."

"I was already aware of that. In fact, I told Inspector Stevens as much when he called to see if Lucy had returned home, as if

I wouldn't have called him straight away if she had. Surely you haven't come here to tell me what I already know."

Mitchell shook his head vigorously. "No, of course not, but I assume, when you spoke to Kelly..."

"I didn't speak to Kelly," Theresa said quickly. "It was Anna who called Lucy's friends."

"Yes, of course, Kelly did say as much, she also told us that as far as she knows, Lucy left school at lunchtime to return here to Oakhurst, so she could meet someone; she couldn't say who though, Lucy didn't tell her."

Theresa responded to that without hesitation. "It must be Oliver Ryder. I can't tell you how many times her father and I have spoken to her about that hooligan – too many times. I swear, she only goes out with him to annoy us. If Sir Virgil should ever find out the sort of person she is seeing, well, I don't know how he would react, but he wouldn't be happy. Have you spoken to him yet?"

"Sir Virgil?" Mitchell couldn't think why he should speak to the famously tough entrepreneur.

"Oliver Ryder. Why on Earth would you think I meant Sir Virgil?" Theresa gave Mitchell no chance to answer the question. "Surely you realise that Oliver has to be your prime suspect in Georgina's...her murder," her voice stumbled for a moment, "and Lucy's disappearance. You've never been the brightest of people, Lewis, but even you must see the connection; first his cousin disappears, after apparently leaving his house, and then Lucy, his - his girlfriend, disappears after leaving school early to come back to the village to see him."

"We don't know that it was Oliver Lucy came back to see," Mitchell said, not reacting to Theresa's out of character display of emotion. "But we will be asking him about Lucy, and about Georgina, just as soon as we catch up with him. First, though, we have some questions we need to ask you, and we need to take a look around Lucy's room."

"What on Earth for?" Theresa asked, startled. "Surely you don't think you'll find Lucy there. I can assure you, it was the first place Anna and I looked."

Mitchell hastened to reassure Theresa. "Of course not, but we do need to search the room for anything that might tell us who Lucy was coming back to see." He continued hurriedly when he saw that Theresa was about to speak again, "Kelly couldn't tell us who that was, but Lucy did, apparently, indicate that the person she was meeting was someone who could make her dreams come true. Her dream, as far as Kelly is aware, being writing. Because of that, we believe she may have been intending to meet Mr Wild; we want to see if there's anything in Lucy's room that might indicate she knew, or had any connection with, Mr Zack Wild."

The startled look on Theresa's face grew. "Writing? Are you talking about Lucy's scribblings?" She shook her head in disbelief. "You can't believe she has a dream that has anything to do with writing. The only things Lucy dreams about are money, shopping, and causing problems for her father and me."

"You may be right," Mitchell said. "But we still need to check to be sure. And if it isn't Mr Wild she was coming back to see, we might be able to find out if it was Oliver Ryder, or someone else. We might also be able to find out if there's anyone we should be talking to that we haven't previously thought of, anyone that might have a grudge against Lucy."

Briefly, Theresa looked as though she was going to debate the suggestion that someone could have a grudge against her daughter. "Very well, do whatever you need to," she said finally.

"Thank you." Mitchell was about to leave the office when he thought of something. "If you don't mind, can you tell us where you were yesterday afternoon, from about half one onwards?" He figured that was the earliest Lucy could have made it back to the village.

Theresa looked mortally offended. "Are you trying to suggest that I may have had something to do with Lucy's disappearance?"

"No, of course not," Mitchell said hastily. "I didn't mean that at all. I just want to find out where everyone was, so I can be certain of their movements."

Theresa did not look mollified, but she did deign to answer him after a brief pause. "I was in town from ten o'clock yesterday morning until a little after five. I was in a meeting with Beth Weald from Action on Homelessness until about midday, and after that I was working with the committee to organise the event we are running next month. If you wish to check, you'll find that I have more than half a dozen witnesses, including Anna – she was there to help me."

"Thank you, that saves me asking Anna where she was," Mitchell remarked. "I'll try and finish my search of Lucy's room as quickly as possible, so I can get out of your hair"

MELISSA TURNED HER attention from the bookcase to the housekeeper. "What should be here?" she asked, indicating the large gap on the second shelf from the bottom.

Anna left her post by the doorway and bent to examine the gap. It was a few moments before she straightened up. "Six or seven books," she said, without seeming to be aware that her answer was all but useless since it was obvious that it was books that were missing.

"Who are they by?" Mitchell asked, guessing at the thinking behind Melissa's query as he joined the two women.

Anna's brow furrowed. "They're all by the same person, I remember that, a man, but I can't remember his name." She bent again to run her eyes over the other books on the shelf. "It begins with a W. They're big books, heavy, hardbacks; Lucy won't take them from the room, they're so heavy, she only reads them here. You'd think, given how many times I've seen Lucy reading them, I'd remember who they're by, and what they're called."

Melissa frowned. "If they're too heavy for Lucy to take them out of the room," she said slowly, "why would she have taken them all off the shelf at the same time? You haven't seen them anywhere around the house, have you? They're not anywhere in the room as far as I can see."

"No. If I had, I would have brought them back up here."

"Do you remember when you last saw the books, and where they were?"

"Yesterday morn..." Anna started to say, before stopping so she could cast her mind back. After several moments, she nodded. "Yes, they were there yesterday morning. I did my dusting, and I remember the only gap was here." After a brief search for the right spot, she put her finger on a book on the third shelf. "This one wasn't here when I dusted yesterday."

"You're certain that that book was missing, and the other books were here, when you dusted yesterday?" Mitchell asked. When Anna nodded, he went on, "What time did you do the dusting?"

"Between half-past eight and nine o'clock; after Lucy left for school, and before I went into town with Mrs Goulding."

"Is it possible that someone other than Lucy could have taken the books?" Mitchell asked. It didn't surprise him when Anna shook her head. "Okay, so if Lucy is the only one who would have taken the books, and they were here when Lucy left for school yesterday, she must have come home at some point."

"Could the books have been by someone called Zack Wild?" Melissa asked.

Anna's face brightened, and she nodded quickly. "Yes, that was it; I can't think how I could have forgotten it, it's such a simple name to remember."

Melissa looked significantly at Mitchell, though her gaze quickly moved from him to the desk. "Do you want me to check it?" she asked, indicating the laptop that sat on it.

"You'll have to," Mitchell told her. "I wouldn't have a clue what to do. While you do that, I'll check the rest of the room."

Immediately, Melissa crossed to the desk and settled into the luxurious, padded swivel chair. It was only when the Windows logo appeared on the screen that she thought to worry that the system might be password-protected – fortunately, it wasn't.

Melissa sat and stared at the desktop screen for more than a minute, unsure how to proceed. Finally, she decided that the place to start was Lucy's email and social media accounts; sixteen was recent enough for her to remember how keen teens were on social media, and how often they used it. The moment she accessed her email account, she saw that Lucy got more emails in a week than she got in a month. Most of the emails were notifications, of one sort or another, from social media, indicating that it was a good idea for her to check Lucy's Facebook, Twitter and other accounts.

It took a while to go through the emails, and when she was done Melissa moved on to the social media accounts themselves. She didn't expect to find anything on any that she hadn't already seen in the notifications, which had had nothing to do with Lucy's disappearance, but she had to check anyway.

"What do you make of this, Mel?"

The distraction was a welcome one and Melissa spun the chair away from the desk to get to her feet. When she reached the bed, she saw that the small pile of clothes Mitchell had dumped out from the laundry basket was made up of a school uniform and some underwear.

"When did you last empty this basket, Mrs Becker?" Mitchell asked.

"Yesterday morning," Anna answered straight away. "I put a load of laundry on before going into town with Mrs Goulding."

"It definitely looks as though Lucy came home yesterday afternoon," Mitchell observed.

Melissa nodded her agreement as she reached out to pick up the underwear, saying, "This is odd, though."

"Why d'you say that?" Mitchell wanted to know. Looking extremely uncomfortable, he stared at the items in Melissa's hand.

"Well, I can understand Lucy changing out of her uniform, if she was planning on meeting someone, especially someone like Mr Wild, she would have wanted to wear something better, but why would she change her underwear." The look on her face conveyed her confusion. "I imagine she already put on clean underwear before going to school."

"Yes," Anna confirmed that.

"Then why change, unless..." Melissa's voice trailed off as a thought occurred to her.

"Unless what?" Mitchell asked.

"Unless...unless she was planning something more than just meeting Mr Wild, or whoever it is she was going to see," Melissa finished.

"What do you mean?" He realised what she meant before she could answer. "Surely you don't think she could have been intending to...to have sex with Mr Wild."

"Or whoever she was planning to meet," Melissa said. "I can't think why else she would have changed her underwear.

Speaking as a woman, the only reason I'd change my underwear, if I already had fresh on, was to put on something sexy for whoever I was meeting. How well do you know the clothes in Lucy's wardrobe?" she asked of Anna.

"Pretty well," Anna said. "I can't tell you how many times I've washed everything, so I should know it."

"Can you tell us what's missing, what she might have changed into?"

"I think so." Anna's voice betrayed a touch of doubt, nonetheless she moved away from the bed and over to the wardrobe, so she could look inside.

"Did you find anything on the computer?" Mitchell asked of Melissa while the wardrobe was being checked. "Anything that shows if it was Wild she was planning on meeting, or someone else?"

"Not so far. I've checked her emails and her social media accounts, but there's nothing there; if she was talking to someone about meeting up with them, or about meeting up with someone else, she wasn't doing it through any of them."

"Could she have done it in code or something?"

"It's possible I suppose," Melissa said doubtfully. "But I can't see why she'd have done so; she didn't even have a password on the laptop, so she obviously didn't worry about anyone looking at her stuff. If she did have a code she used, it'll be almost impossible for us to figure out what she was saying; we don't even know who she might have been saying it to, since she apparently didn't talk to Kelly about it."

"I'll have a look at her internet history, maybe there will be something there to help us."

Mitchell left Melissa to work on the computer and joined Anna at the wardrobe. "Can you tell us what Lucy changed into?"

Anna nodded, her eyes on the colourful array of clothes in the wardrobe. "A mini-skirt, a red micro thing that's positively indecent - her parents don't normally worry themselves about what she wears, but if they'd seen this skirt, they'd have had plenty to say about it - and a low-cut top, red, like the skirt."

"If that's what she was wearing, I don't think there's any doubt she wanted to get attention," Mitchell observed unhappily as he wrote down the details of the outfit Lucy was most likely wearing when she left the house the last time.

Melissa listened with half an ear to the housekeeper, but she was more interested in her search of Lucy's internet history. It didn't take her long to discover that there was only one thing on there of interest, and it was the site Lucy had visited before leaving the house to see whoever it was she came back to the village to meet.

"It seems pretty certain now, doesn't it; Lucy was planning on seeing Zack Wild," she said, showing the author's website to Mitchell.

"Yes. We'll have to go back later and find out what he knows."

"You don't want to go now?" Melissa asked.

"No." Mitchell shook his head. "We'll speak to Oliver first, see what he knows, if anything, then try and speak to Mr Wild. He might, genuinely, not have been home when we tried earlier, so we should give him some time to return from wherever he's gone. If he's not home later, we'll have to think about how we're going to find him."

Melissa shut the computer down once she had determined there was nothing more to see and went with Mitchell as he returned to Theresa Goulding's office.

"I ASSUME YOU DID NOT find Lucy in her bedroom," Theresa said when Mitchell was once again standing in front of her desk.

"No, we didn't. We did find evidence that Lucy came home and got changed, and evidence to suggest who she might have come back to see."

"And who might that be?" Theresa wanted to know. "Not Oliver Ryder, I take it."

"No, not Oliver." Mitchell debated for a moment whether to say anything more, in the end he decided he should. "We believe Lucy was intending to pay a visit to Zack Wild. She has a number of books by him, according to Anna, all of which are missing, and the last thing Lucy did on her computer before leaving home yesterday afternoon is check Mr Wild's website."

"Do you really think that's proof? I realise I have not met Mr Wild yet, but I cannot imagine he would be involved in whatever has happened to Lucy. I don't suppose you are aware of it, but Mr Wild is not just a successful author, he is a former detective inspector."

"How do you know that?"

"One of the committee members from my charity told me; since we are interested in gaining his help with the charity, it was necessary that we know as much about him as possible."

11

Melissa watched as a ball landed on the fairway visible through a gap in the trees. The ball bounced forwards, landed on the edge of the green, and then rolled down the incline towards the water she could see only because of the sun that was bouncing off it.

"Is there a penalty if your ball goes in the water?" she asked of John Knight, whose office it was.

The head grounds-keeper offered an amused smile. "That depends on how good a golfer you are," he said, "and how deep the water is. If the water's shallow, and you're a good golfer, you can get the ball out, you might even be able to get it somewhere useful. Most people, though, will take a penalty and drop a replacement ball near the edge of the water; in the long run, it saves a lot of time, effort and aggravation. I take it someone's just put a ball in the water on the sixteenth."

"If that's the hole out there, then yes," Melissa said. "The ball bounced twice, then rolled down into the water."

Knight's smile broadened. "A lot of people make that mistake," he said. "There's a bit of a nasty bunker to the right of the green, you have to aim just past the edge of it if you want to stay on the green, and not many people manage it, especially if they don't know the course."

"That doesn't sound like much fun."

"Depends on how you look at it. I'm paid to make the course a challenge for people who know how to play a good round of golf."

Mitchell had no interest in the golf talk, and paid little attention to it, instead he focused on watching out for Oliver Ryder. His vigilance was rewarded when a short while later he saw Ryder. "He's here," he told the other two.

It was another couple of minutes before a knock sounded. "You asked me to come in, Mr Knight," Oliver Ryder said as he entered the office. He stopped the moment he saw the two uniformed officers with his boss. "What d'you want?" he asked of Mitchell, not even trying to conceal his dislike of the sergeant.

John Knight took his cue from the look directed at him by Mitchell and excused himself.

"Hello, Oliver, how are you?" Mitchell asked. "How does it feel to be gainfully employed, for the first time in your life?"

"What d'you want?" Oliver repeated his question, ignoring the pleasantries.

"We need to speak to you about something," Mitchell said. "A couple of somethings, actually."

"Yeah, well, I don't wanna speak to you, so you can get lost," Oliver told him. "You only ever come looking for me when you think I've done summat. Well, I ain't done shit, other than go straight. I've got a legit job, I'm learnin' to be a grounds-keeper, and you'd better not have messed it up for me coming here. If you have I'll..." He cut himself off before he could finish the threat he was thinking of.

"We're not here because we think you've been involved in anything," Mitchell said. "We're here about Georgina."

"What about Georgie?" Oliver demanded. "Don't tell me you useless plods have actually managed to find her. No, if you'd found her, Uncle John would've called to tell me, he wouldn't have left it to you lot."

Mitchell hesitated for a moment before saying, "We have found Georgina, or rather, she has been found."

"Then why hasn't Uncle John called to tell me himself?"

"Because, and I really hate to have to tell you this, Oliver, Georgina was..." Mitchell paused before plunging on. "Georgina is dead, she was killed," he said that in a rush, and braced himself for the inevitable reaction – he was not disappointed, though he was not sure that was the right word.

For several, long seconds Oliver simply stood there, staring at the sergeant. His fists were clenched at his side, and his chest rose and fell heavily as he sought to control himself, without success. After about three or four seconds, Oliver gave up trying to control himself, he turned and ran from the office, surprising both Mitchell and Melissa, both of whom had expected him to explode and rage at them. He was gone before either officer could recover from their surprise.

Melissa recovered first and quickly set off in pursuit, unsure why Oliver was fleeing, only that she had to catch him. She stopped to look around when she got outside; at first glance it appeared that Oliver had disappeared, but she guessed where he must have gone when she heard the roar of an un-muffled car exhaust. She hurried for the corner, so she could make for the car park at the side of the building, and reached it just in time to be forced to dive out of the way to avoid being run down by Oliver Ryder's speeding car.

"How could you let him get away?" Mitchell demanded when he caught up with Melissa, who was still on the ground, and saw the Volkswagen Golf disappearing rapidly down the road.

"I didn't let him get away," Melissa said, disbelief on her face as she pushed herself up. "Oliver's faster than me, always has been. In case you've forgotten, he was the hundred metres champion for the county two years running. He was already out of sight by the time I got out here, and in his car by the time I got to the corner. I didn't have a hope in hell of stopping him.

"Oh, and I'm fine by the way, thanks for asking."

Mitchell fumed, but didn't allow himself to react to the sarcasm in Melissa's voice. He had more important things to worry about, namely the fact that Oliver Ryder was getting away. Without checking to see that Melissa was with him, he hurried away, so he could give chase.

Melissa felt like swearing but held her tongue and followed Mitchell. She caught up with him just before he reached their patrol car, and slid into the passenger seat, while he got behind the wheel and started the engine.

"Why d'you think he's run?" she asked as they raced down the narrow drive that led to the rear entrance of the golf course. "We've got no reason for thinking he's involved in what happened to Georgina, at least we didn't 'til now; running definitely makes him look like a suspect. And where's he running to? He can't be heading home, that'd just be asking for him to get caught."

"He's not heading home, he's got someone he wants to talk to," Mitchell said.

12

Mitchell drove through the ruins of the gate Oliver Ryder had smashed and brought the car to a stop in front of the Wright farmhouse. Together, he and Melissa quickly got out and looked around; Ryder's car was a short distance away, the driver's door standing open, suggesting he had abandoned it the moment he reached the yard, but of Ryder himself, there was no sign.

"That didn't sound like Ollie or Kieran," Melissa said when a scream sounded from the house. Hurrying around the car, she could make for the front door, which stood ajar.

"I know, it sounded like a girl," Mitchell said, unhappy with the development. "You take the front, I'll go round the back; give me a minute to get there, then we'll both go in."

Melissa could not remember a longer minute. The moment she reached sixty she burst through the partially open door; she expected to find Oliver on the other side, instead she found an empty passage and had to hurry down it to the kitchen, from which the sounds of fighting were coming.

She threw open the kitchen door the moment she reached it, and heard a sudden cry of pain, high-pitched and obviously female. Melissa guessed that the person she had just hit with the door was one of Kieran's sisters, the other being a short distance away, she didn't have time to worry about her, though, for in the middle of the room was a wrestling match. One of the wrestlers was Oliver, Melissa could see enough to recognise him easily, the other was not so easy to see, but she guessed it was Kieran Wright.

Without waiting for Mitchell, who should have been there already, Melissa moved forward to try and break the fight up. If she didn't, she suspected Kieran was going to be killed, or at least left permanently injured, given the energy and enthusiasm with which Oliver was smashing his head onto the floor. It quickly became clear that it was not a good idea for her to wade in; the moment she got within a foot of the fighting pair, she was caught across the cheek by a wild swing from one of Oliver's fists.

She reeled away from the fight, but the moment she recovered her balance, she threw herself back into the fray. As best she could, she avoided the flailing arms as she sought to separate Oliver and Kieran, with only minimal success. Fortunately, Mitchell arrived before she could receive more than a few painful and annoying bruises, and between them they managed to drag Oliver away from Kieran and hold him long enough to get cuffs on his wrists.

"It might be a good idea if you take the girls into the living room, while I speak to Oliver and Kieran," Mitchell said once he had the two young men on opposite sides of the kitchen.

"Okay." It took some persuasion to get Emily and Tara, Kieran's sisters, out of the kitchen and along the passage to the living room. Emily went willingly, but Tara had to be all but dragged away.

Mitchell waited until Melissa and the two girls had reached the living room, and then he turned to Kieran. "Are you alright?" he asked.

"What the hell are you asking him for?" Oliver demanded. "He's the sick bastard killed Georgie." He launched himself across the room, catching Mitchell by surprise, and threw himself on Kieran. The fact that his hands were cuffed behind his back didn't stop him, he rammed into Kieran with his shoulder, driving him backwards into the upturned table. When he stepped back, Kieran fell to the floor, and there was just enough time for him to lash out with a booted foot, burying it in Kieran's stomach, before he was dragged away.

"You okay?" Mitchell asked of Kieran, bending to help him to his feet after shoving Oliver across the room.

"Sure. That pussy couldn't hurt a flea," Kieran said dismissively, ignoring the fact that the so-called 'pussy' had just floored him.

Oliver sneered at that. "Who the hell are you trying to kid? If anyone's a pussy here, it's you, and you know it. You couldn't fight your way out of a wet paper bag. If your daddy hadn't been here with his shotgun last week, I'da had you in hospital, and if the pigs hadn't turned up today, I'da finished the job I started the other month. You're a sick sonofabitch, and you need to die." As he raged, he struggled against the handcuffs that kept him restrained, even though he had enough experience with handcuffs to know that it was impossible for him to break out of them.

"Shut up, Oliver," Mitchell ordered. He righted one of the upturned chairs that had previously been around the table and pushed him down onto it. "You sure you're okay?" When Kieran nodded, Mitchell got down to his reason for being there. "I'm sorry to have to be the bearer of bad news, Kieran, but..."

"You never said you was sorry when you told me," Oliver butted in angrily as he half rose from the hard, wooden chair he had been put on.

Mitchell pushed Oliver back down, glad of the handcuffs that made the violent twenty-year-old easier to deal with. "I would've said sorry, but you never gave me a chance," he said, fixing him with a hard look. "You ran off the moment I told you what's happened, before I could say anything else, so you could come here and attack Kieran, for no reason other than you don't like him."

"Don't like him, I fucking hate him," Oliver snarled as he continued to struggle. "Uncuff me, I wanna kill that sick sonofabitch."

"Shut-up and behave yourself," Mitchell told him. He shoved Oliver down again, this time with enough force to rock the chair back on two legs momentarily. "If you don't, I'll have Melissa take you out to the car while I talk with Kieran."

"Fuck you." Oliver leaned forwards to stop his chair falling over, and then surged to his feet, so he could launch himself at Kieran. Before he could cover half the distance, he was dragged to the floor by Mitchell.

"Melissa," Mitchell called out as he struggled to keep Oliver on the floor.

Melissa skidded to a halt in the kitchen, having run down the passage to find out what was going on. It didn't surprise her to find that Oliver Ryder had been causing trouble. "What do you need?" It looked to her as though everything was under control.

"Take this pain in the ass out to the car," Mitchell told her. "Lock him in the back; we'll take him to the station once we're finished here."

Melissa nodded and moved to take charge of the prisoner. She got him to his feet, with help from Mitchell, and then led him from the kitchen.

"OKAY, NOW OLIVER'S out of the way," Mitchell said once he was alone with Kieran. "I'm sorry to be the bearer of bad news..."

"It's okay, I know why you're here," Kieran said sadly. "You've found Georgie." He didn't look at Mitchell as he said that, instead he focused on righting the table and chairs overturned during his fight with Kieran.

"Who told you?" Mitchell asked, bending to help with the table, he would not have liked to lay odds on who had contacted Kieran, the list of possibilities was too long.

"I must have been called or text by half the village in the last hour and a half," Kieran said. He gave a short, humourless laugh. "You know how it is around here, nobody can wait to pass on any news they hear, especially if it's bad news."

Mitchell nodded, aware of how much the villagers liked to gossip. "So, what has everyone been telling you?" he asked, wondering how accurate the gossip had been – not very, was his guess.

"They all said pretty much the same thing," Kieran said. "That Georgie was found this morning, and that she was – she was killed." He could not bring himself to say murdered.

"That's right," Mitchell said. "I'm sorry, I wish it wasn't necessary to trouble you with this, and I wish you hadn't had to hear about this from the village gossips, I had to tell the family first, though."

"I understand, of course you had to tell Georgie's parents first."

"I hope you also understand that I need to ask you some questions. Some of them I might have asked before, but I need to ask them again, in case you've remembered something you didn't think of before."

"What sort of questions?" Kieran wanted to know.

"Well, first off, where were you on Friday evening, a week ago?"

"You already asked me that, last week."

"I know, but as I said, some of the questions I need to ask, you've already answered, but I need to be sure you didn't forget something that you now remember," Mitchell told him. "So, where were you last Friday?"

"At the cinema."

"What time was that?"

"I got there, musta been about half-eight."

"As I recall, you said you were supposed to meet Georgina."

Kieran nodded. "We were supposed to go to the cinema together. She text me just after six to say she was stopping at her cousin's, and would meet me at the farm after, then we could head into town. She never turned up, though. I hung around for ages, waiting for her, then I went looking, but couldn't find her. In the end I gave up and went into town on my own. I never saw her."

"Weren't you worried when she didn't show up like she was supposed to?"

Kieran thought about that briefly and then shook his head. "I think I was more annoyed than worried. When she didn't turn up, I figured Georgie had let her bloody cousin talk her into sticking around and cleaning up after him and his moron friends, like he always does. I thought, if that's what she wants to do, it's fine with me, I'd just go and see a film I wanted to see, instead of the stupid, sappy romance I was supposed to see with her."

"What time did you get back from the cinema?"

Kieran shrugged. "Half-twelve, one a.m., something like that I'd guess. I don't really remember. It was definitely after midnight, 'cause the film didn't finish 'til about eleven, and it's over an hour's drive to get back here from the cinema."

"Can any of your family confirm what time you got home?"

"No, they were all in bed, so it was definitely after midnight 'cause Em's usually up 'til 'bout midnight. Wait, yes, Tara can. She might not know exactly what time it was, but she can give you a rough idea," Kieran said as he remembered. "A ninja I'm not, I dropped my phone on the way up the stairs, and it bounced all the way down; the noise woke Tara, she came to see what was going on, had a go at me for waking her, went to the bathroom for a pee, and then went back to bed."

"Why didn't you pick Georgina up, instead of her coming out here to meet you?" Mitchell asked. "You could have met her at Oliver's, it would have been more sensible than her walking up here."

"I was supposed to meet her down in the village," Kieran admitted. "But I was having problems with my car. I've been trying to save up enough to get it fixed for good, but I can't afford it right now, so I'm having to bodge it. Damn thing conked out on me just as I was leaving to pick Georgie up, took me and dad about twenty minutes to get it going again. I text Georgie to let her know what was going on, that's when she said she was gonna stop in at her cousin's, and head up here if she didn't hear from me first."

"Why didn't you head down to Oliver's to pick her up once you got the car going?"

Kieran snorted. "You've seen what he's like, he hates me, attacks me every time he sees me. Georgie hates it when I fight with her idiot of a cousin, so I avoid him as much as I can."

Mitchell doubted that that was the only reason Kieran avoided Oliver; he suspected it was more because he wasn't as tough as his girlfriend's cousin and didn't want to get beaten up.

"I didn't want to get into a fight, that's why I stayed away; besides, I figured if Georgie was gonna choose to hang out with her cousin, instead of going to the cinema with me, I was better off going on my own." He shrugged, as if it didn't really matter, but his indifference was quickly replaced by a deep sadness. "When I – when I heard the next morning that Georgie was – that she was missing..." He fell silent for several long moments. "I wished I'd looked for her, wished I'd done more than just text to ask where she was, and then gotten annoyed when she didn't answer.

"Maybe – maybe if I'd been able to make her see how obsessed Oliver, that fucking asshole," he snarled, "is with her, she would – would've been alright."

Mitchell saw the accusation implicit in the teen's words and knew he would have to ask more questions before he could move on. "What is it, exactly, that makes you think Oliver might have had something to do with Georgina's disappearance, and how she was found?"

"Come on, you can't tell you don't know about his obsession with Georgie," Kieran said. "He acts like she's his girlfriend, not his cousin. He texts and calls her all the time, has her at his house cleaning up after him and his friends, running errands; he's always touching her as well, like he wants her; you know what I mean?"

Mitchell didn't need to be a genius to understand what Kieran was trying to say, even if he didn't believe it, so he nodded.

"I think that's what happened," Kieran said. "He forgot Georgie's his cousin, not his girlfriend – I mean, he gets aggro whenever she starts seeing someone – tried it on with her, and then snapped when she threatened to tell her parents what he'd done."

"It's certainly a theory we'll have to look into," Mitchell promised. "There's something else I need to ask you about."

"What?" Kieran didn't even try to conceal his frustration. "Dad'll be home for lunch any time, he'll want his food ready, and he won't want to see this mess."

"I'm sorry, I'll be as quick as I can," Mitchell said. "Did you see Lucy Goulding yesterday afternoon? Specifically, at any point from lunchtime onwards."

Kieran nodded. "Sure, I saw her yesterday," he said without hesitation. "Is she in trouble?"

"No, but we are concerned about her. As far as we've been able to tell, nobody has seen Lucy since she got on the bus in town yesterday lunchtime to come back to the village. She would have made it back here a bit before one; did you see her after that time?"

"Yeah, I saw her, must have been about two, something like that."

"Where?" Mitchell asked, hoping that he was about to hear something that would advance his investigation.

"Just down the road actually. I was heading out to get some stuff done after a late lunch when my bloody car conked out again. I was trying to get it going again when I saw Lucy, she was at the old Henshaw cottage, being let in by that new guy, I forget his name, the one Emily's been helping with his gardens."

"Zack Wild?"

"Yeah, that's the guy."

Mitchell could not believe it had been as easy as that to get confirmation of what he and Melissa suspected. "Thank you, Kieran; I've got just one last question for you, then I'll be out of your hair." He could see that the teen was frustrated to the point of swearing, so he got straight on with it. "Do you know how long Lucy was with Mr Wild for?"

"No." Kieran shook his head. "But it was a while. I was fifteen, twenty minutes fixing my car, and she hadn't come back out by the time I was done. Mind you, I'm not surprised, given what she was wearing."

"What was that?"

"The shortest skirt I've ever seen her wearing. It was so short I didn't think it was a skirt at first – she had a hell of a lot of leg on show." A smile played about his lips at the memory. "If I was that guy, Wild, I'd've wanted to keep her there for as long as possible, if only for the view."

"I'll leave you and the girls to get things ready for your dad," Mitchell said. "Thanks for your help." He left then, collecting Melissa from the living room on the way out of the house.

13

Mitchell left Melissa to secure Oliver Ryder in one of the station's two cells while he responded to his superior's summons.

"How's the investigation going?" Stevens asked once Mitchell was seated. "Have you made any progress?"

"If you mean with what happened to Georgina, then no; all I've got on that front so far is the theory that Oliver got confused about whether Georgina was his cousin, or his girlfriend and he killed her when she rejected him after he made a move on her," Mitchell answered.

"Is that why you brought Oliver in?"

Mitchell shook his head. "No. He's here for assault and resisting arrest. He attacked Kieran Wright, and Melissa caught a wallop while trying to break the two of them up; she's going to have a lovely bruise come morning, thankfully, that's all she suffered."

"Okay, so you've got nothing on Georgina's murder so far, beyond a theory that doesn't have anything to back it up. What about Lucy's apparent disappearance? Have you got anything on that?"

"I still don't know where she is," Mitchell admitted. "But I have discovered that she came back to the village yesterday afternoon to meet someone. I don't yet have proof of who the someone she was meeting is, but I've got reason to think it's Zack Wild..."

"The gentleman who found Georgina's body this morning?" Stevens asked, surprised. "Why would Lucy have wanted to see him?"

"Because, according to what I've discovered, she wants to become an author, and she wants whatever help he can give her." Mitchell allowed that to sink in. "Lucy's best friend, Kelly Hunter, told us about her desire to be an author, and we found evidence of that when we searched her room; we also found that after she returned home yesterday afternoon, and before she left again, she visited Mr Wild's website, she also took a number of books written by Mr Wild with her when she left the house."

"That's all well and good, Lewis, but have you got any proof that Lucy actually visited Mr Wild? Have you asked him about it?"

"He wasn't home when Melissa and I went to speak to him, we're going to try again later. We do have confirmation that Lucy went to Mr Wild's house, though, and that she went inside, she was seen being let in yesterday afternoon around two."

"Did she leave again?"

"No idea on that score. Kieran, he's the one who saw Lucy go in, was down the road, fixing his car for about twenty minutes and didn't see her leave."

"So, Mr Wild is the last person to have seen Lucy?"

"As far as I know right now. Hopefully I'll be able to confirm that when I catch up with Mr Wild."

Inspector Stevens contemplated Mitchell for a short while. "Do you think Mr Wild could be involved in Georgina's murder and Lucy's disappearance?" he asked.

"I don't want to leap to conclusions based on what may just be a coincidence, but he found Georgina's body in an out of the way place, where almost no-one goes, and he's currently the last person known to have seen Lucy. He's also the person in the village we know the least about. Again, I don't want to leap to any conclusions," Mitchell said, before doing exactly that, "but I can't imagine anyone else from the village being a killer; we know them, if that was the sort of person they were, we'd have discovered it by now." He ground his teeth in frustration. "This would be a lot easier if we knew anything about Zack Wild beyond what he's told us, which isn't much. I know he's definitely an author, but we don't know anything other than that for sure."

"In that case, this might help." Stevens slid a file across the desk to his subordinate. "It's only a summary of Mr Wild's service record with the Southampton police, but it's bound to give you some idea of the sort of person he is. The full file is being couriered over, it should be here later this afternoon. I've added whatever other information I've been able to find out so far, it's not a huge amount, but it might help." He watched Mitchell pick up the file and flip open the cover. "You're due a break, why don't you have a read of that while you take it, then you can take John Ryder into town to identify Georgina."

"HERE, I THOUGHT YOU could do with a fresh coffee," Melissa said, putting the mug she had brought down in front of Mitchell, after moving the old, cold coffee out of the way.

"Thanks," Mitchell said absently, without looking up from the file he was reading.

"Is there anything good or interesting in there?" she asked, curious to know what had been discovered about Zack Wild. She had time to sip about a quarter of her own coffee before she got a response.

"Haven't you read it?" Mitchell asked, and then immediately answered his own question. "No, of course you haven't. Here, have a look." He passed the folder over. "It makes for interesting reading," he said. His attention no longer on the file, he lifted the mug, so he could sip his coffee.

It was interesting, Melissa thought as she read, but also very brief. It took her barely a minute to get through the file, which only made her more curious about the author who had so recently moved to the village and become mixed up in the first murder there had been in more than a decade.

"It makes Mr Wild seem a viable suspect, doesn't it," Mitchell said. "Multiple violent incidents, several against women; it's not proof-positive, but it definitely looks like he could be our murderer to me. Don't you agree?" he asked of his partner.

"Not really," Melissa disagreed with a shake of her head. "We've got nothing but a few coincidences and some incomplete information. The coincidences mean nothing right now, and we don't know enough about the supposed violent incidents to tell if they have any relevance; for all we know, he could have been justified in the things he did. If you're going to make Mr Wild a suspect on that basis, you've got to make Oliver one as well, he's definitely violent, and he's connected to both Georgina and Lucy – one's his cousin and the other's his girlfriend, if that's the right word to describe their relationship."

"Surely you think Zack Wild's a better suspect than Oliver," Mitchell said, speaking with a mouth so full of sandwich it was almost impossible to make out what he was saying. "We know Oliver, we don't know Zack Wild."

"That doesn't mean anything," Melissa protested. "We still don't know there's a connection between what happened to Georgina and Lucy's disappearance; we still don't know that Lucy has disappeared, she could be anywhere, doing anything.

Even if Lucy has disappeared, and there is a connection, we don't have a clue what it is or who's responsible, because we don't have a clue what happened to Georgina before she was found this morning. For all we know, it could be just about anyone in the village who's responsible."

"Oh, come on, Melissa, you can't believe that someone we know could have done what we saw this morning."

Melissa didn't respond to that, instead she took a chocolate bar from her pocket, tore open the wrapper, and stuffed half of it into her mouth to keep her from saying what she was thinking.

14

"Can I help you?"

"Sergeant Mitchell from Oakhurst; we're here about Georgina Ryder."

The morgue attendant looked from the sergeant to the two with him. "I'll get someone to help you," he said before disappearing through the double-doors behind the counter. He returned almost immediately with another attendant, who took charge.

Silent and solemn, Mitchell, Melissa and John Ryder followed the attendant along the passage, past several doors, and through a set of double doors at the far end. The room they entered was the storage area, with three of the walls made up of cabinets, which held the bodies of the recently dead.

"It's Georgina Ryder you're here for, isn't it," the attendant said. "Came in this morning?"

"That's right," Mitchell said with a quick nod.

"Okay, she's in thirty-eight," the attendant said after checking a list on the desk in the corner of the room. "If you'll sign in, I'll show you her."

Mitchell, Melissa and John Ryder all filled out the sheet on the clipboard they were given, and with that formality taken care of the attendant led them over to the appropriate cabinet.

"I assume you're here to make an identification," the attendant said.

John Ryder nodded, unable to bring himself to speak, though he did gasp when he caught his first sight of the girl believed to be his daughter, and the damage done to her face.

"Is that Georgina?" Mitchell asked in a low and compassionate voice.

It was a minute and more before John recovered sufficiently from his shock to react to the sight before him. "My baby, oh my poor baby; who could have done this to you?" With a wail of grief, he threw himself, weeping, on the body.

Melissa turned away, embarrassed by the obvious and painful display of grief. It was not that she was heartless, but John Ryder's reaction was hard to watch.

Mitchell was shocked by his friend's reaction, which seemed excessive. "Come on, John, you've got to get control of yourself," he said, placing a comforting hand on his friend's shoulder. "Georgina wouldn't want you acting like this, and Verity's going to need your support, she's barely managing as it is. If you collapse, who's going to help her through this."

"You-you're right, Verity needs me to be strong," John said as he fought back his tears. "It's just..." He sniffed. "How could anyone have done this to my baby, my Georgie? Who did it? D'you know?"

"I'm afraid not," Mitchell admitted. "We've barely begun investigating. It's liable to take us some time to figure out what happened, and who's responsible. We're doing everything we can, though," he assured him, "and we do have a suspect we're looking at. As soon as we have proof, we'll arrest him."

"Who is it?" John asked desperately as he grasped at the front of Mitchell's uniform. "Please, Lewis, you have to tell me, who did this to my beautiful baby girl? She never did anything to anyone, she was an angel; how could anyone hurt her like this?" He reached out to stroke Georgina's face, in doing so he dislodged the sheet covering her body. It was only the timely reactions of the morgue attendant that kept him from seeing the full extent of his daughter's injuries. What he saw was enough to break the thin veneer of control he had in place over his emotions and make him collapse again. "Oh god, oh god, oh my poor baby."

Melissa guessed that the suspect Mitchell had referred to was Zack Wild, and that made her uncomfortable, for in her mind they had nothing to justify making him a suspect. Even if Wild was guilty of the assaults listed in the file she had read, and that was not certain, it did not follow that he had committed murder. It seemed to her, and she did not like the thought, that her superior had latched onto Zack Wild as a suspect because he did not want the murderer to be someone he knew, someone he was friends with; she could understand him thinking like that but didn't agree with it because of the chance that the real suspect might get away.

She said nothing of her misgivings, however, sure that Mitchell wouldn't want to hear them.

"Are you certain it's Georgina back there, John?" Mitchell asked, a hand on his friend's shoulder as he steered him gently but firmly away from the sight that had caused him such distress. "I'll understand if you're not positive, it's hard to make an identification under such circumstances," he said, making it sound as though he had attended dozens. "There are other ways to be certain whether it's Georgina – dental records and the like."

John Ryder shook his head. "No. No, I'm sure, it's Georgie." Now that he could no longer see his daughter's brutalised body he was much calmer, though no less grief-stricken. "I'd recognise her anywhere, even after what – what - what was done to her."

He sobbed a couple of times before managing to finish what he was saying. "Even if I couldn't, she's wearing the earrings Verity and I gave her last Christmas." Silent tears ran down his cheeks as he allowed himself to be guided along the passage.

"How - how did she die?" John asked as they approached the double-doors at the end of the passage.

Mitchell hesitated before answering, and Melissa was sure he was trying to decide how best to answer the question, without adding to his friend's distress.

"I'm afraid we don't know at the moment," Mitchell said, hoping he sounded believable. "We won't know the answer to that until the post-mortem; when is that happening?" he asked of the morgue attendant who was escorting them out.

"Not sure it's been scheduled yet," the attendant said. "It'll probably be Monday sometime, though, depending on how busy the pathologist is. If you want to know a definite time, you'll have to ring up Monday morning."

"Thanks, I will." Mitchell hoped the post-mortem would provide him with something that might prove who had killed Georgina. He suspected it was Zack Wild, but without proof, suspicion was all he had.

"Was, was..." John couldn't bring himself to finish the question, instead he closed his mouth with a snap and continued out of the building.

15

While she waited for the kettle to boil, Melissa paid a visit to Oliver Ryder in his cell.

"I hear you've been behaving yourself," she said as she peered through the small viewing window in the door of the cell. "What's wrong? You ill?"

When more than half a minute passed without a response from the normally loudly vocal Oliver, Melissa changed tacks. "Do you want something to drink?"

Another half a minute ticked by before Oliver finally spoke, "Stella."

It didn't surprise Melissa that Oliver would ask for something like that, it was in his nature to be a pain. She sighed and resisted the urge to swear. "You know I can't get you that, you can't have alcohol in here. I can do you a cup of tea or coffee, or water – I think there might be a can of coke in the fridge, if you'd rather have that."

Oliver was tempted to tell Melissa where to go, and to hell with her offer of a drink. He didn't, because he knew if he did it would be hours before he was offered anything else to drink, and since he was already a little thirsty, he preferred not to give Melissa, or any of the other cops, a reason to leave him without refreshment.

"Coke then, and make sure it's cold," he couldn't resist adding.

"I'll do my best, but I can't promise anything," Melissa told him.

The kettle had boiled by the time she returned to the kitchen, and she filled the three mugs she had prepared. Two of the mugs she delivered to Mitchell and Constable Pritchard, while the third, she kept for herself. With the mug in one hand, and the last can of coke from the fridge in the other, Melissa headed back to Oliver.

"I'm very sorry, Oliver," she said sincerely when she had unlocked the cell and handed over the can. "Sergeant Mitchell and I have just come back from taking your uncle to town; he's confirmed that the body found this morning is your cousin, Georgina."

"No!" Oliver launched himself off the bed with a howl of anguish. Coke fountained from the can in his hand as he crushed it and threw it aside. His eyes flashed angrily, his nostrils flared, and his hands clenched and unclenched themselves into fists as though they ached to be smashed into something or someone.

Melissa had always been frightened of Oliver Ryder – not so much of him as a person, but of the violence he was capable of when angry. She stood her ground, though, determined not to show what she was thinking or feeling, and sipped at her coffee in an outward show of calm that was almost betrayed by the minor trembling of her hand.

"It's okay, everything's fine, there's no need to panic," Melissa told her colleagues when they hurried along the passage to find out what was going on.

"You sure?" Mitchell asked, looking past Melissa and into the cell, where Oliver was pacing up and down and swearing under his breath.

Melissa nodded. "It's fine, Oliver's just blowing off some steam, aren't you, Ollie," she said with a quick glance over at her shoulder at the pacing prisoner. "I just gave him the news about Georgina, and he's a little upset."

"Okay, well, I'm just along the passage if you need me," Mitchell said. "You behave yourself, Oliver."

Melissa was trying to decide what to say next, and how to say it, when Oliver surprised her with a question.

"Have you arrested him yet?" he asked as he stopped his frenetic pacing to face Melissa with his hands balled into fists at his sides.

Perplexed, the mug in Melissa's hand froze on its way to her lips. "Arrested who?" she asked, though she realised straightaway who he must be talking about.

"That psycho prick, Wright, who d'you think I mean?"

"No, we haven't arrested him, we have no reason to. What've you got against Kieran Wright?" Melissa wanted to know. "I know you think he's a prick, but I've never heard anyone else say anything bad about him, other than that he can be a bit full of himself, and you're just as bad there. Personally, I'd pick you as a murderer ahead of Kieran, especially after earlier."

"If you guys hadn't come, I'd have finished that asshole."

"Exactly. But why? You must have a reason for hating Kieran so much, and for thinking he killed your cousin. If you know something, you have to tell us," Melissa insisted. "This isn't just about Georgina, Ollie, Lucy's missing as well."

"What're you talking about?" Oliver surged to his feet again. "Why hasn't anyone told me Lucy's missing? How long's she been gone? What's happened to her?"

"If you hadn't acted like such an idiot earlier, racing off to attack Kieran the moment you were told about Georgina, you'd have found out then. It's part of what we wanted to talk to you about," Melissa told him. "Her mum reported her missing last night. Of course, we couldn't do anything then because she's sixteen, but her mum still hadn't seen or heard from her by this morning.

"After Georgina was discovered, we realised we had to take her absence seriously; so far, we've discovered that the last time she was seen is yesterday afternoon, about two..."

"Let me guess, by Wright!" Oliver spat the name. "Can't you see, you should be arresting him, not standing here talking to me like it's any other time you've got me banged up. That sick bastard killed Georgie, and he's probably killed Lucy by now as well. I don't even wanna think about what he did to them before he killed them, the sick fuck!"

"What is your problem with him? Come on, what is it? There must be a reason for you to hate him so much."

"You wanna know what my problem with that asshole is. He's a rapist, that's my problem with the bastard, he's a fuckin' rapist!"

"Are you saying Kieran raped Georgina? When did this happen?"

"No, I don't know, maybe; she never said anything if he did. I'd've killed him already if she told me something like that, even with his daddy protecting him."

"Then what are you talking about?"

"Lucy."

"Kieran raped Lucy?"

"As good as. He sure as hell tried to." Oliver's face darkened, and he punched one fist into the other palm, hard enough to make Melissa wince. "That's why she dumped his ass. He got her one night, up at the picnic area, when they were seeing each other. He tried it on, and when she said no, he attacked her.

"If she hadn't managed to get away, he'd've raped her." He saw the look on Melissa's face. "You don't believe Lucy would be seeing someone and not sleeping with them."

"Her reputation does make it difficult to accept."

Oliver gave her a look of amused bemusement. "Don't ask me to understand women, especially Lucy. She were with Wright for months and wouldn't let him go further than copping a feel, but she jumped me the first night."

"Did she tell you Kieran tried to rape her? She never reported it to us. At least not that I heard, and I'm pretty sure I'd have heard about it if she had."

"Yeah, she told me, she told me after he attacked her the second time." As he spoke, Oliver rhythmically slammed his fist into his palm; a smacking sound gave testimony to the strength with which he did so. "He was seeing Georgie by then, but that didn't stop him when he saw Lucy walking home after he dropped Georgie off one night. He grabbed her and tried to rape her again.

"She got away and bumped into me. I took her back to my place to calm her down, that's where she told me what happened, and that it weren't the first time."

"And that's when you attacked him." Melissa recalled the incident easily, she had gotten a black eye while trying to break up the fight. "Why didn't she tell her parents, or report it to us, the first time he attacked her?"

"Would you have believed her? You already mentioned her rep; you know what people think of her. I doubt anyone'd believe her over Wright. They'd just assume she was lying to cause trouble."

"So instead, she told you."

"Yeah. We'd hooked up a few times and started seeing each other when it happened, if that's what you want to call what we do. So, when I took her back to my place and calmed her down, she told me. She needed to tell someone, and knew her parents wouldn't listen, and you guys wouldn't believe her."

"And you decided the best way to deal with the situation was to find Kieran and attack him."

Oliver shrugged, as if it was what anyone else would have done in his place. "I knew it weren't worth looking for him that night, he would've been home by the time I got to him and attacking him there were a stupid idea. He's got a shotgun, and so's his dad. I did it the next time I saw him in the village.

"He were just coming out o' the pub when I nailed him, and I nailed him good." His satisfaction evident in his face and voice. "I would've finished the job if you guys hadn't come along and dragged me off him."

"It's just as well we did, if we hadn't, you'd be in jail now for murder."

"Better that than leaving him alive to do whatever he did to Georgie and Lucy. I'd have gone to jail happily if it kept Georgie alive. So, are you gonna arrest that bastard now?"

"That's not up to me," Melissa told him. "It's up to Sergeant Mitchell. I'll tell him what you've said. I'm sure he'll want to talk to you about it later. I know he was planning on talking to you anyway. He'll be the one who decides who we arrest."

"If you don't arrest that prick for what he's done, I swear to God, I'll fucking kill him the next time I see him."

"SO, YOU DON'T THINK we should pay any attention to what Oliver said." Melissa's voice was disapproving. "You think we should just ignore him."

"I didn't say that," Mitchell said, pausing in the act of getting out of the car. "I just don't think we can do anything, when all we have are the suspicions of a guy we know has a problem with Kieran. We have absolutely no reason for thinking Kieran's responsible for Georgina's murder, other than Oliver's accusation. It's not like Kieran has a history of violence, nor has anyone complained to us about his behaviour.

"If Lucy had come to us, or even told her parents what Kieran supposedly did, or tried to do, we might be able to do something with it, but it's an accusation made by someone we know has no problem lying to us, against someone we know he can't stand. For all we know, Oliver could be trying to cause trouble for Kieran, just to be a pain in the ass."

"Maybe," Melissa agreed. "But it could also explain why Ollie's attacked Kieran three times in the last month, when he's barely paid any attention to him before. And Ollie explained why Lucy didn't come to us or tell her parents, she didn't think she'd be believed, or that we'd do anything about it, though I'd like to think we'd have looked into it, even if we weren't convinced she was telling the truth."

"Of course we would," Mitchell said quickly. "We'd investigate any accusation, no matter what it was, or who made it." With that he got out of the car and started up the path, signalling that he was done discussing the matter.

16

Zack was showering when the doorbell rang. He cursed briefly and hoped that whoever was at the door would go away. A second chime told him the person on his doorstep was not going to leave so easily, and it was then that he remembered his neighbour telling him the police had been looking for him.

Stepping out of the shower, he crossed to the window, so he could poke his head out.

"I'll be right there," he called out, before returning to the shower long enough to rinse himself off. Once he had done that he dried himself off quickly and left the bathroom, wrapping the towel around his waist as he headed down the stairs.

Answering the door wearing just a towel was not something he would do usually, he didn't consider it decent, but on that occasion, he thought it better to let the police in and then get dressed.

"Forgive my appearance," he said once he had greeted the two officers on his doorstep. "You caught me in the shower. If you'll wait in the living room, I'll get dressed and be right down."

Melissa took a seat on the sofa, while Mitchell took a position near the fireplace, so he could see the whole room and get some idea of what sort of person Zack Wild was, and whether he could be the killer he suspected he was.

Zack was back in under five minutes, having swapped the towel for a pair of well-worn blue jeans and a dark blue t-shirt. "Can I get either of you anything to drink?" he asked from the doorway.

"No, thank you," Mitchell said before Melissa had a chance to say anything.

"Okay, in that case, I guess we should get down to your reason for being here." Zack left the doorway and took the armchair. "I assume this visit has something to do with the body I found this morning."

Mitchell nodded. "Yes. We have some more questions we need to ask you about Georgina Ryder, and about another matter that has come up. Do you have the time to talk?" he asked. He was ready to arrest the writer if he answered in the negative, but he didn't want to do that without good cause; he suspected it would cause problems.

"Sure, I haven't got anything else I need to do today."

"Okay, well, first off, you said earlier that you normally follow the road through the village and head out towards town when on one of your runs; have you ever gone down by the river before today?"

"I've been that way before, only the once, though. I've explored most of the village, and the countryside around it – not in any great depth, but well enough to get around."

"When was it you explored the riverbank along from the pub?"

A shrug was Zack's immediate response. "Not sure exactly, it was a while ago, back around the time I first moved here."

"So, you haven't been that way in the past week or so? You wouldn't know if there had been anyone hanging around the area where you found Georgina Ryder?"

"No, 'fraid not."

Mitchell showed no sign of being bothered by that answer, though he did react when he was posed a question in return.

"Do I take it you've been able to identify the girl I found?" Zack asked.

"Yes. Did you know her?"

"As I said at the station when you questioned me, I'd heard the name around the village," Zack said. "As I understand it, she was missing for about a week, but I don't think I ever met her – in passing maybe, but not properly."

Mitchell responded to that by taking out the photograph of Georgina Ryder that had been provided by her mother when she was reported missing. "This is Georgina," he said. "Do you remember meeting her now?"

Zack took the photograph but soon shook his head. "Sorry, never met her; I did see her around the village a couple of times, in the shop or something, I never spoke to her, though."

"When did you last see her?"

"No idea."

That was not the answer Mitchell was after, and he had to stop himself grinding his teeth in frustration. Once he had the impulse under control, he said, "So you didn't see her last Friday evening? Only we have a report that she was seen heading up the road outside on her way to the Wright Farm."

"I wish I could help, but I didn't see anyone last Friday."

"You're sure about that?" Mitchell asked. When Zack nodded, he said, "Where were you last Friday evening, from about six?"

"At home, I was home all evening."

"And you definitely didn't see Georgina, or anyone who could be responsible for what happened to her?"

Zack shook his head. "Like I said, I didn't see anyone."

"So, you were at home all evening and you didn't see anyone," Mitchell said dubiously. "What were you doing?"

"This and that, nothing special, mostly just pottering around, keeping myself busy."

Mitchell couldn't conceal what a hard time he was having believing the author. "Is there anyone who can confirm where you were, or what you were doing?"

A rueful smile touched Zack's lips. "I wish I could say yes, but I can't, I was on my own. You'll probably be able to find time stamps for things on Facebook and on the emails I sent out, but that's all the alibi I have."

Since he had nothing, yet, to contradict Wild's alibi, Mitchell had no choice but to accept it and move on. "Do you know a Lucy Goulding?" He wondered if the lack of surprise shown by Wild meant anything.

"I wouldn't say I know her," Zack said. "She turned up on my doorstep yesterday afternoon."

Such an open admission was the last thing Mitchell expected. He had been sure he would have to reveal that there was a witness before getting Zack Wild to admit to knowing her. "She came to see you? What time was that?"

"A little after two; I'm not sure of the exact time," Zack answered. "Has something happened to her?"

Mitchell ignored the question. "How long was she here? Why was she here?"

Melissa thought the second question a little pointless – it seemed obvious to her why Lucy had visited the author – but supposed it had to be asked, for the sake of thoroughness.

"She was here for about an hour, something like that. She got here not long after two, and it was getting on for half three when she left. I wasn't looking at the clock, so I can't give you exact times, sorry." Even to his own ears, his apology sounded insincere.

"Why was she here for that long?"

Zack ignored both the suspicion in Mitchell's voice and the question, instead of responding to them he repeated his own inquiry. "Has something happened to Lucy?"

"We're not sure," Mitchell made the admission reluctantly. "She hasn't been seen since yesterday afternoon, and, so far, you're the last person to have seen her. Now, why was Lucy Goulding here? What time did she leave, and is there anyone who can confirm that she actually did leave?"

"Yes, my neighbour, Mrs Hawkins, she was pottering around her garden for most of the afternoon; I'm sure she'll be able to give you a rough idea of when Lucy left."

The moment he heard that Mitchell left Wild's, so he could head next door and speak to his suspect's neighbour.

ZACK TURNED TO THE constable on his sofa the moment he heard his front door close on the sergeant. "Now he's out of the way, how about a drink? I don't know about you, but I could do with a coffee."

"Sure, a coffee would be good," Melissa agreed. She had been annoyed by Mitchell's dismissal of the offer of a drink on her behalf and was happy to take advantage of the second offer.

"How do you like it?"

"White, three sugars," Melissa said, flashing an apologetic, and slightly embarrassed, smile when Zack paused to look back at her. "I've got a really sweet tooth. Everyone's always saying I should be really fat, probably diabetic, and missing at least a few teeth; don't ask me how I'm not, I guess I must have a super-fast metabolism or something."

"Consider yourself lucky, there's plenty of people who'd kill for a metabolism like that. I'd be happy with one half as good," Zack commented. "It seems like since I hit thirty, my metabolism's hit the brakes."

Almost the moment he was out of the living room, Zack heard stealthy footsteps; he guessed that Melissa was looking around to satisfy her curiosity, either about him personally, or about his visit from Lucy. He knew he should be offended, but he didn't care; no matter how hard she searched, he knew the constable would not find anything that would suggest he had had anything to do with either Lucy's disappearance or Georgina Ryder's murder.

"Here you go." Zack returned after a couple of minutes with the coffees and found that the curious constable was once again seated on the sofa, as if she hadn't moved.

"Thanks." Melissa lifted the mug she was handed straight to her lips and let out a satisfied sigh after taking a sip. "Oh, that's good. Strong and sweet, just the way I like. This isn't cheap coffee, is it; it's much better than I'm used to."

Zack smiled. "I'm glad you like it. And no, it's not cheap coffee. I spent years living on cheap coffee when I was a detective, and longer putting up with the fancy teas my wife insisted on. She'd go out of her way to buy the nastiest-smelling teas because they were the latest fad but would just get whatever coffee came to hand for me. The only time I got good coffee was when I bought it myself; now I'm doing all my own shopping, I make sure I always have good quality coffee."

"I can see why; I'm gonna be reluctant to go back to the cheap stuff," Melissa said. "I want to ask how much this stuff costs, but I'm sure the price'll scare me."

"Why don't you ask the question that's been on your mind since you got here instead," Zack suggested. He had not missed the way her gaze kept straying to his chest, and it was not hard for him to work out why. "You want to know about my scars, don't you."

Melissa's cheeks reddened, but she didn't deny that she wanted to know about them. She took several long swallows of her coffee to give herself time to collect her thoughts, only then did she speak. "They are pretty nasty looking, and definitely hard to miss. How did you get them?"

"I was young and stupid," Zack answered without hesitation. "I got them in a bar fight." It was not something he was proud of, but neither did he shy away and try to pretend it had not happened. He saw the constable's curiosity was not satisfied, so he expanded. "I was having a drink in a pub, celebrating an arrest, and drank a few too many; there was a group of lads there, they'd had way too much to drink and were giving the barmaids, and pretty much every other woman in there, a lot of hassle. There was four of them, and I was on my own, but I was feeling pretty cocky, so I confronted them."

Zack watched the constable as he related his story and was amused to see that she was hanging on his words as though he was telling a spellbinding story.

"It started off as just words, but soon enough one of them pulled a knife, and another was smashing a bottle to attack me with. By the time it was all over, me and the two guys who attacked me were on our way to hospital, and I was left with the scars you saw. They got lucky on the scars front, but not so lucky on the staying out of jail side of things – they both went down for attempted murder, eight years apiece."

"Wow, you must be a really good fighter to beat four guys in a fight," Melissa said admiringly.

"Not really," Zack said with a shake of his head. "I got lucky. Besides, only two of them were actually fighting, the other two backed off when things got physical, and they were so drunk they didn't really know what they were doing. Even so, I was lucky to get away with just a few scars." He was all too aware of exactly how lucky he was – he had been left with a punctured lung that cost him over a month in hospital "Since we've broached the subject of your curiosity when it comes to me, why don't you go ahead and ask me whatever else it is you want to know," he invited.

Melissa was a little taken aback by the offer, just as she had been by Zack Wild's ready admission that he had been involved in a pub fight – the incident had been mentioned in the summary of his personnel file, but she had not expected him to admit it or explain it. She couldn't let the opportunity pass.

"How did you go from being a detective to being an author? A pretty successful one as well, from what I've discovered."

Zack was sure that was not all the constable had discovered about him, though he doubted she had found out anything that might be a problem for him.

"I guess you could say it's something I fell into," he said. "I was assigned to help CID with research when I was a young constable, and I stumbled on a cold case that got stuck in my mind – I couldn't stop thinking about it, so I went over the file and learned everything there was to know, then I investigated on my own time. It turns out I'm a better than average investigator - before long I'd solved a thirty-year-old murder." He spoke of it in the tone of someone who considered what he had done nothing significant. "The story got in the paper, I got promoted to sergeant, and a friend of my ex-wife's came knocking – she works for a publishing company and thought the story of how I solved the case would make a good true crime book.

"I wasn't sure, either that it would make a good book, or that I wanted to write one, but Paula can be pretty convincing when she wants to be; she talked me into doing the book, talked her boss into giving me a contract for the book, with a small advance, and then she showed me how to structure the narrative and everything else I needed to know to write a book - when I started the book, I didn't have a clue what I was doing. The book did surprisingly well, much better than any of us expected, and Paula's boss offered me a deal for a second cold case I was working on in my spare time; that time I had a better idea of what I was doing, so my notes were easier to turn into a book." His coffee was all but cold by then, but his throat was dry, so he drank it anyway. "Paula's boss wanted a third book when the second did better than the first, but I didn't have another cold case to write about, I did have an idea for a detective novel with a character I created – he liked the idea and gave me the contract.

"Paula had a falling out with my ex-wife around that time and wasn't able to help me after that; fortunately, she had taught me enough to write the book without her help. I wrote several more books after that, some fiction and some true crime; each one did better than the others, and when I got divorced, I decided to make several changes in my life. The biggest was to resign from the police and take up writing full time."

"You must be doing pretty well at it," Melissa said, "to be able to afford a new house and a fancy car, that Aston Martin must have cost you a pretty penny, after getting divorced."

Zack shrugged. "Probably not as well as you think, not yet anyway. I'm doing alright, but royalty payments are always at least six months behind, so I've got a while to go before my bank account looks healthy again, especially after the number Cathy did on it during the divorce. When the money comes in I'll be able to get myself sorted, until then, I'm only getting by."

17

Mitchell was not sure what to think as he walked down the path and made his way around to the house next door, where he knocked loudly. It was typical, he thought, that this should be the one time that Constance was not to be found pottering in her garden. He had to knock three times, and wait for a couple of minutes, before he got a response.

"Lewis," Constance Hawkins greeting her visitor when she opened the door. "What can I do for you? There's no problem, is there?"

"Hello, Constance," Mitchell returned the greeting. "Have you got a minute, I need to ask you a few questions about your neighbour."

"Mr Wild?" Constance had never been slow on the uptake, and she quickly put together the sergeant's earlier visit in search of Zack Wild with his presence on her doorstep.

"That's right. Do you mind?" Mitchell made a gesture intended to suggest they go inside. "I'm sure you'll be more comfortable if we do this in the living room, where you can sit down."

"Okay, Lewis, what is it you want to ask me?" Constance asked once the two of them were seated.

"First off, and I know I already asked you this last weekend, do you remember seeing Georgina Ryder a week ago yesterday on Friday evening, after six o'clock?"

Constance responded immediately with a shake of her head.

"You're certain about that?" Mitchell held firm against the glare the question provoked.

"Of course I'm certain," Constance said. "I have my dinner at six o'clock, every day, and after that I'm in front of the television until bedtime."

Mitchell accepted that, there was no reason for Constance to lie. "Okay, let's move on to your neighbour. Did you see Lucy Goulding pay a visit to Mr Wild yesterday afternoon?"

"Yes, it must have been around two o'clock when she walked past, wearing an outfit that was positively indecent." Constance sniffed disapprovingly at the memory of what Lucy Goulding had been wearing. "I thought at first she must be going up to the Wrights', but then she stopped next door. She was on the doorstep for a short while, talking to Mr Wild; I couldn't hear what was being said, but he let her in. I was surprised by that, I've spoken to Mr Wild a number of times since he moved here, and I wouldn't have thought him the sort of person to let a scantily clad young girl into his home – he seemed more sensible than that."

"I don't know if you're aware of it, but Mr Wild is an author." Mitchell saw Constance nod. "Well, apparently, Lucy is a fan of his books, and a budding author herself; she went there to get copies of his books autographed, and to get some advice on writing, that's why he let her in. Mr Wild claims that Lucy left after about an hour, between three and three-thirty, did you see her go?"

Constance nodded. "Yes, I was still pottering around in the garden when she came back out. I have to admit; I did wonder what Lucy was doing there for so long."

Mitchell was still wondering; he did not believe that Lucy Goulding had visited Zack Wild, dressed the way she was, and all they had done was talk about writing. "Did you see where Lucy went after she left Mr Wild's?" he asked.

"Of course I did," Constance said sharply. "She headed back down the road to the village. If she had gone to the Wrights', you'd have heard about it when you were up there earlier, and the only other place she could have gone is the old Matthews' place, and no-one goes there except canoodling kids. Why don't you ask Mr Wild where she went, he followed her down the road."

That surprised Mitchell. "He never said anything about that to me. When you say he followed her down the road, do you mean on foot or in his car?"

"In his car," Constance said. "He drove down the road no more than a minute after Lucy walked past me. I didn't think anything of it at the time, I just thought he was going out somewhere, but now; you said yesterday afternoon is the last time Lucy was seen?"

"As far as we're aware," Mitchell said. "From what we've been able to find out, she disappeared between leaving Mr Wild's and reaching the village. Please don't be offended, Constance, but are you certain it was Mr Wild you saw heading down the road after Lucy? I'm not trying to suggest you're wrong, I just need to be certain before I do anything."

"I'm certain. I see that car of his outside of next door every day, and I can't imagine anyone else would have been driving down the road then."

"And you didn't see anyone else around, either before or just after Lucy headed down the road?"

Constance shook her head. "No-one. Until Lucy came along, I hadn't seen anyone since Emily and Tara went off to school yesterday morning, and after Lucy left, the only person I saw was Mr Wild. You know how quiet the road is here."

"I do." Mitchell was aware that it was not unusual for a day or more to pass with no-one going either up or down the road outside of those who lived on it. "Anyway, thank you, Constance, you've been very helpful, now, if you'll excuse me, I think I'd better go speak to Mr Wild again."

"You're welcome, Lewis, I'm glad I could help."

"WHY DIDN'T YOU SAY you followed Lucy Goulding down the road after she left?" Mitchell asked the moment Zack opened the door to let him back in.

Zack looked surprised by the question and didn't answer until he had closed the door behind the sergeant. "Because I didn't."

"Mrs Hawkins says differently; she says she saw you drive down the road just a minute after Lucy left your house. She's very definite about it. Now, why don't you tell me why you were following Lucy, and where she is," Mitchell said as he trailed his suspect into the living room.

"I don't have a clue," Zack said. "Where Lucy is that is, because I didn't leave the house."

"Are you saying that Mrs Hawkins is lying? Because she is known to be a very honest and trustworthy person."

"I'm sure she is, but on this occasion, she's mistaken." Zack scratched absently at his arm as he spoke. "After Lucy left I spent the afternoon out back, wrestling with the jungle I've got growing out there – I didn't come in 'til my stomach said it was time to make dinner. I didn't leave the house until I went for my run this morning."

"I take it you have no-one who can confirm that," Mitchell said, his eyes on Zack's arm; when he stopped worrying at it with his fingernails, Mitchell saw the author had a series of scratches, no more than a day old, midway up the back of his arm. "Where did you..." Before he could finish, his phone rang in his pocket. "Excuse me." He left the room.

Mitchell waited until he got to the kitchen, where he was less likely to be overheard, to answer the phone. "Hello, sir, how's everything going with the search?"

"I guess that depends on your point of view," Stevens said. "We've found Lucy, but her parents aren't going to be happy about it. I'm not happy about it."

Mitchell felt his heart sink into his stomach. "She's dead." It was a statement, not a question. "Is it – was she killed the same way as Georgina?" he asked, wanting to hear that she hadn't been killed, that she had died as a result of an accident.

"I didn't see Georgina, so I can't say for certain," Stevens said. "But based on how you described her body, I think so, yes. I'd say she was killed by the same person, but what he did to her was worse, much worse, and I wouldn't have thought that possible when you described what was done to Georgina."

Mitchell wanted to ask what was different about Lucy's murder, but wasn't sure he really wanted to know. Instead he asked, "Where did you find her?"

"In the woods," Stevens told him. "Her body is not far from where Georgina was found."

"Have you found anything that might tell us who killed her? Or if what happened to her and to Georgina are definitely linked?"

"No," Stevens said regretfully. "We've found some partial footprints near where Georgina was found, but the rain we've had in the past week has washed most of them away, so we can't follow them anywhere. The forensics people are still working at Georgina's scene; maybe when they move on to this scene they'll find something useful.

"Paul said you're with Mr Wild, have you been able to find out anything from him?" he asked, changing the subject.

"He claims he didn't see Georgina at all the night she disappeared, and that he never spoke to her, though he did know the name, and he was aware she was missing."

"What about Lucy, has he been able to tell you anything on that front?"

"Things are a little confusing on that score," Mitchell said. "Mr Wild has admitted that Lucy paid him a visit yesterday, but he claims she left after about an hour and he didn't see her again after that."

"And you don't believe him?"

"Well, I've been able to confirm that Lucy did leave the house after about an hour, but, according to Constance Hawkins, Mr Wild followed her down the road in his car a minute or so after she left. He denies it, of course, claims he didn't leave the house until this morning, that he spent his time gardening and working on some book he's writing."

"Are you thinking he could be responsible for these...deaths." Stevens could not bring himself to say murder; it felt to him as though saying it would make it true.

"At the moment, I think he's our most likely suspect," Mitchell said. "He claims not to have seen Georgina the night she disappeared, yet she would have walked right past his house on the way to the Wright Farm, and he found her body in an out of the way place that just about no-one goes to. Then there's his claim that he didn't leave the house after Lucy's visit, when he was seen doing so, and the scratches."

"Scratches?"

"Yes, he has a series of scratches on his arm."

"What do you want to do?"

"I want to bring him in, so I can question him again, and I want to search his house and cars for anything that might link him to all of this."

"Sounds reasonable; I'll send you a couple of the guys from the search party to help you out, I'll send them as soon as I'm off the phone, it shouldn't take them long to reach you."

"IS EVERYTHING ALRIGHT?" Melissa asked when Mitchell walked back into the living room.

Mitchell shook his head. "No, it's not. Mr Wild, I'm placing you under arrest on suspicion of the murder of Lucy Goulding. We'll be taking you to the station for questioning, and searching your house and vehicles for evidence; with that in mind, where's your other car? Your Land Rover is outside, but not your Aston Martin, where is it, we're going to need to search it as well."

The announcement was not a surprise, given how obvious Sergeant Mitchell had been with his suspicions, but Zack had expected it to be a little longer before he was arrested. He assumed the move had been prompted by the discovery of Lucy's body – he didn't doubt that that was what Mitchell had been told on the phone.

"I think that's a question I shouldn't answer until I've spoken to my solicitor," he said. "Speaking of whom." He got to his feet, so he could get his mobile phone from the desk and make the necessary call.

18

Kieran Wright watched as his sisters left the living room in obedience to their father's command. He could hear them whispering, and knew they were wondering what was going on and what sort of trouble he was in, but he couldn't make out exactly what they were saying.

He wanted to snap at them to stop their whispering, he hated the way girls huddled together and whispered, but knew better, doing so would only make his father angrier than he already was.

"Right, now the girls are out of the way," Glen Wright said, leaning forwards. "D'you want to tell me what happened here this morning? What was Oliver Ryder doing here, and why was he hurting your sisters?" he asked angrily. "How could you let that idiot hurt your little sister?"

"I didn't let him," Kieran protested. "I didn't let him do anything. I heard a crashing noise, I know it was Oliver smashing through the gate now, and went to find out what was going on. I was in the kitchen, and before I could get to the living room to look out, Oliver was through the front door. The moment he saw me, he came charging down the passage and attacked me. We ended up in the kitchen, wrestling on the floor; Tara got hurt when she tried to break it up."

"I didn't even know what had happened to her until Sergeant Mitchell and Constable Turner arrived and pulled Oliver off me."

"That's worse, you didn't even know what was happening with your sisters; Tara's got a black eye and a bruised cheek – if she doesn't have nightmares about what happened, I'll be very surprised. As for Emily, she's still in shock." Glen scowled fiercely at his son. "You're supposed to protect your sisters, how're you supposed to do that if you don't know what's going on."

"I was attacked," Kieran said angrily, the volume of his voice rising sharply. "What the hell was I supposed to do, I had to defend myself or he'd have put me in hospital. It's not like I had any idea he was going to come bursting in and attack me. How the hell am I supposed to protect Emily and Tara when something like that happens? Tara should've had enough sense not to get involved, then she wouldn't have got hurt, and if Emily can't handle seeing two guys fighting, she's got bigger problems than being in shock.

"I'm fine by the way, dad, no major injuries or anything."

"Don't you get smart with me, boy." Glen half rose, one hand coming off the arm of his chair to clench into a fist, which he waved threateningly at his son. "If you didn't have this ridiculous feud with Oliver Ryder, none of this would have happened. Why did he attack you this time?"

Kieran shrugged. "I haven't a bloody clue." He fought to keep his anger under control in the face of his father's. "Oliver had no sooner been told that Geor-Georgie..." He had to pause for a moment to collect himself. "Had been found than he was racing over here to smash my face in. It's just like last weekend, when he came racing over here after he heard Georgie had gone missing. Except you weren't here to scare him off with your shotgun this time, and I didn't have a chance to get mine."

"So, he still thinks you're responsible for her disappearance, and now her death. Why's that? Did you have something to do with it?"

"Jesus, dad! How can you ask me that? Of course I didn't have anything to do with it."

"Are you sure? We both know what a temper you've got, and the kind of damage you can do when you're angry; or have you forgotten what happened when you caught that fox in the chicken coop last year?"

Momentarily, an image flashed into Kieran's mind of a carnage-filled chicken coop – there was blood and feathers everywhere, and, at his feet, the body of the fox he had kicked to death after cornering it, surrounded by the chickens the pest had killed before being dealt with. It pissed him off that his father still wouldn't let what had happened drop, even after all this time.

"If I've got a temper, it's only because I inherited it from you," he snapped. "And there's a big difference between killing a fox and killing a person."

"If you had nothing to do with what I've heard happened to Georgina, who did kill her? And why does Oliver Ryder think you did?"

"I've no idea who killed her, how would I know, and as for why that prick thinks I killed her – he's a prick, who knows why he thinks anything." Kieran couldn't believe his dad thought him capable of murder; he had always known that his father thought more of Emily and Tara than of him, but even so, to be thought capable of murder was a harsh blow. "Maybe he's trying to pass the blame. Maybe he thinks if he accuses me and attacks me, the cops will think I killed her and not pay attention to him.

"Did whoever told you about Georgina also tell you that Lucy has gone missing? And before you start thinking I might have had something to do with that, I saw her going into the old Henshaw cottage yesterday afternoon, and I told the police as much earlier. If they haven't already, they'll be speaking to Mr Wild soon about what happened to her, and to Georgie." Kieran got to his feet then and strode from the living room, he had had enough of dealing with his father just then.

19

Zack was surprised by the level of relief he felt when the door of the cell swung open; he would not have thought himself susceptible to the psychological impact of being in a cell, especially when he had been there for such a relatively short time.

"Realised you've made a mistake and letting me go, are you?" Zack asked from the uncomfortable bed, where he had been mentally writing the next few pages of his novel.

"No, Mr Wild, you're not being released," Mitchell said, pleased to be able to disappoint him. "Your solicitor is here. If you'll follow me, I'll take you to the interview room, so you can talk to her." It only took a few moments to get there. "Here you are, Mr Wild." He ushered his suspect into the interview room. "I'll be back in a quarter of an hour, so we can get this interview started."

"The interview will start when I say it does, sergeant," the woman seated at the small table said sharply. "Now, I'd like coffee for myself, and for my client, thank you."

Mitchell stared at the solicitor, not quite able to believe that he had been dismissed with a drinks order. He was not used to being treated in such a way, nor was he used to being told when he could do his job – it was a few seconds before he recovered from the surprise he had been given. His jaw clenched angrily, he turned and left the room.

"Hello, Izzy," Zack said the moment the door had been shut. "Thanks for coming."

"Don't Izzy me, Zack Wild," Isobel Faulkner said in a voice that was as sharp as the one she had used on the sergeant. "I was out with Cathy when you called; I had to lie and tell her it was Sophie who needed me because her car had broken down. What have you gotten yourself into? You said on the phone you were being arrested for murder."

"Sorry about that, I didn't know you were with Cathy, but I needed a lawyer, and it was either call you or call her – I thought you were more likely to answer the phone," Zack remarked. "I doubt Cathy would have agreed to help if she had answered the phone. Chances are, she'd have left me to rot." There was no love lost between him and his ex-wife, and he was all too aware of how happy Cathy would be to leave him in the hands of the police. "Will Sophie back up your story if Cathy asks her?"

"Of course she will, she might be Cathy's sister, but Sophie will do just about anything for you. I didn't even have to tell her anything, she agreed to cover for you the moment she heard you need help; you do have to tell her what's going on when you see her tomorrow, though," Isobel said. "How about the story then? What's going on, how have you gone from investigating murders, and writing about them, to being accused of one?"

"The short answer is, because the local sergeant, as you just saw, is an idiot."

Melissa entered the interview room then. She set down the two mugs of coffee she had brought, along with the packets of sugar, and left again. It was only when she was back out in the passage, with the door closed, that she allowed herself to smile. She could not have picked a better time to arrive with the drinks.

Isobel Faulkner grabbed the nearest of the mugs, took a sip, and then turned her attention back to her friend. "That's the short version, what's the long version?" she asked.

"The long version is that this morning, while I was out for a run, I found the body of a murdered girl. A second girl, reported missing this morning, was found this afternoon, also murdered. If the sergeant is to be believed, I'm the last person to see the second girl, Lucy Goulding; she paid me a visit yesterday afternoon."

"She wasn't seen after she visited you?"

Zack grimaced. "That's where things get complicated; my neighbour saw Lucy leave my place after her visit, but she claims I followed Lucy down the road shortly afterwards. Because of that, Sergeant Mitchell believes I'm the last person to have seen Lucy, and therefore responsible for her murder."

"I take it you didn't follow the girl down the road." Isobel was pretty sure she already knew the answer but needed to hear it from her friend. When Zack shook his head, she moved on to the next potential problem she could see. "If you didn't follow the girl, why does your neighbour think you did?"

"At a guess, I'd say she's made a mistake; she's elderly, and doesn't have perfect eyesight, she probably saw someone who looks like me and simply assumed."

"Do they have anything else to connect you to the murder?"

"The scratches on my arm," he said, showing them to her. "Sergeant Mitchell doesn't believe I got them while working in my garden yesterday afternoon; he's decided they were made by fingernails, Lucy Goulding's fingernails."

Isobel leaned over to look at the scratches. "Is that all they have against you?"

"As far as I know," Zack said. "If they've got anything else, they haven't told me about it, and I can't imagine what it might be since I didn't kill anyone."

"In that case, I think we should get this interview started," Isobel decided. "If they've got nothing more than what you've told me, I should be able to get you out of here in about half an hour, which means I'll be able to get home by about eleven. A five hour round trip on a Saturday evening, you owe me big time, Zack."

"I know, and I'll make it up to you, I promise," Zack said, though he was not sure how he was going to do that.

ISOBEL'S PREDICTION of a quick release for her client did not prove as accurate as she would have liked.

An hour and a half after the interview began, it still hadn't finished, and she was far from happy with the way things were going; she had dealt with many difficult police officers over the years, but in her opinion, Sergeant Mitchell took the prize – he had no hard evidence, only three pieces of circumstantial evidence, yet he went over things again and again, worrying at his suspect like a dog with a bone.

Reaching the end of her patience, she slapped her hand down sharply on the table. "That's it, I'm ending this interview right now; my client and I are leaving," she said. Getting to her feet, she made to head around the table to the door, with Zack on her heels.

Mitchell was briefly struck dumb and immobile by the solicitor's abrupt declaration. He recovered quickly, however, and rose so rapidly his chair was thrown backwards. "Your client is not going anywhere, Mrs Walker," he said, moving to put himself between the door and his suspect. "He's under arrest for murder, as I've already made clear, and will remain in custody until I decide otherwise."

"No, sergeant, my client is here until one of three things happen," Isobel responded, without bothering to correct him in the manner of how she should be addressed. She did not advance any further but showed every indication of being willing to walk right through the sergeant to get out of the room, should it prove necessary. "Either you charge my client with the crimes you believe he has committed, you realise he has committed no crimes and release him, or his twenty-four hours come to an end and you have no choice but to release him. Do you know which one of those three things I think is most likely to happen?"

"I have no idea," Mitchell said. He did not like the solicitor who was representing his suspect, she was too assured, and far too dismissive of both him and his investigation; she had done her best, at every step of the interview, to keep him from asking his questions, and to keep her client from answering him when he was able to ask a question.

"I think you are going to realise that my client is innocent - you have no evidence; your witness is, by all accounts, an old woman with suspect eyesight, and you cannot even prove that my client ever met the girl whose body he found, prior to her being murdered," Isobel went on confidently. "If you don't release Mr Wild immediately, I will have an order for his release, signed by the most senior officer I can lay my hands on, by morning. If you should be stupid enough to charge my client, I will be forced to lodge an official complaint against you over your inept handling of this situation – I would not call it an investigation – and petition the court for an immediate dismissal of any and all charges you file.

"Regardless of that, I will be writing to the chief superintendent for this region to insist that the investigation be placed in the hands of someone competent; you are unqualified and prejudiced, sergeant, and you seem intent on building a case out of coincidence and little else - you certainly don't have any evidence - to close this investigation as quickly as possible. Now, are you going to get out of our way and release my client or not?" Isobel stared at Mitchell, daring him to do other than what she wanted; she was unsurprised to find that he lacked the courage.

20

"**D**ammit!" Mitchell swore and slammed his clenched fist down on the counter.

Melissa could see that he was furious at having been forced to release Zack Wild – she was not prepared to say so, but she could understand the position taken by Wild's solicitor; there was no evidence, so he had to be released without charge – and wanted to get out of the way before that anger was turned on her. Unfortunately, a quick exit was not possible, there was still the end of day chores to be taken care of, and Oliver Ryder, who was still in his cell, to be dealt with.

She doubted that Mitchell was going to get around to sorting out Oliver's situation before morning, which meant an officer was going to have to stay at the station overnight to watch him.

"Do you want me to stay and keep an eye on Ollie?" she asked. It was not a job she wanted, it would afford her little opportunity to sleep, but she felt it was better to volunteer than to have the job put on her.

Mitchell thought about that briefly before shaking his head. "No, you head on home, it's been a long day, I'll sort Oliver out."

Melissa was relieved not to be getting the annoying, if easy, job of babysitting Oliver Ryder through the night, but could not help wondering what Mitchell meant by 'sort Oliver out'. There was something vaguely ominous about the phrase, something that made her think he had a meaning other than that he would be the one to spend the night at the station.

She dawdled over her closing up chores, delaying so she could try and find out what the sergeant was going to do.

Mitchell headed down the passage to his office, where he fell into his chair before reaching for the phone on his desk. As angry as he was with how the situation had turned out, he disliked what he had to do next, tell his superior that he had been forced to release Zack Wild, even more.

Like him, Inspector Stevens had been hoping the arrest of the author meant a speedy resolution to the case, before Sir Virgil Foulds could hear that anything had happened to his beloved great-niece. They could not avoid Sir Virgil finding out that Lucy had been killed, but Mitchell, along with Stevens, had been hoping that by having her murderer in custody before he knew what was happening, they could show they had done everything possible in regard to the case.

He was about to pick up the phone when a thought occurred to him. He turned the idea over in his mind a couple of times, while he looked for anything wrong with it; there wasn't, as far as he could see, so he took his hand from the phone and got to his feet. The phone call to Stevens could wait.

OLIVER RYDER PAID NO attention to the footsteps that approached his cell, he had been checked on several times since he was put in there and was sure the steps merely preceded another check. His eyes flew open, however, when he heard the rattle of keys and the sound of the door being unlocked.

"What d'you want?" he asked sharply of Mitchell when he saw the sergeant in the doorway. "Isn't it way past time an office monkey like you was home? You don't normally work this late."

"I'll be on my way home soon," Mitchell said. "I thought you'd want out of here first, though."

Oliver looked at Mitchell in surprise, not sure he had heard him right. "What're you talking about? You don't normally release me 'til you have to."

"If you want to stay here, you can," Mitchell told him. "I thought I'd save someone the job of keeping an eye on you, though. I can't see the point in putting anyone out for the sake of a pain in the ass like you." He made to shut the door and lock Oliver in again, but the young man was on his feet in an instant.

"If you think I'm staying here any longer than I have to, you're a bigger idiot than I thought," Oliver said, slipping quickly through the door before Mitchell could change his mind. The moment he was out of the cell, he stopped; he wanted to head straight for the nearest door, so he could find something to eat and drink, especially something to drink. He also wanted to find Kieran Wright and finish what he had started before being dragged away by the cops. Before he could leave, however, he had to get the things that had been taken from him prior to him being put in the cell.

Mitchell saw the eagerness in the teen and moved to curtail it. "There is a condition to me letting you go tonight," he said. "Under no circumstances are you to go near Kieran Wright. I'll be speaking to him in the morning, and I'm sure I can convince him not to press charges; if you go anywhere near him again, though, I'll have no choice but to charge you with assault, attempted murder, and anything else that occurs to me. I don't think you'd like that; if you add up all the sentences you've had previously, I don't think they'd come close to what you'd get for attempted murder." He was not sure how long a person could expect to get for attempted murder, but he had seen someone in the news recently who got ten years for it, and that was longer than any other sentence Oliver had got.

"That bastard deserves whatever happens to him, and if I have to be the one to give him what he deserves, so be it," Oliver said, heedless of the possibility that he could end up right back in the cell he had just left. "If you'd do your job, I wouldn't have to deal with the sick bastard. Why the hell haven't you arrested that murdering rapist?"

"Because Kieran Wright isn't a murderer," Mitchell said. "Nor, as far as I know, is he a rapist."

"Didn't Mel tell you what I told her earlier, about what that bastard did to Lucy?" Oliver demanded.

Mitchell nodded. "She told me, but as I explained to her, even if Kieran did attack Lucy and try to rape her, there's nothing we can do because it happened a while ago, and the report hasn't come from Lucy herself. Since we can't establish that the incident took place, we've got no reason to question him over what has happened to Georgina and Lucy, especially when we already have another suspect."

"Who?" Oliver had no sooner asked that question than he realised what else the sergeant had said. "What's happened to Lucy? What's happened to Lucy?" He repeated the question without giving Mitchell, whom he grabbed by the front of his shirt, a chance to answer the first time.

Mitchell freed himself from Oliver's grasp, at the cost of a button, and straightened his shirt as best he could. "The same thing happened to Lucy as happened to Georgina," he said. "Inspector Stevens and the search team found her body in the woods while examining the area around Georgina's body; as far as we know right now, they were killed by the same person. And before you go off on one about Kieran, we believe they were both killed by Zack Wild."

"Who?"

"He's the guy that moved into the old Henshaw Cottage."

"How d'you know it's him?" Oliver wanted to know, his whole body trembled as he fought the urge to race from the station in search of Zack Wild.

"I can't go into the evidence I have," Mitchell said pompously, as though he actually had evidence, rather than just a belief that Zack Wild was guilty of the murders. "But trust me, Wild's the one who killed Georgina and Lucy, not Kieran, so stay away from him and you'll stay out of trouble."

"If you're so certain he killed them, why the hell haven't you arrested him?"

"I did, but he's got an expensive lawyer and she forced me to let him go. Believe me, I'm no happier about it than you are, but until I can find enough evidence to charge him, he's a free man."

DOWN THE CORRIDOR IN the small locker room, Melissa listened to the conversation taking place between Mitchell and Oliver Ryder in disbelief. It was not the fact that Oliver was being released without charge that she had a problem with, she could understand that, even if she didn't wholly agree with it; what she had a problem with, was Oliver being told that Zack Wild was their one and only suspect in the murder of his cousin and his girlfriend, when he had already been arrested for attacking the person he believed responsible.

Her first thought was to confront Mitchell and demand to know what he was doing. No sooner had the thought occurred to her, than she realised that confronting her superior would be asking for trouble, which she didn't want, especially when she couldn't say that he had done anything wrong. Her mind raced as she considered her options, but she came up with no answers; she needed advice and could think of only one person to get it from – her gran.

Not wanting to give Mitchell reason to think that she had been listening to his conversation, even though that was what she had been doing, Melissa grabbed her things and headed for the door.

21

It was a walk of a little over five minutes from the police station to her gran's, and Melissa spent it thinking not only about what she had overheard, but also about recent events in the village. She could not believe how quickly the atmosphere had changed; always before, Oakhurst, even at night, had seemed a pleasant and peaceful place, almost idyllic. Now there was a sense of unease in the air, it made her look around constantly and walk more quickly than she would have normally.

The lights were out, a sure sign her gran had gone to bed, when she got to her destination. She could have knocked, Melissa was sure it would not be a problem, but she hated the thought of getting her gran up, especially when she knew how much of an effort it would be for her.

Since she couldn't talk over what was troubling her, Melissa headed for the pub; it wasn't as good as a chat with her gran, but she hoped a few drinks would relax her, and put the conversation she had overheard from her mind, at least for a short while. She found the pub crowded, as though everyone in the village over the age of eighteen had come in for a drink, including several people who were just about never seen there, and assumed news of the two murders had reached them all and they were there in the hopes of learning something about the situation.

On her way to the bar she saw Oliver Ryder, he was in a corner with his house-mates, knocking back shots as if he was trying to make up for lost time. While she waited for her drink to arrive, Melissa watched Oliver; she had not yet shaken the presentiment of trouble inspired by the conversation she had overheard between Oliver and her superior, and she wanted to know if Oliver was plotting that trouble.

Before she could slip along the bar to a position where she could listen in on what Oliver was saying, she was distracted by a loud conversation Mitchell was having with some of the others at the bar.

"...kilt them girls," Terry Dickens, who had the thickest accent in the village, and was fond of pointing out that his family had been farming in Oakhurst for more than fifteen generations, said. "Who were it?" he wanted to know.

"Zack Wild," Mitchell answered the farmer after draining half his lager in one long swallow.

"Who's tha'?"

The question made Melissa wonder how many people in the village, or how few to be more accurate, knew who Zack Wild was. She had always thought Oakhurst a friendly and welcoming village, but the day's events made it hard for her to believe that – it seemed that only about half the residents knew the name of their newest neighbour, and only a fraction of those who did knew anything about him beyond his name.

"He's the guy bought the Henshaw Cottage a few months back."

"What makes you think it's him?"

Melissa didn't have to see the speaker to know that the question came from Rod Baylor – his accent was not as prominent as Terry Dickens', but his voice was still easily recognisable.

"I don't think it's him, I know it is," Mitchell snapped angrily, unable to stop himself overreacting after the worst day he could remember. Draining his glass, he slammed it down on the bar and called for another.

The answer failed to satisfy the mechanic, who asked another question the moment he heard it. "How d'you know? Just because he found the girl, don't mean he killed her," Rod Baylor said. "If anything, I'd say that makes it less likely he killed them."

"That's not all I've got on him," Mitchell said, stung into revealing more than he intended. "He didn't just find Georgina Ryder, and her body was where just about nobody goes, he's the last person to see Lucy Goulding – she went to see him yesterday afternoon, and he followed her down the road after she left his place. Plus, he's got scratches on his arm, fresh ones, no more'n a day old. He claims he got them in his garden, but I'm sure they came from Lucy."

"So, you've decided this Wild guy's guilty 'cause he's a fitness nut who chose a scenic route for his morning run, and 'cause after Lucy left his place, he took the only road that leads from his place to the village, or even from his place to town." This time it was clear as day that the mechanic thought Mitchell wrong. "You're clutching at straws, Lewis."

"The hell I am," Mitchell snatched up his second pint and began gulping it down as quickly as he had the first. "He's the killer."

"Then why ain't you got him in custody? All of youse is here, 'cepting the inspector; if you had someone in custody, one of you'd be at the station, keeping watch, or driving him to the station in town. If you're so sure he's the one kilt them girls, why ain't you arrested him?"

Mitchell glared angrily at the mechanic, and when he didn't back down said, "We did arrest him, and we questioned him for hours, but his lawyer, some fancy bitch, probably from London, forced us to let him go 'cause we ain't got enough evidence to charge him yet."

"If you ain't got enough evidence to charge him, how in hell can you be sure it's him? Mebbe the killer's someone else, and you're leaving him free to 'tack other girls 'cause you've already decided this Wild guy's guilty."

"Come off it, Rod," Jack Peters, landlord of The Village Green, said as he poured drink after drink to meet the demands of his larger than usual crowd. "If it's not this Wild, who in hell could it be? You're not really trying to suggest it could be one of us, are you? We all know one another," he gestured around the pub. "If one of us was a killer, we'd know about it. Wild's the only stranger 'round here, it's got to be 'im. If you've not got the evidence to charge 'im yet, Lewis, you'd best find it, and soon, before he attacks anyone else."

"Believe me, Jack, I know that," Mitchell said. "I should get something I can use from either the post-mortem or the forensics team, then I'll nail him."

Melissa was a little disturbed by how willing her friends and neighbours seemed to be to believe that Zack Wild was responsible for the two murders that had occurred. Not knowing the man seemed to be all they needed to think him capable of killing not one but two girls. It was only a small comfort to her that of all the people in the village, Rod Baylor was not willing to make Zack Wild a murderer simply because he was a stranger.

She had hoped to find some relaxation in a quiet drink at the pub, while she tried to work out what to do about the conversation she had overheard. That now seemed impossible since it was clear that the sole topic of conversation was the murders, and that was the last thing she wanted to listen to.

Finishing her drink, she left so she could head home, in the hope of getting some peace there.

22

Zack woke with a start. His eyes flew open and he sat bolt upright in bed. For several long moments, he searched the darkness of his bedroom for what had woken him. Just as he was about to give up and return his head to the pillow, he heard it, the sound of people moving around furtively downstairs.

He was out of bed and reaching for the torch on his bedside cabinet in an instant. The torch he snatched up was a foot long and heavy, perfect for either lighting up the darkness or using as a weapon, which was why he kept it close to hand.

He kept the light off as he crept towards the door on tiptoe and pulled it open as slowly and as silently as he could. He didn't want to alert whoever was downstairs to the fact that he was awake until the last possible moment.

"What's going on?"

The question startled Zack and he reacted without thinking. He spun round, his torch raised in readiness to strike. It was only at the last moment that he remembered he had a guest. He managed to stay his hand before the torch struck home, but it was a close thing.

"Dammit, Izzy," he hissed in a voice that was made up of equal parts anger and fright. "You got any idea how close you came to being brained? I was half a heartbeat away from smashing you on the head with this thing." He waved the torch in his friend's face to emphasise his words, not that either of them could see it all that clearly, for the only light in the upstairs passage came from the moonlight shining through the small window in the bathroom.

"Sorry," Isobel apologised in a whisper. "Didn't mean to surprise you. Have you got burglars?" she asked as more noises reached them from downstairs.

"Sounds like it," Zack said. "You go back to the room and keep quiet; I'll be back as soon as I've dealt with whoever's downstairs." He was about to start down the stairs when Isobel caught his arm.

"Shouldn't you call the police instead of putting yourself at risk?" Isobel asked in a barely audible whisper.

"It's only a burglar, nothing to worry about," Zack whispered confidently. "They'll run off as soon as I give them a good scare."

It was Isobel's turn to hiss in a mixture of anger and fright. "What if you're wrong? What if whoever's down there isn't frightened, or they're not just here to rob you?"

"Why else would they have broken in?"

"That sergeant believes you killed those two girls, maybe someone wants to do something about that."

Zack wanted to tell his friend that she was imagining trouble, but before he could do so, he realised that she might be right. He knew well enough from his time as a detective that the murder of someone, especially a young girl, could inspire strong feelings in people, even inspire them to acts of revenge.

"Okay, you go and call the police," he told Isobel, "while I head downstairs; I'm not going to do anything," he said quickly before he could be interrupted. "I'm just going to see if I can find out who it is and what they're doing here."

Before Isobel could stop him, Zack slipped down the stairs. He was stopped halfway down by a crashing sound; listening, he tried to figure out who had broken into his home, and what they were doing there. The moment he did, he had to stifle the urge to laugh – what he could hear was comical rather than threatening.

"Watch what you're doin', ya friggin' moron."

"You watch what you're doin'; if I weren't too busy tryin' not to walk inta you, I'da seen it."

"You've walked into everything else, you might as well walk inta me. Why didn't ya bring a torch so you could see what you're doing?"

"Why didn't you? Here, I'll pull the curtains, so we can see what's worth takin', and be quiet, we don't wanna wake anyone up."

"You be quiet, you're the one making all the noise."

Zack could quite easily have believed that he was listening to a farce; the two men in his living room were clearly drunk, that much was obvious from their slurred speech, and the fact that their efforts to tell one another to be quiet were louder than the noise they were making stumbling into things. He should have been annoyed that they had broken in and were breaking his things, but the situation was too much like something from a Three Stooges film for him to be anything but amused, at least until another voice spoke up – the new voice sounded far more serious than the other two.

"Shut up, the pair o' you. Jesus! Anyone'd think this is the first time you've broken in somewhere." The new voice may have spoken in a hoarse whisper, but it contained a level of menace that silenced the other two immediately. "And we're not here to rob the place, we're here to kill the guy kilt Georgie and Lucy. I'm gonna slice the guy's heart out. He's gonna be upstairs, in bed, not in here, so come on. If you wanna take his stuff, you can get it after I've done what I came here to do."

Zack felt himself go cold when he heard that, and he froze for several heartbeats. It was not the first time his life had been threatened, but all the previous occasions had been in the heat of the moment, and he had known that the people making the threats were not serious. As much as he wanted to believe otherwise, he knew that this occasion was different – whoever had come to his house had done so with the intention of hurting him, and he had brought friends, that made the threat a serious one.

The moment he recovered from his surprise, he turned and hurried back up the stairs as quietly as he could.

"Have you called the police?" he asked once he reached Isobel, who was still near the top of the stairs.

"No," Isobel said with a shake of her head that was only just visible. "I don't know the number for the local police and calling nine-nine-nine would be a waste of time, I doubt they could get anyone here in less than an hour. Anything could happen in that time." She took a couple of deep breaths to calm herself, realising that she sounded panicky, and thought it ironic that for all the times she had represented criminals, both serious and petty, this was the first time she had been on the receiving end of a crime.

"Go into my room and get my phone, the local police station is on speed dial four. Lock yourself in and call them."

"What are you going to do?"

More calmly than he really felt, Zack said, "I'm just going to wait here and keep an eye, or an ear, on what's going on downstairs. Go on, everything'll be alright, just go and call the police." He was relieved when Isobel, after a brief hesitation, made for his bedroom.

Once Isobel had shut herself in, and he was sure she was as safe as she could be while still in the house, Zack tightened his grip on the torch and moved to a position near the head of the stairs. He was certain his friend would not approve of what he had in mind, but he had a plan for dealing with the trio who had come to kill him, or at least to assault him.

He remained tensed by the head of the stairs while he listened to the noisy intruders begin their ascent and draw near. How they thought they were going to be able to sneak up on him while he was sleeping, when they were making so much noise, he did not know – even the heaviest of sleepers would have been woken by their racket - but under the circumstances he was glad they were too drunk to be quiet.

When they were almost at the top of the stairs he jumped out, yelling, "What the hell are you doing in my house?" as loudly as he could. At the same time, he flipped the switch on the wall, bathing the stairs and the upper passage in light.

The suddenness of his appearance, combined with the light and his shout, had the desired effect on the ascending trio. The foremost of the three staggered back a step from the noise and the light, lost his footing as he missed the step he had just left and fell. His arms flailed wildly as he sought something, anything, to keep him upright, but there was nothing, and after about half a second he succumbed to gravity. He collided with his friends, who were only a couple of steps behind him, and together the three of them tumbled down the stairs in a tangle.

Zack hurried down the stairs after the trio, jumping the last four steps so he could avoid the jumble of arms and legs at the foot of the stairs. He landed awkwardly and felt pain shoot up his leg as his ankle buckled, making him fall forwards and bang his head on the front door.

He shook his head to clear his vision of stars, as he got to his feet and checked on the downed trio of would-be killers. Two of the three appeared to be unconscious, they remained just as they had fallen, and showed no signs of moving. The third, however - Zack could not help thinking it annoyingly typical, that it should be the one with the knife, the one who seemed most eager to kill him - not only had his eyes open but had disentangled himself from his friends and was most of the way to his feet, the knife in his hand moving threateningly.

Hurriedly, Zack brought his torch up to block the knife as it came towards him; he got it in the way just in time to keep him from suffering anything more than a slice to the finger.

He had no time to think of his injury, which was minor but bled profusely, for the knife came towards him again. Once, twice, three times, he blocked as the would-be murderer slashed at him again and again, attacking with such rapidity and ferocity that it was all Zack could do to get the torch in the way and keep the knife from drawing more blood than it already had.

When his attacker changed tactics, and lunged instead of slashing, Zack twisted aside, only just avoiding the point of the knife. His injured ankle buckled as he evaded the blade and he fell against the wall. Before he could recover, the knife came towards him again, this time in a wide sweeping arc that was aimed at his head, and which would have injured him seriously, perhaps even fatally, had it made contact.

There was only one way for him to avoid the danger and he took it; he fell, letting gravity pull him down and out of the way. Unfortunately, as he went down, his arm went up, straight into the path of the knife. Zack yelled in pain as the knife sliced deeply into his arm, making blood spurt. He cried out again when he hit his head on the door for the second time, though he maintained enough presence of mind to lash out with a foot to drive his attacker back, gaining him space to get to his feet.

The kick had an unexpectedly positive double result. He caught his knife-wielding attacker square on the kneecap, which made them both cry out in pain, and caused the intruder to stagger backwards into his still unconscious friends.

Zack saw his attacker catch his foot in the entwined bodies of his friends, stumble, and fall backwards onto the stairs and took advantage of the opportunity. He ignored the pain from his ankle and his arm, as well as the blood that ran from his injuries, and struggled up. On his way to his feet, he swung the torch in an overhead blow that proved to be far better timed than he could have anticipated; he intended simply to connect with his attacker, to injure him and put him off continuing the fight, or even to simply hold him off until the police arrived.

The heavy thud that sounded when the torch connected with his rising assailant's head startled Zack; it was louder than he would have expected, and he worried that he had hurt him more seriously than he meant to, that he might have killed him.

Hesitantly, he moved forwards, stepping carefully over the two tangled figures on the floor so he could reach out and check for a pulse. The relief he felt when he discovered what he was looking for – the pulse was faint, but it was there - was overpowering.

23

Zack parked his Land Rover as close to the entrance of the police station as he could and got out. He winced the moment his right foot touched the ground, the painkillers he had taken when he got up – twice the recommended dose – were not doing a good enough job of blocking out the pain from his various injuries; the ankle he had twisted, while not the most serious injury, was making the most 'noise', which didn't surprise him because he couldn't rest it, so it was constantly being aggravated.

Slowly and painfully, he limped around to the front of the building, and then up the steps to the entrance. Once inside he crossed to the counter, where he had to wait almost a minute for anyone to appear to deal with him.

"Is Sergeant Mitchell in?" he asked when a constable finally arrived.

"I'll see if he'll see you," Constable Pritchard said, without offering any of the pleasantries he might have normally when someone entered the station.

"Thanks." Zack noted the coldness from the constable, but paid it no mind, he had other things to worry about. While he waited for the constable to return, he leaned on the counter to take some of the weight off his ankle and reduce the throbbing that made him want to scream.

"What can I do for you, Mr Wild?" Mitchell asked when he reached the counter. He could not bring himself to be any more civil than that given his suspicions.

"I'm here to make a statement about the attempt on my life," Zack said, ignoring the barely concealed hostility, just as he had ignored that from the constable.

Mitchell looked confused for a second, but then his expression cleared. "You mean the assault on you by Georgina Ryder's cousin. Constable Black told me about it this morning."

"No, sergeant, I mean the attempt on my life," Zack said. "He didn't introduce himself, so I'll take your word for it that he's Georgina Ryder's cousin, but the guy who did this – he held up his bandaged arm – made it very clear why he was at my house."

Mitchell looked as though he wanted to debate or dispute that, but then he gave a little shake of his head and said, "You'd best come through, so you can tell me what happened." He opened the security door and led Zack along the passage to the interview room, where he had spent so much of the previous evening. "If you'd like to wait in here, I'll be with you shortly."

"Do you think I could get a coffee?" Zack asked. He was not surprised when the sergeant looked less than willing.

Mitchell wanted to tell Wild where to go; the last thing he wanted to do was give him what he wanted, even when it was something as simple as a drink, he certainly did not want to listen to him give a statement about the assault that had taken place. After meeting Wild's solicitor, though, he realised that refusing, either to take the statement or to provide a drink, would only give her ammunition to use against him. Reluctantly, he nodded before closing the interview room door on the man he did not want to deal with.

"Mel," he caught the attention of the young constable, who was working in the small office she shared with the other constables. "Mr Wild is waiting in the interview room to give a statement about Oliver's attack, he'd like a drink before we get started, would you see to it?"

"Sure." Melissa jumped to her feet, happy to take a break from what she had been doing – like yesterday, she was researching Zack Wild to discover everything there was to know about him. Ordinarily, she would have been happy to have an excuse to satisfy her curiosity, but not then; she knew she had been given the job because Mitchell was hoping she would learn something that would help to prove Wild was guilty of the murders that had taken place, and she was uncomfortable with that. She had been hoping a good night's sleep would make Mitchell more reasonable, and more willing to consider the other possible suspects, but that was not the case.

"Morning," Melissa said as brightly as she could when she reached the interview room. "Sergeant Mitchell said you'd like a coffee, how d'you take it?"

"Right now, I just want it strong and sweet," Zack told her. "I need all the energy I can get." He barely managed to finish speaking before he was overcome by a yawn so massive it made his mouth resemble the entrance to an underground cavern.

"I can see why; you look about as tired as I feel. I'll be right back."

Zack could hardly deny that he was tired – he had gotten less than two hours sleep before being woken by the intrusion that led to his injuries, and after the fight he'd had to be rushed to the hospital, so his arm could be stitched up. He was only able to get a couple of hours' rest, after returning from hospital, before Isobel was forced to get up and head home so she could take care of her dog.

"Right, Mr Wild, I'm sure you've got better things to do with your time, and I know I do, so let's get this statement dealt with. Why don't you start at the beginning and tell me what happened." Mitchell turned on the recorder in the corner of the room and took out a pad and pen.

Zack was about to start speaking when the door to the interview room opened; both he and Sergeant Mitchell turned towards the door, startled by the interruption, and saw Melissa creep into the room.

"Sorry," Melissa apologised when she saw that both men were looking at her. "I just thought Mr Wild would like a few biscuits with his coffee." She laid a pack of digestives on the table, set a mug of coffee in front of Mitchell, and then joined her superior on his side of the table, putting her own mug of coffee down as she took a seat next to him. She had no sooner sat than she reached out to open the biscuits and grab a couple to dunk in her coffee.

Mitchell scowled at Melissa but said nothing. "Now that we all appear to be settled, perhaps we can get started; as I said, we all have other things we need to do." Mitchell didn't look at Melissa as he said that, but out the corner of his eye he saw her redden, and knew she was aware the comment had been directed at her.

Zack nodded. "Okay, well, after I got home from being interviewed by you yesterday evening, I had a drink and went to bed, with my solicitor in the spare room – it was too late for her to head home," he said, getting straight into his story since he didn't want to take any longer about it than necessary. "I'd been asleep for a couple of hours maybe, I'm not sure how long exactly, when something woke me up. I wasn't sure what it was to begin with, but then I heard noises from downstairs, so I got up to check it out; I grabbed the torch I keep on my bedside cabinet on my way out of the room."

"I take it that's the torch Constable Black logged as evidence," Mitchell said. When he received a nod, he went on. "That's not the usual kind of torch a person has around the house, where did you get it?"

"I got it when I was on the force, but I believe you can buy one like it in most hardware or camping shops. Does it matter?" Zack asked.

"I guess not," Mitchell said unhappily. "But in the future, you might want to be more careful about carrying something that could be considered an offensive weapon, which your torch clearly can be, given the amount of damage you did to Oliver Ryder."

"I'll bear that in mind," Zack said blandly. "Under the circumstances, though, I'm glad I had the torch to protect myself with. If I hadn't, it's entirely possible I wouldn't be around to talk to you now."

'More's the pity,' thought Mitchell, though he fervently hoped neither the constable at his side nor the man across from him could tell what he was thinking.

Zack got on with relating the previous night's events then. "When I realised that someone had broken in, I crept downstairs to try and find out what was going on, that's when I heard Oliver Ryder, at least that's who I assume it was. He was telling his friends, who were stumbling around drunkenly, breaking whatever they didn't plan on stealing, that he was there to kill me, and that they should follow him upstairs to help him do that. I headed back upstairs after that and told Isobel to lock herself in my bedroom, and to call the police while I waited to see what was going to happen."

"Why didn't you lock yourself in the bedroom with your friend?"

"Because I figured it would take whoever answered the call to the police station a while to get to my place, and I didn't fancy getting trapped in my bedroom by three guys who were planning on killing me," Zack answered. "I figured my chances were better if I didn't trap myself, and instead surprised them when they got to the top of the stairs. I figured Isobel would be safer if I did that as well. If Oliver and his friends had come after me in my bedroom, there was every chance Isobel would have gotten hurt as well as me, and I didn't want that." He finished the story quickly after that, ending with a brief description of the injuries he had received at the hands of Oliver Ryder – though serious, they were far from the fatal wounds intended by the teen, for which he was duly thankful. "Given the situation, with Mr Ryder being given the impression that I am responsible for the murders of both his cousin and his girlfriend, I wouldn't normally insist on him being charged – just about anyone would react the way he did to the murder of someone they love. That said, I wasn't alone last night, and as drunk as they were, I don't think either Oliver or his friends would have noticed that they had the wrong person if they had come across Isobel before me.

"Charging him is unlikely to change his mind about what he wants to do to me, only you finding the person who really killed those girls will do that, but at least it'll keep him from putting anyone who happens to be with me in danger."

"I don't think you need to worry about that," Mitchell said, "Oliver's friends will be out of hospital later today, they only suffered minor injuries during their tumble down the stairs, but Oliver's going to be in hospital for a while - you fractured his skull. He's in a coma, and the doctor is unable to say when he might wake up. I hate to say this, Mr Wild – that was about as far from the truth as it was possible for him to get – but I am going to have to speak to my superior, and to the Crown Prosecution

Service, so a decision can be made about whether you should be charged with ABH."

"I guess I'll have to hope that the CPS sees sense then, won't I," Zack said. "I'm sure they will, once Isobel speaks to them, after all, it was self-defence." He was reasonably confident the CPS would make the right decision, but he had known them to make some very strange ones. "Is there anything else you need from me?" he asked. "Only I'm supposed to be meeting a friend in town for lunch, and I'd hate to be late."

MITCHELL STOOD ON THE top step and watched as Zack Wild drove away. Only when the Land Rover had disappeared did he turn to the constable at his side.

"Do you want to tell me why you decided to invite yourself to sit in on Mr Wild's statement, when you knew I wanted you researching him?" he asked, making no effort to hide the anger he was feeling.

Melissa looked thoroughly abashed, but also a little defiant. "After what happened at the interview last night, I thought it best if you had someone with you. I didn't want that solicitor of Mr Wild's to have a reason to cause trouble for you." That was not the only reason she was there, it was not even the main reason, but it sounded good, and she hoped it would satisfy Mitchell. "She's already threatened to do so."

Mitchell was reluctant to accept that Melissa's reason was valid, and instead said, "You'd better get back to your research, I want to know everything you can find out about Wild, everything, especially the details of those incidents that were in the summary of his personnel file. He's clearly a violent person, but I want something that will connect him to the murders. And, if possible, I want you to find out what he's done with that fancy sports car of his."

Melissa had no idea how she was supposed to do that but knew better than to waste her time saying as much. Instead, she nodded and made her way back into the station, so she could get on with her work. She hoped that while she was looking into Wild's life, she would come up with some inspiration for how to find the Aston Martin.

24

Zack saw Sophie almost as soon as he walked into the Litten Tree Restaurant; his former sister-in-law was sipping a drink at the bar. She was looking away from the entrance but seemed to sense his presence, for he had barely walked through the door before she turned towards him.

The smile of pleasure that lifted the corners of her lips when she saw him, changed to a look of curious concern at the sight of his limp, and the grimace that crossed his face with each step. The moment he reached her, and before he could say hello, Sophie asked, "What's with the limp?"

"Hi, nice to see you," Zack said, he kissed his ex-wife's sister on the cheek and took the stool next to her.

"It's good to see you too, but what's with the limp? Does it have anything to do with you needing Izzy's help so urgently yesterday? Why was that, by the way, she didn't say."

Zack had to smile. He always forgot, when he hadn't seen Sophie in a while, just how energetic and full of questions she was; she never stopped, either moving or questioning what was going on, not until she had worn herself out completely, which rarely happened before everyone else was exhausted, and she knew everything that had happened or was happening.

He did not respond to any of the questions until he had caught the attention of the bartender and ordered himself a pint of cider; even then he settled for saying, "I'll tell you everything that's been going on, but let's see if our table's ready first, I'd rather not be interrupted, and I could do with taking the weight off my ankle."

"Be right back then." Sophie hopped off her stool and went to check on their table.

"Right, now that's out of the way," she said once they had given their orders to the waiter, "what have you been getting yourself involved in? Why did you need Izzy's help yesterday?"

"I was arrested for murder," Zack said. He anticipated the response from his friend and was not disappointed – she reacted almost exactly as he had expected her to.

"What the hell? What d'you mean you were arrested for murder?" Sophie flushed when she realised she had asked the question more loudly than intended, and that it had drawn attention. "Sorry," she apologised.

"Don't worry about it." Zack ignored the curious looks being thrown his way from the neighbouring tables. "Like I said, I was arrested for murder. I found the body of a teen first thing yesterday on my run..."

"You still go running first thing? What the hell for? You're retired, you can go running whenever you want, if you really must do something that stupid. Personally, I don't see why you do it, I can't see the point in running and getting all sweaty just to stay in shape. Eat what you want, drink what you want, and do what you want, that's my philosophy. It's better to be happy than to be in shape."

"Easy for you to say, you can eat and drink whatever you want without putting on weight, so you never have to worry about staying in shape. We're not all as lucky as you, and some of us don't fancy ending up resembling a fat blob." With that said, Zack got on with his story. "When a second teen was found in the woods, and the sergeant in charge of the case discovered I was the last person to see her, he decided that I killed both girls..." It took him a short while to fill Sophie in on everything that had happened from the moment he discovered Georgina Ryder's body to when he was released the previous evening.

"It sounds to me," Sophie said once Zack was finished, "as though the sergeant is a moron. Is that where you got the limp? Did he try to beat a confession out of you?" Her eyes swept over Zack, searching for other injuries.

"What?" The question surprised Zack so much he spluttered and sprayed Sophie with the cider he had just taken a sip of. He apologised quickly, but still had to laugh, both at the question and what had resulted from it. "You should be the writer, with an imagination like that. Of course he didn't try and beat a confession out of me, but now you mention it, I think he might have tried that route if Izzy hadn't been there. I don't think I've ever known anyone to be so fixated on a suspect without a scrap of evidence to back it up.

"Would you believe he even wanted to know where my Aston Martin is – he seemed to think there might be some evidence in there; that I'm kidnapping teen girls, stuffing them into a car with a small boot and just enough space for a willing person, and taking them away to kill them." He shook his head disbelievingly.

"If you didn't get the limp through the sergeant trying to beat a confession out of you, how did you get it?"

"After Izzy persuaded the sergeant to let me go, told him to is probably closer to the truth, I suppose," Zack remarked. "The cousin of the girl I found, who's also the boyfriend of the other girl that was found, decided to get drunk and break into my place with a couple of friends so he could attack me – he decided not to say that Oliver Ryder's intention had been to kill him, it sounded too melodramatic, and was likely to prompt an overreaction from Sophie, which he didn't need just then - Izzy called the cops while I dealt with them..." He couldn't help thinking, as he listened to his own description of events, that his actions sounded a lot braver and less fraught with danger than was the truth.

"Jesus, Zack! In the space of, what, four months, you've gone from investigating murders, to writing about them, to being accused of them." Sophie could not keep either her amazement or her concern from her voice as she stared across the table at her friend. "What's next? No, I don't even want to think about that. You should never have moved to that village," she told him. "I know you wanted to get away from Cathy, and all the trouble she caused, but there was no need to move so far away, so quickly, especially when it makes it so tough for you to see Jo, she misses you."

Zack could not deny that he disliked not being able to see his daughter as much as he wanted to, nor could he deny that his decision to move more than two hours away from where he had lived had been a hasty one. He was stuck with the move he had made, however.

"You know how the saying goes, 'act in haste, repent in leisure'. I'm repenting in leisure." He gave a short, humourless laugh as he said that. "And this investigation, led by the idiotic Sergeant Mitchell, is my punishment. Fortunately, Izzy should be able to make it go away soon enough; she's already made it clear she's not happy with the way things have been handled. Maybe once I'm no longer in the frame for murder, times two, I can try and figure out what I'm going to do – I'm not sure I fancy staying somewhere that finds it so easy to consider me a murderer – but that's going to depend on what money comes in over the next two or three months."

"Are things as tight as all that?" Sophie knew her friend's finances had been strained by the divorce, and the actions he had taken afterwards, but she had not suspected to just what a degree he had overextended himself in trying to get away from his troubles.

Zack answered with a shrug that suggested the problem didn't matter, though he did admit, "Tighter than I'd like. Tighter than I anticipated. It'll be alright," he said. "It'll just take me a bit of time to get myself sorted, and into a more comfortable position. The new book's going alright, though, so I'm sure everything will be okay. That's enough about me, though, what's going on with you, has anything exciting happened since we last spoke?"

Sophie snorted. "Even if we hadn't spoken only a week ago, there's little chance of anything exciting happening to me, I don't live an exciting life, you should know that by now. About the most exciting thing that happens to me is the coffee machine at work having a fit and spraying hot water everywhere; thankfully, that hasn't happened in a couple of weeks. I swear, it doesn't matter how many times the bloody thing breaks, Larry's not going to replace it 'til someone gets scalded."

"Still not getting on with the boss I take it," Zack said.

Sophie shook her head. "I honestly don't know why he made me assistant manager, he doesn't listen to a thing I say; I don't know how many times I've told him about the machine now."

"Maybe because he'd be out of business in next to no time without you, and if he goes out of business, he's got no hope of selling the place, at least not for a price worth getting."

The two friends continued talking about the things that had happened to them since they last spoke while they finished their meal.

25

Melissa couldn't help wishing she was somewhere else as she waited nervously with Sergeant Mitchell. It was not that she didn't want to see her grandmother, she was always happy to see her, it was the reason they were there she had a problem with.

"Hello, Lewis, Melissa, to what do I owe the pleasure of this visit?" Constance Hawkins asked when she saw who was on her doorstep.

"Hello, Constance, sorry to disturb you on a Sunday," Mitchell said. "But we need to ask you some questions, I hope that's alright."

Constance smiled. "Of course it is, I'm always happy to have visitors, no matter what the reason. You've timed your visit well, I've just put the kettle on for a cup of tea, would either of you like one?"

Mitchell and Melissa nodded in unison.

"I didn't see you in church this morning, Melissa," Constance said disapprovingly as she shut the door.

Melissa flushed. "I was busy, nan, I had to work." It sounded like an excuse, even to her. "I'll go as soon as I've got a chance." Thankfully, nothing more was said about her absence from church.,

"So, how can I help you, Lewis?" Constance asked once she had made the tea and the three of them were seated in the living with their drinks. "You said you have some questions for me."

"That's right. I want to ask you about Friday afternoon; I know I spoke to you about it yesterday, but I need to confirm a few things," Mitchell said, putting his cup back on its saucer and then setting it down on the coffee table. "I hope that's okay." When Constance nodded, he got down to business. "Can you remember what time it was when you saw Lucy Goulding leave Mr Wild's place on Friday afternoon?"

Constance made a sincere effort to remember but was forced to shake her head. "I'm sorry, I know it was sometime between three o'clock and half past, but I don't know the exact time."

"That's okay, Mr Wild wasn't able to give us an exact time either," Mitchell said. "Can you tell us what happened after you saw Lucy leave Mr Wild's?" He saw the unhappy look on Constance's face and anticipated what she was going to say. "Mr Wild has said he didn't leave the house after Lucy left, and his lawyer has suggested that because of your age you might have been mistaken about what you saw; that's why I had to let him go.

"Because of that, I need to check that you're sure of what you saw, so I can add it to whatever other evidence we're able to find and make an airtight case against him."

"His lawyer doesn't know you like we do, gran," Melissa said, almost choking on a large mouthful of fruitcake as she tried to swallow it quickly, so she could speak. "She thinks because you're a bit older, you must have problems with your eyes; we know you don't. Even if you did, it's not like you can't recognise an Aston Martin when you see one; you might not be able to say what model it is, but when it's been parked next door for months, you know it when it goes past."

Constance nodded, but then said, "It wasn't that fancy car of Mr Wild's I saw on Friday, it was his Land Rover."

Mitchell felt his heart sink. "You are certain it was Mr Wild you saw driving down the road after Lucy, though, aren't you?" His heart sank into the pit of his stomach when he heard Constance's answer.

"Of course I'm sure. Even with the sun in my eyes I know my neighbour."

"The sun was in your eyes?" It was several long moments before Mitchell could bring himself to say anything more than that.

Constance nodded. "It was that sort of day," she said. "It didn't seem to matter where I stood, or which way I turned, the sun was constantly in my eyes, fair blinded me it did. I'm not likely to make a mistake about seeing my neighbour drive down the road, though, even when I couldn't see him all that well. I mean, who else could it have been in that Land Rover."

It took every ounce of self-control he could muster to keep Mitchell from swearing, loudly and repeatedly. The situation was going from bad to worse, and he could only wonder what his witness was going to say next to scupper the case he was trying to put together. "To my knowledge," he began, picking his words carefully. "There are three Land Rovers in the village, and probably more in the local area, that look almost identical to Mr Wild's, it could have been any one of them if you couldn't see who was behind the wheel properly.

"Did you see the license number, or anything about the vehicle that would enable you to pick it out as Mr Wild's ahead of any of the others in the village?"

A shake of Constance's head answered the question. "I'm sorry, I wish I could say I had but I didn't. Who else could it have been, though?" she asked. "Neil Stuart has no business being over this way; I would never have thought it was Mr Wild if it was Chris Peake – even with the sun in my eyes, I can tell the difference between a man and a woman, and I saw Glen Wright head down the road in his other Land Rover earlier, before two that was."

"Could you perhaps describe any of the clothes worn by the driver?" Mitchell asked hopefully. "Maybe we can identify Mr Wild that way."

"WELL THAT WAS A WASTE of time," Mitchell said as he unlocked the patrol car he and Melissa were using. He couldn't keep the frustration he felt from his voice, though he did hold it in until Constance had closed the front door and he was reasonably sure he was not going to be overheard. "Your gran can't be certain it was Mr Wild she saw driving down the road after Lucy, which means we've got nothing we can pin on him but a bunch of coincidences. If we try and arrest him again without getting some real evidence, that lawyer of his is going to eat us alive."

Melissa felt some sympathy for the predicament Mitchell was in but couldn't help thinking that if he had waited until he had evidence, rather than rushing to a conclusion he couldn't support, he would not be in his current position.

"Hopefully, the post-mortem will give us some evidence we can use," Melissa said, speaking over the top of the car. "Or the forensics team will find something; they had most of yesterday at the two crime scenes, and they're back again today. Whoever killed Georgina and Lucy, whether it's Mr Wild or someone else, I can't see that they'll have managed to avoid leaving any evidence at all, it's just a matter of time before it's found."

"And how many girls could he have attacked before then?" Mitchell wanted to know. "No girl in the village is going to be safe until Wild is behind bars."

Melissa wondered if the girls of the village would be safe even with Wild behind bars; she wasn't convinced the author was responsible for the murder. She said nothing of what she was thinking, though, sure that Mitchell would not take well to the suggestion he was wrong. Instead of voicing her thoughts, she said, "Why don't we take a walk down the road and see what we can see. We know Lucy didn't make it as far as the village, at least not as far as we've heard; that means she must have been grabbed between here and the church. We might be able to find something that will tell us what happened to her and where."

Mitchell considered the idea briefly before deciding it was a good one. He had been about to suggest they get some lunch and consider the next thing they should do, but they could do that after searching the area for clues, which he doubted would take them long.

"I'll take this side of the road, you take the other," he said, locking the car again.

Melissa nodded, pleased that he thought her idea worth following. She had taken just a couple of steps, her eyes on the ground at her feet, when she absently reached into her pocket for one of the chocolate bars she kept about her person. She tore open the wrapper and chewed noisily as she scrutinised the ground before and around her; she didn't want to say as much, but she had very little idea of what she was looking for and could only hope that any evidence there might be would leap out at her.

Mitchell reached the end of the row of three houses before he realised Melissa was not keeping pace with him. Looking around, he saw that she was about ten yards back, standing at the gate in the wall and looking down the path that ran along the side of the field. He glanced in the direction Melissa was looking but could see nothing to explain why she had paused in her search of the road.

"What's up?" he asked. "Have you spotted something?"

"No," Melissa admitted. "There's nothing along the road, not that I've seen, anyway, but I was just thinking, we've assumed Lucy was grabbed between here and the church, within about five minutes of her leaving Mr Wild's, because she would have been seen if she made it as far as the church or the pub. What if we're wrong, though, what if she didn't head for the village; Lucy would have made it home in about half the time if she cut across the fields and followed the river, and if she did take the short-cut, she could have been grabbed at any point between here and the other side."

Mitchell considered that theory, as he again looked over the gate at the field and the dirt path. "Would Lucy take the shortcut?" he asked finally. "It might save her twenty minutes or so, but would she really have crossed the fields to do so?"

"I don't see why not, it's not like she's afraid to get dirty, and if the outfit she was wearing really was the sort that would get a reaction from her parents, she'd have wanted to get home before them, so she could get changed," Melissa said. "I think it's more likely that she went across the fields than down the road towards the village; whoever it is that grabbed her, Mr Wild or whoever," she added quickly when she saw that Mitchell was about to say something, "would have been taking a hell of a risk in grabbing her off the road – anyone could have come along and seen him, especially since she would have been nearly at the church by the time he could have caught up to her. Going across the fields would have given her attacker more time to grab her, without being seen. He could have taken her to wherever it is he killed her then, which he's got to have done by car because it's over a mile from here to where she was found, and probably longer from wherever she was grabbed."

Mitchell was not happy that the idea had come from Melissa, rather than him, but couldn't deny that it had merit. "We'll continue on down to the church, checking the ground between here and there, then we'll come back up and start a search of the field. If we find anything, we'll mark the spot for forensics."

THE SEARCH OF THE ROAD revealed nothing – Mitchell and Melissa made it as far as the church and the pub, which faced one another across the road, without finding anything to suggest that Lucy Goulding had ever been that way – so they returned to the field, where they hit pay-dirt, at least Mitchell did.

Mitchell had gone about a hundred and fifty yards, when he spotted something up ahead in the narrow strip of scrub grass that grew alongside the wall. He hurried forwards and dropped to his knees the moment he reached the object he had seen - it was a book, one of several that were scattered over half a dozen feet. He was about to pick up the nearest of the books to take a closer look at it, when he saw the name on the cover – Zack Wild; a quick glance at the other books revealed that they were all by his one and only suspect, and when he used a pen to flip open one of the covers without disturbing any evidence, he saw that the book had been autographed by the author with a short message to Lucy Goulding.

"It looks like you were right, Mel," Mitchell called out, more annoyed than before that checking the field had not been his idea, though he was glad that the evidence had been found. "This seems to be the spot where Lucy was attacked; Wild said he autographed several books for her before she left his place."

Pleased that her idea had borne fruit, Melissa hurried over to join Mitchell. The moment she reached him she saw the books; a couple were piled together, while the others were scattered along the wall and partially concealed by the scrub grass. She also saw the remnants of the bag they must have been in, and something else.

"Sergeant, I think you should see this." Following the example set by her superior, she used a pen to lift the item she had found from the clump of grass it lay in.

Mitchell was surprised by the note of revulsion in his subordinate's voice, she sounded just as she had upon catching sight of Georgina Ryder's body. When he saw what it was that Melissa had found, he understood her tone. Dangling from the pen Melissa held was a scrap of cloth, bright orange, and so lacy as to be sheer, a scrap of cloth that had once been a thong. He knew, without thinking or asking, that the once-thong had been Lucy Goulding's, and that it had been ripped from her body when she was grabbed by the man who went on to kill her.

"Jesus!" Was all Mitchell could bring himself to say for quite some time. He had been told what condition Lucy's body was in when it was found, along with the fact that she was naked, which had led to his guessing – just as he had when he saw Georgina Ryder's body – that Lucy had been raped before being murdered; there was something about the sight of an item of intimate clothing, so obviously torn from the body, that made his guess seem so much more real.

"Are you okay to stay here and keep an eye on the area, while I go and arrange for the forensics people to come over and check this place out?" he asked once he recovered the ability to speak.

Melissa nodded hesitantly, not trusting herself to speak. She wasn't about to say as much, but the idea of staying alone where someone had been attacked, and possibly raped and murdered, made her feel distinctly uncomfortable.

26

Zack brought his Land Rover to a stop at the side of the road and watched in the rear-view mirror as the figure ran down the road towards him. He was not normally in the habit of stopping for people who waved him down at bus stops, but on this occasion, he recognised the person doing the waving. Even then he wouldn't usually have stopped, but she looked so desperate that he couldn't simply drive on without at least finding out what was up.

"Thank God you stopped, Kier..." Emily cut herself off when she realised that it wasn't her brother in the Land Rover she had just flagged down. "Sorry, Mr Wild, I thought you were Kieran; I can't imagine why, up close, the two of you look nothing alike."

"That's okay, Emily, I've got no problem with being mistaken for someone half my age," Zack said with a smile. "And given how difficult it can be to see through a windscreen on a moving car, it's not really a surprise that you thought I was your brother – there are superficial similarities between us: height, build, hair colour. So, why were you flagging your brother down?"

"I was after a lift home," Emily said. "I missed the bus, and it's ages till the next one. I thought my luck was in when I saw Kieran, or thought I did. If I have to wait till the next bus, I'll be late getting home, and late getting dinner ready, and dad'll kill me."

"You could still be lucky," Zack told her, noting the concern in the voice of the teen who had been helping him to tame the jungles that had once been gardens at his house. "If you ask nicely."

"Please, can you give me a lift, Mr Wild, I'd be really grateful," Emily said with what she hoped was a suitably coy look.

"Sure, I'll take you home, and it's Zack, remember," he said. "I'm not keen on being called Mr Wild, it makes me feel old."

"Thanks." Emily threw her bag onto the floor in front of the passenger seat and then climbed in. "And for the record, you're not old."

Zack made no comment on that, instead he concentrated on pulling away from the kerb and re-joining the flow of traffic. Despite it being a Sunday, that was no easy feat, there seemed to be far more traffic on the road than was usual for an apparent day of rest. Fortunately, once he merged with the vehicles heading past the bus stop he made good time and was soon on his way out of town.

The journey passed without conversation until they were on the road from town to Oakhurst. That was when a wince from Zack as he pressed down on the clutch while shifting gears prompted Emily to break the silence.

"Did Oliver do something to your foot when he attacked you last night?" she asked.

"You know I was attacked?" Zack asked in surprise.

Emily nodded. "The whole village knew by about eight this morning. Everyone knew why he attacked you as well."

"And why's that?"

"Because Sergeant Mitchell thinks you killed Georgie and Lucy," Emily told him. "Raped and killed them even. Oliver attacked Kieran when he thought it was him who killed Georgie and Lucy, but now he thinks it's you because Sergeant Mitchell arrested you yesterday, so he went after you. I know Oliver's in hospital, that went round the village as well, but no-one's said if you were hurt by Oliver and his moron friends."

Zack was not pleased to hear that he was the subject of village gossip. He suspected he had been previously, but then it would only have been idle gossip about who he was, what he had done or did for a living, and why he had moved there; now it concerned whether he was a murderer of teenage girls. While a part of him refused to care what a group of gossiping villagers thought of him, a more significant part was distressed by the thought that the community he had chosen to join was willing to believe him guilty of such nasty crimes. There was something else about the situation that bothered him.

"If you know I was arrested on suspicion of rape and murder, two counts no less, why on Earth did you get in the car with me?"

"Because Sergeant Mitchell's an idiot," Emily said, as though that was all the reason she could possibly need. "I know you didn't kill Georgie or Lucy, you didn't rape them either."

"What makes you think that?" Zack asked. It wasn't that he was not glad that Emily thought him innocent, it was just that he could not help wondering how she could be so certain; she knew him better than anyone else in the village because of the time she had spent working with him in his gardens, but that didn't mean she knew him all that well.

"Because you're not that kind of person. You wouldn't rape anyone." Emily showed absolutely no concern for the fact that she was in a vehicle with someone who had been accused of such an horrific crime, if anything she seemed amused, perhaps even thrilled by the situation. "Because, if you were going to rape anyone, it'd be me."

Zack was so shocked by that, he lost control momentarily; the steering wheel twitched in his hand, and he had to straighten up quickly before the Land Rover left the road and ploughed straight into one of the many trees that lined the route to the village. Once he recovered, and was no longer in danger of crashing his car, he turned to look at the teen in the passenger seat.

"Why d'you say that?" he asked, swallowing against the dryness in his throat.

"Because you fancy me. I know you do," Emily said when Zack opened his mouth to deny it. "I've seen the way you look at me when we're working in the garden, especially when you think I'm not looking. You like to check out my butt when I'm in shorts or tight trousers. Don't worry about it." She laid a reassuring a hand on his arm, a mischievous smile on her lips. "Why d'you think I wear shorts and tight trousers whenever I come round to work on your garden? I like it when you check me out, it makes me feel good." Her hand stroked along his arm briefly before returning to her lap. "If I didn't, I'd've told my dad, and he'd've come and sorted you out."

Zack didn't know how to respond to that; he couldn't deny that he had checked Emily out – as the teen described it – not when she had made it so clear she knew what he had been doing. She had said she was not bothered by his checking her out, but that didn't make him feel any better about the situation. To cover his discomfort, he turned on the radio, letting music fill the silence and drive away the urge to make idle conversation.

THE JOURNEY FROM BRANTON to Oakhurst took a little under an hour, and a few minutes longer to get from there to the Wright farm. Zack drove into the yard that fronted the farmhouse – there was no gate for him to get out and open, thanks to Oliver Ryder – swung the Land Rover around, and pulled up near to the front door.

"Well, here you are," he said, glad to have the awkward journey over with. It wasn't that he had not enjoyed Emily's company, but he was still uncomfortable after their conversation, which had made him painfully aware of every instance in which his eyes strayed to the teen at his side – why his gaze kept doing so, he couldn't explain, and no matter how hard he tried to stop it doing so, he couldn't; it made no sense to him, she was attractive enough, for someone who was only sixteen, but hardly a stunning beauty.

"Great, there's still time for me to get dinner ready," Emily said, the relief she felt at that evident in her voice. "Thanks, you saved my life, dad would've gone nuts if dinner wasn't ready on time; he only let me go to town because I said I'd be back in time to cook. I owe you big time."

Zack turned his head to respond to that, and got as far as saying, "You don't owe..." before he was interrupted, not by Emily speaking, but by her lips on his.

Before he had a chance to realise what he was doing, Zack found himself kissing Emily back. It was a quarter of a minute before he came to his senses and pushed her away with a feeling of regret and shame.

"No, no, we shouldn't be doing this, it's wrong," he said.

"No, it's not, why should it be wrong?" Emily wanted to know. "You like me, and I like you, why shouldn't we kiss each other if we want to?"

"Because it's wrong," Zack said in a tone that was part apologetic and part regretful. "Even if Sergeant Mitchell, and probably at least half the village, didn't think me a rapist and a murderer, it wouldn't be right – you're only sixteen."

"It's the age of consent," Emily protested. "We're not breaking the law by kissing. We wouldn't be breaking the law no matter what we did."

"That may be true." Zack could hardly deny it since he knew very well that it was true. "But it doesn't really matter. Age of consent or not, you're only sixteen, and I'm more than twice that. Can you imagine your father, or anyone else you know, being alright with you being involved, in any sense, with someone twice your age?"

"Who cares what anyone else thinks," Emily said, too caught up in the moment to worry about anything.

"I do," Zack said. "Nothing bad's likely to happen to you if something were to happen between us, but it almost certainly would to me. I've only met your father a couple of times, but I'm sure he'd be furious if he thought I was trying to take advantage of you, and having been attacked once already, I don't want it to happen again. Not only that, but if I let something happen between us and my ex-wife found out, she'd be so happy she'd probably dance in the street."

"Why would she do that? What difference does it make to her what you do?"

Zack shrugged. "Not a lot really, at least it shouldn't. Cathy's interest in what I do or don't do, extends only to how it affects her ability to keep me from seeing my daughter, and to get money from me, if she can do both at the same time, all the better as far as she's concerned. Cathy would see something happening as a great way to stop me seeing my daughter, or at least to extort more money from me in exchange for not keeping me from seeing her.

"You're a great person: attractive, funny, smart, and very handy around the garden, but I have to think about my daughter, do you understand?" He hoped she did; he didn't like to think what might happen if she didn't understand or became resentful of what he had said.

Emily regarded Zack for a short time before finally saying, "Your daughter's lucky to have you." She got out of the car and was about half way to the front door when she suddenly darted back to the Land Rover.

Before Zack knew what was going on, she had jumped up and pulled herself through the open window of the driver's door, so she could kiss him again. "Maybe next time I come round I'll dress like Lucy, that'll give you something to look at."

Zack was so surprised by Emily's actions that she was in the house, with the door closed, before he could recover, let alone react. Still dazed, he started the engine, shifted into gear, and left the yard. He spent every second of the sixty-second drive home berating himself for what he had just allowed to happen. He could not believe he had been so stupid.

Emily was over the age of consent, he knew that, but kissing her was still one of the stupidest things he had ever done – being a suspect in two rapes and murders, both of which involved teenage girls, only made his actions more stupid. Especially when he knew Sergeant Mitchell was looking for any excuse to arrest him again; he didn't doubt that if the sergeant were to find out what had just occurred between him and Emily, he would be in handcuffs before he could utter a word in defence of his actions. His only consolation was that there had been no-one around to witness the kiss.

He was so distracted by what had happened, and by thinking about the possible consequences, that he didn't realise there was a car parked in his drive until it was almost too late.

27

Emily was on her bed, reading a book, one eye on the clock on her bedside cabinet so she wouldn't be late taking the meat out, when she heard a vehicle pull into the yard outside. Pushing herself up, she craned her head around to look out the window to see who it was; it was too early for it to be her dad or her brother, they were unlikely to get home until just before dinner was ready to be served.

The moment she saw the Land Rover in the yard, she leapt to her feet, pleased that Zack Wild had returned. As pleased as she was, she was also a little nervous. She knew she had caught Zack by surprise when she kissed him, she had caught herself by surprise as well, to such an extent that she had forgotten to grab her bag when she got out of his car, and now she had had time to think about her actions, she realised what a fool she had made of herself.

On her way out of the bedroom and down the stairs, Emily imagined the possible reasons for his return: he could be there simply to return her bag, or he could be there to make sure she was not going to tell anyone what had happened between them; he might even be there because he had changed his mind about what he had said earlier.

She hesitated with her hand on the front door catch, reluctant to open the door and discover how her next encounter with Zack Wild was going to go. After half a minute, she took a deep breath, summoned her courage, and opened the door so she could step out into the yard.

Zack was nowhere to be seen. Emily had thought to find him outside the front door, about to ring the bell, but he wasn't there. She looked around the yard but couldn't see him, which made no sense to her; she couldn't think where he might have gone. She walked to each corner of the house to see if he was there, but there was no sign of him. Bewildered, she walked to where the Land Rover sat in the middle of the yard.

She wasn't normally the sort of person to go rummaging around in someone's car without permission, it wasn't polite, but on this occasion, she thought it okay since she was after her bag. Her bag wasn't where she had left it, though. It should have been in the foot-well in front of the passenger seat, but the foot-well was empty; leaning further into the vehicle, she searched under the passenger seat, where she found a number of items, none of them her bag.

The desire to find out more about the man who lived down the road, and with whom she had made such a fool of herself, made her take out each item in turn so she could examine it. She discovered little, other than that Zack Wild was messier than she had previously thought, at least initially; the first few items she pulled out were a road map of the county, an empty crisp packet, a couple of chocolate wrappers, and a hammer – she had no idea why he had a hammer under the passenger seat, it seemed a strange thing for him to have there, but it wasn't as strange as the next thing she pulled out, a pink mobile phone.

For several long moments, Emily simply stared at the phone; it was familiar to her, she was sure she had seen it before, but she knew it wasn't Zack's. She couldn't work out where she knew the phone from, and that annoyed her because she was sure it was important; whose phone it was, and where she had seen it before, came to her in a flash when the voice sounded from behind her.

"What are you doing?" The voice that uttered the question was curious but evidenced no concern until she turned around and its owner saw the phone in her hand. "Where did you get that? Give it to me," he demanded, holding out a hand insistently.

In an instant, Emily knew who had killed Georgina Ryder and Lucy Goulding, and it was the last person she would have thought capable of murder. So great was her shock, she was left frozen to the spot, unable to react to her discovery except by staring at him. Only when he lunged at her, demanding, "Give me that phone, you nosey bitch," did she recover the ability to move.

At the last second, right before his grasping hand closed around her wrist, Emily twisted away. She felt a small amount of satisfaction when his momentum carried him into the side of the Land Rover, which he collided with heavily, but didn't allow that to stop her racing across the yard to the still open front door. Once she was through the door, she slammed it closed and, with fumbling fingers, dropped the catch; she didn't suppose that was going to keep him outside for long, but any delay was good.

When the front door, against which she was leaning, shook under the impact of something heavy, Emily left it and hurried up the stairs. As she ascended she sought to unlock Georgina Ryder's phone – she had seen it previously in the hands of her brother's girlfriend, which was why she had found it familiar the moment she picked it up – so she could call her father, but her fingers continued to display a reluctance to obey the commands from her brain. She was beginning to think the phone was dead when the screen lit up; unfortunately, that was as far as she got, for Georgina had her phone secured with a password.

Inspiration struck her as she closed the door to her bedroom with a bang and twisted the key in the old-fashioned lock. The relief she felt when Georgina's birthday unlocked the phone was amazing, she had never felt anything so powerfully before. That relief quickly disappeared, however, when she got no answer from her father's number.

Again, and again she tried to get hold of her father, while she listened with one ear to the front door smash into the wall of the passage, followed by the thunder of footsteps on the stairs.

"Come on, dad," Emily pleaded, the phone pressed to her ear so hard it was liable to stay there even after she let go of it. "Pickup, pickup, pickup. Where are you when I need you?"

When the thunderous footsteps reached the top of the stairs and stopped, only to be followed by a crash as something heavy slammed into the door of the bedroom, Emily abandoned her efforts to contact her father, and instead dialled the number for Oakhurst's police station. She hoped, while dialling, that the solid, and old, oak door she had always hated would prove strong enough to keep out Georgina and Lucy's killer; so far it had stood up to the job – it shook and shuddered within its frame but remained secure.

More than she feared being murdered, if it was possible for her to fear something more than that, she feared what he might do to her before he killed her. As she had told Zack Wild on the drive back to the village, she knew what Sergeant Mitchell believed had been done to Georgina and Lucy before they were killed. Until a few minutes ago, she would not have believed that someone she knew so well could be capable of either rape or murder, and she certainly would not have believed him capable of committing either act on her.

Having seen his face when he tried to get the phone from her, though, she found herself scared that he was prepared to do anything, to anyone, including her.

Sturdy the door might be, sturdy enough it wasn't. Once, twice, three times, he threw his body against the door, and on the fourth time it burst open in a shower of splinters that made Emily duck for fear of being struck. When she straightened up, she saw the menacing figure of the person she had cared about approaching her through the ruins of her door. His face was a twisted, barely recognisable, mask of rage that made her tremble violently.

"Gimme the phone," He demanded in a voice that was so harsh and full of hatred it combined with the look on his face to give him an air of insanity.

Emily could only wonder how it was that she had not seen how crazy he was before. It didn't seem possible that he could have concealed what kind of person he was for so long. Someone should have seen through the act he was putting on, she thought during the millisecond in which she was able to think with some semblance of clarity.

"I said gimme the fucking phone."

Emily twisted away as he lunged for her. She tried to slip past him and out of the room, thinking that if she could get out of the house without getting caught, she stood a chance of making it to the village – once there she would be safe. The idea was good, but it failed at the first hurdle; she was caught before she could even get out of the room. She was almost at the door when she was brought up short by a sharp jerk on her top, the back of which had been grabbed by the killer she was trying to elude.

"Where the hell d'you think you're going?"

The question was accompanied by a yank that sent her spinning and stumbling across the room. She hit the bed and fell over it, landing heavily on the floor on the other side. Unaware that her call to the police station had been answered, Emily lost her grip on the phone, which bounced out of her hand to disappear under the bed.

More concerned with protecting herself from the maniac who was obviously intent on causing her serious harm, and most likely on killing her, Emily gave no thought to the phone she had just lost as she struggled to her feet. At least she tried to, before she could make it further than her knees, she was grabbed and thrown onto her back.

"What the hell were you doing looking around in my car?" he demanded, punching Emily in the face as she tried to sit up. "Why are you so fucking nosey? I said, why are you so fucking nosey?" Grabbing Emily by the front of her t-shirt, he pulled her up, so he could punch her again for not answering him, not that she could have done so for the first blow had rocked her head back, so it struck the bedside cabinet behind her.

He repeated the question several times, in different ways, and each time Emily failed to answer him, he hit her. Finally, it sank in that he was not going to get an answer because Emily was incapable of providing one. Once he realised that, he let go of her t-shirt, leaving her to drop to the floor with a thud. While the thud echoed around the bedroom, the madness that had overcome him began to fade; sense, or some semblance of it, began to return to his mind, though not before he was struck by a last – for the time being – burst of open insanity.

"Look what you've made me do. Look at the mess you've made me make." He kicked her in the stomach. He felt like kicking her a second time, but now that the madness was gone, and he was thinking a little more clearly, he realised he had to move quickly if he wanted to avoid getting caught.

He had no idea how much time he had before Tara got home, and he had to get Emily's body out of there before she did, before she could see what he had done. He didn't know where he could take her – he certainly couldn't dump her body where he had dumped Georgina and Lucy, that would be the first place the police looked, but having a destination wasn't half as important as getting her out of the house.

He took a quick look out of the window quickly, to be sure the yard was clear, then bent to grab Emily by the front of her t-shirt. It took all his strength to get her dead weight to his shoulder, and he staggered a little as he made his way out of the room.

28

"Oakhurst Police Station, how can I help you?" Melissa answered the phone. "Hello, is anyone there?" Hello. Hello." She pressed the phone to her ear as she strained to hear anything that would suggest there was someone on the other end of the call.

"Why are you so fucking nosy?"

Melissa flinched, and quickly pulled the phone away from her ear, though not before she heard the unmistakeable sound of a fist striking flesh.

"Sergeant, I think you should hear this," she called down the passage after covering the mouthpiece of the phone. While she waited for Mitchell, she listened with growing horror to the sound of someone being violently assaulted.

"What is it?" Mitchell asked upon reaching the counter.

Melissa answered the question by putting the call on speaker. "I want to be wrong," she said, after silencing the microphone so she could speak without being heard by whoever was on the other end of the call, "but that sounds like someone getting beaten up."

Mitchell nodded his agreement. "You're right, the question is, who; who's being attacked, and who's doing the attacking, and where's the attack happening? Do you know the number?" he asked, looking at the phone's screen.

Melissa wracked her brain but had no more luck recognising the number than Mitchell. "No idea," she said with an unhappy shake of her head. "If I've seen it before, I don't remember it." That didn't surprise her, she had a lousy memory for numbers; to be sure it wasn't a number she should know, she took out her phone.

The number didn't match any of those in her phone book, nor those in Mitchell's when he thought to take out his phone to copy her; despite that, both officers were sure the call was coming from someone in the village.

"What're we going to do?" Melissa asked, afraid that they were listening to the person who had killed Georgina and Lucy as he attacked a third young girl.

Mitchell was quick to answer that. "You're going to stay here and call everybody. I want the inspector here to help you try to figure out who's being attacked, and I want you to send Paul, Michael and Adrian to meet me at Wild's place, and tell them to hurry, I want them there before he can do anything permanent to whoever he's attacking."

"But we don't know that Mr Wild's attacking anyone," Melissa said, not happy that Mitchell was leaping to the conclusion that the author was responsible for what they had heard on the phone. "We've got no reason for thinking that he's attacking, or has attacked, anyone. That voice is familiar, but I'm not sure it's Mr Wild."

"We've got plenty of reason," Mitchell told her, starting down the passage to his office; he returned almost immediately with a file, which he slapped down on the counter in front of Melissa. "Read that. But call everyone before you do." With that he strode around the counter and out of the station, so he could get on his way.

Since the phone line was still open and on speaker, in case anything was said that could be used to identify either attacker or victim – it would have been good if they had been able to record the phone call for future use, but that was not something they had the technology to do – Melissa used her mobile to make the calls she had to, at the same time she flipped open the file so she could see what it was Mitchell wanted her to read. She saw straight away that it was Zack Wild's personnel file from Southampton police, the full file, not the summary they had received before.

It took only a short while for Melissa to see what had caused Mitchell to react the way he had; the file presented the image of a man who was prone to violence, including violence against women. By the time she got to the end of it, however, she realised that Mitchell had only taken what he wanted to from the file.

The confusion she had already been feeling about Zack Wild and Sergeant Mitchell, and the latter's certainty regarding the former's guilt, was deepened by reading the file. She couldn't deny that Zack Wild had control issues when it came to violence, but the report made it clear that the incidents were either self-defence, the result of provocation, or, in the case of the allegations made by two young women, which were most likely the incidents on which Mitchell was basing his presumption of guilt, false.

She was relieved when Inspector Stevens agreed with her that Zack Wild couldn't be arrested on what they had, and that if he was arrested it might jeopardise any case they tried to put together against him in the future.

She doubted Mitchell was going to be happy with her when he realised what she had done, but she found she didn't care; all that mattered to her just then were stopping her superior endangering the investigation, and figuring out who they had heard being attacked, and who was doing the attacking - neither of those last two were easy since beyond the 'nosy bitch' phrase, which suggested the victim was female, and the number the call came from, they had no clues.

29

"Hi, is Tara home?"

Hastily, He pulled the blanket he was arranging down and spun around; the panic he felt at the thought that Emily's body had been seen subsided when he saw that it was only Daisy Hawkins, and she showed no sign of being aware of what he had done, or of what he was doing.

"Not yet," He said, pleased that he sounded completely normal.

Daisy might not have seen anything suspicious, but when Emily was discovered missing, she was bound to mention that she had seen him at the house, and when. No matter how stupid Sergeant Mitchell was, He didn't imagine he would have any difficulty connecting his presence at the house with Emily's disappearance. Since that was the case, He couldn't allow Daisy to tell anyone he had been there, he wasn't sure what to do about her, though.

After a moment, he was struck by what he could only think of as an inspiration. "Actually, I'm on my way to meet her, why don't you come along."

"Okay," Daisy said without hesitation, showing no sign of being afraid or concerned, rather she looked excited at being invited to go with him.

"Get in then," he told her. "I've just got to finish sorting something out back here, then we'll be good to go." He waited until Daisy had climbed into the passenger seat of the Land Rover and couldn't see what he was doing, then he adjusted the blanket covering Emily to be sure she wouldn't be revealed by accident. Only when he was satisfied did he close the boot and get behind the wheel.

"Where are we going?" Daisy asked as he turned off the road less than half a mile from the farm. She had never been down the dirt path they were on now, but she knew it led to an old farm, and she couldn't imagine why Tara would be there; despite that she didn't feel afraid, only surprised.

Fear replaced her surprise, however, when she saw the way he was looking at her.

He had seen Daisy several times, but never thought of her as anything but a young girl, when he thought of her at all. Now, though, and he couldn't have said why his thoughts had changed, he found himself looking at her as he would a girl he was interested in taking to bed, and he liked what he saw. She was young, but she was developing into an attractive girl, and he found himself becoming aroused.

"Where are we going?" Daisy repeated her question. With an effort, she tore her gaze from his; the hint of lust in his eyes – she had never been looked at like that before, but some instinct told her what was behind the look – scared her, at the same time it gave her a tingly feeling she didn't understand, but which made her squirm in her seat. "Why would Tara be out here?"

"She isn't," he told her. There was an edge to his voice that he quickly suppressed. "I've got to take care of something before we go and meet her. You don't mind, do you?" As he asked the question he dropped a hand to her leg and began stroking it up and down, caressing her thigh through the denim of her jeans.

The tingly feeling that had begun with the look increased at his touch, but so did her fear. Despite her excitement at his sudden interest in her, Daisy could not help feeling that there was something wrong. "What do you have to do?"

"D'you always ask so many questions?" He wanted to know. "Hasn't anyone ever told you that men prefer girls who know how to be quiet?"

"S-sorry." Daisy was glad when the hand was taken from her leg, but the sudden sharpness with which he spoke to her made her tremble in fright.

His temper, which had seemed to be just below boiling point for the past week, since he killed Georgina, erupted at this minimal provocation and he lashed out.

"I said shut up," He snapped as Daisy groaned in pain. "Why can't you girls ever do what you're told?" he demanded.

The drive to the farmhouse took no time at all, and he was soon pulling up in the yard in front of the partially destroyed house. He glanced around briefly but didn't give the yard and the house more than a cursory look because he couldn't afford to waste time if he wanted to avoid anyone becoming suspicious. Throwing open the door next to him, he got out, shouting for Daisy to do the same.

Daisy was stunned and horrified by what had happened; she had never been hit before, not properly, and she didn't know how to react to it other than to be afraid. Releasing her seatbelt when he got out of the Land Rover and started towards the rear of it, she threw herself across the car, so she could pull the driver's door closed and lock it. After that she reached over to hit the lock on the passenger door, before dropping into the driver's seat.

She had never driven a car before, she had never even started the engine on one, but she had seen her parents drive often enough to be reasonably confident she could manage. There was just one problem with her plan, the keys were not in the ignition; a tapping sound on the window next to her made her look round apprehensively and she saw that He had the keys. Her heart, which had already been beating a rapid tempo against her ribcage, threatened to burst out of her chest.

When He saw that he had her attention, he stopped and unlocked the car.

"That was very – fucking – stupid," He said angrily, speaking slowly and deliberately to emphasise his words. Reaching into the Land Rover, he grabbed Daisy and dragged her out. She fell to the ground when he let go of her and simply lay there, sobbing. "Get up," he ordered in a voice so harsh it made her sob all the harder. "I said get up. Get up and get inside." He accompanied the order with a kick that lifted her half off the ground and drove the air from her lungs in an explosive gasp.

Daisy lay there for several long moments, overwhelmed by pain and struggling for breath, and then slowly pushed herself up. He seemed satisfied that she was obeying him once she started to get up, and she used that to her advantage; while He was focused on what he was doing at the rear of the Land Rover, she, instead of heading towards the farmhouse, began moving slowly back the way they had driven. She wanted to run, to sprint for the road that led to the village as fast as her legs would carry her, but she was afraid that running would attract his attention, which was the last thing she wanted to do.

She had gone no more than a couple of feet when she saw what he was taking from the boot of the Land Rover. The moment she saw the body – she couldn't see the face, so she had no idea who it was, but she could see it was female – she screamed, a prolonged sound of terror that made him drop his burden and spin towards her. The anger in his face gave Daisy a burst of adrenaline that sent her racing away, like a hare pursued by a pack of hounds.

He forgot all about Emily's body as he sprinted after Daisy – Emily was not going anywhere, but if Daisy got away he would be in serious trouble. He was not as fast as the fleeing girl, he saw that almost immediately, so he did the only thing he could think of, He threw himself into a diving tackle. He caught Daisy around the legs with one arm, knocking them out from under her and sending her to the ground.

Untangling himself, he rolled the teen over and pulled her towards him. "That was really – fucking – stupid." He punctuated each word with a punch that threatened to dislodge Daisy's teeth. "You had to make things worse, didn' you." He continued to berate her between blows until he was out of breath and his knuckles were beginning to get sore, at which point he got to his feet. After several long moments, during which he regained his breath, he bent to grab Daisy's foot, so he could drag her into the farmhouse.

30

A little out of breath after running up the road Tara hurried across the yard to the house. She was late home and dreaded what her father was going to say; she was too old to be spanked, but that was only a small consolation. She hadn't meant to be late, if it hadn't been for her friend distracting her with videos on YouTube when she was about to leave, she would have been home on time.

All thought of the punishment she might receive was driven from her mind when she pushed open the door, which stood ajar and a cloud of thick black smoke billowed out to engulf her. She stumbled away, choking, until she found fresh air and could breathe again.

It took her a short while to recover enough to wonder what was going on, and once she did she cautiously approached the door; the worst of the smoke had cleared, but she still felt her throat close as she stepped over the threshold and started down the passage.

"Em. Em. Emily!" Tara called out as she headed along the passage to the kitchen. She realised before she got to the kitchen that the smoke was coming from the dinner Emily was supposed to have been cooking; how the dinner came to be burned, she didn't know, but she was certain it meant Emily was going to be the one in trouble, not her.

There was no response from Emily by the time she got to the kitchen, and no sign of her dad. Tara's first thought was to go looking for them; she resisted that instinct, however, realising that it was more important to deal with the situation in the kitchen.

She paused long enough to collect the fire extinguisher from the cupboard under the stairs, and then she entered the kitchen with her breath held to avoid choking. The smoke made her blink rapidly, but she found her way to the stove, and once there she put the fire extinguisher down – there were no flames for her to deal with just then.

Since there was no fire, she focused instead on the smoke. Grabbing the pans off the top of the stove, she carried them to the sink, where she turned on the cold tap to douse the contents – at one time it might have been described as food, but that was no longer the case. That done, she returned to the stove.

She groped through the smoke until she had turned off all the hobs, and the oven, and found the oven-gloves. As ready as she was going to get, she pulled open the oven door, releasing a fresh cloud of smoke that threatened to choke her, and reached in for the roasting pans. She dumped them in the sink with the other pans, and with that done she yanked open the back door so she could make for fresh air.

Tara remained outside until the last of the smoke had cleared, returning to the kitchen to turn off the water before the sink could overflow and flood the kitchen when it was safe. The last thing she needed was more mess, even if she wasn't responsible for the state the kitchen was in; she had no intention of being the one to clean it up. Once the water had stopped, she checked the oven to be sure it was out and there was no fire to be dealt with – there wasn't, thankfully – and went in search of her sister.

As she headed nervously up the stairs, afraid of what she was going to find – she knew that something had to have happened for Emily to have let the dinner burn – Tara took out her phone to call her dad.

"Where are you, daddy?" she wanted to know, almost sobbing into the phone, when it had reached the answer phone for the second time. "Why aren't you answering. I need you. I think something's happened to Emily; the dinner's been burned and...and..." Her voice stumbled when she reached the top of the stairs and she saw the mess that had been the door to her sister's bedroom. "I'm s-scared d-daddy," she stammered as she edged towards her sister's bedroom; she wanted to turn and run down the stairs and out of the house, but she couldn't, she had to know if Emily was there. "Emily's door's broken."

She saw the messed-up quilt straight away but wasn't troubled by that. It wasn't until she reached the end of the bed and saw that Emily was not in the room, and that there was blood – her brain leapt to an answer for what the red stuff was – on the bedside cabinet that she lost control of herself. Screaming, she fled the room with such haste that she tripped when halfway down the stairs and fell the rest of the way. Bruised and shaken, but somehow still in possession of her faculties and her phone, Tara got to her feet, so she could run from the house; she had always felt safe and secure at home, but now she felt scared to be there.

She wanted to keep running, across the yard, out the gate, and down the road, but she forced herself to stop in the yard, so she could call for help – not from her father, since he was clearly not answering his phone.

31

Glen Wright was surprised and alarmed to find both of Oakhurst's patrol cars in the yard outside his house when he got home. He brought his Land Rover to a stop and threw open the door, almost falling out of the vehicle in his haste; once on his feet he ran across the yard and into the house – the front door was already open, so he didn't have to waste time fumbling for his keys, but that only made him more concerned.

"Emily, Tara," he called out as he started down the passage. He stopped almost immediately as he caught sight of his youngest daughter out the corner of his eye. "Tara, what's going on?" he asked as he strode across the living room to the sofa, where the fourteen-year-old was sitting with Melissa.

"Where were you, daddy?" Tara asked in a desperate voice. She was torn between the urge to leap to her feet and throw herself into her father's arms, and the desire to remain where she was on the sofa, where she had been made to feel safe by Melissa. In the end she stayed where she was; the distress she felt at her failure to get hold of her father kept her from going to him. "I called and called, but you didn't answer. Where were you. I needed you!"

"I'm sorry, honey," Glen apologised, pulling his daughter up and into his arms so he could comfort her. "But you know how I am with that damned phone – if I'm not right there when it rings, I don't have a clue that anyone's tried to call me. Are you alright?"

"I-I guess so, d-daddy," Tara half sobbed into her father's chest. "I just got really scared when you didn't answer."

"What scared you? What's going on, Lewis, and where's Emily?" Glen asked over his daughter's head. "She should be home, and dinner should be ready to go on the table." He sniffed at the air, as though searching for some sign of the dinner he was expecting. "All I can smell is something burned."

"We don't know for sure what's happened yet, but if you'll come with me. I'll tell you what I know," Mitchell said. "Would you stay here and look after Tara a little longer?" he asked of Melissa.

Mitchell led his friend from the living room and down the passage to the kitchen; only when they reached the smoke-blackened room did he speak, and then it was in response to a question from Glen.

"What the hell happened here?" Glen wanted to know. He crossed to the sink to look down on the pots and pans encrusted with food that was too far gone to even be called well done; he knew straight away that it should have been the dinner he had spent all afternoon looking forward to.

"We don't know," Mitchell said. "But I'll tell you what I do know. Tara came home a little after six and found the dinner burned; she did the right thing and got the stove turned off and the pans in the sink, and she opened the back door to get rid of the smoke. Once she did that she tried calling you while she looked for her sister." He led the way back down the passage and started up the stairs. "She found the door to Emily's room busted, as you can see." He had to hurriedly put out a hand to stop Glen before he could rush into his eldest daughter's bedroom. "Emily isn't in there; we don't know where she is.

It looks – I'm really sorry – but it looks as though she's been kidnapped. We've got the room sealed off, so the forensics people can make an examination of it when they get here; in the meantime, we're trying to work out who could have taken her, and where."

"What the hell d'you mean you're trying to work out who took her?" Glen demanded angrily, his gaze moving between Mitchell and the broken mess that was all that remained of his daughter's bedroom door. "You know who did it, that maniac down the road, the one you let go. If you'd kept him locked up, like you should have, he wouldn't have been able to hurt my Emily. I blame you for this." In his anger he seemed to grow, until he loomed menacingly over Mitchell.

Mitchell opened his mouth to protest but could not get any words out because he agreed with Glen, up to a point, the point where he was supposed to take the blame for Zack Wild being released. He could not deny that if Wild had remained locked up, Emily would almost certainly not have gone missing, but he disagreed with the idea that he was responsible for Wild being released – that was solely down to Wild's solicitor as far as he was concerned.

"I didn't want to let him go," he said once he was able to speak. "I didn't have a choice. If I hadn't released him, his solicitor would have had my job. Don't worry, I'll get Emily back."

Glen ignored Mitchell's efforts to reassure him, and instead glowered angrily at the older man. "You'd better get her back, quick, and unharmed, and you'd better put him away where he belongs, so he can't hurt anyone else. If you don't..." He didn't get a chance to finish his threat, for just then Kieran came through the front door.

"What's going on, dad?" Kieran called out in a worried voice.

"It's your sister," Glen told his son as he slowly descended the stairs. "It looks as though Emily's been kidnapped by that sick bastard down the road."

"What is it, Kieran?" Glen asked, seeing the concerned look on his son's face. "What's the matter?"

Hesitantly, Kieran said, "I saw him, Wild, earlier, he was here with Emily."

"What do you mean?" Glen demanded.

"I saw him. My bloody car broke down, again, and I had to come back for a part; I was in the shed when a car pulled into the yard, and when I looked out I saw his car, you know, that Land Rover he's got that looks like mine; he wasn't alone, though, Em was with him. I was about to go out and confront him when...when..." Kieran's voice tailed off until he was prompted.

"When what, Kieran?" Glen asked of his son.

"When Emily kissed him," Kieran said. "I was so surprised I just sort of froze where I was. I thought at first he'd made a move on her, was about to attack her or something, then I realised she wasn't objecting to what was happening, wasn't trying to stop it. I couldn't believe what I was seeing. By the time I recovered and grabbed a wrench, so I could sort him, Em was out of the car and in the house, and he was heading out of the yard and down the road."

"So, you did nothing, while the monster who killed your girlfriend and your ex attacked your sister. What the hell kind of brother are you?" Glen wanted to know.

He glowered so angrily that Mitchell felt it prudent to place himself between father and son to keep Glen from doing something he might regret later.

"You should have protected your sister," Glen said, fighting the urge to push past Mitchell and attack his son.

"I thought she was alright," Kieran protested. "She was in the house, and he was gone. I was gonna tell you first chance I got. I wanted to confront Em about what I'd seen, her kissing that sick bastard – I don't know how she could do it, when I know she knows what he did to Georgie and Lucy, but you know how she is, she'd never have listened to me.

"Since I knew she'd just tell me to mind my own bloody business, I went to get my car, so I could come back and tell you everything. It took longer to get the damned thing going than I expected." His face fell in an expression of horrified dismay then. "It's all my fault. He must have realised I was there or something, waited 'til I left, then come back. It's my fault Em was attacked," he all but wailed. "If I'd just forgotten about my car and stayed here, I could have protected her, kept her safe from that maniac; she'd still be here, and he'd be in handcuffs or hospital, where he couldn't hurt anyone else."

"It's not your fault," Glen said, reversing his accusation of just a minute ago. "You thought Emily was alright. It's his." He rounded on Mitchell, who retreated quickly from the anger that radiated from every pore of the younger man's body. "He had that sick sonofabitch in custody, he had him in a cell; he knew what that bastard did to Georgina and Lucy, he arrested him for it, and then he let him go."

"It's not my fault," Mitchell protested. "I didn't want to let him go, I had no choice, his lawyer forced me to – I didn't have enough evidence to charge him. If I hadn't released him, she'd have had me fired."

"You let him go, and now he's grabbed my Emily," Glen snarled. "If he's hurt her, I'll kill him."

"You can't talk like that, Glen," Mitchell cautioned his friend.

"I'll talk any way I bloody well want," Glen said angrily. "Especially in my own home. Either you get my Emily back safely, and deal with that perverted murdering bastard, or I will. If I have to deal with him, there's no way in hell he's ever gonna be able to hurt anyone again."

32

Isobel could only stare when she saw the state of her client. She had gotten the impression that something wasn't right when she spoke to him on the phone, but she hadn't expected what she was seeing.

"Jesus!" she said finally. "What the hell happened to you? You look as though you've gone twelve rounds with Mike Tyson."

"I wish," Zack said through gritted teeth. "At least then I'd feel better about being in this kind of shape." Limping around the table, he settled onto the seat next to his solicitor. "Sergeant Mitchell and his constables were a little overzealous when they came to arrest me."

"A little overzealous." Isobel couldn't keep her incredulity from her voice. "This is more than just someone being a little overzealous," she said. "You were a detective; you know how bad this is. It's assault, Zack, they assaulted you, and if the way you're moving is anything to go by, quite badly. Look at you, they've broken your nose, blacked both your eyes – you can barely see; you've got a split lip, a cut on your forehead and your cheek, and that's just what I can see. And your arm's bleeding, you must have pulled at least one of your stitches.

"This is disgraceful. We're going to sue them over this, they're not getting away with it."

Zack shook his head, slowly to try and minimise the pain the movement caused. "I don't want to do that," he said. "Suing will just cause more hassle, and I've had enough of that the last couple of days. I just want to put all of this behind me as quickly as possible, so I can move on."

"And just how do you expect to manage that?" Isobel wanted to know. "This sergeant has made it pretty clear he thinks you're guilty of the murders he's investigating – if you can call what he's doing investigating – and whatever else has happened; which is what? You didn't say when you called, just that you'd been arrested again."

"I didn't tell you because I don't know myself," Zack told her. "All I got was a demand to know where a girl was; I don't have a clue what girl they were talking about, let alone what I'm supposed to have done with her."

Isobel's sense of outrage over the treatment of her friend increased. "Are you trying to tell me that not only were you assaulted, they didn't tell you why you were being arrested?"

"Yes, but let's not make a fuss about it, all I want is to get this interview done, get home, and take as many painkillers as possible."

"You can't just let this slide, Zack; that sergeant is a menace, and given how unwilling he is to even consider the possibility that someone else is responsible for the murders, he's never going to find the real killer until he's forced to back off from you," Isobel said. She couldn't understand why he wasn't more interested in punishing the prejudiced sergeant, he was not normally so passive. "Not only that, but you need to go to the hospital and get checked out; who knows how bad your injuries are."

The two of them argued back and forth about what they were going to do for several minutes, before finally coming to an agreement, at which point Isobel called for Sergeant Mitchell.

"Are you ready to get this interview started?" Mitchell asked the moment he entered the interview room.

"If I had my way, no," Isobel said bluntly, seeing no reason to sugar-coat her words. "My client wishes to get the interview over and done with, however. Before we start, I wish to make it clear how unhappy I am with the treatment he has received at the hands of you and your officers; it is nothing less than appalling, and I can assure you I will be registering a complaint at the highest level possible – not only was my client physically assaulted during your ham-fisted arrest of him, he was prevented from making the phone call he is legally permitted for over an hour, he has not been told why he was arrested, and, worst of all, he has not been seen by a doctor. He could be suffering from internal injuries for all we know."

"The doctor is busy," Mitchell said sharply, not at all happy with the way he was being spoken to. "He is dealing with the family of the girl your client kidnapped and has most likely murdered. As for the suggestion that your client was assaulted, that's utter nonsense – he resisted arrest, and my officers had to use force to restrain him."

"In order to resist arrest, he would have had to know that he was being placed under arrest," Isobel said. "Given that he was hit in the face by his own front door when you and your officers smashed it open, without identifying yourselves..."

"He knows who we are, he's seen us before."

"Even if he had been able to see and recognise you, which is unlikely given he was half-blind as a result of having his nose broken, you are required to identify yourselves and your reason for being there – you did neither. After the attempt on his life last night, it's no surprise that my client defended himself when someone, several someones, broke in and assaulted him. I'm certain you would have done the same under the circumstances." Isobel took several deep breaths to try and calm herself, which wasn't easy. "If it were up to me – she threw Zack a dirty look – I would insist that my client be taken to hospital immediately to be checked out. However, since my client has made up his mind to get this interview out of the way, I will settle for him being examined by the doctor."

"I already told you, the doctor is busy with the family of the girl your client kidnapped, which is more important than dealing with the few bumps and bruises he has." Mitchell nodded at Zack Wild.

"I will be making note of your attitude in the letter of complaint I intend writing to the chief constable," Isobel said. "If you don't want me to insist that this interview be postponed until my client has been thoroughly examined at hospital, and you have been replaced by someone competent to handle this investigation, I suggest you find someone with some level of medical training who can clean my client up and deal with his cuts, and who can replace the bandage on his arm."

Melissa had been sitting silently beside Sergeant Mitchell but now she spoke up. "I've got my first aid certificate; I can take care of it. I'll be right back."

What should have been a simple piece of first aid took longer than any of them anticipated. Cleaning and dealing with the two cuts on Zack's face, and his bloody lip, took little time; it was the injury on his arm, the cut made by Oliver Ryder, that most delayed the start of the interview. The cut had bled freely after the stitches were pulled, and the blood had then dried, sticking together the layers of bandage that covered it.

Melissa worked as carefully as she could to remove the bandage without adding to Zack's pain, but it wasn't easy. The final layer proved especially difficult, and after a couple of minutes of trying, she was reluctantly forced to simply yank the bandage off; in doing so, she pulled another of the stitches, which caused a fresh surge of blood to wash down Zack's arm onto the table beneath it.

There was nothing Melissa could do about the three stitches that had been torn out; she could, however, attempt to stop the blood, clean up the arm, and replace the bandage. Once all of that was done, she cleared away the mess her first aid had created.

"CAN WE GET ON WITH this interview now?" Mitchell asked once Melissa was finished, he couldn't keep his impatience from his voice, and he didn't try.

Reluctantly, Isobel nodded, though she wanted to refuse and insist that Zack be taken to hospital to get his arm re-stitched.

It took Mitchell a few moments to get the recorder set up, once he had he launched the interview with the question he had been itching to ask for more than half an hour. "Where's Emily Wright?"

Zack was shocked to hear that it was his neighbour – in the broad sense of the word - he was believed to have kidnapped, and it was a short time before he could respond. "No idea," he said, knowing he was not going to be believed.

"Are you sure?"

"Of course I'm sure, why would I know where Emily is?"

"Because you were seen with her; you were seen with her, and you were seen attacking her," Mitchell said. It wasn't what Kieran Wright had told him, but he hoped that if Wild believed there was a witness, he would confess.

"Either your witness misunderstood what he or she saw, you misunderstood what you were told, or you're deliberately trying to make what you were told sound worse, to get me to admit to something that didn't happen," Zack said in as calm a voice as he could manage; he had used the same tactic he suspected Mitchell was using when he was a detective, so he knew how it worked. "Yes, I was with Emily this afternoon, but I didn't attack her."

Mitchell looked at his suspect disbelievingly. "What were you doing with Emily?"

"I gave her a lift home. I was on my way back to the village after lunch in town with a friend, when Emily flagged me down; she'd missed the bus she was waiting for, thought I was her brother, and was after a lift home."

"You expect us to believe that Emily mistook you for her brother; you're twice his age and look like nothing like him."

Zack ignored the scepticism in Mitchell's voice. "There are superficial similarities between us," he said. "Similarities that make it easy to get us confused when seen through the windscreen of a Land Rover travelling at thirty miles an hour. Anyway, since I was heading back to the village, and I didn't have to go out of my way, I said I'd give her a lift."

"Did you take her straight home?"

"Yes. She flagged me down at the bus stop at, I don't know, about a quarter past three, and I dropped her off at the farm at just before half four. I remember because Emily commented that I got her home with just enough time to get the dinner cooked, which she was glad about, because she had thought she was going to be late after missing the bus and was afraid of the fuss her father was going to make."

"Did you leave straight away after dropping Emily off?"

Zack nodded. "I dropped her off, and then I headed home."

"Then why do I have a witness who claims to have seen you kiss Emily, and then attack her?" Mitchell wanted to know.

"I wouldn't have a clue since I don't know who your witness is," Zack said. "I do know they're wrong, either deliberately or otherwise, because I never attacked Emily."

"So, you didn't kiss Emily?"

The idea of lying and denying the whole incident occurred to Zack, but he dismissed it after only a moment. Lying was only going to cause more trouble for him, and he didn't want that.

"We kissed," he admitted, ignoring the disappointed and dismayed look that was shot his way by Isobel. "But I didn't kiss her, she kissed me. I know you're not going to believe me," he said before Mitchell say anything, "but that's what happened."

A heavy silence fell over the interview room after that statement and lasted for more than a minute. At the end of that time Mitchell, in a voice so thick with sarcasm and disbelief that it could have been served with a spoon, said, "Let me see if I've got this straight, Mr Wild; you were flagged down at a bus stop in town by Emily Wright, who thought you were her brother, you agreed to give her a lift and brought her home, where she, for some reason, decided to kiss you – an action which you, of course, had no control over. Following the kiss, you left Emily to make dinner for her family and headed home. Have I got all of that right?"

"More or less," Zack agreed. "I was caught by surprise by Emily's kiss, and it was a few moments before I could think clearly enough to stop what was happening. Once I could, I told Emily it was wrong and shouldn't have happened and won't be happening again. That was when she went into the house, and I headed home."

"If that's what happened, Mr Wild," Mitchell said. "How did Emily's bag come to be at your house? We found it in the cupboard under the stairs when we searched your house."

"Emily had it with her in town and was in such a rush she left it in my car when she headed into the house. I didn't realise she'd forgotten it until I got home; I put it in the cupboard out of the way, thinking I'd take it back to her later, but, obviously, I never got a chance."

"Is there anyone who can confirm what time you got home?"

Zack almost smiled. "As it happens, there is. When I got home my agent was waiting for me, he had some things he needed to talk about, and he wanted to see how the next book is coming along; he was there until about quarter past five, and when he left I called my daughter – I always call her on a Sunday – and we spoke until her mother called her for dinner, which would have been about six o'clock.

"It wasn't long after that, that you guys went racing past my house on the way to the Wright farm, and a while later you came bursting through my front door."

"Are you sure you wouldn't like to change your story and tell us the truth, Mr Wild?" Mitchell asked. "Things will go a lot better for you, if you admit what you did and tell us where we can find Emily, especially if she's still alive when we find her."

Zack sighed and shook his head, a move he immediately regretted. "I am telling the truth, so I can't change my story," he said. "I hope you find Emily, soon, and that she's alright, but there's nothing I can do to help you."

"I doubt you're aware of this, Mr Wild," Mitchell decided that it was time to play his trump card, "but we received a phone call here at the station this evening; a phone call in which we heard Emily Wright being attacked, by you."

"You must be mistaken, since I never attacked Emily. What time did you receive this phone call?"

"It was about half past five, wasn't it," Melissa said without thinking, something she wished she had done when she saw the angry look directed her way by Mitchell.

Zack was about to respond to that when Isobel beat him to it. "There must be some misunderstanding on my part," she said. "But if you received this phone call at around half past five, and you knew that the people you could hear were my client and this girl, Emily Wright, and you knew that what you were hearing was Emily Wright being attacked, why did it take you more than half an hour to get to this girl's house? If you ask me, sergeant, the answer is one of three things: either you're lying, and you didn't know who you could hear; the phone call never happened; or you're guilty of criminal negligence for not responding sooner to a phone call from someone in distress."

Isobel paused to see if Mitchell was going to respond, and when he didn't she went on, "If the phone call occurred at half-past-five, it couldn't have been my client you heard, because, as he told you, he was on the phone to his daughter. I'm sure if you call his agent and his daughter's mother, they will confirm what he has told you, then we can end this farce and you can release my client."

Zack wasn't about to say as much, but he had his doubts about his ex-wife confirming his story; she was likely to enjoy having the opportunity to cause trouble for him. Fortunately, he didn't have to rely on his ex-wife and her fickle, and occasionally vindictive, behaviour, his phone and the records from the phone company would confirm his alibi.

33

"Goddammit!" Mitchell swore. "I can't believe I've got to let him go, again!"

"He's got an alibi," Melissa said. "He couldn't have been the one who kidnapped Emily."

"Only if it was Emily we heard being attacked on the phone," Mitchell said as he struggled to control his anger. "If it wasn't her, then we don't know when she was attacked, and Wild's alibi goes out the window. I still say it's him. He was seen kissing her, for god's sake."

"Kissing isn't attacking," Melissa pointed out. She couldn't quite believe she was defending Wild, especially after he had admitted kissing Emily – how he could have done such a thing when he was more than twice her age, she didn't know – but she believed in doing her job right and didn't like the thought of Mitchell remaining so focused on making him a suspect when there was no evidence against him whatsoever. "And if it wasn't Emily being attacked, who was it? It's not like we're a town or a city where people are attacked all the time; it's rare enough for one person to be attacked here, the odds of two people, two girls, being attacked on the same day, around the same time, are ridiculously high."

"I don't know who else it is that could have been attacked, I just know that Wild's the one that attacked Emily." There wasn't so much as a trace of doubt in Mitchell's voice. "That solicitor of his may have forced me to let him go, again – anger flashed in his eyes as he said that – but I'm gonna prove it's him. I'm gonna prove it's him, and I'm gonna put him away for the rest of his life. I'd better go and let Glen and the inspector know what's happened." He stalked away down the passage to his office.

Melissa started after Mitchell, it was unbelievable to her that he should remain so certain of Wild's guilt, but she couldn't see a way to make him accept that someone else might be responsible for the disappearance of Emily and the murders of Georgina and Lucy. When he disappeared into his office, she pushed aside her concerns, temporarily anyway, and got on with the end of shift chores so she could get out of there and, hopefully, relax for a bit.

The chores were done, and Melissa was on her way past Mitchell's office, when she heard something that made her stop in her tracks.

"...do anything to him and I'll have to arrest you," Mitchell said in a low voice that was clearly intended not to be heard by anyone other than who he was on the phone with. "I know you're angry he's been let go, I'm angry too; I didn't want to let him go, but he's got an alibi that makes it look as though he couldn't have taken Emily – his solicitor used that to force me to let him go."

Based on what her superior was saying, Melissa guessed he was speaking to Glen Wright, who was angry that Zack Wild had been released, and ready to make good on the threat he had made at the farm. She hoped that any threats he was making towards Zack Wild were just that, threats; the last thing the village needed, in her opinion, was a revenge attack against the author, especially after Oliver Ryder's attack of the night before.

"I'm telling you, it's not my fault," Mitchell insisted after allowing the person on the other end of the call a chance to speak. "If it was up to me, he'd be in a cell, and wouldn't be getting out." There was another pause then, followed by, "I have no idea how he managed to fake an alibi, he had plenty of time to set it up, though," and then, "No, we don't know where Emily is; I'm sorry, I truly am. What did you expect me to do, beat the truth out of him? I'm in enough trouble as it is for the mess we made of Wild when we arrested him, I could lose my job over it. His solicitor's talking about writing to the chief constable. If we'd beaten him up any more seriously, he'd have ended up in hospital, then there wouldn't be any question about it, I'd lose my job."

Melissa stopped breathing at that point as she made sure she didn't make a sound. She hadn't want to be caught listening to her superior's conversation before then, but now he had all but admitted having taken part in assaulting a suspect, she was certain that getting caught would be very bad for her.

"Of course I don't want him to get away with it," Mitchell snapped. "There's nothing I can do, though, except keep looking for Emily, and for evidence that will help me prove he's the guy doing all of this. The post-mortems should be done tomorrow, and with a bit of luck, we'll get some of the forensics reports, then I'll be able to arrest Wild again, and this time I'll be able to charge him – once I charge him, he's bound to tell me where Emily is.

"What makes you say that?"

Melissa was torn between walking away before she could be discovered and staying where she was so that she could hear more, in case Sergeant Mitchell was going to say something else that it might be important for her to know.

"If she is already dead, there's nothing you can do about it, Glen," Mitchell said, confirming to Melissa, albeit unknowingly, who he was talking to. "And nothing you do will bring her back."

There was a brief pause as he listened to what his friend said. "Maybe it will make you feel better, for a short while, but what about after that? You'll be a murderer, you'll be in trouble, and so will I, because you've told me what you're planning. I told you what's happened because I didn't want you to hear it from someone else; I owe you that. Now go to bed and try not to think too much about what's happened, it won't make you feel any better."

Sensing that her superior's phone call was coming to an end, Melissa slipped away. She grabbed her things from her locker and left the station as hastily as she could, before Mitchell saw she was still around and could have overheard his conversation.

GLEN WRIGHT SLAMMED the phone down angrily, not caring that he was in danger of breaking it, and stood there in the darkness of the living room, his mind racing. He was so lost in his thoughts he didn't hear the footsteps on the stairs, he had no idea his son was there until he spoke.

"What's up?" Kieran asked from the doorway of the living room. Having been woken by the ringing of the phone, he had arrived in time to hear part of the call, enough to know that something was up, without knowing what.

Glen scowled as he turned towards the doorway and his son. "That was Lewis," he said. "He's had to let Wild go, again!"

"What the hell! So, he kills Georgie and Lucy, and he kidnaps Em, but he's still free? What the hell does he have to do before Lewis puts him away where he belongs?"

"He said Wild's got some kind of alibi; he can't prove it's fake right now, but he will, and when he does he'll arrest Wild again, which'll be too late for your sister. It's probably too late for her already." The expression on his face was a mixture of anger and frustration, and his hands were clenching and unclenching themselves into fists; he looked around the dark room as though searching for something to either throw or smash.

Kieran was reluctant to draw attention to himself, when it was obvious that his father was looking to vent his feelings, he couldn't help asking, however, "What are you going to do?" Given the way his father was fidgeting about, Kieran was sure he was planning on doing something, even if he hadn't quite decided what.

"I don't know," Glen admitted. "You go on up to bed, though, I'll be alright, I just want some time to think."

About fifteen minutes later, Kieran watched his father cross the yard and start down the road as he stood at the window of Emily's bedroom. He hadn't heard the front door either open or close, but he hadn't needed to, he had already been in Emily's room, waiting for his father to leave the house and take matters into his own hands, as Kieran had been sure he would, which the shotgun Glen appeared to be carrying strongly suggested he was going to do.

34

"Bloody hell, Zack," Isobel swore when she saw the mess in the living room. "That sergeant and his cronies did this?" she asked, looking around the room.

"Uh huh." Zack nodded. "I think they thought I might have Emily hidden in the sofa or something," he said, seemingly unconcerned by the damage done to his things. "It's not that bad really, they could have done worse." His laptop, which was the thing that mattered most to him, was still intact, even if very little else was."

Isobel looked at her friend as though he had gone crazy. "How on earth can you think this isn't that bad?" she wanted to know. "The only way this could be worse is if they actually set off a bomb. I don't care what you say, we're suing them for this, this and your injuries. If this is what it looks like in here, I hate to think what the rest of the place is like," she said, more to herself than to Zack. "I don't suppose you've got a camera around here, have you?"

"What's the matter with the camera on your phone?" Zack asked, more harshly than he intended. "Sorry. It was in the desk, so it could be anywhere now, assuming the cops didn't take it in the hopes of finding some evidence on it." He looked around at the mess on the floor surrounding his desk, the majority of which had either been in or on the desk prior to the visit from the police.

"If it's somewhere in amongst that lot, it's probably best if I leave it there," Isobel remarked. "I don't want anything moved 'til I've had a chance to take pictures of the mess Sergeant Mitchell and his men have made. This is probably going to be the easiest lawsuit I've ever had to deal with; it's like they were trying to give us everything we could need to sue them."

Zack was glad that if there was going to be a lawsuit, it was going to be an easy one; he knew how difficult they could get from watching his ex-wife when she handled such cases. "Do you want anything to eat?" he asked from the doorway. "I'm going to make myself a fry-up and get some painkillers."

Isobel didn't answer straight away, she was distracted by fiddling with her phone. Once she was ready with the camera function, though, she realised what it was Zack had said. "Please. You couldn't get us a drink as well, could you?"

"Sure, a glass of wine?" Zack was not a wine drinker, he preferred cider or spirits, but he always kept a bottle of red and a bottle of white in the house for guests.

Zack produced the glass of wine – white – almost immediately, but it took the best part of twenty minutes for him to put together a fry-up for himself, and another for Isobel. When he entered the living room with the two plates, he found Isobel still taking photographs.

"Alright, get your top off."

Zack froze just inside the living room. "I beg your pardon."

"Get your top off," Isobel repeated. "I've done everything in the house – this room's the worst, by a fair margin, but they didn't spare any room in the place, they're all a mess, so now it's your turn. If we're going to nail Sergeant Mitchell, and the police, as fully as they deserve to be, we need pictures of what was done to you."

"Can't it at least wait 'til we've eaten?" Zack asked. He looked around for somewhere to put the plates down, and for somewhere to sit; that was when he saw movement outside the window. He reacted instinctively, shouting, "Get down." The plates he was holding, along with the food they contained, went up in the air as he dived for cover; he couldn't have said how he knew the movement he had seen heralded danger, but his quick reactions saved him, for no sooner had he let go of the plates than the main window of the bay exploded in a crash of thunder.

Zack landed alongside what remained of his sofa, which protected him from the flying glass, though it didn't protect him from the fry-ups he had thrown. A mix of bacon, sausage, mushroom, egg, and baked beans rained down on him, messing up his hair and leaving him with bean juice running down his neck.

It was only when he looked up from his position on the floor, and saw that Isobel was covered in blood and swaying on her feet, that Zack put together what he had seen and heard and realised what had happened. Scrambling to his feet he launched himself at Isobel, so he could protect her, since she didn't seem able to protect herself. He crashed into her just as the shotgun went off again and felt a wave of pain, unrelated to the injuries he had received at the hands of Sergeant Mitchell and his constables, sweep over him.

He ignored the pain and focused on making sure that Isobel was safe.

He saw straight away that his friend was in bad shape, having been struck many times by the pellets from the shotgun – covered in blood as she was it was impossible to tell how many of the pellets had hit her, or where she had been hit - her breathing was shallow, and her skin was pale beneath its mask of blood. Worst of all, the blood on her lips bubbled and frothed in a way that made Zack fear she had been hit in the lungs; whatever other injuries she might have, the possibility of a punctured lung worried him the most, and he reached into his pocket for his mobile phone.

35

Goosebumps stood out on the exposed flesh of Mitchell's arms as he stared skyward, watching the lights from the air ambulance disappear into the distance.

Once it had vanished from sight, bearing Zack Wild and Isobel Walker away to the hospital in Branton, Mitchell refocused his attention on things a little closer to home.

"Will you be alright if we talk about what happened?" Mitchell asked of Constance Hawkins, who was at his side, and who, unlike him, showed no sign of being affected by the night's chill, thanks to the dressing gown that covered her from her ankles to her neck.

There wasn't much to talk about, based on what he had seen when he took a quick look around, being careful not to get in the way of the paramedics as they worked on Zack Wild and his solicitor. It was clear what had happened, and after the conversation he had had with Glen Wright following the release of Zack Wild, he could guess who was responsible for the attempt on Wild's life. Before he could do anything about the situation, though, he needed to know what Constance had seen and heard.

"If you'd prefer, we can leave it 'til morning, but I think it might be better if we do this while everything is fresh in your mind."

Constance thought about it for a couple of seconds before responding. "I don't imagine I will be able to sleep much for the rest of the night, not after this, so you might as well ask your questions now. Would you like a cup of tea?" She started up the path to her front door without waiting for an answer, leaving Mitchell with no choice but to follow her.

"Thank you." Mitchell accepted the cup of tea Constance brought him and lifted it straight to his lips. The first sip was hot enough to burn on its way down his throat, but he put up with that, it was a small price to pay for feeling warm for the first time since receiving the call about the attack on Zack Wild. "Do you think you could tell me what happened tonight, from the beginning?"

"Of course." Constance took a moment to sip at her own tea, and then she began. "I went to bed at my usual time, about ten o'clock, and read for a little bit, then I put my head down. I dropped off almost straight away – I've never had a problem getting to sleep, but it seems as though the older I get, the harder it is for me to stay asleep; the slightest little thing wakes me up. I hadn't been asleep for more than an hour when I was woken by a car passing the house and stopping next door; I guessed it must be Mr Wild getting home, but as easy as it is for me to wake up, it isn't so easy for me to get out of bed.

"I had barely made it back into bed, at least that's how it seemed, the clock on my bedside table said about half an hour had passed, though, when I heard the shotgun blasts next door."

"You knew what the noises were straightaway?" Mitchell asked.

Constance looked at him for a moment. "Of course I did. You can't live your whole life in the countryside without knowing a shotgun when you hear it."

Mitchell accepted that with a quick nod since he could hardly deny what Constance had said; he hadn't grown up in the country as she had, but twenty plus years of living there made him sure he would recognise a shotgun when he heard one being fired.

"So, you heard the shotgun, how many times was it fired?"

"Twice."

"What happened after that?"

"I struggled out of bed and made my way over to the window. I was hoping to see who had been shooting, and at what, though after Oliver Ryder's little escapade last night I was reasonably certain what, or rather who, was being shot at." Constance paused in her narrative to sip at her tea; only when it was finished did she put her cup down and resume speaking. "By the time I made it to the window, though, they were gone. Since I was concerned about Mr Wild, I put on my dressing gown and headed next door to make sure he was alright. Thank goodness Mr Wild was able to remain conscious long enough to call for an ambulance; who knows how long it would have been before help was on the way if they had had to wait for me to find them."

"Yes, very fortunate," Mitchell said. "You said you didn't see the person who fired the shots, I take it that means you can't tell me anything about the person who tried to kill Mr Wild." He didn't even consider the possibility that Zack Wild's solicitor might have been the intended target.

"I'm afraid not, sorry." Constance felt bad that her lack of speed had prevented her seeing anything that might be of help. "Do you think it might have been Oliver again? He already tried to hurt Mr Wild once, and he's never been the sort to let up on a grudge."

"He would have been my number one choice," Mitchell admitted. "But he couldn't have done it, he's still unconscious in hospital after last night's adventure; I would have been notified if he'd woken up." He sighed briefly, as though annoyed that Constance couldn't tell him anything. "You didn't see anything, but is it possible you heard something that might help me to figure out who tried to kill Mr Wild?" he asked.

"You mean like a car or something?" Constance shook her head when Mitchell nodded. "Sorry, no, I didn't hear anything, other than the two shots. I didn't hear a car after Mr Wild got home, either coming or going, and I'm pretty sure I would have."

It took Mitchell a few seconds to realise the implication of what Constance had just said. "Whoever did this must have walked here," he said. "Not that I suppose that means all that much – it wouldn't take long for someone to get here on foot, even from the other side of the village." He sighed again. "Do you suppose Barry might have seen or heard anything?" he asked, referring to Constance's neighbour on the other side from Zack Wild.

"I guess anything's possible," Constance said. "I wouldn't be too hopeful, though; Barry's deaf as a post, I doubt if he had any idea anything was going on until you turned up with your siren going."

"Surely he would have heard the blasts from the shotgun." Mitchell couldn't see how Barry Whitelaw could have heard the siren if he didn't hear the shotgun.

Constance offered an uncertain shrug.

MITCHELL BANGED NOISILY on the door, and then stepped back to wait impatiently. When almost a minute passed without a response, he hammered on the door again with his fist.

Glen Wright yanked open the door, ready to yell at whoever had disturbed his sleep, but the words froze on his lips when he saw who was on the doorstep. "Lewis, what's going on?" he wanted to know.

Mitchell didn't answer straight away, instead he grabbed the younger man by the front of his t-shirt and pulled him out of the house, he didn't want either Kieran or Tara to hear what he had to say. Heedless of the fact that his friend was bare-footed, Mitchell dragged him across the yard and into the shadows on the far side of it.

When they were out of the moonlight, and far enough from the house to avoid drawing the attention of Glen's children, Mitchell spun him round and shoved him up against the side of the chicken coop. He did so with enough force to rattle the coop and disturb the occupants, who squawked their protests noisily for half a minute before settling down again.

"Why'd you do it?" Mitchell demanded over the noise from the chickens. "I told you not to do anything, why didn't you listen to me?"

"What're you talking about?" Glen wanted to know, his voice as sleep-filled as his eyes.

"Don't play games, Glen, I'm not in the mood." Filled with anger over the situation he had been put in by someone who was supposed to be a friend, Mitchell shoved Glen up against the chicken coop again, re-awakening the occupants. "I know you went down to Wild's place after I told you I had to release him. I told you not to do anything, to leave him alone, but you went down there, and you shot at him through the bloody living room window."

"You're damned right I did," Glen said, matching Mitchell's anger with his own. "I told you what I'd do if you let that sick sonofabitch go. You let him go; I had no choice. That bastard took my Emily, and he's almost certainly killed her – I can't let him get away with that. Being shot's nothing compared to what he deserves; he deserves a much more painful death than that, he deserves to be tortured, slowly."

"Except he's not dead," Mitchell snapped. "You came closer to killing his solicitor than you did to killing him; it's just as well you didn't manage to kill either one of them, just as well also that Constance is old and can't move too quickly. She didn't make it to the window in time to see you, so she's got no clue who tried to kill Wild, which is good news for you and for me. If she'd seen you, or had any clue it was you, I'd have to arrest you." He looked far from happy at that thought. "As it is, I might still have to arrest you if Wild or his solicitor saw anything that points to you. You'd better hope that when they wake up, they either saw nothing or they remember nothing, otherwise, you're looking at a lot of time in jail for attempted murder."

"I don't care, if you wanna arrest me, go ahead," Glen told his friend. "I'll tell the world what I did, I'm not ashamed; I'm glad I did it – I just wish I'd made sure I killed the sonofabitch; the world would be a better place without people like him in it."

"Don't be such an idiot." Mitchell had to bite his tongue to avoid snapping at his friend as he sought to get his temper under control. "Do you really think what you've done only affects you, that if you go to jail declaring yourself a martyr for justice, or whatever bollocks you choose to claim, it'll only make a difference to you. What about Kieran? What about Tara? What about Emily – she might not be dead; I know you're sure she is, but she might not be, and if she is still alive, she's gonna need you when she's found. Even if she is dead – Mitchell hated having to speak so bluntly, but knew it was necessary if he was going to get through to his friend – Kieran and Tara still need you; Kieran can't manage the farm on his own, if you go to jail, you'll lose it. Even if he could keep the farm going, he couldn't manage it and Tara. I doubt he'd be allowed to try given he's only seventeen.

"Going to jail would cost you the farm and Tara, she'd either have to go and live with relatives or, more likely, be taken into care, is that what you want?" Not only that but I'd probably lose my job, since you told me what you were going to do, and I didn't stop it, Mitchell thought, but didn't add.

Glen seemed to deflate at the mention of his two, still definitely alive, children. "What do I do?"

"Nothing, for now," Mitchell told him. "Just go about your life as if you did nothing, and pray that when they wake up, Wild and his solicitor either saw nothing or remember nothing." He let go of the younger man's t-shirt and was about to walk away when he thought of something. "There is one positive to be had from you shooting Wild – with him in hospital, there's no way he can hurt any other girls, and by the time he's ready to be released, we'll have the evidence to put him away."

"Fat lot of good that does my Emily," Glen said.

36

Melissa had no idea her grandmother was there, despite her name being called repeatedly, until a hand landed on her shoulder. The touch shocked her out of her reverie so violently that she jumped visibly.

"I'm sorry," Constance apologised as she sank onto the pew next to her granddaughter. "I didn't mean to make you jump. You didn't seem to know I was here."

"I didn't," Melissa said with an apologetic smile. "I was lost in my own little world. I started off in the café, and the next thing I knew, I was in here."

"It must be serious, whatever it is that's got you thinking so hard, I don't normally see you in here." Constance meant it only as a general comment but couldn't help sounding faintly accusatory as she looked around the nearly empty church. "I don't see many people in here during the week, and especially on a Monday morning; most folk seem to think they get enough church on a Sunday to last them through the week." As though sensing how embarrassed she was making Melissa, she switched subjects and asked, "So, what is it that has you so troubled that you've come to church to try and figure it out?"

Melissa's eyes strayed from her grandmother to Father Wozniak, who was pottering around, doing his daily housekeeping chores.

Constance grasped her granddaughter's concern without Melissa needing to say anything; the priest was about twenty feet away, but the acoustics were such that when the church was as empty as it was then, a whisper could be heard from anywhere. If that wasn't bad enough, Father Wozniak was a man who loved to gossip, and one who considered anything said outside of the confessional to be fair game for passing on to anyone who might have an interest in it. He dispensed good advice, but no-one went to him unless they were okay with everyone in the village knowing what they gone to him about within a few hours of them seeking advice.

"Why don't you come back to my place for a nice cup of tea and a slice of cake; you don't have to go to work, do you?"

Melissa shook her head. "No, I don't have to be at the station until later. I'm down for the afternoon shift, though I suppose that could change, with everything that's happened. Still, nobody's called to say they need me in this morning." She got to her feet and took her grandmother's hand to help her up.

IT DIDN'T TAKE LONG to get from the church to Constance's house, and once there Melissa sat at the kitchen table while her grandmother bustled about, making tea and setting out a plate of biscuits and cake. Melissa would have helped, even made the tea herself, but she knew better than to offer; her grandmother was a proud and vigorous woman, who insisted on doing everything possible for herself, claiming that it was good for her to keep busy.

Nothing was said by either woman until the pot had been filled and set in the middle of the table.

"So, what is it that has you so troubled that you're lost in thought in the church first thing on a Monday morning?"

Constance asked of her granddaughter. "Something to do with recent events, I take it."

"Yeah." Melissa nodded. "The murders, and the shooting next door last night, and – and everything; at first I didn't think Mr Wild was the killer, he seems too nice, but now I'm not sure, and I think Sergeant Mitchell had something to do with the attack on Mr Wild last night. Oh, I don't mean he was the one doing the shooting or anything like that," she said quickly. "It's just that I think he knows who did it, and he knew it was going to happen before it did, and I think he knew Oliver was going to attack Mr Wild on Saturday." The words tumbled from her lips with little coherency. "It's all so complicated, I don't know what to think or do."

Constance allowed Melissa to ramble on until she was finished. "I can see why you're so confused," she said as she took the cosy off the pot and poured them both a cup. "Why don't you start at the beginning, maybe if you talk it out one step at a time, things will start to make some sense, and you won't feel so overwhelmed."

"I don't know where to begin: with Mr Wild, or with Sergeant Mitchell, or with the murders, or something else. It's all such a jumble up here." Melissa banged herself on the side of the head, as though doing so would knock her thoughts into some semblance of order and allow her to see things more clearly. When that didn't work, she wrapped her hands around the mug her grandmother had filled with tea and sipped at it miserably.

Constance patted her granddaughter's arm sympathetically for a moment. "You're thinking too much. Close your eyes. Don't think, just speak – what's the first thing that comes to mind?"

Melissa obeyed her grandmother, though she felt more than a little stupid sitting at the table with her eyes closed. "Zack, Mr Wild," she said.

"What is it about Mr Wild you have a problem with?"

"I don't know really," Melissa admitted. "When I first met him, god, was it only a couple of days ago?" She couldn't quite believe that only two days had passed since Georgina Ryder's body was found. "He seemed so charming, nice and funny, and normal; not at all the sort of guy who'd hurt anyone, let alone kill them. The more I find out about him, though, the more I wonder what to believe. I've read his personal file from when he was a detective, and I've spoken to him about things, but it's just left me more confused.

"He's been involved in violent incidents, and he's been accused of attacking girls – he explained them, and the file I read explains them as well, and they're either false or understandable, but last night he admitted that he kissed Emily. She's only sixteen and he kissed her!" she exploded. "How the hell could he do that? It's sick and it's wrong, and if he's willing to do that, how much more is he willing to do. What if he is the one who killed Georgina and Lucy, and now Emily as well? I know you've heard what's supposed to have been done to the girls before they were killed. What if he kissed them, or tried to, and wouldn't stop once he got started."

Constance had a few things to say on that subject – she was surprised and disappointed by Melissa's closed-minded attitude – but chose not to voice them just then, instead she said, "Put all of that from your mind for the moment, don't let it bother you. What's the next thing that comes to mind?"

"Sergeant Mitchell," Melissa said. "He seems obsessed with Mr Wild, he's absolutely certain he's the one responsible for the murders, even though we don't have a scrap of proof against him. We've got a pretty good idea of when yesterday evening Emily was kidnapped, and Mr Wild was on the phone with his daughter when it happened, he couldn't possibly have taken her. If he didn't kidnap Emily, chances are he didn't kill Georgina or Lucy. Mitchell isn't willing to accept that, though; he thinks we must be wrong about when Emily was kidnapped. I don't see how we can be, though." She shook her head. "From the moment he heard that Mr Wild was most likely the last person to see Lucy before she was killed, Mitchell's been convinced that he's the killer, and he's not willing to consider that he might be wrong.

"I was told – even when talking with her grandmother she knew to be discreet – that Kieran Wright could be the killer, he's apparently attacked Lucy in the past. Mitchell didn't want to know when I told him, though. He won't even consider the possibility that someone else could be responsible for the murders. From the start he's only been interested in proving that it's Mr Wild. And he's gotten really angry both times he's had to release him; the first time, he immediately let Oliver out and told him that as far as he was concerned, Mr Wild was the killer, not Kieran. We both know what happened after that."

It took Melissa some time to finish unburdening herself, and by the time she was done the pot was empty, the cake was gone, and there were only a few biscuits left on the plate.

"Do you feel any better after getting all of that off your chest?" Constance asked.

Melissa nodded. She couldn't speak just then because she was nibbling her way through another of her gran's home-made cinnamon biscuits. "A little better," she said once she could speak without spraying crumbs all over the table. "But it hasn't really changed anything, all of my problems are still there."

"I realise that," Constance said, "but sometimes just telling someone a problem makes it easier to deal with. Now that you've told me what's wrong, I want you to get a pad and pen and write it all down. I want you to write down everything that's happened since the start of all this, even if you don't think it's relevant, in the order it happened. By the time you're done, you might just realise that you've got what you need to make a decision about what to do.

"Before you do that, though, I want you to answer one question."

Melissa looked at her grandmother curiously. "What's that?"

"Has your opinion of Mr Wild's innocence changed because he admitted kissing Emily, and you genuinely believe it's wrong for someone his age to kiss a sixteen-year-old girl, or because you wish it was you he kissed?"

Melissa's cheeks coloured. "I'm not sure," she admitted. "I do think it's wrong for someone his age to kiss a teen, it's not right at all – he must be twenty years older than her. Emily's sixteen, that's the age of consent, so it isn't wrong, legally, for him to kiss her, but I still think it's wrong. If you're asking whether I'm jealous that he kissed someone else – she nodded – yes, I am; he's attractive, and charming, and I wanted him to kiss me. And now I'm even more confused about everything.

"I don't know if I thought he was innocent because there's no evidence against him, or because I think he's attractive and I fancy him. And I don't know if I now think he's guilty because Emily is the same age as Georgina and Lucy, and if he was prepared to kiss Emily, what might he have done, or tried to do, with the other two, or because I'm jealous it wasn't me he kissed." Her head in her hands, she stared miserably at the table.

Constance permitted herself a small smile for the dilemma Melissa had gotten herself into, though it didn't stay on her lips for long. "It's good that you can admit you're confused, and why," she said. "It's also good that you're willing to accept that just because you believe Mr Wild was wrong to kiss Emily, doesn't mean he actually did something wrong; some people can't do that. Take Lewis for example, in all the time I've known him, I don't think I've ever heard him admit to being wrong about anything. That's a bad trait in anyone, but especially in a police officer.

"I remember your grandfather used to say, 'it's better to say you're wrong, even if you're right, than it is to say you're right, even when you're wrong.'"

Melissa had to smile at that; she hadn't known her grandfather all that well, he had died when she was young, but she did remember him coming out with sayings like that.

"I'm not an expert on this kind of thing, and I don't pretend to be," Constance said. "But it seems to me that if you really want to figure out if the killer is Mr Wild or young Kieran, you need to acknowledge that you're attracted to Mr Wild, and then forget all about that attraction and concentrate on the facts you have."

Melissa doubted that was going to be as easy as her grandmother made it sound. "What do I do about the attempts on Mr Wild's life, though? If I report what I suspect, and I'm wrong, I could lose my job, or at least end up with a black mark in my file; that would mean I can't go for sergeant next year. But if I don't report it, and I'm right, then I could be letting a would-be murderer go free, and letting the sergeant get away with abuse of power, or whatever he could be charged with."

"On that subject, I don't really know what to tell you, except that you should do what you think is right."

MELISSA ARRIVED AT the station well ahead of the start of her shift, and immediately put the kettle on.

Once she was seated with a coffee, she found a pad and a pen and got to work. Putting together a chronological account of everything that had happened since Georgina Ryder went missing proved more difficult than Melissa anticipated. The task was complicated by the need to make sure that none of what she put down was coloured by her personal opinions or feelings.

The arrival of Sergeant Mitchell forced her to stop before she could finish; she didn't want him to see what she was doing, in case he disapproved of it, which he almost certainly would.

"What are you doing this afternoon?" Mitchell asked when he found Melissa; he didn't notice the several sheets of paper she whipped out of sight upon seeing him in the doorway.

"Whatever you need me to," Melissa said. She had been expecting to be on the counter for her shift, with a couple of runs around the village during the afternoon and evening to keep an eye out for potential trouble, but the question made her think Mitchell had something in mind for her.

"Good, because I've had a message to say the post-mortems have been completed, so we need to go into town and speak to the pathologist. We also need to speak to Mr Wild," he said, though he seemed far from pleased by the thought, "to find out what, if anything, he knows about the attempt on his life."

Going to see a pathologist about the results of a post-mortem was one of the last things she would have chosen to do, had she an option, but it beat spending an afternoon at the counter. As horrible and horrific as the events of the last few days had been, she couldn't help thinking that they had shown her how boring her work was usually; it wasn't that she wanted to have to deal with murders and other serious crimes on a daily, or even a regular, basis, it was just that she didn't want to go back to a life where she had little to do beyond breaking up the occasional drunken argument in the pub.

37

M elissa liked her third visit to the morgue no better than she had the previous two – she didn't think she would have liked it any better if all three visits hadn't occurred on consecutive days – but that was no surprise given that two of the visits had been to identify bodies, and this one was to get the results of a post-mortem, something she had never thought to have to do.

The two police officers introduced themselves to the young man at the counter and were directed to the office of the pathologist.

"Come in."

"Hello, Sergeant Mitchell, from Oakhurst," he introduced himself as he entered the office. "You called to say the reports on the post-mortems of the two murder victims we discovered over the weekend are ready."

The pathologist looked blankly at Mitchell for a moment and then nodded. "Ah, yes, I remember now; it wasn't me that called, though, it was my assistant - she must have garbled the message, because I've only completed one of the post-mortems. I'm good, but two posts in a morning is more than I can manage. I won't be doing the second 'til this afternoon. Do you want the report on this morning's PM, or would you rather wait until I've done this afternoon's?"

"I'll take the report." Mitchell accepted the file and leaned back in the chair he had been directed to. He flipped open the file and began to read with an expression that could only be called perplexed; he didn't want to say as much, but he could barely understand a word of what the report had to say - for all the sense he could make of it, it might as well have been written in a foreign language.

Harry Doherty didn't laugh when he saw the sergeant was having trouble, he was used to detectives with far greater experience not understanding post-mortem reports, so it didn't surprise him that a village sergeant was struggling. "Would you like me to explain it to you?" he asked in his most non-offensive tone.

As much as he wanted to be insulted by the suggestion that he didn't understand the report, Mitchell knew it was true, he also knew his inability to understand it was obvious. Reluctantly, he swallowed his pride and nodded. "Thanks, I've never had to read one of these before, and, I've got to be honest, it's like it's in Latin or something."

Doherty permitted himself a smile. "You're not the first person to say that," he remarked. "This is the report on Georgina Ryder, who I understand was the first of the two bodies to be found. I won't trouble you with her gross physical characteristics, I'm sure you know them well enough, I'll just skip to the bits you need to know."

Mitchell was glad about that, he was sure there was a lot of details in the report that were only of interest to a pathologist, or a coroner, or someone with a morbid interest in knowing every last detail of someone's life and death. He did not fit into any of those categories, he was simply after evidence that would prove that Zack Wild was the murderer he knew him to be.

"First, and most importantly, the cause of death – she was strangled, with sufficient force to leave more bruising than would be considered usual. There are photos of each of the injuries I catalogued in the back of the report, but I'll spare you them just now. The extent of the bruising to Miss Ryder's throat, coupled with the other injuries, indicate that the killer is naturally strong, but was also angry at the time of the attack; strength alone would not account for the severity of the injuries I catalogued.

"The chances are good that she would have died even if she wasn't strangled. The injuries she suffered: punctured lung, lacerated kidney and liver, bruising to the heart, fractured jaw, multiple broken and fractured ribs, internal bleeding, all would have made it unlikely that she would have survived to reach hospital, even if she had been found straight away, which I understand was not the case. And none of that takes into account the cuts and bruises she suffered."

A feeling of horror crept over Mitchell as he listened to the range of injuries Georgina had suffered before being strangled. He had seen the cuts and bruises, and the other outward marks of injury, especially the words cruelly carved into her stomach, when he examined her naked body at the scene; none of that had prepared him to hear the level of internal injury she had suffered, though.

Despite his certainty that he knew who was responsible for the murder, he couldn't imagine the type of person it took to inflict such damage on another human being, it didn't seem possible that anyone could. Even harder to believe, was that someone sick enough to brutalise a person in the way described could walk around without anyone being aware of what they were capable of.

It took a short while for Mitchell to recover enough to speak; fortunately, the pathologist understood his silence and waited patiently for him to recover from his shock.

"What about what was – what was cut into her stomach?" Mitchell asked. "Can you tell me anything about that that might help me prove who killed her?"

"Not much," Doherty admitted. "The words were made with a series of precise cuts from a narrow-bladed knife."

"Precise cuts? You mean they were made by someone professional, like a surgeon or something?" Melissa felt compelled to ask.

Doherty shook his head. "No, sorry, that's not what I meant. When I say precise cuts, I mean there was no hesitation in any of them, each one was made with one exact stroke; that suggests that whoever made them knew exactly what they were going to do and wasn't bothered by the fact that they were cutting into human flesh."

"Is that significant?"

"Maybe, maybe not," Doherty said unhelpfully. "It's not the kind of thing everyone would be untroubled by. Inflicting the level of damage that I found is one thing, but carving words into a person's body is not normal killer behaviour. I'm not a psychologist, but it's possible it means the killer didn't see his victim as a person, and that's why he was able to cut into her as he did."

"Can you tell me what type of knife was used?" Mitchell asked, focusing on something that didn't leave him feeling quite so disturbed. He had seen several knives when he searched Zack Wild's house but hadn't thought to take any of them for forensic examination.

"A switchblade, or something like that, I'll need some more analysis to be certain."

That was a type of knife he hadn't seen during his search, and Mitchell decided he would have to make a second, more thorough search. He had other things to concern himself with just then, however, and he focused on that. "She was naked when she was found, does that mean..." He had to pause for a moment before he could finish his question. "Does that mean she was raped?"

Doherty bobbed his head in a slow, regretful answer. "Yes, I'm afraid she was. Do you need the details?" he asked with a quick glance at the young constable, a glance that made it all too clear what he thought the answer should be.

Mitchell couldn't help copying the pathologist and glancing at Melissa before answering the question with a brief shake of his head. "If I need them, I'm sure I can muddle through the file and figure out what it says."

"If you get stuck, you can give me a call," Doherty said. "Anyway, to get back to it; the rape was as brutal as the rest of the attack, that's all I'll say on that, but on a positive note – and I appreciate there aren't really any positives that can be taken from this situation – I did find plenty of DNA on the body. I've got semen, pubic hair, skin from under the fingernails, and saliva; if you've got a suspect, forensics will be able to match his DNA against what I've found. They've already got the samples I collected, so if you're lucky and your killer's in the DNA database, they'll have a name for you in the next couple of days."

That was a possibility that pleased Mitchell. He wasn't sure whether Zack Wild's DNA was in the National Police Database, but he didn't think that was likely to matter; he had no idea of the exact procedure for doing so, it was something he would have to check when he got back to the station, but he was confident he could get a sample of Wild's DNA, and once he had that it would only be a matter of time before what he believed was proved.

"Is there anything else you can tell us?"

Melissa would have been amused by her superior's use of the plural, given that she had so far been all but ignored, but she was too sickened by the description of what had been done to Georgina. She was thankful Mitchell had declined to see the photographs; after how she had reacted upon first catching sight of the teen on Saturday, and how she was feeling just then, she thought it likely that seeing the photographs would make her throw up, and that was the last thing she wanted to do.

Doherty nodded. "As I said, it's going to take a couple of days to get anything back from the DNA samples I sent to the lab, but I can tell you the killer is O positive; it's a fairly common blood-type, the most common amongst Caucasians in fact, but it might help you to narrow down any suspects you have."

38

"**D**addy!"

The cry announced the arrival of Zack's daughter, who reached him before he had a chance to react. In seconds, the ten-year-old had clambered up onto the bed, given him a big kiss and a hug, and settled down to cuddle with him.

"Hello, honey." He pulled his daughter close, so she wouldn't fall off the edge of the bed. He was both pleased and surprised to see her and looking beyond the end of the bed he saw his ex-wife. "Hello, Cathy, what are you doing here? How did you know I was here?"

"I called her," Sophie said from the seat she had been occupying at the side of the room since her arrival before dawn. "I thought Cathy should know where you are."

"Why are you in hospital, daddy?" Joanne asked, twisting around on the bed so she could look at her father.

"Yes, why are you here?" Cathy wanted to know. "What the hell have you been doing? Sophie said someone tried to kill you."

Zack glared furiously at his ex-wife, he couldn't believe she had mentioned that while his daughter was able to hear; fortunately, Joanne was too distracted to register what her mother said. "I got hurt," he said, speaking to Joanne rather than to Cathy. "I'm okay, though, I've got to be here for a couple of days, until I'm feeling better, then I can go home."

"What about Isobel?" Cathy asked, forcing her ex-husband to pay attention to her. "Sophie said she was with you. What the hell was she doing here? What the hell has been going on?"

"Aunt Izzy's here as well?" Joanne asked of her father. "Where is she? Is she alright?"

"We can talk about that later," Zack said to Cathy; he had no intention of discussing his situation while his daughter could hear, he didn't want her knowing or worrying about the trouble he was in. "Izzy's upstairs in another room, honey," he told his daughter. "She's hurt, like me, but she'll be okay."

Cathy looked as sceptical as a person could. "You expect me to believe that after what Sophie told me? I'm not a fool, Zack, you should know that by now. We'll talk about this later," she said, as though Zack hadn't already said as much. "Right now, I'm going to find out what helping you with your problems has cost my friend. Come on, Joanne. I said, come on." When her daughter made no effort to move from the bed, she strode across the room and took her by the arm.

"Oww! Don't mummy, you're hurting me," Joanne cried when she was pulled by the arm and all but dragged from the bed; it was only her father's arm around her waist that kept her from falling to the floor. "Oww!" she cried for a second time as her mother continued to pull at her arm.

"Let her go," Zack told his ex-wife as he held onto his daughter; he was concerned about hurting Joanne by holding onto her too tightly, but more worried about how she would be hurt if he let go of her and allowed his ex-wife to yank her away. "I said let go," he snapped in a sharper voice. "She's a kid, you can't treat her like this."

Cathy let go of her daughter's arm as though she had been slapped. She glared at her ex-husband for a long moment before storming from the room.

"Are you alright, honey?" Zack asked of his daughter when he saw her rubbing her arm where her mother had grabbed her.

Joanne nodded while cuddling her father more strongly.

MELISSA WAS SURPRISED to see there were no guards at the door when she and Mitchell reached the room they had been directed to. With the circumstances being what they were, she would have expected to find a hospital security officer, if not a police officer, outside the door; it was not her place to say anything about it, however, though she was tempted to.

"Mr Wild," Mitchell greeted the man in the bed. "How are you feeling?"

Zack wasn't bothered by the lack of a genuine greeting, nor was he bothered by the perfunctory nature of the inquiry about his health; given how the sergeant had treated him since discovering he was the last person, supposedly, to see Lucy Goulding, he would have been surprised to hear any warmth or genuine concern in Mitchell's voice.

"I'm as well as can be expected."

"Shall we go to the shop and get daddy some chocolate or something?" Sophie asked as she got to her feet. She assumed the sergeant was the same one Zack had told her about at lunch yesterday, and she could see he was keen to talk to her friend about something, most likely the incident that had resulted in him being hospitalised; she didn't think it a good idea for Joanne to be there if she was right.

Joanne looked from her aunt to the two police officers, and then at her daddy. Having lived through the divorce of her parents, which had been far from amicable, she knew when someone was trying to get her out of the room, so an adult conversation could be had. She didn't want to leave her daddy just then, she got to see him so rarely that she wanted to enjoy every moment before she had to go home, but she knew when to do as she was told.

"Can I have some chocolate as well, daddy?" she asked.

Zack smiled at his daughter. "Of course you can, honey, not too much, though, or your mother will kill me." He accepted a kiss, and then watched as Joanne jumped down off the bed and accompanied Sophie from the room.

Only when he was confident his daughter was out of earshot did he address Sergeant Mitchell, who was now standing at the end of the bed. "I take it you're here to talk about last night."

"Yes," Mitchell said with a quick nod before getting straight down to business, he didn't want to be there any longer than necessary. "What happened?"

Zack allowed himself a moment or two to order his thoughts. "After I left the police station, Isobel drove me home, where she had a lot to say about the state my home was left in, and my physical condition. She started taking pictures of everything, so she could prepare a lawsuit – he took pleasure in the alarm that showed on Mitchell's face at that – while I went into the kitchen to make some food and get something to drink. It must have been about half an hour, no more than that, after we got to my place before the food was ready, and I was just carrying it into the living room when I saw something move in the garden outside the window."

"What did you see?"

"At first I wasn't sure, it was just a dark blob, a little darker than the sky outside the window," Zack admitted. "Then I realised it was a person, and he was holding something. An alarm went off in my head and I yelled for Isobel to get down while I threw the plates I was holding and dived for cover. There was a loud blast I thought was thunder, before I realised the window had been shattered and Isobel was bleeding; that's when I guessed it must have been a shotgun. Isobel was still on her feet, don't ask me how, so I scrambled to mine and dived on her to get her down and safe. That's when the shotgun went off again.

"I was the one who got hit that time, though I didn't know it; I was too focused on making sure Isobel was alright, or at least as alright as she could be under the circumstances. I didn't know I'd been shot 'til I got up to take a look out the window to see who had tried to kill me."

"You're sure whoever it was, was there to kill you?"

"Of course I'm sure," Zack all but snapped. "People don't generally shoot at you with a shotgun if they're not trying to kill you."

"Okay, so the person in your garden was there to kill you, with the unfortunate result that they came closer to killing your solicitor."

"I'd hardly call it merely unfortunate."

"Yes, I'm sure, sorry," Mitchell apologised with as much sincerity as he could muster. "You said you saw a dark blob, can you tell me anything about your attacker?" He mentally crossed his fingers.

Zack thought about that for several long seconds while he conjured up an image in his mind of what he had seen. "He was about six-foot-tall, maybe a fraction over, and big built, not fat, I don't think, but definitely not slim or medium build. I only saw a silhouette, as I said, but I'd say he was wearing dark clothes."

Mitchell frowned. "You've said 'he' a couple of times, what makes you so sure your attacker was male?"

"It's just my impression," Zack said. "I suppose there's a chance it could have been a woman but given the height and build I'd say it's a bloke. That's all I can tell you, except I'm pretty certain the person who tried to kill me got to and from the house on foot."

"What makes you think that?"

"I didn't hear a car," Zack said straightaway. "I might not have heard one when he arrived because I was in the kitchen, but if he had a car, I should have heard him drive away, I didn't. The only reason I can think of is that he was on foot."

Mitchell was trying to think of something else to ask or say when his thoughts were interrupted by the return of Zack's daughter. How she had got to the hospital shop and back so quickly he didn't know, but it annoyed him.

Despite the carrier bag she held in one hand, Joanne soon made it onto the bed, where she again nestled against her father. Ignoring the two police officers, she said, "We got lots of chocolate, daddy. Dairy Milk and Fruit & Nut," she took the bars out of the bag to show him, "Aunty Sophie says that's your favourite, and some toffees and some Maltesers – they're for me. We got you grapes as well; Aunty Sophie says you always get grapes for people when they're in hospital. Is that true?" she asked with a suspicious glance at her aunt.

Zack looked over at his former sister-in-law and saw her shrug an apology, which he suspected had more to do with their unexpectedly quick return than the grapes. He then turned his attention back to his daughter. "Of course it's true, honey," he said. "Grapes help you get better quicker."

"We got you some magazines as well," Sophie said. "They didn't have a very good selection, but it was better than the books, so we got you what I thought you'd like."

"Thanks." Zack glanced at the titles as Joanne took the magazines from the carrier to show him: Total Film, National Geographic, Heat, and a couple of others, none of which were his usual reading material, but he supposed they were better than nothing if he was going to be stuck in hospital for a few days – he had been surprised when the doctor told him he would only be there for a short time, surprised but pleased; he could only guess that his injuries were minor enough, all things considered, that he could do most of his recovering at home, which would free up the bed for someone who needed it more.

Mitchell finally recovered from the surprise caused by the arrival of Wild's daughter and resumed his questioning. "Do you have any idea where the figure you saw went after he left your garden?"

Zack wasn't comfortable with being questioned while his daughter was there, but he doubted any notice would be paid if he asked to put it off. He shook his head. "No idea; I suppose he could have gone anywhere, but I guess it's most likely he headed back down the road to the village."

"Most likely. Going up the road would only have got him to the Wright Farm, and I wouldn't have wanted to try and cross the fields at night," Mitchell remarked. "Even with the moon out, it would have been risking a twisted ankle or some other injury. What did you do after you went to the window to look for the guy who attacked you?"

"I called for an ambulance and you guys," Zack said after a quick, worried glance at his daughter. Fortunately, Joanne was engrossed in unwrapping and breaking up the giant bar of Dairy Milk chocolate. "Thank you, honey." He accepted the square of chocolate she gave him and pretended not to notice that while he received one square, and another square was tossed to Sophie, Joanne took two for herself. "After that I must have passed out, because the next thing I remember is waking up here."

"Daddy," Joanne said in a tone that Zack recognised only too well, despite the mouthful of chocolate she was talking around, as her 'I want something' voice. "Can I stay with you during the summer holidays?"

"Joanne!" Cathy chose that moment to return from the ITU. "Didn't I tell you not to mention that? I told you I would discuss it with your father when there's an opportunity. There's a long time to go until the summer holidays, a lot could happen between now and then," she said with a look that made it clear that if it was at all possible, she would find a reason not to let Joanne go to her father's. She turned to the sergeant then. "I suppose you're here because of the attempt on Zack's life."

"That's the main reason right now," Mitchell said with a nod. "There's other stuff I need to question him about, but it can wait." He really wanted to wait to talk to Wild about the murders, and about the missing Emily Wright, but he could see what a bad idea it would be to try and do so just then, while his suspect was being visited by his daughter and his ex-wife. "For now, I'll settle for one last question – what's your blood type, Mr Wild?"

Zack could only shrug; he had never needed to know what his blood type was.

"O positive," Cathy answered. "Why do you want to know that?"

"It's nothing important," Mitchell said quickly. He didn't want to get into the situation with someone who wasn't involved. "We just need to compare Mr Wild's blood-type against a sample we have."

MELISSA WAITED UNTIL the doors of the lift had closed, only then did she ask the question that was on her mind. "Have you got any idea who could have tried to kill Mr Wild?"

"I wish I did," Mitchell said, sounding as genuine as he could. "The last thing Oakhurst needs right now, after everything else that's happened, is a vigilante, or whatever Wild's attacker was, we've got enough to deal with. Unfortunately, Wild's description is so vague it could be just about anyone; we can't even say for sure whether it's a man or a woman. Unless his solicitor can tell us anything extra when she wakes up, or someone confesses, I don't see how we're going to figure out who did this, we've got absolutely no evidence to help us."

"Since we're almost certain Mr Wild's attacker is from Oakhurst, I think we can be pretty sure it was a man," Melissa said. "I can't think of a single woman in the village, or even anywhere around it, that fits the description we just got. I can't even think of any women who comes close to it; those who are tall enough are too slim, and those who are the right build are too short."

Mitchell glanced at his partner briefly. "I take it you've never met Agnes Jameson," he said. When Melissa shook her head, he went on. "She works over at Caldern House, over near Shilverton; she's one of the gamekeepers there, and she's a pretty scary-looking woman, a real Amazon, with strong, not very complimentary, opinions about men. If there's any woman in the local area who's likely to take a shotgun to someone she thinks is responsible for raping and murdering girls, it's her – she was attacked a few years ago, and ever since then she's been of the opinion that pretty much all men are rapists, and should be killed for the good of humanity, or some such thing.

39

Jonathan Farrell noticed the police tape marking off a section of the field to his right and glanced quickly to the passenger seat. Thankfully, his girlfriend showed no sign of having seen the crime scene, he was sure she would have said something if she had.

"Where are you taking me?" Cynthia Potter asked, a touch of concern in her voice as the car turned off the narrow road they were driving along; the dark path they were now on looked as though it belonged in a horror movie. "This doesn't look like the kind of place we should be."

"Don't worry, it looks worse than it is," Jonathan told her. "When the sun's out – it was typical, he thought, that after a sunny weekend, this evening had to be cloudy – this area looks great, trust me, I've been here before."

"With other girls?" Cynthia asked, more than a trace of jealousy in her voice.

Jonathan smiled at that, though he was careful to turn his head away, so she didn't see. "Of course with other girls. It's not like there's many places around here where you can get some privacy. Come on, don't act like it's news that I've had other girlfriends; I've had other girlfriends, and you've had other boyfriends." He reached out to give her leg a reassuring squeeze.

"We're together now, and you're the only one I want to be with, here or anywhere else."

"Well, alright then," Cynthia said. "I still don't like it here, though, it's creepy." Her opinion didn't improve when they reached the end of the short drive and entered the yard surrounding the farmhouse.

"I know it's not the best looking of places," Jonathan admitted, "but like I said, there aren't many places you can go around here if you want some privacy. We can't go to my place, my family's there, and if we go to your place in town, your house-mates will be there. I've got a few things that will make the place a whole lot better, you wait."

He brought the car to a stop half a dozen yards from the front door of the burned-out farmhouse and got out. "Come on, give it a chance," he said when he saw that Cynthia was reluctant to move from the passenger seat. "You go inside while I get the things I've brought. I promise, if you really don't like the place, we'll go back home."

Cynthia stayed where she was for more than half a minute before finally slipping the seatbelt off and exiting the car. She moved slowly across the yard to the doorway, where the door hung off its hinges, and made her way inside. She entered the dim interior with a feeling of trepidation; she didn't think she had ever seen anywhere, let alone been anywhere, that would make a more perfect setting for a horror movie.

Jonathan waited until his girlfriend had disappeared through the doorway, and then he made his way to the boot, so he could get the things he had brought. He had the blanket slung over his shoulder, and the radio in one hand, and he was just picking up the picnic hamper, when the scream sounded from inside the house.

He dropped everything as he spun away from the car and darted into the house. He nearly knocked over Cynthia, who was frozen like a statue just inside the doorway, when he reached the living room. It was only by twisting and half-jumping aside that he was able to avoid running into her.

When he saw what it was that had made his girlfriend scream, he felt an urge to do likewise. The scream that threatened to un-man him subsided slowly as he turned Cynthia, who showed no sign of being aware he was there, and steered her from the room and the house. Once he had his girlfriend in the passenger seat of his car, wrapped in the blanket he had brought for them to sit on, he returned to the house.

Jonathan stopped the moment he was over the threshold, so he could steel himself, and so he could take out his mobile and call the police station. While he listened to the phone ring, he hesitantly entered the living room and slowly approached the nearest of the two objects on the floor; as much as he wanted them to change, they didn't, they remained a pair of bodies, bodies belonging to two young girls: one clothed and the other naked.

"Hello, Oakhurst Police Station," Constable Black answered the phone. "How can I help you?"

"It – it's Jonathan F-Farrell," he stammered into the phone as he checked the throat of the girl on the floor before him for a pulse and fought the urge to throw up; he had seen enough of the body as he crossed the room to know the girl was no older than his little brother, which made her about fourteen, and she had suffered a great deal. "I'm at the old Harwell Farm; I've found – I think it's Emily Wright and Daisy Hawkins, they've been attacked."

There was a period of stunned silence, while Black took in what he had just been told, before the constable was finally able to speak again. "Did you say you've found Emily Wright and Daisy Hawkins? I didn't even know Daisy Hawkins was missing."

"Neither did I," Jonathan said.

"Are you certain it's her?"

"Not certain, no, but I think it's her, I recognise the hair. She's naked, and, oh Jesus!"

"WHEN WAS THE LAST TIME you saw Daisy?" Mitchell asked of Jonathan Farrell.

"I don't know. She's just a kid," Jonathan said quickly, defensively. "I don't pay attention to when she's around and when she's not. Maybe Neil would know, he goes to school with her, I think he even fancies her."

"But doesn't she live just down the street from you?" Mitchell asked.

Jonathan nodded. "Two doors down, but that doesn't mean I know when she's home and when she's out, or where she goes."

"When's the last time you do remember seeing her?"

"Saturday morning," Jonathan said after some thought. "She was walking along the street, heading away from home. Don't ask me what time it was, I don't remember, and I don't have a clue where she was going."

"LEWIS," STEVENS GREETED his subordinate sombrely when Mitchell had finished questioning Jonathan Farrell and his girlfriend.

"Sir," Mitchell returned the greeting. With a barely concealed look of distaste he glanced around at the crowd that was being kept to the edge of the yard by his constables. He didn't like that so many people had come from all over the village – he liked it less that so many people had found out so quickly about the discovery that had been made – it didn't seem right to him that they should express their curiosity in such a way, especially when their presence was likely to get in the way of his investigation. "Isn't there anything we can do to get rid of them?" he asked.

Stevens glanced over his shoulder to see who Mitchell was referring to. "I don't think so," he said, though he didn't sound certain. "I think as long as they're keeping out of the way, and not doing anything that's obviously wrong, they're allowed to be there. Just ignore them and be thankful what's been going on around here hasn't reached the ears of the local press." He couldn't help wondering how much longer it would be before that happened, it could only be a matter of time, he thought. "What exactly is the situation here?"

Mitchell sighed, "What did Black tell you when he called?"

"Not much. Almost nothing," Stevens admitted. "He told me that Emily's been found, and that Daisy Hawkins' been found as well – I didn't even know she was missing," he said that last in a slightly accusatory tone, as though his officers had been keeping him in the dark about things.

"You're not the only one," Mitchell said. "As far as I can tell, no-one knew she was missing." He heaved another sigh. "I don't get it, she's only fourteen, someone should have realised she was missing: her parents, school, somebody. Mr Farrell thinks he saw her on Saturday morning, but isn't sure; she's got to have been missing for at least a day – Wild was at the station from seven, and in the hospital from one a.m. – without anyone noticing, how's that possible?"

"I don't know, Lewis, it's something we're going to have to find out," Stevens said. "Is it definitely Daisy Hawkins?"

"Yes." Mitchell nodded reluctantly. "How the hell Mel's coping, I don't know." He glanced over at Melissa and marvelled once again at how she was holding herself together; he would not have blamed her if she had fallen apart with grief upon hearing that her young cousin was now a victim of the killer who had already taken the lives of Georgina and Lucy; that hadn't happened, however. Melissa had withdrawn into herself, but that was her only reaction to the tragedy.

"Okay, so Daisy Hawkins is our fourth victim; what else can you tell me about the situation here?" Stevens asked. He knew he sounded cold, speaking so baldly, but he had to do it, he was sure that if he didn't shut off his emotions as much as possible, he would not be able to cope; he had felt a twinge in his chest, and a shooting pain his left arm, when he heard what Constable Black had to say, and he worried he was on the verge of having the full-blown heart attack the doctor had been warning him about for the past year.

"There is some good news," Mitchell told his superior, who looked at him as if he had said something truly crazy. "Emily's alive." He let that sink in. "I don't know how, but she is, just about. The paramedics say that since she's made it this far, she's probably going to be alright, though how long it's going to take her to recover, and whether she'll recover fully, they don't know. If we're lucky, though," he smiled with bitter irony as he said that, "Emily will wake up and tell us who attacked her; that, plus the DNA evidence the pathologist said he found on Georgina – I assume he's going to find more on Lucy – will be enough to convict Wild. I only wish I'd been able to get the evidence to charge the bastard before it got this far."

"So do I," Stevens admitted. "Because the chief inspector is far from happy with the situation here, and that's without hearing the latest. He hasn't insisted on a detective taking over the case, yet, but there's every chance he will after this, especially given the pressure he's almost certainly getting from Sir Virgil; about the only thing that'll stop him is us catching the killer – are you absolutely certain it's Mr Wild?"

Mitchell nodded emphatically. "I'm positive. I haven't figured out how he managed to kidnap Emily and half-kill her, or when he took Daisy, but I've got a bit of a theory running around my head, and I am positive Wild's our man. The pathologist was able to give me the blood-type of our killer while I was at the morgue, I checked, it matches Wild's."

"Well that's good news. I'll tell the chief inspector, I'm sure he'll be able to tell Sir Virgil that we've caught the guy who killed his great-niece, it might be enough to help us all keep our jobs."

The two officers stopped speaking to watch as the stretcher bearing Emily Wright was wheeled out of the house. They followed it with their eyes on its way round the side of the house to the air ambulance. Only when the helicopter had lifted off and disappeared from view did Mitchell and Stevens return to their conversation.

"What's your next move?" Stevens asked. "Aside from passing what you've got on to the CPS, so they can charge Mr Wild."

Mitchell didn't need to think about that. "I need to go and see Glen, tell him we've found Emily and she's alive – I'm surprised he isn't here already, he should have been able to see the air ambulance from just about anywhere on the farm – he'll want to get to the hospital as quickly as he can. Kieran and Tara should probably go as well, just in case the paramedics are wrong and Emily isn't going to make it." His voice remained steady only with an effort. "After that I need to find Daisy's parents, so I can find out how she could have been missing for so long, without being reported missing, especially given recent events. I just hope nothing's happened to them, Wild's got enough to answer for as it is."

Stevens could see how angry Mitchell was and laid a comforting hand on his shoulder. "You worry about Glen and his family," he told him. "I imagine they're going to need the support of a friend. I'll find the Hawkins and speak to them, find out what's going on there. I think you should take Melissa with you, it might help her if she has something to concentrate on other than her cousin, and if it doesn't, you'll be able to get her some proper help at the hospital."

Mitchell nodded. He was about to get Melissa and head up the road to see the Wrights when a thought occurred to him. "Why didn't we think to check this place out?" he asked of Stevens. "It's such an obvious place for Wild to have brought Emily; I'll bet Wild realised Kieran had seen him, so he left, then went back to grab Emily once the coast was clear, stashed her here, fixed up his alibi, and then returned while we were at the farm, so he could have his fun – the sick bastard." There was no mistaking the disgust Mitchell felt.

"Don't beat yourself up. I was with the search party going through these woods on Saturday, remember; I never thought to check here either." He shook his head. "Emily hadn't been taken then, but chances are this is where he killed Georgina and Lucy before he dumped their bodies in the woods. Maybe if we'd checked here, we could have found the evidence to charge Mr Wild, rather than being forced to let him go. If we'd done that, Emily would never have been taken, and maybe Daisy would have been safe as well." He was as unhappy as Mitchell about what they had and hadn't done, but also more realistic about things. "We can't change what's happened, all we can do is make sure our case against Mr Wild is airtight, so he can't ever hurt anyone else."

"And hope Sir Virgil doesn't blame us for failing to catch Wild after Georgina went missing and before he could grab Lucy," Mitchell said pessimistically.

40

When his phone rang, Mitchell excused himself and moved away from the waiting area, leaving the Wrights: Glen, Kieran and Tara, to their wait for someone to come and let them know what the situation was with Emily. Melissa was there as well, though so lost in her grief over the murder of her cousin she was oblivious to just about everything around her.

"Have you been able to find the Hawkins?" Mitchell asked once he had exchanged pleasantries with his superior.

"Yes, but it wasn't easy," Stevens said. "It seems they're away at the moment, which is why they didn't report Daisy missing; they weren't aware she was, though you'd have thought the school would have been in touch to find out why she wasn't there today. I had to get their contact details from a neighbour; they left on a family emergency yesterday, Ursula Hawkins' father had a heart attack. They were going to take Daisy with them, but didn't want her to miss school, so they made arrangements for her to stay with a friend last night and go to school with her this morning."

"What friend?" Mitchell's eyes strayed to the Wrights in the waiting room, he had a horrible feeling he knew who Daisy was supposed to have stayed with.

"Tara Wright," Stevens answered. "According to Frank Hawkins, Daisy couldn't go to the Wright Farm straight away because all the family had things to do; she was to stay at home and make her way to the farm in time for tea and was then to stay the night there. I figure it would have taken her about three quarters of an hour to get to the farm from home on foot, which fits, because the neighbour I spoke to said she saw Daisy heading up the street at about five, and the Wrights were supposed to have tea at about six, if I remember what you said Glen told you."

"That does fit," Mitchell said, suppressing his sudden excitement. "Wild most likely bumped into her while he was taking Emily from the house and grabbed her, so she couldn't tell anyone where she had seen him." The last of his excitement drained from him as a thought occurred. "What if Emily is still alive because he bumped into Daisy? What if she's still alive because he was too busy raping and murdering Daisy?" He was struck with horror at the thought. "Jesus! How do I tell Glen his daughter's alive right now only because Wild was too busy raping and murdering a second, younger, girl to realise she wasn't dead?"

"I have no idea," Stevens admitted.

"Have you been able to find out anything else?" Mitchell asked after half a minute or so of silence.

"Not so far, no," Stevens said regretfully. "I've been trying to find out if anyone saw Daisy after her neighbour did yesterday, so we can be certain she was heading for the farm, but no luck yet. I want to look more closely at Wild's alibi as well; I know you've proved his blood-type matches the killer's, and you'll have the DNA results back in the next couple of days, but it will help our case if we can prove he lied about his alibi.

"What's the situation over there at the hospital?" he asked in a change of subject.

"Unknown at the moment. Unless someone's come up with some news while I've been talking to you, we're still waiting to hear what the results of the scans are, and we won't know how good or bad Emily's situation is until we get them."

MITCHELL REACHED OUT to shake his friend's shoulder, bringing him back to the here and now, as he squatted in front of him. "I need to talk to you about something."

It was a few moments before Glen became fully aware that Mitchell was before him, and a similar amount of time before he found his voice. "Wh..." He cleared his throat when his voice died in a croak and tried again. "What?"

"I need to talk to you about something," Mitchell said. "I know this is a difficult time for you, but I need to know; why didn't you tell me Daisy Hawkins was supposed to be staying at the farm last night?"

"Oh god!" Glen gasped, wringing his hands until his knuckles were as white as his face. "Oh god! How could I have forgotten about her?" There was a brief silence as he mentally castigated himself. "Her mum called yesterday morning, they had some kind of family emergency and had to go away; they didn't want Daisy to miss school, so she asked me if I'd have her for the night, so she could go to school with Tara this morning. I said yes, but she couldn't come to the farm 'til dinner time 'cause we were all busy.

"I can't believe I forgot she was coming."

"It's alright, it's not your fault," Mitchell reassured his friend. "It's no surprise you forgot about Daisy, the arrangements were made at the last minute, and you had much more important things to worry about."

Glen nodded, though it was clear he didn't quite believe Mitchell. "Is she alright?" he asked. "What happened to her? Why didn't she come out to the farm?"

Looking at his friend, Mitchell realised Glen wasn't thinking straight, he was too distracted by concern for his daughter, which was perfectly understandable. "We think she did come to the farm," he said in a gentle voice, not wanting to add to the distress his friend was clearly suffering, though he realised it couldn't be avoided. "We think she was on her way to the farm when she ran into Wild, and that he took her, so she couldn't tell anyone she had seen him. Her body was found a short distance from Emily in the Harwell Farmhouse."

"My god!" Glen's left hand went to his mouth, while his right shook, spilling coffee from the cup he held. "You mean she's – she's dead? That if she hadn't been coming to the farm, if I hadn't said she could stay the night, she'd be alright? Oh god! It's my fault isn't it, that's what you're telling me; it's my fault she's dead." The paper cup fell from his hand, spilling the last of the coffee it held over his shoes. "I should have made certain..."

Mitchell cut him off quickly before he could say anything that might incriminate either of them. "It's no good thinking about what you should or shouldn't have done or blaming yourself for something that isn't your fault; you didn't kill Daisy, or Georgina, or Lucy, it was Wild, and now we've got the evidence to prove it." He couldn't keep the satisfaction he felt from his voice. "There's something else; I'm going to have to have a forensics team search your house and yard for evidence that Daisy made it as far as the farm before Wild grabbed her. The more evidence we can find, the better our case against Wild."

MELISSA FOLLOWED HER superior through the door and into the private room occupied by Zack Wild, though it felt more like she was swept along in his wake. If she could have, she would have chosen to be just about anywhere else in the world rather than in Wild's hospital room; following her grandmother's suggestion had only left her more confused than before regarding Wild's guilt or innocence, if that were possible, and that confusion, worsened by what had happened to her cousin, left her deeply uncomfortable in his presence.

The shock of her cousin's murder was massive, and it was all she could do not to break down in floods of tears – why Mitchell had insisted on her accompanying him, first to the hospital, and then to this room, she didn't know, but it felt cruel. She wanted to be with her cousin's parents, or with her own, though that was not easy since they no longer lived in the village, or her grandmother, she would even have preferred to be at home on her own with a large bottle of something for company while she allowed her grief to run its course.

ZACK WAS SURPRISED when he looked up from his book and saw that it was not a nurse who had just entered - Sergeant Mitchell was the last person he would have expected to see at that time.

"You're here late, sergeant," he remarked as he set aside his book and reached for the cup of water on the cabinet next to him. "What can I do for you?" Even if the lateness of the visit hadn't told him that something more had happened, the look on Mitchell's face would have. "Have you found Emily?"

Mitchell nodded, his head jerking up and down in short, sharp movements as he said, "We found her alright; we found her and she's still alive. Does that surprise you?"

It was Zack's turn to nod. "Given what you've said of what was done to Georgina Ryder and Lucy Goulding, I'm very surprised. She must be tougher than she looks."

"More like luckier, certainly luckier than the other two," Mitchell said. "She's only alive because you were too busy raping and murdering Daisy Hawkins."

"Who?" Zack had no idea who his supposed victim was, though he suspected, given that they shared a last name, that she was related to his neighbour, which meant she was also related to the constable at the end of his bed, who looked about as miserable as a person could.

"Who?" Mitchell went red in the face. "Who?" he said a second time, a moment before he launched himself across the room.

The sudden move caught Melissa by surprise. Before she realised what Mitchell had in mind, let alone could react to it, he had Wild by the throat and was choking him.

"Who?" Mitchell demanded. "She was only fourteen, you sick sonofabitch. Fourteen! You rape and murder a fourteen-year-old girl, and you don't even know her name."

Zack tried to pull himself free from Mitchell's grasp, but it wasn't easy. Not only was he growing steadily weaker as the life was choked out of him, but he had been half-dragged out of bed, and now hung down with the blood rushing to his head. His fingers scrabbled against those around his throat, but he lacked the strength to break their grip, and what strength he did have was disappearing rapidly as blackness crept in at the edges of his vision.

Melissa was horrified by what her superior was doing right in front of her, but she was unable to move to do anything about it. It wasn't until a nurse entered the room, stopped dead for a moment when she saw what was happening, and then hurried forward, bumping into her on the way past, that Melissa found the will to move. Coming to her senses, she rushed to help the nurse pull Mitchell off Wild, whose eyes were mostly closed, and whose lips were starting to go blue by the time they were successful.

"Are you alright, Mr Wild?" the nurse asked as she heaved her patient back onto the bed, proving that even a medical professional could ask a stupid question when someone was hurt.

"Is he alright?" Mitchell asked in disbelief. "That sick sonofabitch should be dead. He's a goddammed murderer, who the hell cares if he's alright."

It took every ounce of strength Melissa had to keep hold of Mitchell and stop him finishing what he had started. She was glad when two more nurses, and a security guard, entered the room in a rush, responding to the alarm the first nurse had sounded.

The nurses went to help their compatriot with the patient, whose face was beginning to regain some of its colour. They got him straightened up and checked him over, making sure that he was as alright as he could be under the circumstances; fortunately, the attack had done no apparent lasting damage. While the nurses did that, the security guard helped Melissa to guide Mitchell from the room. Only when they got him out into the passage did Mitchell calm down and allow himself to be led away.

Melissa felt the eyes of both the security guard and the senior nurse watching them as they headed down the passage towards the lift; she could tell they wanted to say something about what had happened, so did she, but she couldn't think what to say – Mitchell's actions had come as a complete shock to her.

41

Melissa was on the doorstep for a couple of minutes before a light came on in the passage; she had to wait another couple of minutes for the door to open, and the moment it did she burst into tears.

She felt vaguely ashamed at collapsing emotionally, but that disappeared as her grandmother stepped out of the house and wrapped comforting arms around her. They remained like that for a minute or so, until her sobs subsided, at which point Melissa allowed her grandmother to lead her into the house and down the passage to the kitchen, where she was pressed into a seat. She put the batch of papers she had brought with her on the table, but that was as much as she could bring herself to do, after that she simply sat there, her cheeks wet with tears as she stared ahead, looking at nothing.

"Here, drink this." Constance pushed a glass into her granddaughter's hand and then guided it to her lips.

Melissa gasped as the strong liquor burned its way down her throat. She hadn't realised what it was she was being given to drink until it was too late to worry about. Now, though, she knew it was some of her grandfather's favourite whiskey, which her grandmother kept around for special occasions and emergencies, and this was definitely an emergency. The second sip went down a little easier than the first, though it still burned and made her eyes sting with tears that had nothing to do with grief.

"Do you feel any better now?" Constance asked once Melissa had finished the whiskey.

"A little." Now that she was more with it, Melissa could see that her grandmother's eyes were puffy and red from her own tears and she reached out to take her hand. "How are you?"

"I've been better. As you get older you think nothing can shock you, and you can cope with anything, even the death of those near to you; somehow, though, life has a way of proving you wrong. I can't believe Daisy's gone," she said. "She was so young. Too young to die, especially like that." She closed her eyes for a moment and took a couple of deep breaths.

Melissa gave her grandmother's hand a quick squeeze, and then released it so she could get to her feet and put the kettle on. She barely had a chance to pick it up before her grandmother recovered, as much as she was going to just then.

"Is this that thing you were going to do, everything that's happened since Georgina went missing?" Constance asked, pulling the small stack of papers across the table so she could take a look at them.

Melissa nodded as she filled the kettle from the tap. "It's not finished, though; I haven't had a chance to add everything..." She had to stop for a few long seconds to collect herself before she could go on. "Everything that's happened today, especially tonight."

"Well then, you sit yourself down and finish it, I'll make the tea." Constance got to her feet and took the kettle from her granddaughter, she then nudged her towards the table while she set about preparing the pot and their cups. "I called your parents after I heard what happened."

"What did they say?" Melissa asked. She couldn't help wondering if her parents were going to come back to the village because of her cousin's death – she couldn't bring herself to use the word murder, even in her mind, because she was sure it would make her break down again; her parents hadn't returned to Oakhurst since leaving the village several years before, when her father got a job in London.

Constance returned to the table while she waited for the kettle to boil. "Your mother will be here sometime today; she couldn't say when, but she thinks it will be before lunchtime. Your father..." She hesitated for a moment, which was as close as she came to showing disapproval for the man her daughter had married; it wasn't that she disliked Eric Turner, she just thought him more interested in work than in people, even family. "Your father will be here for the funeral, once he knows when that will be, but he apparently has a couple of meetings he can't get out of today, and too much work that he can't afford to leave."

The news upset Melissa a little, though it wasn't unexpected. She was pleased – as pleased as she could be under the circumstances – that her mother was going to be around, but she would have liked her dad to be there as well; she had only seen him a couple of times since her parents moved to London, and both times she had had to all but force him to spend time with her. She would have liked to think he could put work aside at such a difficult time to help support his family.

"Where's mum going to stay?" Melissa asked. "Does she want me to make up the spare room?" It only occurred to her then that she hadn't checked her phone to see if anyone had tried to call or text since she was given the news of her cousin's murder.

Constance shook her head as she filled the teapot and brought it over to the table. "She's going to stay here. I've got the space, and it will be easier than putting you to any trouble."

Melissa was relieved by that news; as much as she wanted to have her mum in the spare room, close by, it would have felt awkward for the house she lived in belonged to her parents until they moved.

IT TOOK MELISSA UNTIL after two in the morning to bring her account of events up to date, at which time her grandmother read it. Despite the hour, neither of them thought about going to bed, they were both sure they would only lie awake, thinking about Daisy and what she must have gone through as her life was taken from her.

Melissa was especially keen not to have the time or the opportunity to think about it since she had seen Georgina's body, and so was more aware of what her young cousin had almost certainly endured.

Instead of trying to sleep, they did everything they could think of to keep themselves occupied, both physically and mentally. In Constance's case that meant filling the kitchen with the heavenly aroma of fresh-baked cakes and biscuits, enough to fill a shop; Melissa's way of distracting herself was to finish the chronology, and then to make herself more than a little sick by eating her way through as much of what her grandmother had baked as she could, which still left a significant amount for someone – about half the village it seemed – to eat.

"Is this everything that's happened?" Constance asked once she made it through the last page of what her granddaughter had written. When Melissa nodded, she asked another question, "Lewis really tried to strangle Mr Wild?"

"He didn't just try, he nearly succeeded," Melissa said. "I was so shocked by it, on top of everything else that happened tonight, I didn't know what to do, I just stood there like an idiot.

It's just as well one of the nurses came in, and then a couple of others, with one of the security guards; if they hadn't shown up, I think I'd have had to arrest Mitchell for murder. As it is, if Mr Wild makes an official complaint, and I'm sure he will, I'm going to have to arrest him for assault, maybe even attempted murder." She sighed more heavily than she had ever sighed in her life; it seemed as though Mitchell was determined to make an already terrible situation worse.

"At least you don't have any doubts about what the right thing to do in that situation is," Constance remarked. She was as shocked by what Mitchell had done as Melissa and could only imagine how much more shocking it must have been to witness the incident. "Have you made up your mind about any of the things that were troubling you before?"

"Not entirely," Melissa admitted. "Mr Wild is apparently the same blood-type as the killer, but he has an alibi for when Emily was attacked, most likely attacked," she amended. "If his alibi is true, and it almost certainly is, I don't see how he could be the killer." She gave a quick shake of her head and then went on. "The only things I'm certain of right now are that Sergeant Mitchell can't be allowed to stay in charge of the case; even if Mr Wild is the killer, the way Mitchell's acted is going to put the case against him in jeopardy; and more attention should have been paid to the possibility that Kieran Wright is the killer. He might not be, but Mitchell hasn't even considered the possibility that he might be, let alone looked into it."

"What are you going to do about it?"

"Speak to the inspector first thing," Melissa said, she couldn't think of anything else she could do.

42

Melissa yawned mightily as she leaned on the doorbell at her superior's house. Her mouth gaped like the entrance to a cave suitable for roosting bats, but she closed it hastily when the door opened.

"Melissa, what are doing here so early?" Irene Stevens asked when she saw who was on the doorstep. "Constance." If she was surprised to see Melissa, it was nothing to how she felt at seeing who was with her. "Has something happened? Something new?"

Melissa hesitated briefly and then nodded. "You could say that," she said, wondering if Mitchell had told the inspector any of what had happened at the hospital the previous evening; she doubted it, it was past midnight when they made it back to the village, and she didn't imagine Mitchell would have wanted to admit what he had done. "I know it's early, but I really need to speak to the inspector, it's important."

Ordinarily, Irene would have told Melissa to come back later, but she knew the constable wasn't the sort to come knocking without a very good reason. "Come in, I'll get Robert." She stepped back from the door, so Melissa and her grandmother could enter.

Stevens found his guests on the sofa when he reached the living room. "So, Melissa, to what do I owe the pleasure of this visit?" he asked once they had exchanged pleasantries. "I take it you're the one who wants to see me." He glanced at Constance, but most of his attention was on his subordinate.

"It's about Sergeant Mitchell, sir, and Mr Wild," Melissa said. She was a little worried about how Stevens was going to take what she had to say, he had always been a fair and reasonable boss, but she couldn't help remembering that he was good friends with Mitchell and had been since she was a baby. "And about the murders." She fell silent for a moment, waiting for Stevens to say something, when he didn't, she continued, "I think Sergeant Mitchell needs to be taken off the case, I think we need a detective to take over."

"Why's that?" Stevens asked. "Lewis has already caught the killer. I know he hasn't arrested Mr Wild yet, but he has assured me that Mr Wild's blood-type matches that of the killer, and he will arrest him once he has proved his alibi is false."

"The blood-type match means very little, sir; the killer's blood-type is the same as that of a third of the male population. That aside, Mr Wild's alibi is solid, so the only way he could be the one who attacked Emily is if we're wrong about when she was attacked, and given all the information we have, and the phone call we got at the station, that seems unlikely. If he can't be responsible for the attack on Emily, he can't be responsible for the murders of Georgina and Lucy either."

"You're certain of that?"

Melissa nodded while trying to read the look on her superior's face. "Yes, sir, very certain," she said. "At the time we received the call in which we heard someone – we still haven't been able to confirm that it was Emily, though I can't see that it could have been anyone else – being attacked, Mr Wild was on the phone to his daughter. We've confirmed that both with his ex-wife and through his phone records, and before that his agent was at the house. If Emily was the one we heard being attacked,

I don't see how Mr Wild could have been responsible, it's all but impossible.

"There's more, sir; Sergeant Mitchell has been so obsessed with proving that Mr Wild's the murderer that he hasn't even considered that it might be someone else. Oliver Ryder gave us reason to make Kieran Wright a suspect, but Sergeant Mitchell hasn't considered the possibility at all; he never properly checked whether Kieran saw Georgina the night she disappeared, he never checked his car or anything, he just took his word for it that he hadn't seen Georgina." Melissa saw that Stevens was about to say something and hurried on, "I also think Mitchell may have been involved in the two attempts on Mr Wild's life..."

Stevens' face darkened, and he leaned forwards angrily. "Are you really trying to suggest that Lewis Mitchell, a man I have known for almost as long as you have lived, would have had anything to do with attempted murder? I'll give you one chance to withdraw that claim, Melissa, before it has serious repercussions for your career. I know you are ambitious, as ambitious as anyone, but a claim like this could put an end to your career."

"I realise that, sir," Melissa said. She went pale at the mention of serious repercussions for her career but didn't back down; now that she had made the decision to tell Stevens her suspicions, and what had led her to them, she was not prepared to back away from them just because they might harm her career. "But I have good reason for what I've said, and I believe it can be proved if you want to check it. In fact, there's worse even than him being involved with the two attempts on Mr Wild's life..." She hesitated for a long moment and then plunged on. "Last night at the hospital, I witnessed Sergeant Mitchell try to kill Mr Wild. After we left the Wrights, we went down to speak to Mr Wild; Sergeant Mitchell got very angry, and ended up with his hands around his throat, trying to strangle him. It took me and a nurse to pull him off, and I needed a security guard to help me get him out of the room. If the nurse hadn't arrived, I don't think I would have been able to stop him killing Mr Wild."

A lengthy silence fell over the living room as Stevens considered what he had been told. Without tears, he could not have looked unhappier. "Why are you here, Constance?" he asked to give himself time to think. "This has nothing to do with you," he said, his words harsher than he intended them to be.

"I'm here to support Melissa," Constance said. "And to make sure you listen to what she has to say." She had no illusions about her lack of authority over Stevens, she could not compel him to do as she wished, but she did have a position of respect in the village that made it more likely that he would listen to Melissa if it was clear she supported her. "I think you should read the file Melissa has put together; she makes a good case for all she says."

With a degree of reluctance, Stevens reached out to take the file. It took him some time to get through the pages, which were more detailed than anything he had been told or shown by Mitchell, and by the time he was finished he was far from happy. He was unhappy with his friend for claiming to have solved the case, when it appeared that he had actually made it worse, and he was unhappy with Melissa for making him aware of the situation.

"You heard Glen Wright threaten to harm Mr Wild if Lewis didn't deal with him and find his daughter; and then, when he was forced to release Mr Wild because of a lack of evidence, you heard Lewis on the phone to Glen Wright, telling him not to do what he was thinking of doing." When Melissa nodded, Stevens sighed heavily. "Yet he hasn't arrested him."

"No, sir," Melissa said with a shake of her head. "Mr Wild hasn't filed an official complaint yet, either, but I think that's probably just a matter of time."

"If the attack was as serious as you say, I'd have to agree." Stevens shuffled the papers together. "Okay, you'll get what you want, I'll call the chief inspector and request a detective to take over the case and look into your allegations. You'd better hope he or she agrees that Lewis has a case to answer to, though; if the detective we get disagrees with you, I think you'll have to give serious thought to finding a new career."

43

Melissa was asleep, having been sent home to try and catch up on some of the rest that grief and circumstances had denied her during the night, when her phone rang, vibrating noisily on the bedside cabinet. She woke with a start and groped for the phone without opening her eyes.

"Hello," she croaked once she had the phone to her ear. She stayed with her face half-buried in the pillow, hoping the phone call was going to be a quick one so she could go back to sleep – she could not remember when she had ever felt as tired as she did then.

"Mel, it's Paul," Pritchard identified himself. "You're needed at the station."

"What for?" Melissa hoped she sounded more with it than she felt. With the greatest of reluctance, she pushed herself up until she was sitting on the edge of the bed; looking down she saw that she was still dressed in her uniform. She must have been really tired if she had gone straight to bed without getting undressed, she thought.

"The case has been handed over to a detective inspector, he's here now, and he wants to see you," Pritchard told her.

Blinking, Melissa sought out the radio alarm clock, so she could see what the time was. It surprised her to see that it was not quite half past ten; she had thought it would take longer for

Stevens to explain everything to the chief inspector and convince him to give them a detective – she hadn't expected them to get a detective inspector – let alone for one to be found who could be spared, and for that detective to get to the village.

"I'll be there as soon as I can." Melissa hung up before Pritchard could say anything more. She didn't really want to go anywhere but back to sleep, for about twelve hours if she could manage it, but she could hardly ignore a summons from a detective inspector, especially when she was the reason for him being there, so she tiredly got to her feet.

A LITTLE OVER HALF an hour after being woken, Melissa walked into the station, dressed in a fresh uniform.

"Where's the DI?" she asked as she screwed up the wrapper from the chocolate bar she had eaten on the way there and threw it in the bin. The chocolate had given her a bit of energy, but she still felt as though she needed about a gallon of coffee if she was going to make it through what remained of the morning, let alone the rest of the day.

"He's in Mitchell's office," Pritchard said. "He's been waiting for you."

"Thanks. What's he like?" Melissa asked. It was because of her the inspector was there, but she couldn't help feeling a significant amount of nerves, which slowed her pace to a crawl as she headed down the passage.

Pritchard shrugged. "He seems alright. I've barely met him, though; he's been in the office practically since he got here. He's spoken to the inspector and to Mitchell, and he's been reading the case file; mostly, though, I think he's been waiting for you. Asking for you was just about the first thing he did after speaking to the inspector."

Melissa's nerves didn't diminish with that news, if anything it made them worse. "I guess I'd better go see what he wants," she said, relieved that her voice betrayed nothing of what she was feeling.

"Come in," an unfamiliar voice called out from behind the closed door of Sergeant Mitchell's office when she knocked.

Melissa stopped the moment she was through the door. "Constable Turner, reporting as ordered, sir," she told the man seated behind her superior's desk. He appeared nice enough, as Pritchard had said, but she was beginning to appreciate just how deceptive appearances could be; someone she knew was a murderer, and a brutal one, yet there was nothing about any of them that made it easy to pick him out.

"Good morning, constable, I'm Detective Inspector Harrison, I'm now in charge of the investigation into the murders you've had here in Oakhurst," he said.

Melissa studied the DI for a moment, he was a fair bit taller than her at just about dead on six feet in height and slender, almost skinny, with close-cropped brown hair, hazel eyes and the remains of a tan. None of what she saw, including the dark, casual-smart suit he wore, told her what she really wanted to know - whether he was a good detective who would solve the murders and deal with the question of whether Sergeant Mitchell was connected with or guilty of the attempts on Zack's life.

"I understand from your Inspector Stevens that you're responsible for this," Harrison held up the wad of papers Stevens had given him. "Is that true?"

Melissa nodded nervously. There was no point in her denying authorship of the file when he clearly knew she had written it. "Yes, sir."

DI Harrison smiled briefly. "It's very detailed, more so than the official file," he remarked. "How accurate is it?"

Melissa opened her mouth to protest the suggestion that what she had written might be wrong, but quickly shut it again. "As accurate as I could make it, sir," she said. "I've probably missed a few things out, or not put in all of the details of something, but for the most part it's everything that's happened since Georgina went missing."

"Good, this is likely to save me a lot of time," Harrison said with a second smile that disappeared as quickly as the first. "Now, on the basis of this," he held up the report again. "I have requested that your inspector assign you to me to help with my investigation – I could get more help from my own station, but I'd rather use you, you know the case and the people involved, which will help – and he has agreed on the condition that you also agree to the assignment, he seemed to think you might have reasons for declining."

She definitely had reasons, Melissa thought. "I'm related to one of the – one of the victims," she said. "Daisy Hawkins is my cousin. And I'm a witness to Sergeant Mitchell's attack on Mr Wild."

"Ordinarily, those things would keep you from being a part of this case, but I've discussed the situation with your inspector, and he agrees with me that if you're okay with assisting me to investigate your cousin's murder, there shouldn't be any problem with it," Harrison told her. "As for the assault on Mr Wild by your Sergeant Mitchell – I will be investigating it and your other allegation against the sergeant, just not yet, the murders are my priority. Once that case has been resolved, I'll look into the rest of it, though, truth be told, I don't think it will take long to deal with your allegations."

Melissa was relieved to hear that she was being taken seriously, even if it was going to take a while for anything to come of what she had reported. "As long as you're sure there won't be any complications with me being involved, sir, I'll help you." It was tempting to use the excuse she had available and leave the investigation into the murders to other people; that would leave her unaware of how the investigation was proceeding, however, and she preferred to know.

"I'm pleased to hear that. Our first stop," Harrison flipped open the covers on the files that detailed Georgina's disappearance, and the murders that had taken place in the village, "is to get the post-mortem report on your cousin; I've phoned the morgue, and it should be ready by the time we get to town. I know that the murders of Georgina Ryder and Lucy Goulding have been linked through the preliminary tests that have been run, now we need to be certain that your cousin's murder is linked to the other two – if it is, we'll know that the attack on Emily Wright is also linked. I realise you're already pretty certain they're all connected," he said when he saw that the constable who would be partnering him was about to say something, "but we need to be certain of that."

It only took Melissa a moment to realise he was right; as confident as she was that the murders were connected, there was a chance she was wrong. She didn't want to stay fixed on an idea that might not be right, not when that was what had prompted her to go to Inspector Stevens about Sergeant Mitchell; her thinking continued along that line until it made her say, "Sir, can I ask..." she hesitated for a moment and then went on with her question. "Do you think Mr Wild is the killer?"

Harrison didn't answer straightaway, instead he allowed himself a brief period in which to consider the question. "Based on what we have right now," he said finally, "I'd have to say it's unlikely. Except for Mr Wild's blood-type, which isn't rare enough to be conclusive, all the evidence against him is circumstantial; not only that but the same witness reported last sightings of two of the girls in the company of Mr Wild. That could be coincidental, and is certainly more likely out here than it would be in town, but I find it suspicious, especially when that witness is someone you've identified as a possible suspect." He frowned. "This would be easier if I had been brought in right at the start; at this point the water's been muddied a little too much for my liking." After a quick sigh of regret, he shook himself off. "Come on, let's go get that post-mortem report, we can discuss the case on the way."

"THE ONLY THING WE KNOW for certain right now, if I've read your report right," Harrison said as he drove them towards town, "Is that all four of the girls we believe are victims of our killer were either at the Wright Farm or on the road that leads to it when they were attacked."

"But we don't know where Daisy was when she was attacked," Melissa said, determined not to get caught in the trap of believing something was certain until it was proven. "We know she left home just before five, and that she should have been on her way to the Wright Farm, but we don't know that that's where she was actually heading, and we haven't been able to find anyone in the village who saw her between the end of the road she lives on and the farm."

"That's true," Harrison agreed. "But the fact that she was found in a farmhouse off the road we're talking about does suggest that the attack on her fits with the others. It gives us somewhere to start, and that's important. The map you included in your file indicates that the road to the Wright Farm runs for about a mile from the church to the farm; we can probably discount about half of that distance, the area from the church to the three houses you marked, as being where the attacks took place – the odds of three girls being snatched along that stretch, where there's most likely to be a witness, are too low.

"I think it far more likely the killer would have grabbed them on the latter stretch of the road, where there was less chance of him being spotted."

"I guess so, the only place where we know for sure that one of the attacks happened, other than the attack on Emily, which happened in her bedroom, is the field belonging to the Wright Farm, that's almost parallel with the houses, but the actual spot where the attack happened isn't easy to see from them." Melissa grimaced. "That doesn't really help us, though, does it."

"Maybe, maybe not. If there were no houses along that stretch of road I'd be inclined to agree with you, but with them there it means the killer is almost certainly either Zack Wild or Kieran Wright. The attacks occurred on at least three separate occasions – if someone who had no reason for being there was seen on the days the attacks happened it would have been noted by one of Zack Wild's neighbours, who I'm sure are aware of everyone who goes up and down the road; it's doubtful, however, that they would take much note of the comings and goings of either Zack Wild or Kieran Wright.

"Since Wild has an alibi for when one of the attacks appears to have taken place, we need to focus our attention on either proving that Wright is responsible for the murders, or on finding the evidence that proves he can't be."

"We've got DNA from Georgina and Lucy," Melissa said. "That should prove who the killer is."

"It will certainly prove whether Mr Wild is the killer or not," Harrison said. "We can get a DNA sample from Mr Wild no problem; we can't with Kieran Wright, he would have to volunteer, and I can't see him doing that. I do have a tentative idea for how we can get a sample from him without arousing his suspicions, however. The problem we have is that they are our only two suspects, if the DNA eliminates both of them, we're left with no idea who the killer is, and nothing to point us to him unless Emily Wright wakes up."

44

Zack waited until his former sister-in-law was off the phone to ask about the conversation he had overheard.

"What did you mean, you don't know when you'll be back at work? I'm being released today, so there's no need for you to take any more time off, especially if it's going to put your job at risk."

"My job's not at risk," Sophie assured him. "I might wonder why Crandall made me assistant manager, and he certainly blusters and moans a lot, but he's not going to sack me, not when I'm the one that keeps that business afloat. I'll pick up some paperwork and do it from home, your home that is, that'll keep him quiet. I'm not going back to work 'til you're no longer in danger of going to jail for murder." She held up a hand when she saw that Zack was about to say something. "I'm not having a debate about this; you're in trouble because that Sergeant Mitchell is a prejudiced idiot who either isn't capable or isn't willing to conduct a proper investigation, and you have no-one who can alibi you. Since that's the case, I'm going to stick around and shadow you until the real killer is caught, so the next time they try to arrest you for something, you'll have someone who can vouch for where you've been and what you've been doing."

Zack wanted to protest, to tell Sophie that there was no need for her to effectively put her life on hold simply to help him, but he couldn't bring himself to do so. He didn't want his friend to put herself to so much trouble, but he couldn't deny that it would be a help; having someone who could vouch for his movements would make it a lot more difficult for him to be hit with fresh allegations.

"It's your decision," he said, realising that it would be a waste of time to try and talk Sophie out of what she was intending. "But you probably won't be very comfortable, my place wasn't very tidy the last time I saw it."

"Tidying it up will give us something to do while you keep out of trouble," Sophie remarked, making it clear that she was not going to be put off.

"GOOD AFTERNOON, MR Wild, I'm Detective Inspector Harrison," he said as he approached the bed. "I've been put in charge of the investigation into the murders you've been accused of in Oakhurst. Sorry to disturb your lunch but I'm here to ask you a few questions, if you don't mind."

"Given that you've probably saved me from a bout of food poisoning, I don't mind at all." Zack swung the table that held his tray of 'food' away from the bed, so he wouldn't have to look at it. "I take it Sergeant Mitchell is no longer involved with the investigation." Involuntarily, his hand went to his throat, which was still sore from the previous evening.

"That's right. After last night's incident, it was decided that the investigation would be better off in the hands of someone not so closely connected to it," Harrison said.

Zack was sure the attack on him was not the only reason Mitchell had been taken off the case; he imagined the fact that there were now four victims, three of whom were dead, had something to do with it. Picking up his glass of water from the bedside cabinet, he sipped at it while he waited for the inspector to get on with his questions, which he was sure he could guess at.

"I understand you were a DI yourself until recently," Harrison noted the nod that confirmed that comment but didn't respond to it, "so I'm sure you can appreciate that I'm probably going to have to ask you some of the same questions that Sergeant Mitchell did, just to be certain I've covered everything. I'll try not to repeat things any more than necessary."

"Do you want me to go, or would you rather I stay?" Sophie asked from her chair at the side of the bed.

"You go on," Zack told her, sure that she would only slow things down if she stayed. "I'm sure I'll be fine."

"I'll be back later." Sophie stopped when she reached the door. "I forgot to say, the garage called earlier, they said your car's ready to be collected. I told them I'd pick it up later."

"Thanks."

Harrison waited until there was just him, Melissa and Zack Wild in the room to speak again. "If you don't mind, just for my own peace of mind, I'd like to start at the beginning and run through the events of the past couple of weeks to clarify your role in events, and to see if you might have remembered something that slipped your mind previously."

"Sure, no problem," Zack said, aware that the real reason for going over everything was to see if he would change anything he had said before, or reveal something he hadn't mentioned previously, something which might help to firm up the case against him. "First, though, can I ask, do you know how Emily is doing? Has she woken up yet?"

Melissa was about to answer Wild when she stopped herself. She had no idea what the DI she was now working with wanted Wild to know and what he didn't. She kept quiet and left it to

Harrison to reply in whatever way he wanted; when he did, she was surprised by what he said.

"Yes, she has." Harrison watched Wild closely as he said that, searching his face for anything that might indicate concern. "According to the doctor, she woke briefly this morning, which is good, but until she remains awake for more than a minute, they can't judge the extent of the damage to her brain, or the likelihood of her making a full recovery. Personally, I'm inclined to think that her waking so soon after the attack, even if for only a short time, bodes well for her being able to tell us who attacked her."

"That's good news, I'm relieved to hear that her condition is looking up," Zack said with genuine feeling.

Harrison saw that Wild appeared untroubled by the news that Emily Wright had woken, but he had encountered many good actors and actresses during his time as a detective and knew that appearances could be deceptive. For now, he accepted Wild's apparent relief and got on with the questions he was there to ask.

"Georgina Ryder went missing on the evening of the third, after leaving her cousin's house in the village of Oakhurst, where you live, so she could head to the Wright Farm to meet her boyfriend, Kieran Wright. Her route to the farm would have taken her right past your house on Oak Road; did you see her that evening?"

It took over an hour of questioning for Zack to answer all the inquisitive inspector's questions, by which time he was tired and hungry and ready for something that didn't look as though it would be rejected by a starving refugee.

LEAVING ZACK WILD'S hospital room at Harrison's side, Melissa made her way down the corridor towards the lift. As they walked, she wondered what Harrison had made of the answers they had been given, which were all but identical to those Wild had given previously. She wondered more about something else, however, and once they were far enough from the room to be sure they couldn't be heard, she asked about it.

"Why did you tell Mr Wild that Emily woke up this morning, sir? She didn't, and the doctor thinks it will be at least a couple of days before she will, if she ever does."

"I know," Harrison said. "But I've had an idea for how we can catch the killer. If it isn't either Zack Wild or Kieran Wright, we're going to need something more than the DNA samples the pathologist has for us - they're only any good for confirming that we've got the right guy once we have a suspect. My idea, if the superintendent is willing to go along with it and give me the officers I'm going to need, will help us catch the killer in the first place."

Melissa was no more enlightened than she had been before, but instead of saying so, she chose to wait and see if her new superior would explain further, which he did, though it took him a while.

"How long do you think it would take you to spread the story I gave Mr Wild?" Harrison asked. Reaching the lift, he pressed the button and then waited with his eyes on Melissa for an answer.

"I don't know, a couple of hours maybe," Melissa said. She didn't like admitting that her village was a place prone to gossip – it was bad enough that Harrison assumed it was – but she couldn't see the point in denying the truth, especially when she was beginning to understand how he was thinking, at least she thought she was. "Are you thinking that if the killer believes

Emily is going to wake up, he'll worry she might be able to identify him and try to finish her off?"

Harrison nodded. "That's exactly what I'm thinking. Whoever the killer is, he won't want Emily to identify him, especially when up to now Zack Wild has been the only suspect under investigation; he'll want us to remain focused on Wild. If by some chance the killer is Mr Wild, which I don't consider likely right now – even ignoring how hard it would be for him to have attacked Emily while establishing his alibi, there is the fact that as a former detective inspector, as well as a writer of crime novels, he should be well enough versed in forensic procedures not to have left the amount of evidence the pathologist found during the post-mortems – he won't want to be identified by one of his victims." The lift arrived then, and he stepped on board. "My plan is to have you spread the rumour of Miss Wright's waking as far and as wide as you can, just in case the killer is neither Kieran Wright nor Zack Wild, and then for us to be waiting here tonight with a team to arrest the killer when he tries to silence her.

"Before you begin your part of this, however, I need to speak to the superintendent, he's not always in favour of this kind of operation, and I don't want to put Miss Wright in danger unnecessarily."

45

After a brief stop to look at the ruined farmhouse where Emily and Daisy had been found, which was still being examined by the forensics team from Branton, Harrison and Melissa continued up the road to the Wright Farm.

"Do you think anyone's home?" Harrison asked as he got out and headed across the yard to the front door of the farmhouse.

"It doesn't look like it," Melissa said. "Neither Kieran's Land Rover nor his dad's are here; I guess they've got to keep the farm going, despite what's happened. Tara could be here, though. If I was her, I wouldn't want to go to school after everything; mind you, I wouldn't really want to stick around here on my own either."

Harrison considered that as he reached out to knock on the door. He had come to the farmhouse in the hope of finding Kieran Wright, and he didn't fancy having to search the entire farm for him. When there was no response after almost a minute, he knocked again, louder.

"Someone's home," Melissa said after the second knock. "I saw the curtain twitch." She pressed her face against the window to try to see into the room. She was pretty sure she knew who was in the house, but it wasn't easy to see anything. "Tara, it's Melissa, Constable Turner, can you come to the door," she called out; there was a sudden movement near the doorway of the living room, and a few seconds later the front door opened, stopping when it reached the extent of the chain.

"Who's with you?" Tara asked suspiciously through the narrow gap. Her eyes, which were about the only part of her that was visible, darted from the constable, whom she knew, to the stranger.

Melissa was not surprised by the way the young girl was acting, she was sure she would have acted the same way if she was in Tara's position. "This is Detective Inspector Harrison, he's here to investigate the – what's been happening here recently," she said, quickly changing what she had been about to say to try and avoid upsetting the girl.

"Hello," Harrison said in the friendliest tone he possessed. "I know you don't know me, but you know Constable Turner, don't you." When the eyes bobbed up and down in a way that suggested the girl had nodded he continued, "Well, Constable Turner will tell you there's nothing to worry about, we just need to speak to your brother; do you know where he is?"

Tara nodded quickly and then made to shut the door.

Harrison's hand reached out to stop the door being shut. "Where is he?" he asked.

"I-I think I should call my daddy," Tara said.

"You should," Melissa told her. "And you should lock the door once we're gone. First, though, where's your brother, is he on the farm?"

"He's in the East Field." With that Tara slammed the door and locked it securely, before hurrying back into the living room so she could snatch up her mobile phone. She hadn't wanted to tell the police where her brother was, it felt like a betrayal, but she knew and trusted Constable Turner and, most of all, she wanted to get the two police officers away, she didn't feel safe with them there.

Harrison started to ask, "Where's the East Field?" when the slamming of the door cut him off, leaving him to look at it in surprise.

"It's alright, sir," Melissa said quickly. "I'm pretty sure I know where it is."

WITH HER PHONE PRESSED to her ear, Tara watched from the window as Melissa and the inspector returned to their car and left the yard. She felt a little better when she saw them head down the road, but that was offset by the panic inspired when the phone she was calling rang and rang and rang before finally tripping over to the answer phone after almost a minute. She immediately jabbed at the screen to disconnect the call and try again.

Three times, Tara called her dad's number, trying to get hold of him, without success. "Where are you?" she sobbed into the phone when the call tripped over to the answer machine for the third time. "I need you, daddy, where are you? The police were here, they wanted to know where Kieran is, I think something's up."

GLEN WRIGHT STRUCK the nail one last time. Finished with his repairs, he gathered up his things, ran an eye over the cows in the field to be sure everything was alright, and headed for his Land Rover.

The first thing he did when he climbed behind the wheel was check his mobile phone. His heart leapt into his mouth and he went cold when he saw he had a missed call, which reminded him of Tara's failed efforts to get hold of him on Sunday - he should have been carrying the phone with him, he thought, but quickly reminded himself that it wouldn't have made any difference, he never heard it ring when he did have it about his person.

He felt even worse, if that were possible, when he unlocked the phone and saw that it was actually three missed calls and a voice-mail from Tara.

His heart lurched in his chest briefly, but he ignored it as he concentrated on accessing his voice-mail, so he could listen to the message from his younger daughter – it was short, only a few seconds long, but it was enough to make him grope for his keys, which were still in the ignition, and scare his cows as he turned the Land Rover around and raced for the gate.

He brought his Land Rover to a skidding stop once he reached home, threw open the door next to him and sprinted to the back door, which opened at his touch. He felt a moment's annoyance at that, he had told Tara to make sure she kept all the doors shut and locked while she was on her own, but it quickly changed to fear as it occurred to him that the door might be unlocked because something had happened.

"Tara, Tara! Where are you, honey?" he called out as he crossed the kitchen and started down the passage.

"Daddy!" There was no mistaking the relief in the young girl's voice as Tara appeared from the living room and practically threw herself down the passage and into her father's arms. "Where were you?" she asked accusingly. "I called and called and called but you didn't answer. I thought something had happened to you." Had there been anyone there to witness it, they would have been amazed at the way Tara went from relieved to accusing to scared in the space of just a few seconds.

"Sorry, honey." Glen hugged his daughter reassuringly before continuing to the living room, which wasn't easy because Tara didn't want to let go of him, she clung to him as if she thought he was going to disappear the moment she released him. "But you know how I am, I'm useless with that phone. I was fixing a fence in one of the North fields when you called, so I didn't know about it 'til I was done, but I hurried back as soon as I heard your message.

"You said the police were here looking for Kieran, did Lewis say why, or why he didn't call me?"

Tara shook her head. "It wasn't Sergeant Mitchell, it was Constable Turner, there was a detective with her; they didn't say why they wanted Kieran, they just said they were looking for him. I told them he's in the East field, then I tried to call you. I was scared when you didn't answer, daddy."

"I'm sorry, honey," Glen apologised again. "Do you feel better now?"

"A little," Tara said with a hesitant nod of her head.

"Good. Why don't you go and put the kettle on, make us some tea, while I call Lewis and see if I can find out what's going on."

46

"Where's my son?" Glen demanded the moment he reached the reception counter of Oakhurst's police station. "I know you've got Kieran here, I wanna know why, and what some strange detective's doing scaring my daughter. Tara's had enough to deal with the last couple of days, we all have, without having some stranger come banging on the door trying to find her brother."

Harrison was in the interview room, with the door closed, but he, Kieran Wright, and Melissa all heard Glen Wright's raised voice as he demanded answers of Constable Black, who was unlucky enough to be at the counter.

"You stay here and keep an eye on Mr Wright, Constable," Harrison told Melissa as he left the room. He reached the counter in just a few long-legged strides and came to a stop alongside Constable Black. "Mr Wright?" he inquired politely; the answer was obvious, but he asked anyway.

"Who the hell are you?" Glen asked. He ran his eyes suspiciously over the stranger.

"Detective Inspector Harrison." He showed his warrant card. "I've been asked to look into the murders that have taken place here in Oakhurst, and the two attempts on the life of the man your Sergeant Mitchell has identified as a suspect."

"Who's asked you to do that? We don't need you, we know who the killer is, Lewis already figured it out, it's that Wild bloke," Glen said, not happy to hear that an outsider had been brought in to handle things he thought had been all but resolved. "Lewis told me he's just waiting for some test results to come back to confirm that Wild's the killer, once he gets them, Wild'll be going straight from hospital to jail."

"I'm aware of what your sergeant believes, but fresh information suggests that Mr Wild may not be the killer," Harrison told him. "My superiors are keen for this case to be resolved – three murders, a fourth girl, your daughter, attacked, and two attempts on the life of the only person identified as a possible suspect – and they feel an independent investigator, me, would be better suited to do that. With a bit of luck, I'll catch the killer in a couple of days and be out of your village's hair, leaving everyone here free to go on with their lives."

"So, why've you arrested my son?" Anger reddened Glen's face as he leaned across the counter. "Don't tell me you think he's the murderer."

"Your son has not been arrested, Mr Wright, he is simply here to help us with our inquiries."

"Then I'm taking him home. I'm not having him dragged down here to be accused of murder by the likes of you." Glen made to go around the counter, so he could find his son, but was defeated by the security door, which was there specifically to stop people doing what he was attempting. Frustrated, he banged on the door with his fist and kicked at it with a booted foot. "He could never have hurt any of those girls; one of them's his sister, and another's his girlfriend, for God's sake."

"Calm down, Mr Wright, I have not accused your son of murder, nor is that why I've brought him down here." Though he gave no indication of it and couldn't because doing so would have messed everything up, Harrison was pleased by the display of anger, it was just what he had been hoping for. "Kieran is here because I wish to question him about the attempt on Mr Wild's life on Sunday night, he will be released when, and if, he convinces me he had nothing to do with it."

"He didn't."

A ghost of a smile touched Harrison's lips at that. "You'll forgive me if I don't take your word for it, but you are biased."

"I tell you, he didn't do it," Glen said firmly.

"I appreciate you don't wish to believe your son is capable of such an act, Mr Wright," Harrison said compassionately. "But Kieran has the means, he is the licensed owner of a shotgun; the motive, both his sister and his girlfriend are among those who have been attacked, and Mr Wild has been named as the person responsible for the attacks. He also had the opportunity, he lives just up the road from Mr Wild.

"Unless you have proof, rather than just your belief that your son wasn't involved in the attempt on Mr Wild's life, you'll have to wait 'til I've spoken to him to take him, assuming I feel it appropriate to release him." With that he turned and started back down the passage to the interview room.

Glen started to swear. "I know Kieran didn't try and kill Wild," he called out quickly before the DI disappeared into the interview room he had come from. "I know he didn', 'cause I'm the one you're looking for. I'm the one shot Wild and 'is solicitor."

Harrison stopped in the doorway. "You'll have to do better than that, Mr Wright," he said. "You can't just make a claim like that to try and save your son, that's not how things work. Just standing there and saying you did what I'm about to question your son about isn't going to help him, it's only going to get you in trouble as well. I'm a busy man right now, however, so I'll give you a break." He paused for a moment before playing his trump card. "Withdraw your claim, or back it up with something, if you don't do either, I'll have no choice but to arrest you for obstruction of justice."

Glen didn't hesitate. "Arrest me then, but I'm telling you I'm the one you're after. I walked down the road after Lewis called to say he was releasing Wild again and shot 'im through the living room window. I hit 'is solicitor first, I didn't mean to do that, but if she's gonna go 'round tryin' to get rapists and murderers off, she's got to accept the consequences, then I got 'im. I thought I'd killed 'im, but I guess not. If I'd known that, I'd've kicked the door in and gone inside to finish the job."

Harrison considered what he had just heard for several moments before deciding what to do. "Okay," he said finally. "If you're sure about this. Bring him through, constable." Turning to look through the doorway into the interview room he addressed Kieran, "Looks like you're free to go, Mr Wright, your father's decided to confess to the attempt on Mr Wild's life that I was going to question you about."

Kieran was too surprised by that news to react to it straight away. Once he recovered, he rose and left the interview room, meeting his father in the doorway. "Why'd you say you did it?" he wanted to know.

"I couldn' let them charge you for something I did," Glen told his son.

Kieran shook his head. "They weren't going to charge me with anything. I've done nothing wrong, and they'd have realised that, sooner or later."

"I couldn' take that chance." At the prompting of the inspector, Glen squeezed past Kieran and into the interview room, so he could take the seat previously occupied by his son. "Your sister's gonna be worried when I don't come back soon, so you need to reassure her, make sure she knows everything's going to be alright."

Harrison took the opportunity. "Maybe this will help make your sister feel better; I was at the hospital earlier, and the doctor in charge of your sister's case told me she woke this morning. It wasn't for long, only a minute or so, but apparently it's a good sign. The doctor thinks it's only a matter of time before she wakes up properly – it'll be a while before she's able to come home, but at least she'll be able to tell us who attacked her." He watched Kieran closely as he said that, and thought he saw something in his eyes, but couldn't be certain.

"HOW DID YOU KNOW GLEN would confess if we brought Kieran in?" Melissa asked once they had finished interviewing the farmer.

"I was gambling," Harrison admitted. "Betting he wouldn't want his son to be accused of something he'd done. It was a risk, but it's paid off. Even if he hadn't come in we'd have gotten a result; we were able to get that DNA sample from Kieran Wright before his dad got here, which means we'll be able to tell if he's the killer we're after." He offered the constable at his side a brief smile. "If we're lucky, we'll catch the killer tonight, assuming you're right about how quickly gossip gets round this village – in which case pretty much everyone who lives here should know by now – but if not, we've got the DNA samples to fall back on, and with a bit of pressure the lab boys will take less than the usual two or three days to tell us if they match.

Melissa wasn't all that comfortable with the action Harrison had taken through the afternoon; she didn't like the false hope he had offered to Emily's family, even if she could understand why he had done it. Nor did she like the trickery he had employed – that was how she thought of it – in bringing Kieran in for questioning simply to get his father to confess to the crime he had committed to save his son from a false accusation. She made no mention of what she was thinking and feeling, however, for she doubted it would make any difference, and she had no alternatives to offer.

47

Zack's stomach lurched into his throat as the car came to a sudden stop outside the village shop. Next to him in the driver's seat, Sophie laughed at the look on his face.

"Did you think I was going to lose control and crash your baby?" she asked, amused by his reaction to her driving – she wasn't about to admit it, but her own stomach had given a bit of a jolt when the car stopped more quickly than she expected; the brakes on the Aston Martin were much more responsive than those on her own car.

"You came close a few times," Zack said once his stomach had settled back into its usual location.

"Rubbish," Sophie scoffed. "I was in complete control. I'm a very good driver."

Zack looked at his friend sceptically. "How do you explain your car then?" he asked. "I don't think I've ever seen it looking like it's capable of passing an M.O.T.."

"It might not be pretty to look at, we can't all afford fancy sports cars, but it runs, without any problems, and it's never even come close to failing an M.O.T.." Sophie was proud of that. "I'll be back shortly," she said, throwing open the door at her side. "I haven't had a chance to stock up your fridge, I've had too much other stuff to do, and I don't much fancy going hungry tonight."

Before Zack could say or ask anything, she was out of the car and at the door of the shop.

While Sophie browsed the aisles in the shop, Zack did his best to make himself comfortable in the passenger seat. It wasn't easy, the last batch of pain relief the hospital had given him had worn off, and he could feel a multitude of tiny pinpricks of fire shooting through his back where the shotgun pellets had struck him. The pain was more intense where his back pressed against the seat behind him. His injuries were minor compared to those suffered by Isobel, but he couldn't help wishing for a magical remedy to heal them.

"BLOODY HELL!" THE PROFANITY came from Rod Baylor; the mechanic was standing outside the pub with the rest of the smokers. "That's that Wild bastard, isn't it," he said, pointing down the road with his cigarette to the Aston Martin outside the shop.

"Yeah, looks like," Gary Fredericks agreed as he puffed on his cigarette. "He's the only one in the village with a car like that. What the hell's he doing out of hospital?"

"How'm I s'posed to know?" Baylor asked. He looked around at his fellow smokers, but none of them showed any sign of knowing the answer. "I guess Glen didn't do a good enough job of dealing with him. Useless bastard!" he swore. "He can't have been more than a dozen feet from Wild, with a shotgun, and he still couldn't manage to kill him."

"I suppose you'd have walked up to Wild, shoved the shotgun in his balls, and blown his dick off," Gary said contemptuously.

"Damn right." Rod turned to Sergeant Mitchell, who had come out from the pub to see what was going on. "I thought you said he was going to be in hospital till you had the evidence to prove he's the killer, that our wives and daughters were safe. Why's he out of hospital, and what's he doing back here?"

"Not a bloody clue," Mitchell admitted. It was clear that he was as unhappy with things as the smokers were. "I'm not in charge of the case anymore, some DI from town is, I'm not even in the loop. Did you know he was being released?" he asked of Melissa, who had followed him out with her drink, and was now watching and listening to everything that was happening.

"No, I didn't have a clue," Melissa said. "I thought he'd be in for at least a couple more days, so did Inspector Harrison as far as I know," she continued, pre-empting the next question.

"What good are you then, either of you," Rod demanded. "You guys are supposed to protect us and our families from assholes like him, but you don't even know when he's around, and when he ain't. If we hadn't been out here and seen him, who knows how many girls he could have attacked before we knew he was back. Someone needs to do something about him."

"Who's that gonna be, you?"

Rod rounded on Gary. "Yeah, maybe it will be," he said sharply. "If the cops ain't gonna protect our wives and daughters, someone's gonna have to, and it might as well be me."

"You, ha!" Gary was openly contemptuous. "You're a worse shot than Glen, at least he managed to hit Wild, you can't hit a barn door at twenty paces."

"You can't talk like this guys," Melissa spoke up, while thinking that it shouldn't be up to her to tell the group that what they were talking about was inappropriate, Mitchell should. "If anything happens to Mr Wild, you'll be the ones we come and talk to."

IF HE'D KNOWN HOW HE was being talked about up the road, Zack would have had a harder time getting comfortable. As it was, he was uncomfortable enough to be glad when Sophie returned and slid behind the wheel again, after putting the shopping she had bought in the boot.

"What did you buy?" Zack asked once Sophie had started the engine and pulled away from the kerb. "It looked like about half the shop."

"Not hardly," Sophie said with a shake of her head. "I know it's only a little village shop, so I shouldn't expect much, but the selection in there is terrible. I don't know how the people around here cope with it. I was able to get enough food, so we can eat tonight, and some stuff for tomorrow, but we're going to need to go into town tomorrow and visit a proper shop."

"So how come you had two bulging carrier bags?" Zack felt the eyes of the smokers outside the pub on him as they headed past, but he ignored them as best he could. After all that had happened, it didn't surprise him that his fellow villagers were watching him when they could.

"I got cleaning supplies. I used up most of what you had in the house trying to make the place look presentable, in between driving to and from home, and spending what seems like hours on the phone trying to sort out one thing or another for you."

Zack looked at his friend for a moment but decided against asking what she was talking about; he had neither the energy nor the enthusiasm necessary to care.

"MR WILD."

Zack jumped visibly. He had just grabbed the two carrier bags of shopping from the boot, having endured a heart-stopping moment when he thought Sophie was going to drive straight into the door of his garage, when his name was called. It was only his good reflexes that kept him from dropping the shopping and dooming him and Sophie to a meal of whatever he had left in the fridge.

With his heart beating more quickly than he liked, and a firm grip on his bags, Zack turned around to see who it was that had hailed him. He didn't think he was in any danger, it was unlikely that someone who intended attacking him would alert him to their presence before doing so, but that didn't keep him from being nervously alert. He only relaxed when he saw his neighbour approaching slowly, looking as nervous as he felt.

"Hello, Mrs Hawkins, how are you"

"I'm fine, thank you," Constance said, stopping a few paces from Zack. "How are you? I didn't expect to see you out of hospital so soon, especially after the way you looked when they took you away in the helicopter. I wanted to come and see you, to apologise for everything, but it's such a long bus journey."

"It's okay, I wouldn't have expected you to put yourself through such a journey," Zack told her, touched that she would even think of doing such a thing. They had spoken on a number of occasions since he moved to the village, and on a number of subjects, but he would not have thought them friendly enough for her to visit him in hospital. "I'm as well as can be expected under the circumstances, better in fact, given how my friend fared. And there's nothing for you to apologise for."

"There is," Constance said with a sad look. "If I hadn't told Sergeant Mitchell I thought it was you I saw driving down the road after Lucy Goulding left you, I don't think you would be in the position you are. I'm sure it was that, that made him think you are the one who killed those girls. I'm sorry. If I hadn't led Lewis to make that assumption, you wouldn't have the whole village thinking you're a murderer, and you wouldn't have been attacked."

"There's no need for you to apologise," Zack told her. He couldn't remember the last time he heard someone apologise for telling the police what they believed. "You only did what you thought was the right thing, there's nothing wrong with that. I'm sure Sergeant Mitchell would have decided I'm the killer sooner or later, with or without you; he much prefers the idea that the killer is someone he doesn't know, rather than someone he does. I don't imagine he's alone in thinking that way either."

Despite the reassurance she was given, Constance still felt the need to apologise, and nothing Zack said would stop her.

"THAT WAS NICE OF HER," Sophie said as she shut the door behind Zack.

Zack nodded. "Certainly was."

"I like her." Sophie nodded as though she had come to a decision. "She's a nice lady."

"I have to agree," Zack said. "She's one of the few in the village to actually make an effort to get to know me."

"She said she was a friend as well as a neighbour when she came round this afternoon. She didn't say as much, but I think she was curious about who I was and what I was doing here. When she found out I was cleaning up after Sunday night, she stayed to help; she might be old, but boy can she scrub." As though the house was hers rather than Zack's, she led the way along the passage to the kitchen, where she took the carriers and put them on the side, so she could unpack the shopping. "If it had been left to me, you'd still have stains in the carpet, but she got them out; just as well she came round and helped actually, or I'd never have had the time to sort out having your furniture picked up, so it can be re-upholstered, they're coming to get it day after tomorrow, so're the window people - soonest they can make it out here. And I've ordered you a new TV and laptop, same models as the ones you had before, well, same makes anyway, newer models."

Zack stared at his friend suspiciously for several long moments. "Thanks for doing all that," he said finally. "One question, though, how can you afford to buy me a new TV and laptop – not that I won't pay you back – I was under the impression you're just about permanently skint."

"Not quite. I've got enough money to get by, it's not like I'm gonna starve or anything. Once I clear a couple of outstanding debts I'll be fine. I didn't pay for anything, though." Sophie grinned cheekily as she took something from her pocket and held it out. "Here, you'll want this back."

Only when he took the object did Zack realise that it was his credit card.

"You really shouldn't leave your credit card lying around where just anyone can find it, especially when you're not the only one that knows the pin number."

Zack slipped the card into his pocket. "If I'd known what was going to happen, I'd have made sure I kept my wallet in my pocket." Taking the first items that had been unpacked, he began putting them away. "Do I need to check my bill when it comes in to see what you've tried to sneak onto it?"

"You can if you want," Sophie said unconcernedly. "I didn't put much on it, just a few little things, call them a fee for babysitting you until it's safe for you to be left on your own again."

Zack laughed at that. He wasn't actually worried that Sophie might have used his credit card to buy things for herself, he knew her well enough to be confident she hadn't bought anything at all, and if she had it would be something he could easily afford.

48

The surveillance room in the security suite at St Mary's Hospital was small, barely big enough to hold the two chairs occupied by the guard who had the duty of watching the bank of monitors that took up most of the space and by DI Harrison. There certainly wasn't enough room for either of them to move out of the way, which meant Harrison had to lean across the guard, who was reluctantly sharing his space, to see the image on the middle left monitor better.

"All stations, heads up, we have a possible suspect in the East stairwell, heading up from the ground floor," Harrison alerted the officers he had been given for that night's operation. "Suspect appears to be between five-eight and six feet tall and medium build, wearing dark clothes, including a balaclava or similar.

"Can you follow him on the cameras?" he asked of the security guard next to him as the figure in the stairwell continued up, disappearing out of range of the camera he had been watching.

The guard answered the question with a nod and quickly cycled through the cameras he controlled until he found the mystery figure again, he then followed the suspected killer on his way to the fourth floor.

Harrison found himself torn by conflicted feelings as he watched the figure leave the stairwell on the fourth floor. A part of him was pleased the plan he had come up with appeared to be working; someone, and he didn't want to pre-empt his thinking by putting a name to the figure, was heading towards Emily Wright's room, almost certainly with the intention of killing the teen before she could wake up. A much larger part of him, however, was concerned about the fact that there was now a murderer in the hospital, and the violence he had shown, according to the post-mortems, suggested that he was not going to simply surrender when he realised he had been tricked. If anything, discovering that he had been set up was likely to make him angry and violent.

HE PAUSED WHEN HE REACHED the fourth floor, so he could listen at the door of the stairwell. He had made it that far without being seen, as far as he was aware, and was determined to make it the rest of the way, deal with Emily Wright, and get back out again without being discovered; he hadn't even been seen when he entered the accident and emergency department and headed for the stairwell, and that was where he thought it most likely someone would stop him and want to know what he was doing.

He listened for more than a minute before deciding the corridor on the other side of the door was empty. Once He was sure of that, he eased the door open and slipped through. He had scouted the hospital earlier in the day, so he would know just where to go to commit the murder he was there for, but everything looked different in the semi-darkness, and he was no longer as confident of where he had to go.

Despite the gloom and his uncertainty, he made it to his destination without getting lost, and with only one incident. Halfway to Emily's room the sound of footsteps around the corner he was approaching made him scurry back the way he had come in search of somewhere to hide; he found what he was after in the form of an ITU room occupied by an elderly man who was being kept alive by a variety of machines.

As he had in the stairwell, He pressed his ear against the door and listened until he was sure the way was clear; the footsteps approached his position, making him worry he was going to be found, then passed and receded into the distance. Relieved to have evaded detection, He left his hiding place, and a couple of minutes later reached the room Emily had been put in. He stopped in front of the door and looked around briefly before entering so he could kill the teen who stood between him and safety from the police.

Once in the room He crossed it quickly before stopping at the bed. For several long seconds, he stared down at the barely visible outline of the slumbering form that was his target. There was a part of him that thought he should leave and not do anything to Emily, after all, she was already in a coma, but that was overridden by his instinct for self-preservation, and the selfishness that made him care for himself ahead of anyone else.

Almost of their own volition, his hands reached out towards the place where he was sure Emily's throat was. His fingers bumped against her chin and he quickly altered their position, so he could tighten them around her throat and end the threat she posed to him. That was when a lamp come on over the bed and he saw that it wasn't Emily he was strangling.

"YOU'RE UNDER ARREST," Melissa gasped as she let go of the switch for the lamp and brought her hands up to try and pull away those around her throat. It was a task she found all but impossible; it took her only a moment to realise that she was much weaker than her attacker, and what strength she had quickly faded as darkness crept in at the edges of her vision.

Laughter bubbled up out of him at the words from the constable he was killing; it amused him so much that she was trying to arrest him while he was strangling her he couldn't help it.

"This is the police, release the constable, you're under arrest."

The situation wasn't as funny when the words were repeated from behind him. His laughter died abruptly, and he released Melissa as he spun around, only to be all but blinded when the overhead light blazed on, illuminating every corner of the room. He could see little of the man who had spoken beyond an outline, but that was enough; he charged, barrelling into the officer before the sergeant - he saw the stripes on the uniform sleeve just before impact - could react. The collision knocked the sergeant to the floor, and He quickly straddled him, using his weight to keep him from rising.

While the man beneath him bucked and heaved in a desperate effort to throw him off, He grabbed him by the hair and smashed his head into the floor. Again and again he repeated the manoeuvre until an arm encircled his throat and began to apply pressure, forcing him to let go so he could defend himself.

Having recovered from her own choking, as much as she was likely to just then, Melissa used all her strength to maintain her grip on the killer. She didn't want to kill the man who had murdered her cousin – at least she didn't think she did – but she was determined not to let him get away, and if that meant choking him until he passed out, she was fine with that. While she kept him in a choke hold that was intended to subdue him, she used her free hand to keep him from breaking the grip she had on him.

That task was difficult enough, given how much stronger than her he was, and it became even more difficult when he straightened to his full height, which was about a third of a foot taller than hers. She had to stretch up to maintain her grip on his throat, and when he began throwing himself about to dislodge her, it became almost impossible.

With his vision beginning to fade and his breath coming in short, sharp gasps, He found himself in a position to understand what the girls he had killed had been through before dying. The experience was not one he liked, and it made him even more determined to get free; he thrashed about as if he could shake the person on his back loose, while wrenching at the arm around his throat.

It wasn't until he bumped into the bed and fell over it that the arm loosened its grip and he could breathe properly again. He slammed his head back into Melissa's face, provoking a short, sharp gasp of pain and a further loosening of the grip she had on him, which enabled him to jerk free and scramble to his feet.

He glanced back as he headed out of the room and saw that Melissa was still on the floor. He was tempted to stay and take out the anger he felt at having been deceived on her, but he quickly reminded himself that giving in to his emotions would not help him to get away. He had to move quickly, and not let anything slow him down, if he wanted to avoid getting caught and spending the rest of his life in a prison cell.

He had gone no more than a dozen feet when he found his route back to the stairwell blocked by two constables. His hand immediately went to his pocket, and the knife he always carried with him, the sight of which made the constables hesitate.

He feinted to his left, forcing the officer there to retreat quickly, and then turned so he could barge into the other officer, bowling him over. That left the way clear for Him to escape. He threw himself through the gap between the two officers and was just thinking he was clear and could head safely for the stairwell when his ankle was grabbed, and his leg pulled out from under him.

He tumbled to the floor but rolled quickly onto his back, so he could kick out at the constable who had brought him down. He caught the man square in the face, shattering his nose and leaving his features a bloody mess; a second kick worsened the damage, and left the constable unmoving on the floor.

A jerk of his leg freed it from the grip of the immobile officer, and he slashed the air wildly with his knife to keep the other officer away as he scrambled to his feet. He slashed again to force the uniformed figure back, and then turned so he could race away down the passage. A glance over his shoulder told him that although he was far from the quickest of people, he was quicker than the constable pursuing him, who seemed almost to plod along like he was trying to run on sand. He smiled beneath his balaclava as he turned the corner and sped down the passage towards the stairs.

49

"Talk to me people, what's going on?" Harrison spoke urgently into his radio. He had no idea what had happened in the room where Constable Turner had been playing the part of Emily Wright, but it seemed clear to him that things had not gone well. If it had, the figure he believed to be their killer would not have reappeared in the passage, except in handcuffs, and he would not have been able to leave a constable immobile on the floor while he ran from the other.

"He got away, sir, sorry," Melissa gasped into her radio as she left the room. "Sergeant Tracey's down, I don't know how badly he's hurt, but it looks bad. Help's on its way." It hadn't been an easy decision for her to make, to leave the injured sergeant after pressing the alarm button to summon help, but she was sure she had done the right thing. She had no medical knowledge, beyond her first aid training, so there was little she could do for him, but there was still a chance that she could catch the man who had tried to kill them both. "Constable Walsh is down as well," she reported.

Harrison made a snap decision as he saw Melissa hesitate by the constable on the floor. "Leave him, let the medical staff deal with him, you get after the suspect." He realised that his decision might not be one Melissa agreed with, it might even be one that would land him in trouble when the operation was reviewed, but he was certain it was the right one.

Melissa had already been torn between stopping to help the constable on the floor and continuing her pursuit of the killer; she was relieved to have the decision taken out of her hands.

In obedience to the command she had been given, she took off down the passage. When she reached the corner around which she had seen Constable Yarrow disappear, she saw the fleeing figure of their suspect up ahead, beyond her lumbering colleague. Her throat was sore where she had been choked, she was sure her nose had been broken, and her split lip was bleeding; she didn't let any of that slow her as she gave pursuit, however.

It surprised her when she began to close the distance between her and those she was pursuing - she overtook Constable Yarrow just before they reached the stairwell.

"Which way?" Melissa asked of Harrison after bursting through the door into the stairwell. "Up or down?"

She didn't wait for an answer, the sound of heavy, hurried footsteps from below told her which direction to take, and she descended as quickly as she could.

HARRISON SAT IN THE security room and watched the monitors with a growing sense of dismay. He had said from the start that he needed more officers, four plus himself simply wasn't enough to be certain of stopping someone who had shown a capacity for extreme violence - a capacity that had been demonstrated again with the disablement of two of the four officers given him for the operation. He watched as the medical staff began working on the constable in the passage, and he watched as his suspect pulled away from Constable Yarrow, only to have Constable Turner narrow the gap.

It was good that Melissa was gaining on the fleeing suspect, but it only took him a second to realise that she was unlikely to catch him, and that if she did she was at a serious disadvantage. Barefoot, and dressed in only a hospital gown, with neither handcuffs nor baton, Melissa had little chance of stopping the suspect, especially when he was armed and unafraid of violence. He could think of only one way to prevent what seemed like the inevitable escape of his suspect, and he got quickly to his feet to leave the room.

Harrison radioed control with a request for backup as he ran from the security suite. It wasn't easy to run and talk at the same time, but he moved as quickly as he could, determined to reach the stairwell and put himself between his suspect and escape. He didn't have a baton, an oversight he regretted, but he did at least have handcuffs, and he hoped he could hold his suspect up for long enough for the two chasing constables to catch up; despite the failure so far, he was confident that between the three of them they could make a successful arrest.

He threw open the door to the stairwell and bounded up, amazed to see that he had got there before his suspect could reach the ground floor. He slowed as he reached the first floor, his eyes on the dark-clad, masked figure descending towards him, and on the knife in his hand; above the figure, but closing the gap, was Melissa, and audible, but not yet visible, was another person, who Harrison guessed was Constable Yarrow.

"Stop where you are, you're under arrest."

Harrison was surprised when the murderer neither stopped nor slowed, but instead leapt at him. Before he could react, let alone dodge or defend himself, Harrison was borne to the floor by the weight of his attacker; his breath escaped him in an explosion that carried with it the pain of being stabbed. When he felt the knife pierce his stomach he was reminded that he had forgotten to put on his stab vest, a potentially fatal mistake he hoped he wasn't going to regret.

Melissa saw her superior attacked and reacted without thinking; she rushed down the stairs and launched herself at the man who had killed her cousin. She crashed into him, knocking him away from Harrison and sending him rolling down the stairs; she went with him, and when they came to a stop she found herself on top. Quickly, she pinned his arms with her knees, so she could pull off his mask to see if she was right about His identity.

It seemed a simple enough thing to do, removing a mask, but the murderer under her bucked and heaved wildly in an effort to throw her off. That made it difficult for her to keep him pinned and get a grip on the balaclava he was wearing. She had the advantage of being on top, but Melissa didn't find it easy to control the killer she had caught; she imagined what she was experiencing was similar to how it must be trying to stay on a bucking bronco at a rodeo.

Looking around for help, Melissa saw Harrison pulling himself slowly and painfully towards her and her captive, while Constable Yarrow was still a floor away, continuing his descent at a tortoise-like pace. She couldn't believe how slow her fellow constable was, his running speed seemed to be barely above walking; she felt like yelling at him to speed up, so he could help her, but she needed her energy for other things.

Harrison had managed to drag himself only a couple of feet, and Yarrow was still a dozen or so steps away, when the struggle between Melissa and the killer ended. Before she had a chance to realise what had happened, He wrenched an arm free from the knee pinning it and slashed at her face – she hadn't thought to try and disarm him, so focused was she on unmasking him.

Melissa jerked back away from the flashing blade, but not quickly enough, the razor-sharp weapon opened her cheek from her ear almost to her lip. Before she could recover, from either the surprise or the pain, an almighty heave threw her off her suspect and she saw stars as her head struck one of the stairs.

She struggled to her feet and looked dizzily from her injured superior to the fleeing murderer; she didn't want to abandon the pursuit and let Him get away, but she didn't want to leave someone who was injured either, not again, not after already doing it twice that night.

"Don't worry about me, get after him, don't let him get away," Harrison ordered in a pain-filled voice when he saw Melissa coming towards him.

"WHICH WAY DID HE GO?" Melissa demanded of Yarrow when she caught up to him just outside the entrance to the emergency room, where he was looking unhappily around the dimly-lit car park as though he expected their suspect to appear from the shadow of one of the cars they could see.

"No idea," Yarrow admitted. "He was gone by the time I made it out here. He could be anywhere by now."

Melissa's head whipped around, sending blood splashing from her cut, as the sound of a racing car engine reached her. She hurried along the front of the building towards the corner where the engine noise had come from; she knew the vehicle she could hear might not have anything to do with the suspect she was after, but the timing of it seemed too coincidental for her to ignore.

She reached the corner in time to see a dark Land Rover race away through the car park towards the exit; it was gone so quickly there was no time for her to spot anything that might help her to recognise either the vehicle or the driver during the few instances when it passed through a patch of light.

50

Zack whipped the curtains back, flooding the room with light, and crossed to the bed. "Come on, time to get up."

"No, it's not," a muffled voice replied. "It's still dark."

"If it's dark, why have you got the duvet over your face?" Zack asked. "Come on, get up." He yanked the duvet off the bed and out of Sophie's reach. "You said you're going to be my shadow and keep me out of trouble, well I'm going for a run, are you coming along to keep an eye on me, or am I going alone?"

Sophie opened her eyes, which she had scrunched up when the duvet was pulled away. "Are you out of your mind?" Propping herself up on one elbow, she looked at her friend disbelievingly. "You only got out of hospital last night, your back looks like a mass of freckles, and you had a buggered ankle only the other day; why the hell would you want to go running? And why the hell would you want to do so this early? What time is it anyway?"

"Half-six," Zack answered. "And no, I'm not out of my mind, at least not as far as I know. I'm going for a run because I'm awake and I've got energy to burn, now are you coming or not?" Before Sophie could respond, he said, "I'm going to put the kettle on and finish getting myself ready; I'll be heading out the door in about fifteen, with or without you." He exited the room, leaving Sophie staring after him with an expression that would have killed him, were it possible for a look to do so.

Sophie leaned over and retrieved the duvet, which she pulled up until it covered her so completely she was no longer troubled by the light filling the room. She remained like that for a little over a minute before deciding to give in to what she knew was inevitable; as much as she wanted to go back to sleep, she had promised Zack she would stick with him until his troubles were over, and that was what she was going to do.

Reluctantly, she threw back the quilt and got to her feet, so she could head to the bathroom and get herself ready. It didn't take her long, and she was soon in the kitchen doorway, accepting a mug of coffee from Zack, who handed it to her with an amused smile on his lips.

"I hate you," she said, though that didn't stop her sipping eagerly at the drink, desperate to wake herself up.

"No, you don't," Zack told her "You just hate mornings. You're like Garfield, you hate mornings and Mondays, and you love Lasagne. Now hurry up and drink your coffee, I want to get going."

Sophie regarded her friend over the top of her mug. "Why don't I just break your leg or something and then go back to bed?" she asked.

"'cause you'd have to catch me first." Zack dodged past her and headed for the front door. He stopped just outside to do some stretching exercises while he waited for Sophie, who didn't take long to join him. Despite his joking, he knew that if Sophie wanted to catch him, she could, and probably without too much effort; his injuries aside, he was a fairly fit person, but Sophie was one of those blessed people who remained in great shape no matter what they ate or drank, and without the need to do any exercise at all.

"Can I ask you something?" Sophie asked as she set off down the road at her friend's side, Zack's spare water bottle in one hand.

"Of course you can, anything, you know that." Since he wasn't sure how his ankle was going to hold up, it felt fine while walking but running was different, he started them off slow, which meant they had plenty of breath for talking.

"Where were you last night?"

Zack frowned as he looked ahead, keeping an eye on the road. "What d'you mean?"

Sophie turned her head to study her friend for a moment. "I woke up in the night," she said. "Must have been around one, needing a pee, so I got up and went to check on you while I headed to the bathroom. You weren't in bed, and you weren't anywhere in the house, I checked. And just when I was heading back to bed, worried obviously, I heard a car head up the road."

"You can't have looked very hard," Zack remarked. "I was in the back garden."

"What the hell were you doing out there? It must have been freezing."

"It wasn't too bad," Zack said with a shrug. "A little brisk, but nothing more than that. I was sitting on my rusty old bench, contemplating everything that's happened since I moved here; trying to decide what I'm going to do."

"And?"

A ghost of a smile touched Zack's lips. "I decided that moving here is just about the worst thing I've ever done; few people have made any effort to get to know me, I haven't been any more productive with my writing than I would've been if I'd stayed in Southampton, and the first chance they got, just about everyone who lives here decided I'm a rapist and a murderer.

"I can understand them wanting to believe it's me, a stranger, rather than someone they've known for most, if not all, their lives, but that doesn't make me feel any better about it. Worst of all, being here makes it tough for me to see Joanne, and I miss her."

Sophie didn't need to be told that last, she knew just how much Zack missed his daughter, she also knew why he had moved away – to escape the situation with his ex-wife, where she had made it almost impossible for him to see his daughter. She didn't agree with Zack's decision to move away, she thought he should have stayed and fought, but she could understand it.

"So, what are you going to do?"

"What can I do? I'm stuck," Zack said unhappily. "Between paying for the house and the cars, and my other bills, and the child support Cathy convinced the judge to set, I'm only just making ends meet. Moving here took what savings I had, it's going to be a while before I've got any spare cash I can do anything with, especially with the royalty cheques only coming in every quarter." His frustration was obvious. "I'd move back to Southampton if I could, but it's going to take at least a year to come up with the money to do that, assuming I can find a buyer for the house, which is doubtful after everything that's happened here. I definitely won't be able to find a quick buyer, not one who's willing to pay the full value of the house, and without that I'm stuck here."

"Why don't we sit down with a nice, big fry-up when we get back and see if we can't figure out a way to get you back to Southampton quicker than that," Sophie said, reaching out to give Zack a reassuring pat on the arm. "If it comes to the worst, you can always borrow my spare room."

51

Tara climbed the stairs slowly, carrying a pile of washing she had just taken from the dryer. The washing had been there since Sunday, but she hadn't given it a thought, she was only doing anything with it now because her brother wanted her to empty the laundry baskets and put the washing on before she headed off to school.

School was the last place she wanted to go, she couldn't keep her mind on the things she wanted to do, let alone the things she didn't, but Kieran was insistent, and while their dad was away he was in charge.

When she reached the top of the stairs she crossed to the door of her sister's bedroom, or rather the doorway since there was no longer a door, and stopped. A voice in her mind, which sounded a lot like her father's, told her she was being silly, but she couldn't bring herself to enter the room where her sister had been attacked, just the thought of doing so made her shiver uncomfortably.

Standing in the doorway, she threw the pile of laundry. It landed untidily on the bed, at least most of it did, two pairs of socks went astray, they fell off the bed and rolled under it. Tara swore, and immediately regretted doing so, if her father had been there to hear, he would have threatened her with his belt. She hesitated in the doorway, reluctant to enter, after all it was going to be a while before her sister was back and in need of her clothes, but her father's voice in her mind kept her from doing so - he would never approve of her not tidying up a mess she had made.

It took her a few moments, but finally she did what her father would have wanted, she entered the room and got on her hands and knees, so she could retrieve the socks. She found them easily enough, though it was a bit of a stretch to get the second pair, but that was not all she found.

Dropping the socks onto the bed, Tara sat and stared curiously at the pink mobile phone she had discovered; it wasn't her sister's, she knew that, Emily's phone was on the bedside cabinet, which left her wondering whose it was, and how it came to be under her sister's bed. She pressed the power button on the top of the phone and watched the screen while she waited for it to turn on.

"What are you doing in here?"

Tara's head whipped around. "Nothing," she said quickly, flushing under her brother's gaze. "I brought Em's clothes in and some of the socks fell under the bed."

"So, what are you doing sitting on it, and what's that in your hand?" Kieran went cold when he saw the pink of the object in his sister's hand and realised what she was holding. "Where did you get that?" he wanted to know.

Tara looked down at her hand. "I found it, it was under the bed. It's not Emily's." Automatically, she pressed the power button again.

"Give it to me." Kieran held out his hand expectantly.

For a brief moment, the phone turned on and Tara saw who it belonged to before the almost completely dead battery cut out again. "This is Georgie's phone," she said in surprise. "How did it get here? We should call the police, tell them we've found it."

Kieran ignored that suggestion. "Give it to me. I'll deal with it." He stepped closer to his sister, hand outstretched. "I said give me the phone." When Tara continued to hold onto the phone he lunged for her.

Tara was not the brightest kid in her class, let alone her year, but nor was she was a dummy, far from it. When Kieran lunged for the phone in her hand, her brain made a connection between Emily being attacked, her finding Georgina's phone under Emily's bed, and Zack Wild being released by the police.

"It was you!" Tara couldn't keep the horror she felt from her voice, though it did freeze her in place momentarily. Only when she felt her brother's fingers on her hand as he sought to pry the phone from her grasp did she react physically. Snatching her hand away from Kieran's, she scrambled backwards across the bed; she reached the other side quicker than she expected and fell to the floor before she could stop herself. She got back to her feet as quickly as she could and darted for the doorway.

"Why are you doing this?" she sobbed when Kieran interposed himself between her and the door, forcing her to halt abruptly and hurriedly jump back out of reach.

"You're just like all the rest," Kieran told his little sister in a voice that was so harsh it was almost unrecognisable. "A nosey, whiney, ignorant, little bitch, who won't do what she's told. Give me the phone, that's all you had to do, that's all Em had to do as well, if she'd done that I wouldn't have had to hurt her. I didn't even realise Georgie dropped it in my car till Em found it, which she wouldn't have done if she hadn't been a nosey bitch."

As he talked, he advanced on his sister, a crazed look on his face that made her think him a stranger rather than the brother she had known all her life. It didn't seem possible that she could have known him for so long without seeing this side of him. Fearful, she backed away from him, her eyes darting left and right as she tried to figure out a way to escape; she couldn't come up with any possibilities while he was between her and the door, and she almost threw the phone she held at him as a distraction, so she could slip past and out of the room. Some instinct told her she needed to keep hold of it, however, to show the police.

Tara's retreat came to a halt when her legs hit Emily's bed and she tumbled backwards onto it, sprawling in an inelegant fashion. Before she could recover, Kieran was on her.

Kieran leapt onto the bed to stop his sister getting away and reached quickly for the hand that held the phone which had caused him so many problems. Tara held onto it with a strength and a tenacity he wouldn't have expected of her, it forced him to use both hands to try and pry her fingers away from the phone, which prevented him defending himself as she struck at him again and again and strove to push him off and away.

When she failed to accomplish anything that way - her brother showed little concern for her flailing fist - Tara groped blindly with her free hand for something she could use as a weapon. She was desperate, certain that Kieran was going to get the phone from her at any moment, and her hand closed around the first object it touched, her sister's radio alarm clock. Tara swung the clock with all her might, smashing it into the side of her brother's head.

"Fuck!" Kieran's curse carried equal parts surprise and pain, and he abandoned his effort to get the phone from Tara, so he could focus instead on disarming her, before she could hit him again.

Tara tried to hit her brother with the alarm clock for a second time, and when she failed she dropped it in favour of another tactic. She had never been in a fight before, certainly not one where her life was in danger, but some instinct told her that her best chance of getting away involved going for the eyes, and with that in mind she reached for his face. At the same time, she struggled to get out from under her brother, moving her body in ways she wouldn't previously have thought it capable of managing as she sought to heave him off her; she didn't think much of her chances, he had her well and truly pinned, so it came as a complete surprise when he suddenly fell away, leaving her free.

Her body reacted to the situation before her brain could fully comprehend that the weight pinning her down was gone. She rolled off the bed, going in the opposite direction to that in which Kieran had fallen, and darted for the doorway. She made it out of the bedroom before she heard her brother give chase, and that gave her enough of a lead to make it downstairs and to the front door ahead of him.

She was moving with such haste that she hit herself with the door when she yanked it open; it bounced shut off her foot, forcing her to open it a second time to escape the house.

Kieran leapt the last half dozen or so steps, one hand outstretched towards his sister. His fingers closed on empty air, however, as he missed Tara by the thinnest of margins. By the time he recovered, she was across the yard and at the gateway. He set off after her but stopped almost immediately, even if he had been closer, he doubted he would have been able to catch his sister, at least not on foot – she was much faster than him. Instead of continuing the pursuit as a footrace, which he was bound to lose, he altered direction and hurried over to his Land Rover.

It started the moment he turned the key in the ignition – given how temperamental it was usually, he took that as a sign that he was meant to catch Tara and keep her from telling anyone about the things he had done. Shifting into gear, he raced out of the yard and down the road after his sister.

Tara couldn't help looking back over her shoulder when she heard the Land Rover start up, in doing so she lost sight of where she was putting her feet and stumbled. She hit the ground heavily, bashing her knees on a stone and scraping the skin from her palms, leaving them raw and bloody; she was too stunned to cry out, in pain or otherwise, she simply pushed herself to her feet and continued down the road, albeit with a limp. Her pace was much slower than before, and she was afraid her brother was going to catch her, which was almost certain since he was in a Land Rover and she was on foot, but there was nothing she could do except keep going and hope for a miracle.

She had gone just a couple of slow and painful steps following her fall when she saw something that gave her hope. A distance away, but getting closer, were two people, a man and a woman.

"Help!" she called out. "Please help!"

52

Zack was almost home, having abandoned his usual five-mile run after less than a mile of jogging because of the pain from both his ankle and his back, when he heard the cry. He halted abruptly, which prompted a fresh spasm, and looked around for the person calling for help; almost immediately he saw the girl running towards him, he also saw the Land Rover speeding down the road behind her.

He started up the road at the same walking pace he had used to get home, but quickly sped up when he saw that the Land Rover was angled in a way that would see it run down the young girl, whom he suspected was Tara Wright. The pain that had cut short his morning run magnified the moment he accelerated, reaching a crescendo as he hit sprinting speed, but he ignored it and focused on reaching the girl who appeared to be in danger.

Somehow, and he had no idea how, Zack managed to reach Tara before the Land Rover did. Grabbing her, threw her over the wall into the field on the other side of it; he launched himself over right after, landing heavily just beyond the ditch at the edge of the field before rolling to place his body protectively over Tara's. He barely had time to do that before the Land Rover struck the wall, almost exactly where he and Tara had gone over it. A section of the wall was knocked down by the impact and

Zack felt several pieces of debris hit him in the back, adding to his pain.

Zack continued to protect Tara with his body until he heard the Land Rover drive away. He pulled himself off her then and slowly and painfully got to his feet, so he could look around; when he saw the Land Rover was heading down the road towards the village, he reached down to help Tara to her feet.

"Are you alright?" he asked, and immediately felt like an idiot for doing so – she had just been picked up and thrown into a field to keep from being run down by her own brother, at least that was who he guessed had been behind the wheel; he very much doubted she was alright.

Tara didn't answer the question because she couldn't. Now that she was back on her feet, and no longer running for her life, she was overcome by shock; she began trembling uncontrollably and couldn't stop. Even when Zack wrapped her in his arms to try and comfort her, she continued to tremble, she trembled so violently her teeth chattered.

Zack knew enough about shock to realise that he was unlikely to be able to help the teen while they remained in the field. "Come on, let's get you out of here. My friend, Sophie, will make you a nice cup of tea while I take care of that knee," he said with a glance down at the bloody mess he hoped had not been caused when he threw her over the wall, "and you tell me what's going on."

Tara allowed herself to be led through the corn towards the gate. It would have been easier if they had climbed over the wall and made their way along at the side of the road, she baulked at doing so when Zack suggested it, however. It was just as well she did, for they had not gone far when the Land Rover raced back up the road. A fresh tremor, this time caused by fear rather than shock, went through her as Kieran fixed her with a look of pure hatred on his way past.

"I think he killed them," Tara said in a barely audible voice that wavered and threatened to die away completely. Her eyes stayed with her brother's Land Rover as she spoke, watching as he drove through the gateway and into the yard surrounding her family's house.

"Killed who?"

Tara's eyes snapped back to what was ahead of her once the Land Rover was no longer easily visible. "Georgie and Lucy and...and..." She couldn't bring herself to finish. It was a minute or so before she said anything else, by which time they were almost at the gate. "He said he attacked them, and Emily." It wasn't what her brother had actually said, but her mind made the leap based on what he had said.

Zack didn't say as much, but he was pleased to hear that someone else was now in the frame for the murders he had been accused of. Once DI Harrison heard what Tara had to say, his name would be cleared; he just wished his exoneration wasn't going to come at the expense of Tara's family. In danger of losing her father because of his attempt at vigilante justice, it didn't seem fair that it should turn out that her brother was the killer who had brought such heartache to the village.

"Are you alright?" Sophie asked once Zack reached her with the teen he had saved.

"I'm fine," Zack said, though his back felt anything but. "And I'm sure Tara will be fine once she's had a cup of tea. Tara, this is my friend, Sophie, Sophie, this is Tara Wright, she lives at the farm up the road."

The introductions made, Zack guided Tara up the path and into his house. Once through the door, Sophie's hand on his arm made him stop. "The kitchen's at the end of the passage, Tara," he told the young girl as he looked at Sophie questioningly. "Why don't you go on through, Sophie and I will be with you in a moment."

"What's going on?" Sophie asked quietly once Tara had reached the kitchen, she looked briefly over her shoulder, through the glass panel near the top of the front door. "Did that guy really just try and kill her, because that's how it looked."

Zack nodded. "Yeah, I think he did. Hardly a surprise, she said he's the one who killed the girls I've been accused of murdering."

"Really, Jesus! Did you see who it was? Did you recognise him?"

"Oh yes, I recognised him. I thought I did on the way up the road, and I got a good look at him when he headed back to the farm; it's her brother, Kieran."

"Jesus!"

"Just what I was thinking," Zack said. "Come on, we'd better get along to the kitchen before Tara wonders what's happened to us."

While Sophie put the kettle on, Zack dug out his first aid kit to take care of Tara's knee and her hands. As he did, he questioned her about what had happened that morning; the habits developed during his time as a detective were hard to ignore, and he couldn't suppress the curiosity that made him want to know what he could about the case he was, however reluctantly, involved with.

53

Melissa was as surprised to see DI Harrison pull up next to Oakhurst's police station as he was to see her at the top of the steps, about to enter the building.

"I didn't expect to see you here today, sir," she said when Harrison reached her. "Not after being stabbed last night."

"I could say the same of you, constable," Harrison said as he made his slow way up the steps. "You might not have been stabbed, thank god, but you did suffer quite badly at the hands of that maniac." He reached for the door with a stifled groan, annoyed to discover that the painkillers the hospital had given him were wearing off.

"Are you sure you should be here?" Melissa asked, alarmed by how white Harrison had gone.

"Not really," Harrison admitted in a strained voice. "And the hospital definitely isn't happy with me being here, they were very much against releasing me. I had to insist. I've got a job to do, and I'm not the sort to give up until the job's done. How are you feeling this morning?" he asked in a change of subject.

"About as well as can be expected," Melissa admitted. Her collar was undone because it irritated the bruises around her throat where she had been strangled, and a large dressing covered the five stitches used to close the sizeable cut on her cheek. "I don't think I'm going to be all that quick about getting things done today, but I'm fit enough to work. I'd rather be here than at home feeling sorry for myself anyway," she said, especially since if she stayed at home she would have to put up with the fuss her gran, and her mum when she got there, would make.

"What the hell happened to the two of you?" Johnson asked when he saw the inspector and his fellow constable make their slow, obviously painful, way, across reception. "You both look as though you've been through hell."

"I'd say that's a pretty fair description," Melissa croaked. "It sure felt like hell." She unlocked the security door and made her way through to the rear of the police station without actually answering her colleague's question; she had no interest in relating everything that she and Harrison had been through during the night, not only would it take too long, but talking was painful, and she intended doing as little of it as she could.

Johnson watched Melissa and the inspector head down the passage, his curiosity far from satisfied. The phone rang before he could try again to find out what had happened during the night, though, and he quickly turned back to the counter to answer it. "Oakhurst Police Station, how can I help you?"

"Inspector, I think you should take this," he called down the passage after listening to what the caller had to say.

"Who is it?" Harrison asked as he took two strides back towards the counter and immediately had to slow down because of the pain.

"It's Zack Wild," Johnson answered. "He says Kieran Wright tried to kill his sister, Tara, a short while ago, and that he all but confessed to her that he's responsible for the murders."

Harrison's step stuttered for a moment as he blinked at the constable. Of all the things he might have pictured happening this morning, that wasn't on the list. When he reached the counter, he took the phone. "Mr Wild, DI Harrison, would you mind repeating what you just told Constable Johnson?" He listened intently to what Wild had to say, taking it all in despite his amazement – he was sceptical, he had never found it easy to believe it when one suspect tried to convince him that another was guilty, but there was enough about the story that rang true for him to accept what he was being told.

Whether he believed it or not, he realised he couldn't afford to just ignore what he had been told, he had to check it out. "Thank you, Mr Wild, we'll be there as quickly as we can. Please keep Miss Wright there, and if you see her brother leave the farm again, call us."

Hanging up, Harrison turned to the two constables, his mind racing as he made plans - he couldn't help wishing he was back in town, where there would be more options available to him. He considered calling his superior for support, after the way the operation at the hospital had gone it seemed appropriate, but he didn't like the thought of giving Kieran Wright, if he was the killer, time to make plans of his own, or even to get away. Besides, he figured there was only one way out from the farm, and so long as they were sensible and careful, Wright wouldn't be able to get away.

"Turner, I want you to come with me, now," Harrison told Melissa. "Johnson, I want you to call Constables Black and Pritchard and get them, and Sergeant Mitchell, out to Mr Wild's as soon as possible, we'll be going on to the Wright Farm from there. I want Inspector Stevens to call the chief inspector and ask for backup to be sent out here straight away. I don't want to wait for it, but I do want it on its way here ASAP in case it's needed." He sincerely hoped it wouldn't be. He was reasonably confident that Kieran Wright, if he was the killer, would realise the game was up, when he saw that they had come to arrest him, and that resisting would only make his situation worse. "When you've finished with the phone calls, I want you out at Wild's as well."

"Yes, sir," Johnson said, not at all happy with the thought of taking part in the arrest of a vicious murderer; he wasn't a coward, but he had heard what the killer – Kieran Wright apparently – had done to his victims, and he didn't want to face that kind of violence, it wasn't what he had joined the police to deal with.

54

"**D**amn! Damn! Damn!" With each curse, Kieran slammed his fist down on the steering wheel. He could not believe that so much had gone wrong so quickly; first there was the trap the police had set and almost caught him with, then he had failed to get Georgina's phone from his sister. It should not have been possible for him to fail to do that when his sister was so much smaller and weaker than him. And finally, he had failed even to stop Tara reaching help.

It took more than a minute for him to calm down enough to leave the Land Rover, and when he did he hurried across the yard to the house. He couldn't stay at the farm, not now Tara had escaped him – he simply could not imagine that his sister would keep quiet about what had happened that morning – which meant he had to leave the village; to help him make a quick getaway, he left the keys in the ignition and the front door ajar.

He threw open the wardrobe the moment he reached his bedroom, took out his sports-bag and tossed it onto his bed. He was about to start throwing clothes after it when he stopped; he was normally one for acting first and thinking later, but he realised if he wanted to stand a chance of getting away, he needed to go against his nature and think before doing anything.

Standing by the open wardrobe, Kieran thought harder about his situation than he had about anything in a long time. He had no idea where he was going to go, or what he was going to do for money when he got there; fortunately, he wasn't afraid of hard work, and he was prepared to do almost anything as a job.

For the time being, though, he didn't think it mattered that he didn't have a destination or a job in mind, he could work that out later; what did matter was that he got out of the village and put as much distance between it and him as he could before the police were at his door.

To give him the best chance of avoiding being caught, he needed to take with him everything he was likely to need for the next few days, money, food and water – the less he had to stop, the better his chances of getting far enough away that the police wouldn't find him. Now that he had a plan, limited though it might be, Kieran reached into his wardrobe again.

His footsteps thundered as he descended the stairs in a rush, and once at the bottom he hurried along the passage to the kitchen. When he had filled the rucksack he had taken from his wardrobe with as much food and drink as he could squeeze into it, he took it out to his Land Rover, so he could stuff the bag behind the driver's seat.

The next thing for him to go looking for was money, and he quickly emptied the piggy bank - really a whiskey bottle they all threw their loose change into - his father kept in the living room; unfortunately, there seemed to be far more one and two pence pieces than coins of any other denomination. Any amount of money was going to be useful, but he would have preferred to see more pound coins in the flow as he poured the contents of the bottle into a carrier he got from the kitchen.

From the living room, Kieran made his way upstairs to his father's bedroom. He went straight to the chest of drawers under the window and pulled out the top drawer; rummaging amongst the socks and boxers, he soon found what he was after, the small, red lock-box where his father kept his emergency money. It amused him that his father thought the lock-box so well hidden, when he had known where it had been for years; he thought it equally funny that his father thought the money in the box safe. At first look the lock-box appeared sturdy, but Kieran knew it had weak hinges, and with only a bit of effort he had it open, so he could get at the contents.

"Sonofabitch," he swore angrily, throwing the lock-box aside so violently it cracked the door of the wardrobe. "Cheap, useless bastard," he raged as he counted the money he had taken from the box again and again, failing each time to make it amount to more than the two hundred pounds he had come to the first time. He hadn't expected his father to have a fortune stashed away, the family had never been well-off, but he had expected to find at least twice what he now held.

Kieran put aside his frustration as best he could and focused on what he needed to do; in the absence of any real money, he needed things he could turn into money, jewellery being the best bet, but anything he could sell at a pawnshop would help. He knew that his father still had some of his mother's jewellery somewhere, he just wasn't sure whether it was worth anything; valuable or worthless, it was better than nothing if he could find it, and he went in search of it.

He found a dress watch he had never seen his father wear but had no luck beyond that until he reached the wardrobe he had damaged; it was there that he found the jewellery box containing his mother's rings, earrings and necklaces. He didn't think what he had found would add up to more than a couple of hundred pounds in value, but every penny he could get would help.

He searched Tara's bedroom next, raiding it rapidly for anything that might have value. He doubted he would get much for the small amount of jewellery he found so he left it behind, focusing instead on his sister's CD collection and the small number of electronic gadgets she had: mobile phone, iPod, the tablet she had convinced their dad to get for her last birthday, as well as the few other trinkets of possible worth he found.

He was just checking that he hadn't missed anything when he heard a vehicle pull into the yard. Leaving Tara's room, he hurried into Emily's, so he could look out into the yard; what he saw made him drop the bag and dash back out of the room and downstairs. He kicked the front door shut on the way past and hurried on down the passage to the cupboard under the stairs.

He yanked open the door the moment he reached it and stepped inside. He didn't bother fumbling for the light switch or trying to remember whether he had his key on him, he didn't want to waste the time, he simply put his boot into the door of the cabinet where he and his father's shotguns were kept locked. The first kick cracked the door, while the second destroyed it, leaving it in pieces, which he quickly pulled out of the way.

He was stuffing extra shells into the pockets of the jacket he had pulled on, having already loaded two into his shotgun, when a loud banging came from the front door.

"Kieran Wright, open up, it's the police. If you don't open up, we'll have to break the door down," Mitchell called through the door, banging on it a second time.

Kieran left the cupboard under the stairs and hurried along the passage. He raised the shotgun as he went and pulled the trigger when the muzzle was at stomach height and just a couple of inches from the door.

INTELLECTUALLY, HARRISON knew there was no separation of sight and sound at that distance, he should have seen and heard everything simultaneously, as it occurred. That was not what happened, however. He saw a section of the door explode outwards, and Mitchell fly backwards, a large, bloody hole in his stomach, but he heard nothing until the door swung open. It was then that the sound of the shotgun blast and Mitchell's quickly cut off cry washed over him.

Mitchell's death was shocking, but not so much that Harrison was unable to react to the sight of the shotgun when it appeared around the edge of the door. The pain from his knife wound forgotten, and all thought of making a quick and easy arrest pushed from his mind, he turned and dived for the nearest piece of cover there was, his car - he didn't make it.

KIERAN RAISED THE SHOTGUN and fired the moment he saw the inspector. He didn't care that he was shooting an unarmed man in the back, that didn't matter to him, all that did was increasing his chances of getting away, and he was prepared to do anything to manage that. The blast took Harrison in the back and sent him sprawling. He hoped the shot had killed Harrison, but it was enough to have another of his would-be captors out of action.

He looked around quickly for some sign of the two constables he had seen when he looked out of his sister's bedroom window; when he didn't see them, he assumed they were using one of the cars in the yard for cover.

He didn't care as much about the constables as he did Mitchell and the inspector, so he ignored them for the moment and retreated into the house. Ejecting the spent shells, he reloaded his shotgun as he made his way upstairs to retrieve the bag he had been filling with his family's valuables.

"WHAT WAS THAT?" TARA'S head snapped around from Zack's laptop, which she had been given to distract her from the morning's events, to point, unerringly towards her family's farm. It was like she could see what was going on there, despite the walls that prevented her seeing the road, let alone the half a mile up it to the farm.

"What was what?" Zack asked, he hadn't heard a thing.

"It sounded like a shotgun," Tara said. She had never handled a shotgun, but she had heard her father and her brother using theirs often enough to recognise the noise. "There it is again."

Zack heard the noise the second time, and would have guessed at it being a gunshot, but he wasn't practised enough with the sounds of the countryside to be able to say it was a shotgun blast; four months of country living simply wasn't long enough for him to become an expert on such things. To his mind, it didn't matter what variety of gun it was that had been fired, the only thing that did matter was that someone, somewhere was shooting. Given the situation that was ongoing, he didn't need to be a genius to figure out where the shot had come from, or what it might mean.

Melissa recognised the noise immediately and felt herself gripped by a wave of panic; since none of her colleagues had gone to the farm with a shotgun, she knew Kieran must be the one who fired the weapon, and that made her worry that one or more of them had been hurt. "DI Harrison, Constable Turner, come in please. DI Harrison, come in please," she said, snatching her radio from her belt.

Melissa tried again and again to get hold of the inspector; when she was unsuccessful after repeated attempts, she tried Sergeant Mitchell instead. In the end, it was Constable Black who responded to her radio calls, though he sounded very unhappy to be doing so.

"Mel, it's Mike, the inspector's down, so's the sergeant, he shot them both." His shock was audible despite the crackling of the radio signal. "He shot the sergeant right through the door, and then he shot the inspector in the back."

Melissa went cold at that news.

"What do we do now?"

Melissa found the question incredibly unfair, she was the youngest of the constables, and Black the oldest; if anyone should have been able to come up with an idea of what to do, it was him. Her mind raced for a few moments as she thought about the situation; she hoped that Black would come up with something, but when he didn't she spoke.

"Where's Kieran?" She had been listening for further shotgun blasts and was relieved not to have heard any; she hoped that meant her colleagues were safe, but the absence of such noises told her nothing of what was going on at the farm, which meant she couldn't relax.

"He went back into the house after shooting the inspector," Black said. "He hasn't come out again." He was relieved by that, though he couldn't help worrying about what the teen might be doing in the house. The patrol car he had arrived in sheltered him but did not stop him feeling as though he was being watched, and possibly being sighted on with the shotgun; it was a feeling that made his skin crawl, as though his body was being explored by a tarantula.

"Are you safe?" Melissa hoped so, though she found it hard to believe that he could be under the circumstances.

"Safe enough, for the moment," Black said, he was unable to conceal either the lack of certainty or the apprehension he felt.

"What about Paul and Adrian?"

"Paul's with me, we're both hiding behind a car, Adrian's not with us, he's still at the station 's'far as I know."

Good, stay safe," Melissa told him, as if she expected her friend to foolishly risk his life. "I'll call Inspector Stevens and see what he says; armed backup should be on the way, hopefully they'll be here soon and can sort things out." She ended the radio call and switched to her mobile phone, so she could call her superior.

KIERAN SNATCHED UP the bag of saleable items he had dropped in his sister's bedroom and left again without delay. He thought about searching Emily's room for anything worth taking, but decided against it, the odds were it wouldn't be worth the time it would take to find his sister's 'valuables'.

He opened the front door slowly and cautiously; he didn't think either of the constables he had seen when he first looked out into the yard were armed, if they were, he was sure they would have returned fire when he shot Sergeant Mitchell and the inspector, he wasn't about to risk himself stupidly, however.

He peered around the yard but saw nothing, he assumed the constables were still hiding behind the patrol car, he had seen their heads when he looked out the window after collecting his bag. Just to be on the safe side, and to encourage the constables to keep out of the way and to not do anything stupid, he fired off both barrels from his shotgun as he moved hurriedly across the yard to his Land Rover.

His shots were not intended to harm the constables, whom he couldn't see in any case, they were merely to keep their heads down. In that they succeeded for he saw not so much as a hair to indicate there was anyone in the yard with him by the time he reached the driver's door of his Land Rover.

55

"Mike, Mike! What's going on up there? Are you alright?" Melissa abandoned the call to Stevens, so she could try to find out what the new shotgun blasts indicated; she hoped it wasn't a sign of something bad, though how it could indicate something good, she didn't know. Her concerns grew the longer she waited for an answer.

It was almost a minute and a half before Black responded to the radio call, time in which he cowered behind the patrol car, afraid that the slightest move on his part would draw more fire from the murderer. "I'm uninjured, so's Paul, but I'd hardly say we're alright," he said, speaking in as low a voice as he could manage to keep from being overheard. "We're still using the patrol car for cover."

"What were the last couple of shots about?" Melissa asked. "If you're staying under cover, what was Kieran shooting at?"

"Us!" Black said. He sounded a little calmer, but there was still a note of alarm in his voice. "I don't think he was actually trying to kill us – for which he was more than a little grateful – I think he was just trying to get us to keep our heads down."

"Is he still in the house?" Melissa still had her mobile phone in her other hand and she could hear from it, faintly, Inspector Stevens' voice as he demanded to know what was going on.

There was a prolonged period of hesitation from Black, as he worked up the courage to raise his head above the bonnet of the patrol car, against which he was leaning, so he could look around. He exposed himself for no longer than was absolutely necessary, dropping back down into cover after the briefest of glances. "No, he's not in the house anymore," he said quickly into his radio once he was safe again. "He's in his car. I think he's getting ready to leave; yes, he's just started the engine. What do we do?"

The answer was obvious to Melissa. "Stop him." After everything Kieran had done, they couldn't simply hope that the requested backup would arrive before he got away; in her mind that would be tantamount to aiding and abetting his escape.

"How're we supposed to do that?" Black wanted to know.

"I don't know, any way you can think of," Melissa told him. She couldn't believe that she seemed to be the only one capable of thinking of solutions. "Run his car off the road or something."

"DON'T DO IT, MELISSA," Zack said in his most authoritative voice. He realised what the young constable was intending a heartbeat after she dropped her phone and radio and bolted from the living room and was determined to stop her before she got herself hurt. "Melissa!" He hurried after her but wasn't quick enough to catch her before she made it out the front door.

"What's going on, what's she going to do?" Sophie followed her friend, worried and curious, but, like Zack with the constable, was unable to catch up to him before he disappeared through the front door, which he left open.

Sophie wanted to continue the pursuit, if only to satisfy her curiosity, but stopped when she remembered that Tara Wright was still in the living room; the young girl may have calmed after the ordeal she had gone through that morning, but that didn't mean she could be left on her own. Frustrated, she left the door ajar and returned to the gloomy living room, where she kept an eye on the teen Zack had saved while listening for anything that might tell her what was going on outside. The boards over the windows annoyed her even more than they had before, because they prevented her having any idea of what was going on outside of the house, as well as requiring them to have the light on, despite it being daytime.

Zack reached the end of his drive in time to see the patrol car that had been parked to block the narrow road race away. What Melissa was doing was what he would have done were he in her position, but he would have liked her to show a little more caution.

There was nothing he could do to stop her, however, short of turning into Superman, which left him with just a couple of options: he could remain where he was and watch as Melissa continued up the road on a collision course with the Land Rover that had just left the Wright Farm, or he could give chase on foot and hope that he could somehow limit the potentially fatal disaster he could see looming – he chose the latter option.

56

Kieran was astonished to see the patrol car heading up the road towards him as he left the yard. He didn't know which of the village's constables was behind the wheel, and he didn't really care, he was more concerned with the fact that there was no space for him to get past the vehicle; if he tried to go to his right he would be stopped by the copse of trees bordering the Harwell Farm, while on his left there was the wall, and the ditch on the other side of it, that separated him from his family's field.

His foot lifted from the accelerator momentarily, doing so without him thinking about it consciously, but once he realised what he was doing, he pressed his foot back down, so he could speed up.

He hoped whoever was behind the wheel of the patrol car would lose their nerve, and turn away before there was a collision, after all, his Land Rover was more likely to come out better off. It wasn't until the last moment, when he saw that it was Melissa behind the wheel, rather than one of the other constables, that he realised the car was not going to turn away; by then it was too late for him to do anything but brace himself for the impact.

When it came, both quicker than he had expected and with more of a delay – the final second or so before the two vehicles collided seemed to slow until it passed at a fraction of the proper speed, enabling him to take in every detail, right down to the look of grim determination on Melissa's face – it sent a shock up his arms and made him fly forward, unhampered by the seatbelt he hadn't bothered to put on, and into the steering wheel.

It was fortunate that there was not enough time for either vehicle to accelerate to too great a speed, it meant the impact was less severe than it could have been. His chest hurt, as did his arms, but not so badly that he couldn't move, albeit slowly, and with much muttered cursing.

Kieran threw open the door at his side and stumbled from the Land Rover; the moment he was on his feet, he looked around to determine where the danger he was sure he had not yet escaped was going to come from next.

In front of him was the patrol car Melissa had stopped him with, it looked as though it had been welded to his Land Rover. Neither vehicle was going to be moving any time soon, that much was obvious, and from what he could see, Melissa was as stuck as her car; she was struggling to cope with the air-bag that had opened protectively, which he was glad about. Beyond the patrol car was Zack Wild, who was approaching the crashed vehicles slowly and cautiously and, as far as he could see, without a weapon; since that was the case, Kieran dismissed him as a threat.

When he turned to look back up the road, Kieran saw something that worried him more than either the author or the trapped constable; the second patrol car, carrying the two constables who had come to the farm to arrest him, was creeping towards him. The speed of the patrol car's approach could not have been more than one or two miles an hour, but he still didn't like to see it heading his way.

He reacted to the threat automatically, diving back into the Land Rover, the pain in his chest forgotten, to retrieve his shotgun from the passenger seat. He brought the weapon to his shoulder the moment it was clear of the vehicle and sighted along the barrel at the windscreen of the patrol car.

Kieran watched as the patrol veered suddenly and sped up, crashing through the wall and into the ditch, though not before the driver's window shattered under the impact of the double load of shot he had fired. His eyes remained on the crashed patrol car for a moment, until he felt sure the officers in the vehicle were no longer a threat to him. Zack Wild on the other hand, having almost reached the rear of the patrol car Melissa was trapped inside of, was, even if he still appeared to be unarmed.

Hurriedly, Kieran removed the spent shells from his shotgun and replaced them with fresh ones he dug out from the pocket of his jacket. With his gun reloaded, he reached into the Land Rover to retrieve the bag containing the 'valuables' he had gathered from the house, he couldn't afford to leave that behind, not if he wanted to stand any chance of surviving beyond his escape from the village.

With the shotgun held awkwardly in one hand, he climbed over the crumpled bonnet of the patrol car and dropped down on the other side. After a quick adjustment to the bag on his shoulder, he approached the driver's door.

Melissa was still struggling with the air-bag when Kieran yanked open the door at her side, and she didn't immediately realise what was going on. By the time she did, he had ripped a hole in the air-bag, deflating it, and reached in to undo her seatbelt. She tried to fight him off as he grabbed her by the front of her uniform blouse and hauled her out of the driver's seat, to no avail.

When it became clear that she lacked the strength to fight Kieran off, she used the only tactic she could think of, she went limp. The result of her move was that when she was pulled out of the car she fell to the ground, which forced Kieran to reach down to lift her up; Melissa intended that and took the opportunity presented to her.

The moment Melissa felt Kieran's hold on her loosen, she wrenched herself free and surged to her feet. One hand went for the shotgun, while the other went for his face. She was successful in pushing the shotgun away, so it couldn't be used against her, he caught her other hand before she could do any damage to his face, however, and she found herself being spun around and secured in a grip that she found impossible to break free of, despite her best efforts.

"Get back," Kieran told Zack Wild, raising his shotgun one-handed so it was pointed in the general direction of the author, while he tightened his other around Melissa to stop her struggles. "I said get back." He squeezed the first trigger, more to discourage Wild, who was making his way around the rear of the patrol car towards him, than because he wanted to kill him. Despite that, he was disappointed to see that Wild's sudden dive behind the rear of the patrol car saved him from harm.

"Give it up, Kieran," Zack said as he pushed himself up from the ground, in pain from the numerous injuries he had gathered over the past few days, but glad that his reflexes were still sharp enough to keep him from being shot. "There's nowhere for you to go."

Kieran looked around quickly before smiling nastily. "Who's gonna stop me? You? I've got this." He waved the shotgun. "And I've got her." He indicated Melissa with a nod of his head. "As long as I've got these, there's nothing you can do to stop me, now get outta my way." He took a step towards the rear of the patrol car and Wild, his grip on Melissa tight enough to stop her escaping, while the muzzle of his shotgun, despite the wavering caused by his one-handed grip, remained pointed at Wild threateningly.

"Don't make things worse than they already are," Zack told the teen, speaking in as reasonable a voice as he could manage – he had never done the negotiator's course while he was with the police, but he had some idea of how to handle such a situation. "There are armed police on their way to the village, they'll be here soon, and when they arrive you'll be caught, or killed if you try and force the issue. Things will go better for you if you surrender now."

"I'm not an idiot," Kieran snapped. "Things won't go better for me no matter what I do. Now back up and give me the keys to one of your cars, I don't care which one, I just want a vehicle, and whatever money you've got on you."

Zack grimaced. "I can't do that," he said regretfully. He carried on quickly when anger flashed across Kieran's face. "I haven't got any money on me, nor have I got my car keys. I don't even have my mobile on me."

Melissa felt Kieran tense through the grip he had on her and was sure he was about to try to shoot Zack again; she wasn't going to let that happen if she could stop it, not that she was sure how she could, given how good a job Kieran was doing of restraining her with just the one arm. She knew that working on a farm helped to develop muscles, but she wouldn't have thought it could make a teen that much stronger than her; no matter how hard she tried she couldn't free herself, she couldn't even pull an arm free.

She might not have the use of her arms, which hampered her significantly, but Melissa realised there was something she could do to try and stop Kieran shooting Zack. Hooking her right foot behind Kieran's leg, she threw herself back into him, while twisting her body to throw his aim off should he manage to pull the second trigger on the shotgun.

Zack saw what Melissa was doing and hurried from his position of cover; he closed the distance between him and the two struggling figures as quickly as possible, wanting to reach them before the teen murderer could get control of his captive and his weapon. With one hand outstretched, he caught the long barrel of the shotgun with his left hand and immediately gave it a tug. He had been planning on simply keeping the weapon away from him while he tried to free Melissa, but now he had hold of it he realised it was a better idea for him to disarm the teen.

Kieran had to think and act quickly when he felt the tug that almost pulled the shotgun from his grasp. He tightened the grip he had on the gun with his right hand and abandoned his efforts to subdue Melissa with his left, leaving her to fall to the ground, at the same time he took his finger from the trigger – he didn't want to fire his one remaining shot accidentally, especially when he wasn't in a position to reload.

Zack wrenched and twisted at the shotgun with both hands as he sought to disarm Kieran, who he quickly realised was stronger than him, especially in his current wounded condition. His efforts weren't helped when he stumbled over Melissa, who was in the act of pushing herself to her feet, so she could join the struggle. He fell to one knee and had to let go of the shotgun with his right hand, so he could put it down to keep from falling over completely; releasing half his grip on the weapon was the last thing he wanted to do, but the move was automatic.

Kieran gave the shotgun in his hands a massive tug the moment he saw Zack's hand leave the gun. He was hoping to wrench it free while Zack was off-balance, so he could turn it on the man and use it as it had been intended. Luck was not with him, however, just as it hadn't been during the rest of the morning; somehow, Zack managed to keep the shotgun pointed away from his body while he struggled to get back to his feet.

From her position on the ground, Melissa saw that there was no way for her to untangle herself from Zack without knocking him over. If she did that he would be forced to let go of the shotgun completely, which would mean they were both as good as dead.

Despite being hampered by being on the ground, tangled up with Zack, and squashed against the side of her patrol car, she was determined to do whatever she could to arrest Kieran and bring him to justice for the numerous crimes he had committed, especially for his murder of her cousin. Her determination paid off when a tug and a twist on the double-barrel of the shotgun by Zack pulled Kieran's upper body forward; Melissa immediately snaked out a hand to grab the off-balance Kieran by the belt, and with one almighty heave she pulled him down on top of her and Zack.

It was far from ideal for them all to be in a heap on the ground, but at least there was no way for Kieran to use the shotgun as a weapon.

Zack felt the air explode from his lungs as Kieran landed heavily on top of him, at the same time his injuries, which he had been ignoring as best he could during the struggle, sent a wave of pain rippling through his body. It was all he could do not to scream. The pain was so sudden and so intense that he released his grip on the shotgun without being aware he had done so.

Fortunately, Kieran was too close to be able to take advantage of having complete control over the weapon, and Zack recovered quickly enough to realise that his best bet was to keep Kieran close and negate the shotgun as a weapon. He ignored the gun, which Kieran was stubbornly holding onto, and worked to roll the teen over onto his back, with him on top so that he could gain an advantage.

The awkward and unskilful wrestling match continued for about a minute and a half before Zack and Melissa, though weaker individually, were able to gain the upper hand. When Melissa secured Kieran in a headlock, Zack wriggled out from under the teen, fending off the hand that sought to grab hold of him and keep him from getting away.

An elbow to Kieran's ribs knocked some of the fight out of him, allowing Zack to roll away and get to his feet. He was bruised and battered, and his brain seemed to be receiving signals from just about every pain receptor in his body, but he pushed all of that aside as he grabbed the shotgun Kieran was still stubbornly holding onto. He wrenched at the gun, with more success than before, and reversed it once he freed it from Kieran's grasp.

After watching for a moment for the right opportunity he struck with the weapon, using it as a club rather than as a gun. He slammed the butt into Kieran's forehead with as much force as he could muster and watched as the teen's eyes rolled back into his head and he went limp on top of Melissa.

Switching the shotgun to his left hand, Zack reached down to grab hold of Kieran, so he could drag him off Melissa. That took what seemed to be the last of his energy, and prompted a fresh wave of pain, which he let out in a loud groan that threatened to become a full-blown cry.

"Thanks," Melissa said gratefully, accepting the hand that Zack held out to her; she could have got to her feet on her own, now that she was no longer at the bottom of a pile of bodies, but was glad of the help.

Drained, both physically and mentally, she slumped against the patrol car, sure that if it wasn't there she would not be able to stay on her feet. She simply could not believe everything that had happened over the past day, let alone the past week, and looking from herself to Zack, who was swaying on his feet, she wasn't sure which of them had suffered the most – they were both in bad shape, physically and mentally and in need of a long rest, not to mention medical treatment.

"How long d'you think he'll be out?" she asked after a quarter of a minute, during which time she kept a careful eye on the unmoving form of Kieran at her feet, as though she expected him to wake and resume the fight at any moment.

"No idea," Zack admitted. "He could be out for hours, or he could wake up at any moment. If I were you, I'd get some cuffs on him before he does wake up, and I'd call to see where that backup is, just to be on the safe side. You should get some ambulances on their way as well, you're gonna need all the medical help you can get."

"Where are you going?" Melissa asked when Zack left her and the unconscious Kieran and started up the road past the two crashed vehicles.

"I'm gonna go see if any of your colleagues are still alive, and if there's anything I can do to help them," Zack told her. He had waited until Kieran's hands were cuffed, and he was sure the teen was not going to be getting away if he woke, and now that that had been done, he felt it was safe to leave Melissa with the teen. "If anything happens here, yell, and I'll come running." 'Maybe not running' he thought, given that this morning had shown he was not up to moving at speed.

Melissa nodded. She would have preferred to be the one who went and checked on her colleagues but knew she couldn't ask Zack to stay there and keep an eye on the prisoner. That would not have been right since she was the police officer and he the civilian.

Torn by conflicted feelings – she was unhappy with everything that had happened that morning, though pleased that the murders that had rocked Oakhurst were at an end, and the killer was in custody – Melissa kept one eye on Kieran, while with the other she followed Zack as he made his way up the road. It was only when he disappeared behind the Land Rover that she remembered she was supposed to be checking on the backup and making sure that there were ambulances en-route.

Leaning into the patrol car, she grabbed the spare radio from the glove-box and made the call to the station. With that done she sat on the edge of the driver's seat to wait for help to arrive.

POETIC JUSTICE: THE OAKHURST MURDERS #2

1

Zack Wild's eyes followed the ambulance that held Kieran Wright until it disappeared from view.

There was a patrol car with two uniformed officers escorting the ambulance, and a third officer in the ambulance with the handcuffed Kieran, yet Zack could not shake the feeling that the teen murderer, who had done so much damage to the village of Oakhurst, and whose arrest had been so costly, was not done causing trouble and hurting people.

The situation was not really anything to do with him, a detective inspector once, he was now retired from the police force and made his living as a writer, but old habits died hard. He couldn't forget either what he had seen, or what he knew had been done by one of the worst killers he had ever encountered.

His sense of responsibility was not helped by the fact that it was he who had found the first of Kieran Wright's victims. Nor was it diminished by the fact that until that morning he had been the one and only suspect under investigation by Sergeant Mitchell. Only Kieran Wright revealing himself as the murderer to his youngest sister had changed that.

With the ambulance now out of sight, Zack turned his gaze to survey the mess that had resulted from the ill-prepared attempt to arrest Kieran Wright by Detective Inspector Harrison, who had taken over the case from Sergeant Mitchell.

His green eyes settled first on the Land Rover and the patrol car that stood enmeshed, bumper to bumper, blocking the road and preventing any other vehicles from getting past.

From the conjoined vehicles, his gaze moved up the road to the second of Oakhurst's patrol cars. While the first had been used in a game of chicken that kept Kieran Wright from escaping the village, the second had crashed through the wall at the side of the road before burying itself, nose-first, in the ditch on the other side of it.

The panicked manoeuvre had kept the driver, who was now on his way to hospital in the same ambulance as Kieran Wright, safe from the two shotgun blasts the teen murderer had fired at him but had not protected his partner.

Zack could just make out the figure of Doctor Kelly, the village's elderly GP, as he strove to keep Constable Black alive until the air ambulance could return to take him to hospital. Having seen the extent of the constable's injuries when he went up the road to check on the party sent to arrest Kieran, Zack doubted the younger man would survive, no matter how hard the doctor worked. It was a doubt that had been shared by the paramedic from the air ambulance when he decided to take DI Harrison rather than Constable Black to the hospital in Branton first.

After leaving the crashed patrol car, Zack's gaze continued up the road to the Wright farmhouse, though it didn't remain there for long. The farmhouse, and the yard that surrounded it, were half a mile distant, too far away for him to make out details. He had already seen what was there, though, and he could picture Sergeant Mitchell's lifeless body, a large hole where his stomach had been, on the ground a short distance from the front door simply by closing his eyes.

"What do you think'll happen when the backup finally gets here?"

The question refocused Zack's attention on his immediate surroundings, specifically on the young constable at his side, whom he had helped to arrest Kieran Wright.

"No idea," he admitted. "They don't need to arrest Kieran, we've already done that, but I'm sure they'll find something to do. Most likely they'll search the farm for evidence to connect Kieran to the murders — they'll want proof to help close out the case — and they, or someone else, will want to look into his morning's operation to work out what went wrong, and how it could have been avoided."

"Someone's gonna get the blame for all of this, aren't they," Melissa said unhappily.

"Someone," Zack agreed with a nod. "I wouldn't worry too much about it, though, if I were you. This is one occasion when you can be glad you're only a constable. Sergeant Mitchell and DI Harrison are far more likely to take the blame, they're more senior, and they made the decision to go in without waiting for armed backup." He had enough experience of such circumstances to know that the higher-ups in the police force would want to find someone to blame for what had happened, and though Kieran Wright was the one with the shotgun, it was a police officer who would have to take responsibility for the failures that had occurred. "You might even come out of this with something positive on your record."

"I'd rather have this morning back, so I can tell Mitchell and the DI to wait."

That was a sentiment Zack could understand, though he realised it was not going to help anything. "Best not to think about that too much," he advised. "You can't change what's happened. Come on, let's go and check on Tara, I'm sure she's pretty worried about everything." Without waiting to see if Melissa was going to follow him, he pushed away from the boot of the patrol car and made his way down the road to his home, where Kieran's fourteen-year-old sister was being looked after by his friend, after Kieran tried to run her down to keep her from telling anyone that he was the murderer who had terrorised Oakhurst's daughters.

2

Kieran Wright kept his eyes shut with an effort all through the ride from Oakhurst to the hospital in town. It wasn't easy; every time the ambulance hit a bump or made a turn he wanted to look around to figure out where he was. He was determined not to do that, however. So long as his hands remained cuffed, he had no intention of letting either the crew of the ambulance or the police officer watching over him know that he was conscious.

It did not become any easier to conceal that he was no longer unconscious when he reached the hospital. He was transferred from the ambulance's stretcher to a trolley and wheeled away somewhere, which he struggled to identify as a cubicle in the emergency department using just his hearing — he had never before appreciated how hard it was to work out where he was, or what was going on, without looking, and he could only wonder how much longer it would be before someone realised that he was faking being unconscious.

Fortunately, neither the nurse nor the doctor who appeared gave him more than a cursory examination before sending for a porter to take him for an x-ray.

It was when he and his escort, Constable Pritchard, reached the x-ray department, where he was to be examined for a possible fractured skull or a concussion, that Kieran heard what he had been waiting for.

"You're going to have to take the cuffs off."

Constable Pritchard could only stare at the technician for a quarter of a minute, that was how long it took for him to find his voice. "You've got to be kidding." He eyed the teen on the trolley nervously. He had survived the arrest of the murderer without serious injury but had seen what had happened to Sergeant Mitchell and DI Harrison, and to his partner, whom he was sure must have died from his injuries by now. "Have you got any idea how dangerous he is? There's no way I'm taking those cuffs off."

"How dangerous can he be?" The technician, who was waiting to x-ray the teen, didn't really care whether he was dangerous, so long as he personally wasn't in danger. He had a queue of people waiting to be x-rayed that morning and he didn't want to be delayed. "He's unconscious, and I doubt he's gonna wake up in the five minutes it'll take for me to x-ray him. Come on, man, five minutes, that's all it'll take. You take the cuffs off and help me shift him over to the couch, five minutes for me to run the x-rays, then you can have the cuffs back on him. What can he do in that time? He's unconscious and unarmed, and you'll be right here with your baton thing."

Kieran wanted to laugh, or at least to smile, over the fear evident in Pritchard's voice. Even to him it seemed ridiculous that a man almost twice his age should be afraid of him. He resisted the urge to react to what he was hearing, though, and kept his body as relaxed as possible, despite being sure he was going to give himself away at any moment.

Pritchard looked nervously at the teen who had killed his sergeant, probably killed his partner, and who had tried to kill him, while he thought about what the x-ray technician had said. He couldn't understand where the two officers who were supposed to be with him had got to, and their absence worried him. He could do nothing about their absence, however, and much as he wanted to, he realised that waiting for them would only give Kieran more time to wake up.

Finally, after an agonising period of indecision, he made up his mind.

"Fine, I'll do it." Taking out his keys he undid the first of the cuffs.

Kieran felt it when his wrist was released from the cuff, it was what he had been waiting for. He allowed himself to smile as his eyes flew open and he launched himself from the trolley, catching both the room's other occupants by surprise. He crashed into Pritchard, bearing the constable to the ground, where he proceeded to repeatedly slam the older man's head against the hard surface under them.

Pritchard had no time to react to Kieran Wright's sudden attack. He was on the floor and seeing stars before he had a chance to realise that the teen had been faking being unconscious. He made one, feeble, attempt to protect himself, but that came to a quick end when Kieran shoved his hands away and punched him twice in quick succession, once in the ribs and then on the jaw.

Kieran went back to smashing his head on the floor after that, doing so with energy and enthusiasm. A part of him knew he had done enough to prevent the constable being a threat by the time he had beaten his skull against the floor the third time. He continued, however, only stopping when a rush of noise from behind reminded him that there was someone else in the room.

He let go of Pritchard and surged to his feet. He saw the technician darting for the door and raced after him, shoving aside the trolley on which he had been delivered to the room on his way past. He couldn't afford to let the technician get away, if he did he would have hospital security and the police after him before he could get to the end of the corridor — he intended getting much further than that, even if he was aware that he could not avoid what he had done being discovered.

He caught up to the technician as he was pulling open the door. Grabbing him by the back of his tunic, he yanked him away and sent him spinning across the room to fall into the trolley, which he hit with a crash.

Kieran cringed at the noise of the impact, and quickly yanked open the door so he could look up and down the corridor. By some miracle there was no-one around, and he could see and hear nothing to suggest anyone was coming to investigate the noise.

Relieved by his good fortune, he let the door swing closed and turned his attention to the technician.

"That was really stupid," he snarled as he stalked towards him. "Really...Fucking...Stupid."

CONSTABLE RALEIGH WAS almost at the x-ray suite before he caught up to his partner, whom he was surprised to see wasn't already with the prisoner they had been sent to watch over. He wasn't worried that his partner wasn't where he was supposed to be, he wasn't either, because the constable from Oakhurst was with the teen murderer they had followed from the village, and the teen was unconscious.

"Where've you been?" Raleigh asked curiously as he fell in beside his fellow constable. "You only had to park the car."

"It wasn't easy finding a parking space," Constable Bass replied. "The car park's pretty full, you'd think it'd be quieter, given how much it costs to spend any time there, and I had to get a ticket. Then I had to find the place. What about you, you should have been here already, you didn't have to do anything but come straight up here after I dropped you off.

"I'll bet you stopped to chat up a nurse, didn't you." He knew only too well how easily his fellow constable could be distracted by someone with a pretty face, and even the occasional less than pretty face.

"No, I bloody didn't, I had to stop at the bog," Raleigh said with an indignation that was not entirely genuine. He had made a detour into the toilets on his way past, but that had only taken a few moments; the rest of his delay had been taken up with a young nurse he stopped to get directions, which he didn't actually need, from.

He reached the door of the x-ray room two steps ahead of his partner and was pulling it open when he suddenly stopped and swore.

"What's up?" Bass asked as he stepped up to his partner's shoulder. "You just remember you forgot to wash your hands? Or you realised your zip was open the whole time you were chatting up the nurse you reckon you didn't speak to?"

"No, there's blood on the door," Raleigh said in a quiet voice, pointing to a pair of a parallel bloody smears that looked to have been made by someone's fingers. Automatically his hand went to the holster for his extendible baton, an action his partner immediately copied.

His baton extended, ready to be used at the first sign of trouble, Raleigh slowly pulled open the door to the x-ray room. Once it was wide enough he slipped through, his grip on the baton tightening, though he quickly realised that the weapon was not going to be needed, it was too late for that.

"Jesus!" he swore, lowering his baton as he moved further into the room.

Bass couldn't help repeating his friend's utterance when he saw the room, and the bloody mess that had been made of the technician's face. He recovered more quickly than his colleague and hurried across the room to check for a pulse.

"Thank God!" he gasped in relief when he found one.

"What about the constable from Oakhurst?" Raleigh wanted to know as he looked around the room. "He should be here. And what about the kid, how'd he get away, he was cuffed. D'you think he had help?"

"How the hell am I supposed to know?" Bass asked. Having satisfied himself that the technician was still alive, which he considered a minor miracle based on what he knew of what had happened in Oakhurst that morning, he got to his feet, his mind racing as he tried to work out what could have happened and what he and his partner should do next. "Maybe he took the guy's cuffs off so he could be x-rayed, I'm sure they have to remove everything metal or it messes up the x-rays," he said, remembering that from the last time he had to have an x-ray. "Have you looked everywhere for the constable? How about on the other side of here?" He leaned over the couch of the x-ray machine and saw what he was looking for. "Here he is. You check whether he's still alive, while I get help and radio this in."

TWO FLOORS BELOW THE horrified constables, who were dealing with the aftermath of his escape, Kieran Wright made his way between the cars in the car park at the side of the hospital. He had no idea that the mess he had left in the x-ray room had been discovered, so he didn't hurry as he headed towards the target he had picked out. His pace was slow and steady, and his route indirect, as he sought to avoid drawing attention to himself.

Kieran glanced around, searching the car park for potential witnesses, when he saw his target finally stop at a car, a forest green Ford Focus with several dents and scratches. He could see no-one, which both surprised and pleased him, and he hurried forward, moving quickly between the cars that separated him from the man he had followed from the hospital's side entrance.

As he rounded the bumper of the last car Kieran flicked his wrist, extending the baton he had taken from Constable Pritchard to its full and deadly length. He raised it above his head at the last moment and brought it down with all his strength on the shorter man. His intention was to smash the baton down on the back of his target's head, ending things quickly, but luck was not on his side.

At the last moment Kieran's victim turned his head. The baton, instead of hitting him squarely and ending things quickly, glanced off the side of the skull before smashing into his shoulder.

Though he had anticipated that a single blow would be all he needed, Kieran was already prepared to deliver a second when he saw that the first had not gone as planned. He smashed the baton into the angle where the neck joined the shoulder, smiling at the loud crack that announced the destruction of the collar bone.

Again and again Kieran struck with the baton, battering the body that lay at his feet. He didn't stop until he heard a noise behind him. He spun round, his arm falling so the bloody baton was at his side and out of sight, while he searched the car park for the source of the noise that had disturbed him. It was a few moments before he heard a car engine start up, and his searching gaze homed in on the roof of the vehicle as it pulled away from the space it had occupied.

He watched the car all the way to the car park's exit, only turning away when it was no longer visible, and he was reasonably certain he was safe.

Kieran wiped the baton clean as best he could using the clothes of the man he had just beaten, and then he retracted it, so he could put it in his pocket. After that he searched the pockets of his victim for anything of value or use; the keys to the car were in the door, so he didn't need to look for them, but he did find a wallet and a mobile phone — he took the phone, and emptied the wallet of cash, just as he had done with Constable Pritchard's.

Once he had finished the search and found everything worth taking, what little there was, he took the keys from the door and pulled it open, so he could slide behind the wheel. He had no idea where he was going to go as he started the engine and shifted into gear, but he didn't allow that to trouble him. Just then it was more important that he put as much distance between himself and the hospital as he could, as quickly as he could, than it was for him to worry about something he could decide on later.

3

Zack rose to his feet when the doorbell sounded, an action that required more effort than would normally have been the case because of his injuries, and because he was sitting on the floor, his furniture having been taken away to be repaired and reupholstered because of the damage done to it during the attempt on his life a few nights ago.

"Mr Wild? I'm Detective Inspector Martins." The smartly-dressed coloured lady on the doorstep held up her warrant card.

"I'm Zack Wild," he confirmed, giving the warrant card only the most cursory of glances. He could spot a fake a mile off, and he doubted a journalist with a phoney police ID would be there so soon. "How can I help?" He had a pretty good idea.

"I've been put in charge of the situation here," Martins said. "If you don't mind, I'd like to speak to you about this morning's events, and last night's events at the Southdene hospital, get your account of them. I'd also like to speak to Constable Turner and Tara Wright, I'm told they're both here."

Zack took a step back from the door, so the inspector could enter. "I can't help you with whatever operation went on at the hospital last night, I wasn't involved, and I know nothing about it. I can't help you with Constable Turner either, she's next door at her grandmother's, but Tara is here, and I'd be happy to tell you what I know about this morning. The living room's just through there." He indicated the doorway to his right. "Would you like something to drink, tea, coffee, water?"

"No, I have a lot to do this morning, and I'd rather get on." Martins slipped past Zack and into the living room, where she looked around bemusedly, surprised to find herself somewhere that appeared to be only a step or two up from what might be found in a squat — the room was cleaner than a squat, but the boarded-up windows, which she hadn't noticed from the outside, and the lack of furniture, matched what she had seen in buildings occupied illegally. "I thought you said Constable Turner is next door," she said, her eyes on the woman on the living room floor next to Tara, who was being kept occupied, and distracted from everything that had been going on, by Facebook.

"She is, this is my friend, Sophie," Zack said. "Would you like me to go and get Melissa while you speak to Tara?"

"It'll save me time."

Zack wondered, as he made his way out the front door and down the path, if the inspector always lacked courtesy, or if she was simply reacting to the stress of the situation she found herself in charge of. While he had never had to deal with anything as serious as what had happened that morning, for which he was grateful, he liked to think that he had always remained both kind and courteous, no matter what the situation, and no matter who he was dealing with.

When he returned to his living room with Constable Melissa Turner he found Inspector Martins on the phone. It sounded, from the little he could hear, as though something serious had happened.

"What's going on?" he asked once Martins ended her call, unable to shut off either the need to know what was going on or the desire to take charge.

Martins hesitated before answering. Glancing at Tara, who was pretending to be fully occupied with the laptop, while surreptitiously listening, she indicated with a quick jerk of her head that they should talk somewhere more private.

"Kieran Wright has escaped," she said once she, Zack, and Constable Turner were in the kitchen. "I don't know how, or exactly when. All I know right now is that he somehow managed to get out of his cuffs and attack a constable and a technician at the hospital. I'm going to have to speak to you both about the morning's events another time. Right now I've got to get back to town to coordinate the search for him. The press are going to have a field day with this.

"I doubt there's any real cause to be concerned," Martins said, speaking in what could only be described as a deliberately light voice, "but given that he tried to kill his sister this morning, it might be wise to keep an eye on her."

Zack agreed with her doubts. He didn't credit Kieran Wright with that great a level of intelligence, at least not based on what he had done over the past week, but he didn't think the teen murderer was stupid enough to return to the village, especially not to kill his sister.

"Don't worry, ma'am, I'll make sure nothing happens to Tara," Melissa assured the inspector.

"Good, now, what's the situation in the village? I've got to go, but I want to make sure everything's alright here before I do. You've lost your sergeant and one of your fellow constables, and another is in critical condition, do you have enough officers to help you maintain order here?"

Melissa would have laughed at Martins' phrasing if it wasn't for the circumstances that had prompted the question. "Outside of recent events with Kieran, Oakhurst is generally a pretty quiet place, we don't get a lot of trouble," she said. She wasn't about to admit as much to a senior officer she had only just met, but in a usual week there wasn't enough work to keep her, let alone her colleagues, fully occupied. "I have Constable Johnson, he's at the station at the moment, and there's always Inspector Stevens who can lend a hand if needed, he has more experience than the rest of us combined."

"Okay, good. If you need any support, I'm sure your inspector can arrange it. In the meantime, there will be people back and forth for most of the day, sorting out this mess." Martins left then, without even a goodbye.

Melissa was startled by the abruptness of the inspector's departure, and it was a few moments before she recovered. Once she did she turned to Zack to ask, "What do we say to Tara?"

"Nothing, for the time being." Though he tried not to make it sound as if he was giving an order, Zack couldn't avoid the authoritative note that entered his voice. "It won't do her any good to know her brother has escaped. If anything, it'll put her at risk of going into shock again, and if that happens I don't think the internet will distract her.

"With a bit of luck Martins will catch Kieran quickly, before he can hurt anyone else, and there won't be any need for Tara to know what's happened." He suspected, though he hoped he was wrong, that before Kieran Wright was back in custody more people would be hurt, perhaps even killed.

"I hope you're right," Melissa said, pleased that the doubts she felt didn't make it into her voice. "I know this is a bit cheeky, under the circumstances, but will you look after Tara for me for a while, I've got a few things I need to take care of."

The curiosity that had led Zack to become a detective, and which still led him to investigate anything that intrigued him, made him want to ask what it was Melissa had to do; courtesy kept him from doing so, however. He imagined there was a lot the constable had to do, given everything that had happened that morning and over the past week, so he simply nodded.

"Sure, I'll keep an eye on her. She's already here so it won't change anything. We'll need to do something about getting in touch with whatever family she has, though, she can't stay with me indefinitely. Even if I was equipped to look after a teenage girl who isn't related to me, I doubt social services would let me. I assume she has no family left in the village." He was basing that on the fact that no-one had turned up to take Tara off his hands.

Melissa shook her head. "No. The Wrights are pretty new to the village. I think they're just about the only family that isn't related, by blood or marriage, to every other family in the village. I think there might be an aunt somewhere, though, I seem to remember there being one who moved away years ago."

4

Kieran had been driving around town aimlessly for about half an hour, unsure of either where he was going or what he was going to do, when the news was announced on the radio.

To his horror, the lead story was about the escape of a murder suspect from Southdene hospital. His name wasn't mentioned, but that was small comfort when the news reader revealed that the body of the man he had assaulted in the car park had been discovered, and the police were looking for the man's stolen car.

It was too late for him to change what he had done, nonetheless he couldn't help thinking that he should have taken the wallet instead of tossing it after emptying it of money. Without the wallet the police would have had a harder time knowing who had been attacked and what vehicle to look for.

An even better idea would have been for him to put the man he had attacked in the boot of the car he had stolen. That would have robbed the police of any clue to how he had left the hospital grounds; it would also have made it almost impossible for them to figure out what vehicle he was using.

There was only one thing he could do, he realised, and that was ditch the car he was driving and get himself a new one. Ditching his current vehicle was easy enough, all he had to do was park it and walk away, but without another vehicle to replace it he would be too visible — it was only a matter of time before the police released his name and a description of him. Once they did that, being on foot was almost guaranteed to lead to him being spotted, recognised and reported.

It was another ten minutes before Kieran found somewhere he thought would be a good place to dump his stolen Ford. To be more exact, he almost ran someone down while looking for somewhere to dump his car, at which point he realised he might not get a better chance to replace his current vehicle with one the police didn't know about.

He braked to a screeching halt about fifteen yards further on from the man he had just nearly run down, shifted into reverse, and quickly backed up, forcing the smartly-dressed man to flatten himself against his car again to avoid being hit.

"What the hell do you think you're doing? You could have bloody well killed me, twice."

Kieran was caught by surprise when the passenger door was yanked open and the man thrust his head and shoulders into the car. He wasn't scared by the display of aggression, just surprised by it, it wasn't what he anticipated from a man looking like the one he had almost run down. He reacted by throwing open the door at his side and all but launching himself out of the car.

By the time he was on his feet he had the baton taken from Constable Pritchard out. He gave it a flick to extend it as he hurried around the car but held it low and out of sight.

"Are you bloody crazy?" the man demanded, backing out of the car to watch warily as the teen approached. "Are you trying to intimidate me, because it won't work, I'm not afraid of you."

That comment, so obviously a lie, was enough to make Kieran laugh. He continued to do so as he raised the baton in his right hand and brought it down with all his strength. His target was the man's head, he wanted to cave in his skull and finish things quickly before someone could come along and witness what he was doing, but a jacketed arm got in the way. A loud crack announced that the blow had broken the arm, but that didn't make Kieran feel better about being denied his objective.

He put his frustration into his next blow, and the one after that. Again and again he struck the man, battering at him with the baton until he was on the ground, and even the involuntary twitching of his muscles had stopped, by which time his chest was heaving and sweat stained the armpits and back of his t-shirt.

Kieran looked up and down the side street while he got his breathing under control and he recovered from his exertions. Thankfully there was no-one around, which meant what he had done had gone unwitnessed, and if he was lucky and he worked quickly no-one, especially the police, would have any idea what car he had switched to.

Once he was sure there was no-one around he wiped the baton clean and shoved it into his pocket out of the way. He then rifled through the pockets of the man he had just beaten — Kieran didn't know if he was dead or merely unconscious; he would rather he was dead, so he couldn't be a problem in the future, but he didn't really care just then — searching for his car keys, and anything that might be of use.

It was while he was going through the man's wallet, which he emptied of what money it contained, that the idea came to him. He had the address for his victim, and he had his house keys; he could lay low at the man's place, at least for a short time, while he worked out where he could go and what he could do.

It didn't take long to finish his search, which turned up little, and with that job done Kieran turned his attention to concealing the body. He didn't fancy driving around with a body in the boot of the car he was about to steal; getting stopped and found with a body would only make his situation worse, not that he could really imagine how his situation could be any worse — he had killed and attacked so many people that he supposed it was only a matter of time before the press came up with a nickname for him, something they thought was both clever and witty — fortunately, there was a simple solution to that problem.

Opening the boot of the Ford Focus revealed that his simple solution was not going to be as simple as he thought. The boot was filled with an assortment of things he had to quickly dump out, so he could heave the body into it. Fortunately, the Focus had a good-sized boot, and once he had emptied it he had little difficulty fitting the body in; there was even space for him to squeeze some of the smaller items back in around it.

The rest of the items that littered the road behind the car, which included a spare wheel and a heavy toolbox, he had to shove onto the rear seat. It was all going to be noticeable to anyone who happened to glance into the car on their way past, but he didn't think that was going to matter. He was confident that anyone who did see it would simply assume the car was owned by a careless and untidy person, an impression that was likely to be helped by the vehicle's outward appearance.

By the time he had finished hiding the body and clearing everything away, Kieran's muscles were screaming in protest. He didn't understand why they should ache so much, he was used to spending all day working on the farm without feeling the way he did then. The only explanation he could come up with was that everything he had been through that morning had drained him, more than working did.

Despite the aches and pains he was suffering — reminders of the crash and the fight he had been in prior to being captured by the police, in the form of Constable Melissa Turner, and the interfering Zack Wild — Kieran didn't have time to stop and rest, he still had things to do before he could leave his current location.

Slipping back behind the wheel of the Ford he reversed it up the road so there was space for him to drive Howard Skinner's car out of its parking space — he got the name of his victim from the driver's licence he found in the man's wallet. He swapped cars, drove the BMW, which was much more comfortable than his temperamental Land Rover had ever been, a short distance down the road and then parked the Ford in the vacated space.

He accomplished that as quickly as he could, and once he was done he locked the Ford, tossed the keys under the car, and returned to the BMW.

5

"Can you stop that for a moment, Tara, there's something I need to talk to you about," Zack said. He shifted the pillow he was using as a seat closer to where the teen was lying on her belly while she played on his laptop.

It was a minute or so before Tara finished the game she was playing and tore her attention away from the screen. "What's that, Mr Wild?" she asked.

"Do you have any family outside the village you can contact?"

"Why?"

"You're going to need someone to look after you." Zack saw the distress and panic on his guest's face and hastened to reassure her. "You're welcome to stay here as long as you want and need, I'm not about to kick you out after what you've been through, but I suspect the authorities, child services especially, would rather you were in the care of a relative. If you don't have family who can take you in, at least until we know what's going on with your dad, they may decide to place you in a home, or with a foster family."

"But I don't wanna go to a home or a foster family," Tara protested.

"I'd rather you didn't as well," Zack told her. "I'm sure you'd be much better off with family than with strangers, and there's your sister to think about as well. I'm sure it's just a matter of time before she comes out of her coma, and when she does she's going to need the kind of care you can only get from family. So, can you think of any relatives?"

Tara's face screwed up in concentration as she thought about the question. Finally, she said, "I can't think of anyone in the UK, my grandparents are all dead, but I've got an aunt in Canada. I haven't seen or spoke to her in...I don't know how long...years it must be."

"Is there a reason you haven't kept in touch with your aunt?" Zack asked. He wondered if there was a problem that would lead to her going into care, a prospect he was sure her father wished he could prevent. Unfortunately, Glen Wright was on remand for attempted murder, having been denied bail, and so could do little about his daughter's situation.

A shrug was the only answer Tara had. "Don't really know. I did hear once that dad and Aunt Brenda don't get on, but don't ask me why." She made to turn her attention back to the laptop she was borrowing but had to stop when she realised that Zack wasn't finished with her.

"Do you know how to get hold of your aunt?"

"Dad might have her number or her address somewhere, but I've no idea where. I guess I could have a look," Tara said reluctantly.

Zack was not surprised that Tara seemed far from thrilled by the thought of going home, he was sure he would have felt the same if he was in her position. That didn't matter, though, since he doubted it would be possible to search the house for contact details for her aunt until the police finished with the property.

"Can you think of any other way of getting in touch with your aunt?"

"I suppose I could find her on Facebook," Tara said, though she didn't look too confident about that."

"I think you should try." Zack pushed himself to his feet and crossed to his desk, which had somehow survived unscathed the attempt on his life when the rest of his furniture had suffered damage that required it to be taken away for repair. He returned to his cushion with a pad and pen, so they could work out what to say to Tara's aunt once she was found.

WITH BOTH THE PATROL cars belonging to Oakhurst's small, and now even smaller, police force out of commission, Melissa was forced to walk down the road from Zack's to the station. Ordinarily that wouldn't have been a problem for her, she was in much better shape than her sugar-rich diet would suggest, thanks to an excessively high metabolism.

Today, though, after the night she had had, and the exertions involved in the arrest of Kieran Wright, walking was just about the last thing she wanted to do. She barely had the energy to put one foot in front of the other.

When she reached the station, she expected to be there for only a short while before returning to Zack Wild's. It soon became clear that that was not going to be possible, however, when she approached the counter and her colleague, Constable Johnson, showed no sign of knowing she was there. He remained oblivious to her presence even when she waved a hand in front of his face to get his attention.

Worried, she hurried around the counter, and when she still couldn't get a response from Johnson she called the doctor.

"IT'S SHOCK," DOC KELLY said once he had finished his examination of Constable Johnson, who had been guided away from the counter and down the passage to the office. "If I had to guess, I'd say it's been brought on by this morning's events." He sighed heavily. "It seems as though everyone in the village, no matter what their connection, has been affected by what Kieran has done. I've been getting calls almost non-stop since news of what happened at the farm started going around the village.

"Most of the calls have been people wanting reassurance, and confirmation that what they've heard is either true or false, depending on who called, but, Melissa...." he hesitated for a moment. "Inspector Stevens has had a heart attack. It wasn't a major one, at least it didn't appear to be when I examined him, but Irene has taken him to hospital."

"Christ!" Melissa swore. "What the hell am I supposed to do now? If both the inspector and Adrian are out of action, I'm the only officer left in the village. Well, the only one here for the village rather than here to deal with this morning's mess."

"Adrian will be fine, he just needs a bit of time to get over the shock," Kelly said confidently. "I'm sure you can call your superiors in town and get some help in the meantime." He doubted the chief inspector, or whoever's job it was to make such a decision, would leave Melissa to look after the village on her own, especially when she was only a constable. He considered her as capable as any other police officer, but that didn't mean she didn't need guidance from a more senior officer.

"I'll give them a call if anything comes up that I need help with," Melissa said. "To be honest, though, I think with Kieran in custody — she had no intention of being the one who allowed panic to spread through Oakhurst by revealing that Kieran had escaped custody in town — everything is going to settle down. We didn't have much in the way of crime to deal with before the murders started, and I'm sure it's going to go back to that now they're over."

"I hope you're right, Melissa, I really do."

The phone on the counter chose that moment to ring and both Melissa and the doctor spun towards it. They looked at the phone and then at each other, both wondering what trouble the call heralded. It was a few seconds before either of them moved.

"Oakhurst Police Station, Constable Turner speaking, how can I help?" Melissa answered the phone. She fervently hoped that the call was nothing more than an inquiry about the morning's events from someone who wanted an official answer rather than gossip.

"Constable, it's Miles Hewitt from the Jameson Stables."

"Yes, sir, what can I do for you?" Melissa knew, even before she got an answer to her question, that Miles Hewitt had not called for information on what had taken place at the Wright farm. The owner of the largest horse stables, stud and riding school in the area had little interest in the village, or what happened there, the only things he cared for were horses and making money.

"We've had some vandalism," Hewitt said. "I'd like an officer to come out and take a look at it."

Melissa was tempted to say that it would have to wait, that she was on her own and was too busy. She quickly realised that she couldn't do that, though; no matter the situation in the village, she had a responsibility to deal with any and all crimes that occurred there. "Sure, I'll be there as soon as I can." She took a few details and then ended the call as quickly as decency allowed.

"Is everything alright?" Kelly asked. As human as the next person, he could not help being curious about the phone call, and whether it had any bearing on what had happened that morning.

Melissa grimaced. "Problem at the Jameson Stables," she said, setting the phone to forward all calls to her mobile, in case there should be any other problems requiring her attention. "It doesn't sound too serious, but I'm going to have to go and deal with it. Would you mind taking care of Adrian for me?"

Kelly nodded. "Of course. I'll take him home and get him settled. He'll snap out of it soon enough, I'm sure. He just needs some time."

Melissa had to wait for the doctor to guide her fellow constable out of the station, so she could lock up, before she was able to head off to the Jameson stables. Even then she couldn't go straight there, she had to head home first to collect her car, and on the way, she had to call Zack to let him know what was going on and make sure everything was alright with Tara.

6

DI Martins didn't break the speed limit on her way back to town from Oakhurst, though she was tempted, but she did get to Southdene hospital as quickly as she was able. All through the drive she worried about what the escaped killer was doing, and what was being done to hunt him down. She didn't like not knowing what was going on, it made it hard for her to plan.

She found something else to dislike when she got out of the car at the hospital — journalists, and their counterparts in broadcast media. Since she had not had the radio on in her car, she didn't know that news of the escape had reached the media, so she didn't know to expect a crowd of journalists and reporters at the hospital's main entrance.

The crowd was being kept from entering the hospital by a trio of uniformed officers, which was good, but it didn't keep questions from being shouted at anyone who approached the entrance and looked as though they might know something of what was going on.

Martins thought about avoiding the circus at the main entrance and finding another way into the hospital, she was sure there were several others. Before she could make up her mind she was spotted by one of the journalists, and with teeth gritted against the frustration — she liked the media when they were reporting on the successful conclusion of another case by her, but not when she couldn't boost her career by using them — she continued to the entrance.

"Inspector Martins, inspector, what can you tell us about the suspect who escaped? Is it true he was under arrest for murder? How about that he killed several officers before being arrested, and that he killed several more people while escaping, is that true?"

Martins resisted the urge to stop and answer the questions shouted at her. Until she had more information than she currently possessed, anything she said could only be misinterpreted and make the situation worse, something she wished to avoid.

"How about how this guy was able to escape, can you tell us that? Or what you're doing to keep the public safe and get him back?"

Martins reached the door then, which opened at her approach, and slipped through, glad to be away from the questions. She stopped the moment the doors slid closed behind her, not that they remained closed for long with the number of people going in and out of the hospital, and looked around. A short distance away she saw one of Branton's junior detectives and hurried over to him, hoping to get some answers so she could begin making plans.

"What the hell has been going on here?" she demanded of DC Reid in a louder voice than she intended as she hurried over to him.

"Follow me, ma'am, we've been given an office to use, it's not far," Reid said. As best he could he ignored the hard look directed at him by his superior. Inwardly, though, he winced at the thought of what was going to be said once they were alone.

"Sorry for speaking like that back there, ma'am," he said the moment they were through the door of the office they had been loaned. "But I didn't want anything said where it could be heard or recorded. We've caught three journalists pretending to be patients since we asked them to stay outside, and we caught one genuine patient on the phone to a journalist, trying to make a deal to sell whatever information he could get.

"It's been a nightmare, and it's only been a short time since the shit hit the fan. I'm glad you're here to take charge."

Reluctantly, Martins was forced to abandon what she had been about to say. She might not like the tone in which she had been spoken to, but she couldn't deny that Reid had done the right thing given the circumstances. "Okay then, now that we can't be overheard," she said. "What's been going on here? How the hell did..."

"Kieran Wright," Reid supplied helpfully.

That unlooked-for piece of assistance did nothing to help Martins' mood. "How did he escape?" she asked. "He should have been cuffed and watched by three officers. I was told there was a constable in the ambulance with him, and two more following in a patrol car. They should all have been with him when he got here, so how did he escape?"

Reid looked thoroughly embarrassed, even though neither the escape nor the circumstances that had enabled it were anything to do with him, and no reasonable person could blame him for them.

"We don't know how Wright was able to get out of his cuffs yet; the constable who was with him, the one who was in the ambulance, is dead, his head was bashed in, but the technician from the x-ray suite Wright escaped from is still alive — badly hurt, but alive — and might be able to tell us something when, if, he wakes up."

"What about the two officers who were supposed to be following the ambulance? Where were they?"

Reid reddened still further. "One of them had trouble finding somewhere to park the patrol car, and the other was caught short, he had to go to the toilet. They both swear they were only a couple of minutes getting from the car to the x-ray suite."

"Is that supposed to make this situation better?" Martins asked in a sharp voice. "It only took a couple of minutes for Wright to escape, and he was able to do so because two officers had trouble parking a car and needed the toilet. If this was a film no-one would believe it." The expression on her face could only be described as incredulous, with a large pinch of dismay, and it was almost a minute before she spoke again. "The journalists outside said that more than one person was killed during the escape..."

"Yes, ma'am, about half an hour ago the body of a man in his early twenties was found in the side car park by a visitor. We don't know for sure that Kieran Wright is responsible, we haven't finished searching the hospital yet, but we are working on that assumption, since it seems the most likely explanation for the body."

"You're assuming that Wright killed this guy and took his car," Martins said. It was an assumption that made sense, even if it wasn't helpful. She had been harbouring the hope that the escaped murderer was still in the hospital and would be found after a comprehensive search. If Wright was out of the hospital and in possession of a vehicle, there was no telling where he could be, or where he might be heading.

Reid nodded. "If it wasn't Kieran Wright then we need to be looking for a second killer, and I don't think it likely that someone would be here, killing a man and stealing his car, at the same time that Kieran Wright was escaping from custody."

Martins could hardly disagree with that. To have two killers at the hospital at the same time would be beyond the realms of coincidence.

"As soon as I realised what had happened I told the media, so the public knows to be on the lookout, and to report the car if they see it."

"What exactly did you tell the media?" Martins asked.

"Only what was necessary," Reid said defensively, sensing that his superior was unhappy with him. "They knew a suspect had escaped — I don't know how, someone in the hospital must have called them, they were here almost before I was — so I confirmed it, though I didn't give them Wright's name, and told them about the car he stole. They wanted to know what he was under arrest for, how he escaped, and how many people were hurt."

"None of which you told them, I'm sure."

"Of course not, I'd never tell them anything like that, that should only come from a senior officer."

"Yet when I arrived, the group outside knew that our escaped suspect is wanted for murder, and that he killed an officer while escaping, and several officers before being arrested." Martins was none too pleased with the media's possession of such knowledge. "That last isn't something they could have been told by anyone but a police officer, and when I find out who it was they'll be for the high jump. You do realise, I suppose, that what you've told the press could cause a panic.

"If it goes out on the news that a suspected murderer has escaped from custody, and it almost certainly already has — I can't imagine that any of those outside would sit on such a story — people are going to be looking over their shoulder and jumping at shadows. Worse than that, because you didn't give the media a description, or even a name, people are going to be suspecting anyone and everyone they aren't absolutely certain about." A frown creased Martin's brow. "I can only imagine what's likely to happen as a result of that; if we're lucky, all it will be is a lot of false sightings because someone's spotted a stranger acting suspiciously." Her concern was that someone would try and make a citizen's arrest on someone they didn't like the look of, and that people would get hurt as a result.

"Should I have given the press Kieran Wright's name?" Reid wanted to know. "I couldn't have given them a description, I didn't have one, I still don't."

Martins didn't answer that, she was too busy thinking about the fact that she didn't have a description for the escaped killer either, something she was going to have to fix if she wanted to stand any chance at all of recapturing Kieran Wright.

7

Melissa parked her car to one side of the Jameson Stables' yard and got out, looking around as she did so.

The last time she had been there was ten years ago, when she persuaded her parents to pay for riding lessons. That was before Miles Hewitt married Catherine Jameson and the stables went more upmarket. Everything she could see was new from the time she rode there, but not too different to what she remembered.

There was no sign of the vandalism that had been reported, which left her wondering what was going on. Not only was there no sign of any vandalism, she couldn't see anyone to talk to. She heard noises coming from the stables across the yard, however, so she headed in that direction, only to be diverted by a shout before she could get there.

"Hello, Mr Hewitt," she greeted the owner of the stables, husband of the owner at least, as she altered direction towards the office, where Miles Hewitt stood in the doorway. "How are you?" she asked politely.

"How do you think I am?" Hewitt demanded. "I've got a business to run; I've got more important things I should be doing than dealing with you and the insurance company, so if you'll just give me a crime number for the insurance company, I can get on with business. I'm sure you've got things to be doing, just like me; I've heard all about what happened over at the

Wright farm. Terrible series of events," he said with an obvious lack of sincerity.

"I can't just give you a crime number, Mr Hewitt," Melissa said apologetically, ignoring the unspoken suggestion that the death of her fellow officers was not as important as the work that was being interrupted by the situation that had brought her there. "If I give you a crime number, I have to investigate. Now, what can you tell me about 'this rubbish'? You indicated when we spoke on the phone that there has been some vandalism."

Hewitt looked far from pleased with the constable, and it was clear that he was tempted to say something sharp to her. He resisted the urge, however, and instead said, "All of the stables' vehicles have been vandalised. Dan Morgan, our head stable-hand, found them when he got here first thing."

Melissa fumbled in her pocket for her notepad and pen. "How exactly were they vandalised?"

"Tyres slashed, windows smashed, and graffiti all over them, as I told you over the phone. It'll cost a bit to get them fixed, and more to hire replacements while they're out of action, not to mention the cost of the lost business. If it wasn't for that, I wouldn't waste my time with the insurance company, or with you."

Melissa knew that she was probably being cynical, but she couldn't help wondering if Hewitt had taken the time to calculate whether it was cheaper to cover the cost of the damage himself, rather than paying the extra on his insurance premiums. His attitude suggested he had.

"So the damage is extensive and amounts to a big financial loss for the stables," she said. "Can you estimate the value of that loss?"

"Minimum ten grand, maybe as much as fifty," Hewitt answered promptly.

"Are you including the lost business, and the cost of hiring replacement vehicles while yours are fixed, in that?" Melissa asked. "I was only after the value of the damage to the vehicles," she said when he nodded. "Sorry I didn't make that clear. I can only record the actual loss, not possible losses; they're something you'd have to take up in a civil suit."

"Ten grand then, somewhere around there," Hewitt said, with only a half-hearted effort at concealing the annoyance he felt at her insistence on doing her job, rather than just giving him a crime number so he could file his claim with the insurance company.

"Thank you." Melissa scribbled the figure in her notepad. "Do you think I could see the vehicles? I'm going to have to get photographs of the damage, and then I'm going to have to speak to all your staff to find out what, if anything, they know about the vandalism. I'll also need to speak to you and your wife. It might even be necessary to get a forensics team out to examine the vehicles for evidence."

Hewitt opened his mouth to say something but closed it without speaking. He opened it again almost immediately. "I'll be here all morning, what's left of it anyway," he said with a glance at his watch. "I've got to make arrangements for replacement vehicles if I'm going to limit our losses here. As for Catherine, I would have expected her to be here by now, she has a lesson at eleven."

"Well I'm sure it won't matter if I don't get to speak to her until later, I've got enough to be getting on with. I'll start with the vehicles, where can I find them?"

"I'll have Dan take you to them. We moved them out of the yard to somewhere out of sight." He saw the curiosity on the constable's face and answered the unspoken question. "I didn't want any of our clients to see the vehicles, it wouldn't be good for the business."

Melissa was not surprised to hear that Hewitt had moved the vehicles. It was in keeping with what she knew of Miles Hewitt that he would not want anyone to know what had happened in case it harmed the business. She would have preferred it, however, if he had left the vehicles where they had been when they were vandalised, in case there was evidence at the scene. If any such evidence had existed, she was sure it had been damaged beyond usefulness during the moving of the vehicles.

"DAN!"

Melissa winced at the bellow from the stables' managing director, who had gone no farther than the door of the office before calling for the head stable-hand. There was no question that the shout had carried to the stables, but she would have expected, given his self-professed love for all things equine, that he would have been more careful about startling the horses, especially since many of them didn't belong to the stables, and were merely kept there by their owners.

"You bellowed, sir," Dan said when he reached the office, making Melissa smile.

Hewitt resisted the urge to comment on his employee's cheek, which he knew he should be used to, and said, "Take the constable to where we put the vehicles, she wants to see the damage. Try not to take too long about it, there's a lot to do today if we're going to keep that contract with Fayoud."

"Okay." With a jerk of his head Dan Morgan indicated that Melissa should follow him. "How's things with you?" he asked once they were out of earshot of Hewitt. He answered his own question before Melissa had a chance to do so. "Not good, I'd imagine, if even half of what I've heard of what's happened this morning is true."

"Not good is an understatement," Melissa told Dan, whom she knew from the pub, where he was a regular, and from her riding lessons when she was a teen, during which she had developed a crush — now faded — on the stable-hand. Involuntarily her hand went to her throat and cheek, both of which had suffered at the hands of Kieran Wright during the attempt to trap and arrest him at Southdene hospital, before they knew who was responsible for the murders. "If I never have another day like today, it'll be too soon. Still, the worst is over. Everything that's left to do is down to the police from town."

There was such obvious relief in Melissa's voice that Dan couldn't help smiling, despite the subject under discussion.

Melissa returned the smile, briefly, before changing the subject to ask, "What can you tell me about the vandalism? Mr Hewitt estimated that there's about ten grand's worth of damage been done."

"I wouldn't have thought it was as much as that," Dan admitted. "But you never know. It'll add up to a few grand at least, that's for sure." He looked around in a conspiratorial manner before saying. "It wouldn't surprise me if Miles isn't trying to bump up the insurance claim to get more than the damage is actually worth."

"It wouldn't surprise me either," Melissa said. "He wasn't too happy when I told him I wouldn't just give him a crime number, that I'd actually have to investigate."

The vehicles, it turned out, had been moved about half a mile away from the yard to an old barn that was well away from the main part of the stables. It seemed to Melissa that a lot of effort had been taken to get the vehicles out of sight; she could only imagine how hard it would have been to move vehicles with slashed tyres, and that made her wonder exactly what it was about the vandalism that made Hewitt so keen for it not to be seen.

She guessed the graffiti the vehicles had been adorned with was either rude or embarrassing to the stables.

"Wow, someone really did a number on them, didn't they," Melissa remarked when her eyes had adjusted to the gloom in the barn, and she could see what had been done to the five vehicles that were taking up all the space. She wasn't sure that ten thousand pounds was an accurate assessment of the value of the damage, but she didn't think it was far off the mark now that she could see it. "Whoever did this must really have a grudge against the stables, or someone who works here," she said when she saw that the graffiti amounted to one word, sprayed repeatedly across every available part of all five vehicles in letters of varying size. "It must have taken them a fair bit of time. Didn't anyone see or hear anything?"

Dan shook his head. "It was all done by the time the first of us got here this morning. Whoever did it must have been long gone by then."

"What about the night watchman?" Melissa asked with a frown. "When I was riding here you always had someone on the premises overnight, usually one of the stable-hands who was living in the studio flat over the office, in case something happened to one of the horses."

"Miles stopped that not long after he married Catherine and was sure he had control over the stables. I don't think he liked the idea of having a stable-hand living over the office, he doesn't like or trust them. He doesn't trust me much either for that matter. He acts like we're all going to rob the place or something."

"I can understand him not trusting the other stable-hands, if they're anything like the ones you had in my time here, they don't present a good image. I'd have thought he'd trust you, though, you've been here for I don't know how long without any trouble."

"About twenty-five years now," Dan said, showing no annoyance at the lack of trust from his employer. He shrugged when he saw the disbelief on Melissa's face. "I don't think he actually distrusts any of us, he just doesn't like that most of the stable-hands know more about horses in general, and especially those stabled here, than he does."

"How's that? I thought he was an expert on horses."

"That's what he'd like everyone to think, it's what he tells people. He hasn't been doing this kind of work for as long as most of us have, though. He's a quick learner, I'll give him that, and he listens well, when he's in the mood to do so."

Melissa turned the conversation back to where it had been before the brief diversion then. "Isn't there anyone here overnight at all?"

"We did have a security guard, but Miles sacked him about a month ago — he was a drunk, hardly ever sober — and he hasn't bothered to replace him. Don't tell Miles I told you that, though, I'm sure he'd rather you didn't know, and he definitely doesn't want the insurance company to know we don't have anyone watching the place. I get the impression the insurance is void if we don't have someone here overnight."

"If it's a requirement of the insurance policy, why hasn't he replaced the last guy?" Melissa couldn't understand why Hewitt would have put his insurance at risk like that, though it did explain why he didn't want an actual investigation to take place.

"Because there hasn't been any real trouble during all the time he's been in charge, so he figures there's no point wasting money on someone who only sits on their ass and does nothing all night — his words." Dan shook his head at Hewitt's stupidity. "I tried telling him we need someone here in case one of the horses gets sick or injured, but he wouldn't listen. We had a sick horse the other week and I had to stay here myself to keep an eye on her.

"If we have another sick horse, and things go bad, it'll cost this place more than a security guard would."

With the camera she had taken from her car, Melissa made her way around the vehicles for a second time. She moved slowly as she captured every inch of the vehicles, determined not to miss any bit of the vandalism in case that bit should be the one that helped her figure out who was responsible.

Once she was done she turned her attention back to Dan. "Can you think why anyone would have written 'liar' all over these vehicles?"

"No."

"Can you think who the vandal could have been referring to, Mr or Mrs Hewitt, or perhaps someone else at the stables?" Melissa thought it most likely that it was either Miles or Catherine Hewitt who was being referred to with the accusation. It was unlikely that the vandal would have attacked the stable's vehicles if the object of his or her anger was not one or other, or even both the owners — she doubted it was both, otherwise the vandal would have written 'liars' rather than 'liar'. "How about the guard that was sacked, could he have done this?"

"I suppose so, but I don't think that's the sort of guy he is. If he was going to do anything to get revenge for being sacked, I think he'd have hit Miles, and only then in the heat of the moment. I wouldn't credit him with the gumption to come back and do anything. He might think about it after a few drinks, but I doubt he'd go through with it. And if he was going to do something like this, 'liar' is probably the last word he'd use; he'd have to be deluded to think that Miles lied when he sacked him

— we all knew he had a problem with drink, we just didn't care as long as it didn't cause us problems."

"And you can't think of anyone else who might be responsible?" Melissa asked. "Has anyone else been fired recently, someone who might have a grievance?"

Dan nodded without hesitation. "One of my stable-lads, I say lad, he's in his mid-twenties, was fired last week by Catherine."

"What was he fired for?" Melissa asked.

"Theft. I can't say I was surprised he ended up getting sacked, but theft was the last reason I expected."

"What d'you mean?" Melissa stopped what she was doing to look at Dan. She wondered if she was about to hear a motive as well as a suspect's name.

"He wasn't the best stable-lad I've had work for me, but I wouldn't have said he was a thief. Oh, he was very good with the horses," Dan said when he saw the querying look thrown his way. "Knew what he was doing there, and he was very popular with the clients, especially the female ones, if you get what I mean. He was more interested in chatting up the clients than doing his job, though."

Melissa did. "So, he was a bit of a ladies man, liked to flirt with the clients. Is it still mostly young girls?" She remembered that when she was a student there nearly all the riding school clients had been girls, many of them teens. She didn't know why, but boys had not seemed as interested in learning to ride.

Dan nodded. "I don't think Marius has done anything with any of the girls," he assured Melissa. "He's just very flirty. Though I wouldn't be so sure about the older students, the ones over the age of consent, or the mothers of some of the younger ones."

"Are you trying to say that this guy, Marius..."

"Kowalski, his family's Polish."

"That he was actually sacked because he's too friendly and flirty with the students, and that Mrs Hewitt just said it was because of theft to avoid embarrassing the school or something?" Melissa tried to recall Catherine Hewitt from her days at the school, but only remembered her as being nice, if somewhat distant. It didn't help her decide if she was the sort of person who would accuse someone of something they hadn't done simply to maintain the school's reputation. She could believe it of Miles Hewitt but wasn't so sure about Catherine.

"I couldn't say," Dan admitted. "I only know what I was told by Catherine after Marius was sacked, and what I saw of him before that. Apparently, some money went missing from petty cash; they couldn't prove it was him, but he was caught with a mobile phone that belonged to one of the students. He claimed he found it and was taking it to the office for safekeeping, but the girl it belonged to said it was stolen."

"So, Mr Kowalski could have a reason for spraying 'liar' all over the stables' vehicles, and for trashing them."

"I guess. I wouldn't have thought him the sort of person to do this, though, just like I don't think he's a thief." There was a brief hesitation then before Dan said, with clear reluctance, "But I was told by one of the other stable-lads that Marius got pretty angry when he was sacked, he had a right go at Catherine, calling her a lying bitch and saying she'd be sorry. Jenny told me there was more to the argument, but she couldn't hear it because she had to get on with her work."

"Definitely sounds like I should talk to him, see what he knows about this. Have you got his address?"

"No, sorry. I know he lives somewhere on the Potter Estate, but I don't know exactly where. Miles'll be able to give you the address."

8

It took Kieran a while to figure out how to use the sat nav on the dashboard of the BMW, but he was glad it was there, and even more glad that Howard Skinner had programmed his address into the home function. Without that, he didn't know how long it would have taken him to find the house he was now parked in front of.

He sat behind the wheel for more than a minute while he searched the front of the house for anything that might suggest it was not the safe place he thought it was. He was glad the drive was largely hidden from sight by the hedge that bordered the front garden, he would not have wanted to sit there if anyone in the neighbouring houses or walking along the street could see the car, and him, easily.

Finally, he decided that everything was okay, and it was safe for him to get out of the car. A pleasant lawn, surrounded by colourful flowerbeds, fronted the house but Kieran paid it no attention. He wasn't much for gardens, at least not the floral sort, he was a farmer through and through, and of the opinion that lawns and flowerbeds occupied space that could be better used for growing vegetables or raising chickens, or something of that nature.

Even if he had been interested in the garden, it would have been driven from his mind by the music he heard the moment he unlocked the front door. He froze in the doorway while he considered what to do; he could turn and leave before whoever was listening to the music he could hear realised he was there, or he could stay and investigate.

It didn't take him long to make up his mind. If he left the house, he would be stuck with nowhere to hide out while he tried to come up with a long-term solution to the problem of being on the run from the police. That was likely to lead to him being caught.

Taking the key from the lock, Kieran slipped into the house and quietly shut the door behind him. He took out the extendible baton from his pocket and flicked it open as he started up the stairs to investigate the music.

The music got gradually louder before peaking when he reached the top of the stairs and followed it to the back of the house, and the bedroom it was coming from. The door was slightly ajar, and he pushed it open a little more, his grip on the baton tightening in anticipation of it being needed.

What he saw when he had the door open far enough to see most of the room was enough to make his blood boil. In a matter of seconds his mood went from calm but curious to a murderous rage, of the sort that had driven him to kill three girls in Oakhurst, attack both his sisters, and take a shotgun to the police when they came to arrest him.

He threw open the door and leapt through, reaching for the teenage girl who was on her knees in the middle of the room, giving the similarly-aged boy, who was also dressed in a school uniform, a blow-job. Grabbing her by her ponytail, he hauled her unceremoniously away from the boy she was pleasuring and threw her onto the bed, where she lay, too stunned to move.

Before the boy could recover from his shock, Kieran smashed him across the face with the baton, sending him flying.

He didn't stop with the one blow, he followed and kept hitting and hitting until he had reduced the teen's face to a bloody mess that was barely recognisable as something human. Only when he was sure the boy, who hadn't so much as raised a hand to defend himself, was dead did he leave him and turn his attention to the girl on the bed.

He approached the bed slowly, enjoying the look of fear on the girl's face as much as he enjoyed her appearance. Her blouse was open, her bra had been pushed up to expose her breasts, and her skirt had flipped up to reveal her underwear, which looked more like brief shorts.

Kieran snarled, "Whore!" as he climbed onto the bed and crawled up it to the girl. "You're all whores, every one of you, walking around in your short skirts and your tight tops, teasing every man you come across. You don't care what it does to them, only what you can get out of them, and once you've got it you don't wanna know anymore. It makes me sick. Especially when you start crying rape or assault the moment a guy tries to get a thank you for everything he's done." Anger dripped from every word, and it couldn't be clearer how much he despised the girl, even though all he knew of her was what he had seen when he entered the room. "Girls like you need to understand what it is you do to guys."

Until Kieran touched her, the girl's only reaction was to flinch as though his words were blows. When he placed his hand on her leg she flailed her hands as though trying to get rid of a bee at a picnic. Kieran pulled back to avoid being hit in the face and she quickly scrambled off the bed, so she could make for the doorway.

Kieran rolled off the bed and onto his feet, so he could chase after the girl. He didn't just want to catch her to punish her for what he felt she, and all girls like her, did, he wanted to make sure she didn't get away and tell anyone he was there and what he had done. He lunged for her as she disappeared through the doorway, missed, and bounced off the frame back into the room.

He recovered quickly and hastened from the room to continue his pursuit.

The girl was at the bottom of the stairs by the time Kieran made it half way down. Afraid that she was going to get out the front door before he could reach her, he leapt and knocked her to the floor. He hit his head on the far wall of the passage after crashing into the girl and saw stars for a moment. He recovered quickly and sprang to his feet to chase the girl down the passage towards the kitchen and the rear door.

He brought the girl down with a diving rugby tackle that ended with them in the middle of the kitchen and him on top of her. He pulled his arms out from under the girl and rolled her onto her back; as he did he punched her in the face, knocking some of the fight out of her, a second punch took care of the rest.

With the girl quiescent on the floor, Kieran pushed himself up, so he could enjoy the view for a few seconds. While his eyes were drinking their fill, his hand went to the button on his jeans.

9

Martins swept her eyes around the briefing room at the officers assembled and then turned her attention to the boards behind her. Once she was satisfied that everything was ready she got the briefing under way.

"I'm sure you've all heard that we have a murder suspect on the loose," she began. "Kieran Wright." She tapped the picture on the board behind her, which she assumed had come from his driving licence. "Nineteen years of age, five-feet-eleven and medium build, black hair and grey eyes. He is suspected of being responsible for the rape and murder of three girls, and attacks on two other girls, all teens, in the village of Oakhurst, where he lives. For those of you that don't know, Oakhurst is roughly twenty miles from here in the middle of nowhere. Details of the murders and attacks are up here on the board, and before you leave here you'll all receive copies of the files to read. Wright is a very dangerous young man, and none of you should take any chances if you find him.

"DI Harrison attempted to arrest Wright earlier this morning, with the help of several officers from Oakhurst, and Wright attacked them with a shotgun. He killed Oakhurst's sergeant as well as one of the village's constables, and DI Harrison was left in critical condition, before he was finally arrested."

"If he's been arrested, how's he on the loose?"

"We're not yet sure how he was able to escape," Martins admitted. "We're still trying to establish the details. At present all we know is that Wright was taken to the Southdene hospital here in town to be checked over because he was hit on the head during the arrest, and while in the x-ray suite he managed to escape from his handcuffs.

"A constable from Oakhurst was killed during the escape, and the x-ray technician badly injured. A third person, a civilian, was killed and his car stolen around the same time. We believe Wright was responsible but currently have no proof of that."

DC Reid took up things then. "This is Damon Wilcox," he pointed to another of the photographs on the board, "his car is a green Ford Focus, registration, OU16 28X. The details have been given to all patrol vehicles, and to the media; the media has been told that anyone spotting the car should report the sighting but not approach the car, and all patrols have been told to wait for backup before attempting an arrest."

"Wright no longer has his shotgun, of that we're certain," Martins said. "But we have reason to believe he is armed with the extendible baton which previously belonged to the constable from Oakhurst, and based on the attack on Mr Wilcox he is still very dangerous. This is what he did to the constable and the technician, and to Mr Wilcox." She indicated the photographs taken at the two crime scenes at the hospital, pausing at each to give the officers plenty of time to see the damage that had been done by the murderous teen, both before and after he acquired a weapon. "We anticipate that Wright will be spotted soon, I've prepared a fresh release for the press, this one including the name and a description of our suspect. In the meantime, I want to know everything there is to know about Kieran Wright, and I do mean everything. I want him caught as quickly as possible, and the more we know about him the more likely that is to happen."

With little to nothing known about the lethal, and on the loose, teen there were plenty of assignments to be handed out, and it took a while for Martins to make certain that everything that needed to be done was in hand.

10

Finished with his pleasure, and the release of his anger, Kieran pushed himself off the girl on the kitchen floor and got to his feet. He zipped up his jeans and looked around, unsure what to do next.

His eyes fell on the fridge-freezer in the corner and his stomach responded to the sight by emitting a thunderous rumble. He had eaten breakfast at the usual time, but now he felt as though he hadn't eaten in days. He could only put the hunger, and the incredible tiredness he felt, down to the exertions he had been through that morning. Fortunately, now that he was somewhere he felt safe, temporarily at least, he could take care of all his needs: food, drink, and sleep.

Leaving the body of the girl he had just strangled on the floor, he took three steps to the counter. He filled the kettle at the sink, then took a mug from the tree that sat next to the kettle and filled it with two teabags — he liked his tea very strong, a habit he had picked up from his father — three sweeteners, which he settled for after failing to find sugar, and a splash of milk.

While he waited for the kettle to boil, Kieran looked through the contents of the fridge for something that would satisfy his hunger. It quickly became clear that the family, two members of which he had now killed, were believers in eating healthy. The fridge was filled with things that would never be enough to keep a man going through a day of hard work on a farm: low-fat this and healthy choice that. He was finally forced to settle for making himself a couple of ham, low-fat cheese, and tomato sandwiches.

He poured water into the mug once the kettle boiled, squeezed the teabags, and then dumped them and the spoon in the sink. He was about to do the same with the knife he had used to cut the cheese for his sandwiches when he thought better of it. Cleaning it off he carried it with him as he headed out of the kitchen and upstairs.

A brief glance at the boy he had beaten so enthusiastically assured him that he hadn't moved. Despite that Kieran still approached the body, doing so not because he wanted to check that the boy was dead, but so he could roll him over and conceal the obvious evidence of his maleness.

That done he crossed to the bed and sat down. The knife and the mug of tea went on the bedside cabinet, after he had shoved aside the radio alarm clock and lamp to make space, while the plate remained on his lap, so he could eat.

He was so hungry and thirsty that it didn't take long for him to finish his food and drink. When he was done he shoved the mug and plate aside and rolled over onto the bed to put his head down on the pillow. He was asleep in moments.

11

Melissa made a detour to Zack's house to speak to him, and to check on Tara, after leaving the stables. Much as she wanted to solve the mystery of the vandalism, so she could relax again, she could not bring herself to hurry. She was tired after the morning she had had, on the back of the last week or so, and ready for a good, long rest, which she realised she was unlikely to get, despite her injuries, given the situation in the village.

"Call the chief inspector and ask for some help," Zack advised when he heard what Melissa had to say. They were in the kitchen having a coffee while Sophie kept an eye on Tara, which consisted mostly of leaving her alone while she surfed the internet, watched videos and listened to music, and played games. "I know the village isn't large, but it's too much for you to look after on your own, especially when you're injured."

"Not that badly," Melissa said, as though all she had to worry about was a few minor bruises. The truth was quite different. She had several stitches in her cheek where it had been sliced open by Kieran at the hospital, a ring of bruises around her throat from where he had tried to strangle her, and several other injuries from the collision in which she used a police patrol car to stop Kieran escaping that morning.

"Badly enough," Zack remarked, though he said no more about her injuries, focusing instead on what he considered the more important issue. "Anyway, whether you're injured or not, you need someone to help you out. You've got a case to work on now, what if something else comes up. You can't work on two cases simultaneously. Not only that but you need someone who can back you up when you need to make an arrest or talk to a suspect, and someone who can cover for you while you take a shift off.

"What's stopping you making the call?" he asked when he saw that Melissa was still reluctant.

It was several long moments, during which she finished her coffee, before Melissa responded. "I don't think it'd be very good for the village to have another stranger around. There's enough strangers in the village as it is, even if they'll be going once they've finished what they're doing. We don't get a lot of trouble here, ignoring this last week, but nobody's going to be happy to have what trouble we do get dealt with by someone they don't know. It'll only make things worse."

While he could understand what Melissa was saying, and was sure she was right, Zack could not help thinking that there was something more keeping the young constable from calling the chief inspector. After studying her for a moment he thought he knew what the problem was, she didn't want her superior, and especially not the people she lived with and policed, to think she was incapable of handling whatever happened in the village.

He wondered briefly if fear of speaking to someone so much higher up the chain of command was also a problem for Melissa. He doubted it. He doubted that anyone who was prepared to go to their inspector about their sergeant, as Melissa had about Sergeant Mitchell, would be afraid of that.

"Unfortunately, I think everyone is going to have to accept the situation, including you," Zack told her. "The chances are good that you're going to be sent help, whether you want it or not. It's only a matter of time before someone realises that you're all but on your own. It'll be better for you if you request help before it's sent."

"Why's that?" The confusion on her face matched that in her voice.

"Chief inspector's always prefer junior officers to admit when they need help, it's an indication of good judgement, which will go in your favour when you go for a promotion. I assume you've given some thought to promotion." A smile played about Zack's lips as he said that for he had never met an officer, of any rank, who didn't think about promotion, especially during the early stages of their career.

Melissa nodded slowly, almost embarrassed to admit to her dream, in which promotion to sergeant was only a step. "Okay, I'll call the chief inspector and ask for some help." She changed the subject to the other reason she had made the detour then. "Have you been able to find out anything about Tara's family?"

"Some. As far as Tara knows, the only family she has apart from the known, is an aunt in Canada, and the only way she has to contact her is through Facebook." He didn't say that it had taken a fair bit of searching for Tara to locate her aunt, and to be certain that she had the right Brenda Saul. "We've sent a message but haven't had a reply yet, which isn't really a surprise given she's at least five hours behind us. It won't even be breakfast time where she is. Hopefully she'll get in touch once she sees the message, so we can discuss what we're going to do with Tara."

"Hopefully," Melissa echoed. "Are you alright to keep on looking after Tara while I handle the vandalism case? I hate to keep imposing on you like this, especially when you don't really know Tara and it isn't your job, but I need someone who knows how to handle someone who's been through what Tara has. Nan's great at looking after people, so's mum, but I'm not sure they'd know what to do if Tara goes into shock again."

Zack dismissed the matter with a wave of one hand. "No worries, I've got to stay home anyway." He saw the curiosity on Melissa's face and answered the unspoken question, "I'm waiting for the window people to come and sort my living room windows. They told Sophie they'd be here today, but didn't say when, so we've got to stay in and wait for them."

It was only when he had watched Melissa disappear around the hedge that bordered his front garden that Zack remembered what it was he had meant to say to her. He thought about hurrying after her but decided against it; as sure as he was that it was only a matter of time before journalists found their way to the village and she was pursued for information, he didn't think there was any point in giving her more to worry about than she already had.

MELISSA WAS SO STARTLED when the mobile phone in her pocket rang that she almost ran her car off the road and into a tree. It shouldn't have caught her so completely by surprise, but for some reason it had, and she felt her heart thumping loudly in her chest as she pulled over to the side of the road to answer it.

Digging the phone out of her pocket she glanced at the screen to see who was calling. It was a diverted call from the station and she immediately felt relieved that she had followed the advice from Zack and had called the chief inspector to ask for help. She was normally an optimistic person, but after recent events she couldn't help thinking that the phone call meant something had happened to further disrupt the peace of her beloved Oakhurst.

"Constable Turner, how can I help you?" Melissa watched the road in both directions as she answered the phone. She was not too concerned that someone would hit her, it was daytime and there was good visibility, but the road was only wide enough for one and a half cars. If someone who wasn't paying enough attention came along, there was a chance that she would be hit.

"Constable, it's Catherine Hewitt, my husband said you want to speak to me about this morning's vandalism."

Melissa had not expected to hear from her so soon, if at all; she had thought it more likely that she would have to chase the older woman down to speak to her, and it was a moment before she was able to talk.

"Yes, that's right, I do need to speak to you, when are you available?"

"I'm available now," Catherine said. "And, if you don't mind, I'd like to get this out of the way as soon as possible. I've got work planned for the rest of the day, and I'd rather not have this hanging over my head all afternoon."

If it had been her husband, or any of the other people that worked at the stables, Melissa would have put her off until after she had spoken to the sacked stable-hand, whom she was on her way to see. She didn't want to do that with Catherine Hewitt, however, for she wanted to talk to her about Marius Kowalski's dismissal. There was a chance that she would know or remember something that would be of use when she questioned Kowalski.

"Now is fine with me, I can be at the stables in about twenty minutes." It was fortunate that she wasn't any closer to town because then she would have had to allow for traffic, which began to develop once the road passed the Potter Estate.

There was a second or so of hesitation and then Catherine said, "If you don't mind, I'd rather not meet at the stables. Would you mind meeting me at the cafe? We can have a coffee, and you can ask me whatever questions it is you have."

Melissa wondered why Catherine didn't want to talk to her at the stables but came up with nothing, except the possibility that Catherine didn't want to be overheard, especially by her husband or any of the staff. That raised further questions in Melissa's mind, though, and left her suspecting that the riding instructor knew something about the vandalism and didn't want anyone — anyone that didn't need to know at least — to find out what she knew.

She was tempted to suggest that they meet at the station but stopped herself before she could voice the idea. It occurred to her that Catherine might be more willing to open up and reveal whatever she might have to say if she was somewhere she felt comfortable.

There was another reason for her to agree to a meeting at the cafe, it would give her an opportunity to have the second coffee she hadn't wanted to ask Zack for. She had popped into her grandmother's to use the toilet but had resisted the urge to stop there long enough to have either the drink or the cake that was offered; now she had an excuse to have both, without feeling as though she was neglecting her work.

"I'll meet you there in about a quarter of an hour," she said, glad that she was not going to have to drive all the way through the village and out the other side to get to the stables.

She ended the call as quickly as decency allowed and then carefully turned her car around, which required a fair amount of manoeuvring because of the narrowness of the road, so she could head back to Oakhurst.

12

Melissa sipped at her coffee for a few moments as she fought the temptation to take a big bite out of the slice of cake she hadn't been able to resist buying. She kept both hands away from the plate by holding onto the mug with one and taking out her pad and pen with the other.

She was about to speak when Catherine Hewitt, who was seated across the table they had taken outside of the cafe, beat her to it.

"Miles said you took a look at the vehicles, so you've seen the damage that was done, and you spoke to Dan." Catherine paid very little attention to the coffee that was on the table in front of her. "He also said you asked for addresses for a couple of our ex-employees. If you've got suspects, why do you need to speak to me?"

Melissa studied Catherine for a short while before answering the question. She could not have missed the older woman's concern if she was blind, it was that obvious, yet there was nothing about Catherine that gave any clue to why she should be so concerned. All that Melissa could think was that she was connected to or responsible for the vandalism that had damaged the vehicles at the stables, and that made no sense since the damage could not do anything but hurt the stables, which would ultimately hurt Catherine as well.

"To ask if you know anything about the vandalism, who might have done it or why. And, now that I have a couple of suspects, to ask whether you think they could be responsible. The two names I was given are Ralph Graves and Marius Kowalski, both of whom were sacked recently. Can you think of anyone else who has been sacked in the last two or three months?" She doubted that the vandalism would have been caused by anyone who had lost their job more than three months previously, that was a long time to wait to get revenge. "Or anyone else who might have a reason for vandalising your vehicles?"

Catherine shook her head after thinking about the question briefly. "We've been lucky. Outside of Ralph and Marius, I don't think we've had to get rid of anyone in over a year. We have good staff, most of whom have been with us for a long time, and they don't get into trouble." She took a small bite of the carrot cake she had bought and didn't speak again until she had swallowed it. "I can't tell you anything about Ralph Graves, I'm not sure I ever met him. Miles hired him," she explained, seeing the disbelieving look that flickered across Melissa's face, "and he didn't start work until long after I left each day, and was gone by the time I arrived in the morning. All I know about him is what Miles told me when he hired him and when he sacked him, and I don't suppose you're after second-hand gossip."

"No, that wouldn't help me very much." It was possible that second-hand gossip might get her somewhere, but in her experience, gossip caused more problems than it solved. "What can you tell me about Marius Kowalski? Dan told me you sacked him because of theft."

"That's right. I suspected Marius behind the disappearance of some money from the petty cash box, as well as items belonging to some of the students from the riding school, but couldn't prove it. Then he was caught with a mobile phone belonging to one of the students. He claimed he found the phone and was bringing it to the office for safekeeping; he was nowhere near the office, though, and the girl it belonged to swore the phone was with the rest of her things in the locker she was using." Catherine looked away from Melissa for a moment. "If it had been just the one incident I might have been able to give him the benefit of the doubt but, as I said, money had gone missing from petty cash, and there had been other reports of things going missing. Not only that but I'd had reports that he was too familiar with some of the students, and not just with those over sixteen.

"I'm sure you can appreciate that I couldn't afford to ignore something like that, it could have ruined us."

Melissa nodded agreeably, yet she could not help feeling that there was a rehearsed quality to the older woman's words that suggested she was lying. Whether she was lying about the thefts, or about Marius being too familiar with the students, or both, Melissa didn't know, but her suspicions made her think there might be an additional reason for Marius Kowalski to be responsible for the vandalism, beyond him being sacked. She wondered what the former stable-hand was going to say when she spoke to him.

"I can understand that," she said. "Parents would have insisted you sack him for inappropriate behaviour, either that or they'd have taken their kids to another riding school. Word would have got around and no-one would have brought their kids to your school. I was told there was an argument when you sacked Kowalski, and that the word 'liar' or lies' was used, is that true?"

"Yes," Catherine said with a quick nod. "He got mad, that's for sure, called me a liar and a few other things, and told me

I'd be sorry for sacking him. To be honest, I didn't pay much attention to him. We've been lucky with our stuff recently, but I have had to fire several people over the years, for one reason or another. I've learnt that nearly everyone gets angry when they're fired. Some hide it, or try to, and others don't. Marius was one of those who showed they were angry.

"I figured if he was going to do anything about being sacked, he'd get a solicitor and try for wrongful dismissal or something. I never thought he'd do anything like this."

"So, you don't think Marius Kowalski is responsible for the vandalism?" Melissa asked, her voice thick as she attempted to speak through a mouthful of cake.

Catherine shrugged. "I wouldn't have thought he would do this, but I can't think who else would have."

"You have any enemies, you or your husband?" Melissa was certain the attack had a personal motivation, and one that had been inspired recently; if the Hewitts had enemies, they were more likely of long standing, and would probably not have used the word 'liar', but she was prepared to admit that she could be wrong and so had to ask the question.

Laughter escaped Catherine before she could stop it, and it took her a few seconds to get it under control. "I don't know what kind of people you think Miles and I are, constable," she said once she could speak, "but we're not gangsters, we're just business people, we have business rivals, not enemies."

"And you don't think any of them might be responsible?"

"Of course not." It was clear that the very idea was ridiculous to Catherine. "We're rivals, but that doesn't mean we're not friendly and we don't help one another out. Miles still hasn't got used to that, even after all this time; he's convinced he's going to have to fight with the insurance company to get any replacement vehicles quickly enough to be of any use to us — we've got a horse we've got to get to Aintree in time for a race tomorrow."

It came as news to Melissa that the Hewitts had anything to do with racehorses, beyond using them at the stud farm once they retired from racing.

"I've told him I'll borrow a trailer off Iain Mackenzie, he's an old friend, owns the Branton Stud about twenty miles away," Catherine said as though Melissa should know the place she was talking about, which wasn't the case. "But I don't think he believed me, either that or he was too busy on the phone to listen."

"Okay, well, if you think of anything, you have my number," Melissa said. "I'd better go and speak to my suspects." Now that she had heard what Catherine could tell her, which wasn't really enough to justify her having come back to the village, she wanted to get on with her next task.

13

Constable Pang passed the halfway point of his shift, the point at which he allowed himself to start thinking about the end of it, and what he would do once it was finished, as he started down Guildhall Road.

His thoughts were on what would come after the end of his shift, but that didn't mean he was unaware of his surroundings. He spotted the Ford Focus from three cars away, but it wasn't until he drew level with it that he realised why it had attracted his attention. It was the only vehicle he saw that was likely to be owned by a low-paid person, all the others in the short road were worth at least twice what the Ford was, and they clearly belonged to professionals of one sort or another.

The fact that the Ford contrasted so greatly made him wonder what it was doing there. It was possible that the owner had merely taken advantage of a parking spot convenient to their destination, but he didn't think so, especially since there was something about the car that was familiar to him.

In an effort to try and work out why he thought he should know the Ford he walked around it, so he could look at it from all sides and peer through the windows. His suspicions about the vehicle were increased by the odd assortment of items that filled the back seat, items he would normally have expected to find in the boot of a car, not taking up space inside it.

It wasn't until he bent to look through the window in the driver's door that he saw the blood that stained the road. The moment he did he realised why the car was familiar. He immediately lifted his radio to call the station.

"Five-forty-two to control, come in, over."

"Control here, go ahead, five-forty-two, over."

"What's the reg number for that Focus on the alert that went out a couple of hours ago, over?"

"OU16 28X, over." The reply came after a brief pause while the control room operator scanned the sheet that listed all the alerts that had been sent out since the start of her shift. "It's a green Ford Focus with damage on the driver's side. Have you found the car, over?"

Constable Pang took a moment to check the reg number he had been given against that on the licence plate. "Control, I've found the car, it's on Guildhall Road, over."

"Pang, can you confirm you have found the car that was taken from Southdene Hospital this morning, a green Ford Focus, registration OU16 28X, over?"

Pang was annoyed by the repetition but made sure not to show it for the question had been asked by Sergeant Hardwick, who had watch duty in the control room, and he was not known to be tolerant of officers who acted or spoke out of line. "Yes, sergeant." He was pleased to hear no trace of what he was thinking in his voice. "It's definitely the car from the alert, over."

"And you said it's on Guildhall Road?"

"Yes, just round the corner from Wallis and Leigh, that fancy solicitor's place," Pang told his superior.

"Is the vehicle occupied?"

"No, and there's no-one around either. There is something, though, sergeant. There's blood on the road next to the car, fresh blood by the look of it, and the back seat of the car has been filled with the sort of rubbish you'd normally find in the boot of a car."

There was silence for a second and then the sergeant said. "Stay there and watch the car, make sure nothing happens to it. Someone will be there shortly to take charge. Until they get there, remain alert. The car is believed to have been stolen by a Kieran Wright, and he's considered very dangerous. Perry will give you his description; if you see him, do not approach alone, he's suspected of multiple murders."

DESPITE HER INTENTION of staying in the incident room until they had a definite location for Kieran Wright, Martins couldn't resist heading out to where the stolen Ford Focus had been found.

"What's the situation?" she asked the moment she reached the scene. Her eyes roamed over the Ford, taking in every detail of it before moving on to the stain on the road at the side of it. As she looked around she wondered why Kieran Wright had chosen that spot to ditch the car he had stolen at the hospital, and if it meant he was somewhere nearby.

"We've got the road blocked off, ma'am. Officers are speaking to the people in the surrounding buildings to see if they saw Wright at any point, others are collecting all CCTV footage from within a few streets of here, and another group is attempting to track down the owners of all the vehicles parked along the street," Sergeant Levine answered.

"And I've found a set of keys under the car," Constable Pang said, wanting to make it clear that he had done something other than stand watch over the car after discovering it. "I left them there, I didn't want to disturb any evidence, but there's a Ford key on them, so I'm pretty certain they're the keys to the car."

"Have you put in a call for forensics?" Martins asked of Sergeant Levine, who nodded quickly.

"Yes, ma'am, they're on their way. They said they'd be here as soon as."

"Good, but we can't afford to wait around for them. If Wright took another car after leaving this one here, we need to know what car he took and who it belongs to, and we need to try and figure out where he might be going." Martins suspected the young murderer she was trying to locate had as much of a clue about where he was going as anyone on the team searching for him. It was only a matter of time, though, before Wright stopped drifting and came up with a plan, and she wanted to know what that plan might be before her target got even further away.

From a pocket of her jacket Martins took out a pair of latex gloves. Reaching under the car she retrieved the keys, so she could open the driver's door. It didn't take her long to search the car's interior, which revealed nothing helpful, and with that done she moved on to check the boot.

'Shit!' The profanity rose to her lips when she opened the boot and saw what was inside, but she didn't allow herself to voice it. Instead she said, "Sergeant Levine, I believe we have a problem."

"Bloody hell!" Levine swore when he saw the body.

"I think you had better call for an ambulance," Martins said, though she doubted an ambulance would do any good. Her fingers searched automatically for a pulse, but she was sure the man squeezed into the Ford's boot was already dead and had been for a while. It was standard procedure to call for an ambulance, though, just as it was standard procedure for the duty doctor to be called — it would be the doctor's job to confirm the death, only when that was done would the ambulance be able to leave.

Martins withdrew her fingers once she had determined that there was no pulse to be found and began searching every pocket she could find in the suit that adorned the body in the boot. It was not an easy task to accomplish for she didn't want to disturb the body any more than necessary; if possible, she wanted to keep the body as it was, so forensics could get an accurate record of everything.

"Okay, it appears that Mr Doe is actually Howard Skinner, and he works at..." Martins said when she found the man's wallet, pausing for a moment as she fought the urge to swear. "He works at Wallis and Leigh." She could not imagine what she could have discovered that could be worse than finding out that the body belonged to an employee, and probably a solicitor, of the biggest, most successful, and least liked law firm in Branton. "They're going to have a field day when they find out about this." If there were any choice in the matter, she would delay the solicitors of Wallis and Leigh finding out about the death of their colleague, there wasn't, though, because it was possible they might be able to provide some useful information, such as a time-frame for when Howard Skinner died.

For several long moments Martins simply stood there, her eyes moving between the body in the boot and the business card in her hand, while she considered the situation and what her next course of action should be. It didn't take long for her to decide, there were procedures to be followed which told her what she should be doing.

"Sergeant, I want you to put out an alert for whatever vehicle Mr Skinner drives," she told Levine, unhappily aware that she was going to have to hold a press conference soon to let the public know the situation. The public needed to know that the escaped killer had killed again and was now in a different vehicle to the one they had been told about. They also needed to be made aware of exactly who they were to be on the alert for, and what he looked like, information that was missing from the earlier press announcement.

"Yes, ma'am." Sergeant Levine remained where he was for a moment to see if the inspector had any other instructions for him, and when he was sure she didn't he moved away so he could get on his radio.

Martins turned to Reid then. "You get to notify Mr Skinner's next of kin. Take the constable with you. Here's the address." She held out the wallet, so Reid could copy it down from the driver's licence. "Be diplomatic, and don't give out any more details than you have to. We don't want anyone adding to the fuss we're going to have with this situation."

For herself she left the more unpleasant job, that of telling the solicitors at Wallis and Leigh that one of their colleagues had been killed by an escaped murderer.

14

Louisa Orchard accepted the pint she had ordered and moved away from the bar in The Village Green to take a seat at one of the tables. The pub was not very busy just then, though she supposed it was busy enough for a village pub at lunchtime, or just after lunchtime anyway. She imagined that most people were either busy on their farms or working in town.

The people that she could see, nine by her count, not including the landlord or the woman who flitted in and out of the area behind the bar — she presumed she was the landlord's wife — were split into two distinct groups.

Louisa was sure that the quartet at a table near the door worked together somewhere near the village and were on a late lunch, while the five men and women who were lined up along the bar and talking with the landlord were clearly residents of the village. It was equally clear from the low volume in which they were conversing that they didn't want to be overheard by any of the strangers in the pub.

Unfortunately for them, and fortunately for her, Louisa had exceptionally good hearing, a trait she found enormously helpful in her career as a journalist. Straining her hearing without appearing to do so, she soon determined that the quartet at the table were not talking about anything of interest to her, unlike the group at the bar. As expected, they were talking about recent events in the village, the reason she was so far from her usual field of operations.

Every journalist and reporter of her acquaintance, and quite a few she didn't know, was scouring town for every scrap of information they could find about Kieran Wright and the hunt for him, not to mention the crimes he was believed to have committed. She was the only one, as far as she knew, who had discovered that the on-the-run murderer was not from town, and that his crimes had not been committed there.

Along with excellent hearing, Louisa had a great memory; though she often took notes, she didn't need to because she could remember easily what she was told. She stored away every scrap of information she heard while slowly drinking her way through two pints of cider. By the time she was finished with her drinks she had everything she thought she was likely to get from the quiet discussion in the pub — the group at the bar had begun repeating themselves.

Louisa left the pub without a backward glance, as though she had no interest whatsoever in the people. Her apparent lack of interest did not keep her from noticing the relief expressed by several members of the group at her departure. When she got to her car she retrieved her tablet and notepad from under the passenger seat, she then locked up again and made herself comfortable at one of the tables that sat on the grass by the river. Despite her reason for being there, it was far too nice a day not to sit out in the sunshine while she did her research.

The moment she was online she began researching the names she had overheard in the pub, the first of which being, of course, Kieran Wright. As the murderer who was the reason for her being there, Wright was the most important of those she wanted to know more about.

Barely a minute after she began her search for information on Kieran Wright Louisa gave up on it. There was little to be found on the internet about the teenager; even his social media presence was minimal, and Louisa was forced to conclude that if she wanted to know more about the murderer she was going to have to talk to people about him.

Louisa jotted down the names and details of those from Kieran Wright's social media who might be able to provide her with information on him, and then she moved on to the next of the names she had overheard in the pub, Zack Wild.

When she saw what the internet had to say about Zack Wild she thought she had the wrong man. Even when she had double and triple-checked what she was looking at she couldn't believe it; it did not seem possible that the gamble she had taken in coming to Oakhurst to try and find an angle to the story that her rivals would not have should pay off so handsomely.

Even the papers who already had reporters on the case were likely to be interested in her story once they realised a best-selling author was involved, and that he had been the prime suspect in the murders until that morning. She could name her price and stand a good chance of getting it.

Louisa was distracted from her disbelief by movement out the corner of her eye. She looked up from her note-taking and saw a uniformed female crossing the road to the police station. Since she thought it unlikely that such a small village would have more than one female officer, she leapt to the conclusion that she was looking at Constable Melissa Turner, who was one of the people she had heard mentioned by the gossiping group at the bar, and someone she wanted to talk to.

Briefly she considered approaching the constable to see what she could get out of her. She decided against it, however; the constable looked busy, and Louisa suspected she would have better luck when she wasn't.

With that decision made, she found herself wondering what it was the constable was busy doing. She doubted it was anything connected to the murders because she had seen the officers, obviously from town, who were handling what remained of the investigation into the murders while checking the village out.

Louisa presumed that the constable was involved with some other incident that had taken place in or around the village, and she was tempted to find out what it was in case it was something she could write about. She decided the current story was enough for her to focus on, though, she didn't need to get side-tracked.

15

A quick stop at the station following her coffee with Catherine Hewitt enabled Melissa to check the police database for anything on the two suspects she had been given.

Nothing came up when she looked for Marius Kowalski, which told her only that he had never been caught or accused of anything criminal. It was a good sign, but Melissa knew it was still possible that he could be guilty of numerous things. She got a better result when she searched for Ralph Graves, he had a lengthy record for a variety of alcohol related crimes, primarily drink-driving and being drunk and disorderly.

Although his record was interesting, it didn't make Graves a more likely suspect than Kowalski, so Melissa chose to stick with her original plan and call on the ex-stable-hand first. He was her prime suspect and he lived closer, and she figured that she could go to town to find the security guard after seeing the ex-stable-hand, if it was still necessary for her to do so.

A motorbike occupied the drive out front of the address she had for Marius Kowalski and Melissa hoped it meant he was home. Her research had revealed that he owned a motorbike, but she didn't know the make or licence number so couldn't be certain it was his.

"Hi, I'm looking for Marius Kowalski, I'm Constable Turner," she said when the front door was opened. She knew the man who had answered the door was not who she was after without asking, Kowalski was Caucasian, while the man on the doorstep was not. "Is he home?"

"What d'you want with him?"

"There's been some vandalism at the Jameson stables, and I've been given Marius' name as a possible suspect," Melissa said, hoping to draw a reaction or to get some indication of whether she was at the right place. She got a reaction, but it was not the kind she had expected.

"I bet it was that bitch Catherine that told you that, wasn't it."

"I can't reveal anything about who might have given me the information I have," Melissa told him with all the authority she could muster. "Now, is Marius Kowalski home?" She had heard nothing from the house to suggest there was anyone else home, but she supposed Kowalski could be hiding.

Still without introducing himself, Kowalski's friend shook his head.

Melissa saw none of the evasiveness that would have suggested he was lying, nor did she see anything out of place in his body language, not that she could claim to be an expert at reading body language. "Do you know where he went, or what time he'll be back?"

"He's at the pub." With that Kowalski's housemate, Melissa presumed, disappeared back into the house, slamming the door behind him.

FOUL WAS THE ONLY WORD to describe Melissa's mood as she walked through the door of The Village Green. Tiredness was a large part of the reason for how she was feeling, she was rapidly reaching the point where if she didn't put her head down and get at least a couple of hours rest she thought she was going to collapse, but not all of it.

She was frustrated by having driven out to the Potter Estate in search of Marius Kowalski when he was apparently at the pub. Her frustration was worsened by the knowledge that once she was done with Kowalski, she would have to head back out of the village to track down Ralph Graves.

To top things off she had received a phone call from John Ryder, who had been distressed to be visited by a journalist, though not as much as his wife, who was still suffering from the shock of their daughter's murder.

The news that there was a journalist in the village annoyed her, even if she realised she should have expected that one would turn up sooner or later. Since she could not think what she could do about the situation, she put it from her mind as she stopped just inside the pub and looked around.

She saw no sign of Marius Kowalski in the main bar of the pub, so she made her way through to the back room, where she found the sacked stable-hand on the pool table with two friends. All three were talking loudly, laughing and joking, and generally showing signs of having enjoyed more than just a couple of drinks.

"Marius Kowalski?" Melissa had to raise her voice to be heard over the noise being made by the merry trio.

"What d'you want, pig?"

Melissa ignored the question, and the epithet. She had learnt during her relatively short career as a police officer that it was better to pay as little attention to comments like that as possible. Responding, whether verbally or otherwise, only encouraged people to be insulting.

"Which one of you is Marius Kowalski?" she asked, looking around the trio. She guessed it was the one at the table, he was better looking than the other two, and he had an air about him that suggested he was both aware of how attractive he was and liked having the attention of women and girls. That fitted with the little she had been told about Marius Kowalski. Her guess was soon proved right.

"That's me." Kowalski didn't look up from the pool table as he spoke.

"I'm surprised your housemate didn't call and tell you I was looking for you, Mr Kowalski," Melissa remarked as she approached the pool table, where Kowalski was lining up his next shot. "I need to speak to you about the Jameson Stables."

"What about them?" Kowalski asked without looking up. "Has Catherine decided that sacking me, and making sure I'll never get a job working with horses in this county, isn't enough? Is she gonna try and press charges against me now?"

Melissa had expected anger, or an aggressive response of some kind, but Kowalski seemed almost indifferent, as if he didn't really care what Catherine Hewitt had told the police. He further demonstrated that by striking the cue ball and watching as it ran up the table to knock a yellow ball towards the top left pocket without paying her attention.

As far as Melissa could tell, his lack of interest was genuine, but that left her wondering why that was. She couldn't think why someone who had already lost their job over an incident would not be bothered that their life might be further affected by it. The only answer that came to mind was that he had already gained his revenge, in the form of the vandalism that had rendered the stables' vehicles temporarily unusable.

"I'm not here about the incident that led to your being sacked," she said. "I'm here because several vehicles at the stables were vandalised during the night. Tyres were slashed, windows smashed, paintwork damaged, and graffiti spray-painted over them. The damage is significant, and will cost a fair amount to get fixed, and your name is one of two I was given as possible suspects."

Marius Kowalski did look up from the pool table at that, though he was beaten to a response by the friend who had called Melissa a pig.

"I thought you said you weren't gonna do anything about the stuck-up bitch sacking you. Nice one, mate. I wish I could have seen her face."

"So, what did you graffiti on the cars?" Kowalski's other friend wanted to know. "I hope it was good. Told the bitch what you think of her."

"I didn't do anything," Kowalski said firmly. "Whatever's happened at the stables, I had nothing to do with it."

"Perhaps we should talk about this somewhere more private." Melissa looked significantly at Kowalski's friends. She suspected she would have a better chance of getting sensible and truthful answers to her questions if she got Kowalski on his own, where his friends couldn't interrupt or offer opinions.

Kowalski looked at Melissa for a moment before shifting his gaze to his mates and nodding. "Okay, but I'm not going to the station. We can talk through there." He gestured to the main area of the pub with one hand, while with the other he held out the pool cue to the nearest of his mates.

Melissa accepted that without debate, she had no problem with talking to him in the pub rather than the station. For one thing, the seats were more comfortable.

"Okay, Mr Kowalski," she began when they were both seated in a booth, "as I said, there's been a case of vandalism at the Jameson Stables and your name came up as a suspect."

"And as I said, I had nothing to do with it," Kowalski told her, his pint of lager halfway to his lips.

"So, you weren't upset about being sacked? Most people I know would have been, getting sacked is a pretty upsetting experience." At least Melissa gathered it was based on the reactions of her housemate, who had been sacked several times; she had never been sacked herself, so she didn't have first-hand experience.

Kowalski shrugged. "Sure, I was upset, anyone would have been. Not only did Catherine lie and accuse me of being a thief, she rang every other stable in the county and made sure none of them would hire me. What the hell am I supposed to do?" he demanded, slamming his glass down on the table. "Horses are all I know. If I'd known she was going to do this, I'd have closed my eyes and shagged her, like she wanted."

Melissa was so startled that it was several long moments before she could do anything but stare across the table at her suspect. Marius Kowalski was attractive, she couldn't deny that, almost as attractive as she considered Zack Wild to be — she preferred Zack's attractiveness because it came with an air of experience, and because he wasn't possessed of an obvious self-awareness of his good looks, as Kowalski was — but, and she had to admit she didn't know the woman all that well, she had not thought Catherine Hewitt the sort of person to cheat on her husband.

"What do you mean by that?" she asked once she had recovered.

"Just what I said, Catherine wanted to jump me," Kowalski said with the air of someone used to being wanted. "I wasn't interested though."

Melissa found herself disliking the stable-hand. She was sure he could be very charming when he wanted to be, but she didn't like his clear belief that every woman, including her, would fancy him the moment they saw him or his certainty that he could have any woman he wanted.

"Are you sure about that?" she asked. "Is it possible you misread things?"

Kowalski laughed as he shook his head. "I didn't misread anything. I'm used to having woman want me, so I know the signs, and she made it about as obvious as she could: brushing up against me whenever she could, making suggestive comments, inviting me out to lunch, wanting me to come up to the house to help her with things. I think the only one that didn't know she wanted to get me into bed is her husband, and he's more interested in acting like the Stephen Hawking of horses and making money to have the slightest clue what's going on with his wife."

"The Stephen Hawking of horses?" Melissa knew it was a diversion from the main topic, but she just had to know what he meant by that.

"Yeah, you know, Stephen Hawking, the guy all those scientists go to for advice because he knows everything." Kowalski saw the bemused look on Melissa's face. "I like the Big Bang Theory, he's mentioned on there a lot. Anyway, Miles wants to be like him, he wants to be the one everyone goes to for advice, in his case about horses. Not that he knows enough about them to give advice."

Melissa accepted that with a quick nod and then dismissed it from her thoughts. It was a mildly amusing reference but nothing more than that, so she got on with what she was there for. "I take it from what you've said that you weren't as interested in Catherine Hewitt as she was in you"

"I wasn't interested at all," Kowalski said. "And I told her. I like women, and she's as attractive as anyone, but she's too desperate. I prefer women that are a bit more of a challenge.

I could have Catherine any time, I'd rather have someone that makes me chase them a bit."

"What happened when you told her?" Melissa couldn't help wondering what, if anything, this had to do with the vandalism. She hoped it would lead to that subject soon, and that it would answer the question of whether Kowalski was responsible for it.

"She was pissed off, got really angry and started causing me problems. It was reaching the point where I was thinking of quitting when Catherine accused me of being a thief and claimed there had been accusations made against me by some of the pupils." He flushed angrily at the memory of what had happened. "It was all lies, she just wanted an excuse to get rid of me without anyone asking too many questions about what was going on. Being sacked was bad enough, but she can be a real vindictive bitch when she doesn't get what she wants. Thanks to her I can't work with horses anywhere in the county, she called every other stable, riding school and stud and fed them all kinds of crap to make sure none of them will hire me."

"Which brings me to my reason for being here," Melissa said. "You were recently sacked from the Jameson Stables, are clearly unhappy about it, and you believe Catherine Hewitt lied when she sacked you. As well as being badly damaged, the vehicles belonging to the stables were all graffitied with the word 'liar'." She paused for a few seconds to let that sink in. "Where were you last night and early this morning?"

"I already told you, I had nothing to do with any vandalism. Yeah, I was pissed off with Catherine, but that doesn't mean I had anything to do with this."

"That doesn't answer my question, Mr Kowalski," Melissa said. "Where were you last night and first thing this morning?"

"I was at home, in bed."

"Can anyone confirm that?"

Kowalski scowled. "You mean did I have anyone in bed with me."

"Yes."

"Yes."

"Yes, you had someone with you?" When he nodded, Melissa asked her next question. "What's their name, and how can I get in touch with them?" She saw the reluctance to answer in Kowalski's face and wondered at it, he didn't strike her as the sort to be concerned about revealing who he was sleeping with. She suspected he was more the type of person to brag about it. "If you don't tell me who you were with I'll have to assume that you have no alibi, and that means I'll have to keep you as a suspect." The only reason she could think of for him to be unwilling to say who he had spent the night with was that it was someone he shouldn't have been with. She guessed that that meant his alibi was one of the students from the riding school, and that she was most likely underage.

Melissa soon discovered that she was right, though only in half of what she had guessed.

Kowalski said nothing for almost a minute, he simply sat there, gulping down his drink. Finally, he said, "Her name's Natasha Greene."

"And she'll confirm that you were at home all night?" Melissa asked after she had written down the phone number she was given.

Kowalski nodded, though he immediately revealed his doubts by saying, "At least I hope she will."

"Is there any particular reason why you think she might not?"

"She's married. And she might not want to talk to you in case her husband finds out, apparently, he can be pretty nasty. If he's around when you speak to her, I can pretty much guarantee she won't tell you anything."

"I'll be the soul of discretion," Melissa assured him. All the same, she wondered what she would do if Natasha Greene refused to support Kowalski's alibi. Without corroboration she wouldn't be able to take him off her very short list of suspects, even if she was only unable to get corroboration because his alibi was afraid of her husband.

16

Detective Constable Reid pulled up outside of the house belonging to Howard Skinner and got out. With Constable Pang at his side he made his way round the hedge and up the drive to the front door to deliver the bad news that had brought him there, not that he was sure there was anyone home for him to deliver it to.

He stopped in surprise when he saw the BMW parked in the drive. At first, he couldn't think why he was surprised, he had been hoping to find someone at home, so the presence of a vehicle should have been good news, then he realised what it was — the licence number matched that of the BMW registered to Howard Skinner, the one that Kieran Wright was believed to have stolen. Why it should be there, he didn't know.

"Ma'am, it's Detective Reid," he said when Martins answered her phone. "I'm at the Skinner house, and Skinner's car is here."

"Are you sure?" It was possible, Martins supposed, that they were wrong about Kieran stealing the car after killing Howard Skinner, but she found that so unlikely that she dismissed the notion almost immediately. The only reason she could think of for Wright to have killed the lawyer was to steal his car, which begged the question, why was the car now at Skinner's house.

"Positive, it's his car. What do I do?"

"Is there any sign of Wright?" As incredible as it seemed, the only reason Martins could think of for the car to be there was that Wright was there. It was possible the teen wasn't as stupid as she had first thought; hiding at the house of his latest victim was pretty clever since it was the last place they were likely to look for him.

Reid looked all around, as though he expected the murderous teen to suddenly jump out from behind the car or something. He saw no sign of Kieran Wright, however. "No, ma'am, if he's here, he's out of sight," he said, grasping what his superior was thinking. "He might be lying low in the house, or he could have stolen another vehicle from nearby."

"We'll work on the assumption that he's in the house," Martins said. She suspected that was the case since it made sense for the teen to find somewhere to hole up, for a while at least. "I want you and Constable Pang to watch the house, discreetly, in case Wright tries to leave, or any of the family comes home. If they do, do not let them enter the house." She worried that there might have been someone at home when Wright got there, which would mean they were either dead or a potential hostage. She couldn't operate based on unknowns, however, only on what she either knew for certain or had good reason to suspect. "The superintendent has put an armed response team on alert for us, I'll get them on their way to you, do nothing until they get there. Let them make the arrest if Wright is at the house. Don't risk either yourself or Constable Pang unless it's absolutely necessary."

"Yes, ma'am." Reid was not against taking risks, doing so was a part of his job — every attempted arrest held risks. On this occasion, however, he was more than happy not to be the one taking the risks when it came to arresting Kieran Wright. Having seen and heard what the man was capable of, he could not help but feel that it was a job the armed response team was far better suited to.

"What are our orders, sir?" Pang asked once Reid finished the phone call to the inspector.

"We're to keep an eye on the house and make sure no-one enters or leaves," Reid told him. "The inspector's got an armed response team on the way, they'll handle the situation once they get here. Come on, we should get out of sight. If Wright is here we don't want him to know we're here." He examined the front of the house again, in case some sign of occupancy had appeared since his last check, and then turned away so he could leave the drive and get out of sight.

He was back on the pavement, and about to disappear behind the hedge, when a loud clattering sound made him jump. With his heart thumping loudly in his chest he spun back to the drive to see what was going on. He was startled to see Pang sprawled on the ground, and the wheelie bins that had been positioned just inside the drive now on their sides.

"What happened?" he asked as he reached down to help the constable up.

"A cat, a stupid, bloody cat," Pang said with obvious disgust. "It came out of nowhere and tripped me up. Sorry."

"Too late for that," Reid said, his eyes going to the first floor of the house, and the bedroom window where he had caught sight of movement. He recognised Kieran Wright from the picture he had been shown, so there was no mistaking the young man whose face appeared at the window.

KIERAN STARED DOWN on the drive in disbelief. Only one of the figures was wearing a uniform, but he didn't need to be a genius to figure out that they were both cops.

He couldn't believe the police had found him. He had no idea what he had done that had led them to him, especially so quickly, and no time to try and figure it out, he had more urgent worries, namely how many police there was outside the house, and how he was going to get away.

The answer to the latter of his concerns came to him almost immediately and he turned away from the window, so he could hurry out of the bedroom.

17

Reid reacted the moment he saw the face disappear back into the room, which he took as a sign that the teen murderer was about to make a run for it. He doubted Wright was going to remain there with two police officers, Pang's uniform made it clear what they were, outside.

"Call the inspector, tell her what's going on," he told Pang quickly. "We need all the backup she can get us. When you've done that, stay here and make sure Wright doesn't get past me."

Reid didn't give the constable a chance to react to what he said, he simply trusted that Pang had understood him, and would do as he had said. He hurried up the drive to the front door and threw himself at it the moment he was close enough.

The door shuddered but stood firm.

Reid ignored the pain in his shoulder and threw himself at the door for a second time. The door shuddered again and threatened to break but it wasn't until he slammed his body into it for a third time that it flew open to smash into the wall of the passage.

He stepped over the threshold and into the house the moment the door was open. His eyes went to the stairs leading to the first floor but hurried, heavy footsteps drew his attention to the rear of the house and the kitchen at the other end of the passage.

Reid saw a body on the floor of the kitchen as he headed in that direction, it wasn't Wright, though, so he spared it only a brief glance, long enough to be sure the girl was dead and there was nothing he could do for her. Most of his attention was on the window over the sink, through which he saw Wright disappearing over the fence into the garden of the house next door.

Hurrying to the back door, which stood open, he pursued Wright out into the garden and then over the fence into the neighbouring garden. He dropped to his feet in time to see Wright climbing the opposite fence and he hastened to follow.

With each fence he found himself a little further behind the teen he was attempting to catch, and after surmounting a fourth barrier he found that the garden he was in was empty. There was no sign of Kieran Wright, and nothing to indicate where he had gone.

Reid dismissed the possibility that Wright had left the garden by climbing the hedge on the far side of it. Not only was the hedge too high to have been climbed easily, but he would have seen the teen if that was what he had done.

He looked around for some other way out of the garden and saw the back door of the house the garden belonged to. The door was locked when he tried it, though, suggesting that Kieran had not disappeared that way, so he looked around again for an exit.

FOR ABOUT HALF A SECOND Kieran stared in dismay at the privet hedge that surrounded the garden he found himself in at the end of the row of houses. He didn't even consider trying to climb it, it was obvious that he wouldn't be able to, and equally obvious that trying to break into the house was out of the question. Even if he could manage to do so before the cops caught up to him, it would be clear what he had done, and the time would have been wasted.

There was only one way for him to get out of the garden quickly, the gate he could see at the side of the house. Turning away from the hedge he hurried over to it. A padlock prevented him opening the gate, but after the quartet of fences he had climbed to get there the gate proved no obstacle.

He was over it in seconds, and shortly after that he was crossing the street, so he could put as much distance between himself and the police as possible.

He could see no police other than the uniformed constable standing at the drive of the house he had just escaped from. He was sure they were there and ready to give chase the moment they saw him, though.

REID REACHED THE ROAD, having hauled himself over the gate at the side of the house, in time to see Kieran Wright head around the corner across the road and to his left. He immediately shouted for Constable Pang, waving to attract his attention so he would know where he was, and set off in pursuit of the teen. While he ran he fumbled in his pocket for his mobile phone, so he could call Inspector Martins and let her know about the change in the situation.

"It's Reid," he puffed into the phone as he pursued Wright. Talking and running was not easy, but he could see that even in such a short time he had closed the distance between himself and his target, thanks to the running he did as part of his fitness training. "Wright is on the run. He realised we were there, sorry, ma'am. He went out the back of the house and through some gardens."

"How did he realise you were there?" Martins asked. She kept her voice even to try and avoid giving away to the senior partner of Wallis and Leigh, whose office she was in, what had happened.

Reid grimaced as he said, "A complete accident, Pang tripped over a cat and fell into some bins."

Martins resisted the urge to swear. "What is he now, and where are you?"

"Boxwell Street, heading towards Franklin." It was becoming more difficult for Reid to talk, he needed every bit of oxygen he could get to keep himself running.

GLANCING OVER HIS SHOULDER, Kieran was shocked to see the detective from outside the house pounding down the road after him. He had been sure no-one had seen what direction he took. Not only was he being pursued, he was being caught; the detective was slowly but surely closing the distance between the two of them.

He reacted instinctively to the unexpected situation by changing direction suddenly and running straight across the road. He narrowly avoided being hit by an oncoming car by slipping between two parked cars and up onto the pavement on the opposite side of the road. He then continued along the road in the same direction he had been going before turning to head down the road that led to his left.

A glance over his shoulder just before he turned the corner revealed that the manoeuvre had succeeded in opening the gap between him and his pursuer. It was only a matter of time before he was caught if he continued to try and get away on foot, though, he simply wasn't quick enough. He needed a vehicle, but where he was going to get one from he didn't know.

As if in answer to his question, the traffic lights ahead of him switched from green to red, forcing a line of traffic to come to a stop. He put on a burst of speed, using the last of his strength, and ran out into the road and around the rear of the Honda at the back of the line of three cars.

Yanking open the driver's door he reached in to release the seatbelt, so he could pull the woman out from behind the wheel. He dumped her onto the road, not caring if she was injured, and slid in behind the wheel.

Without wasting time with the seatbelt, safety was the last thing on his mind, he shifted into gear, spun the wheel, and pulled out of the line of cars. He did all of that in the space of just a couple of seconds.

Kieran raced past the other two cars in the line and spun the wheel sharply to speed through the crossing, scattering pedestrians. He straightened up once he was through and put his foot down, accelerating as rapidly as the car he had stolen could manage, sure that he had left the cops behind.

REID ROUNDED THE CORNER in time to see Wright throw a woman out of her car and drive off in it. Despite what he knew of the teen and his crimes, he was surprised by what he had just seen. He recovered quickly and hurried up the road to check on the woman whose car had just been stolen.

"Are you alright?" he asked, dropping to his knees the moment he reached her. "Are you hurt?" He couldn't imagine that she was alright given what had just happened.

"No, I'm okay," she said, though she didn't sound certain and she made no effort to get up.

Reid was relieved to hear that. Given how she had been thrown from the car he had expected her to be hurt badly. "Do you know the licence number of your car?" he asked as he dialled Martin's number to report the latest development and get an alert out on the stolen car.

He was partway through his recounting of what had happened when the face of the woman, whose name he had not yet got, fell. "What is it?" he asked, leaving his superior to wait on the phone for him to finish what he had been saying.

"My...my son," the woman struggled to get the words out, so great was her distress. "He...he...he's taken my son," she sobbed.

It took Reid a while to calm her down enough to find out what she was trying to say, and once he knew he found himself struck by a feeling of horror. It was still with him when he remembered that he had been on the phone to his superior.

"Ma'am, it's worse than I thought," he told the inspector in a voice that was far steadier than he felt. "The car Wright stole," he hesitated for a moment, "there's a kid in it."

"What do you mean?" Martins asked after several seconds. It took her that long to recover from the shock of what she had just heard.

She hadn't thought that the case she had been put on that morning, which should have been about as easy as a case could be, given that all the hard work had been done, could get any worse than it already was. It seemed, though, as if every time she turned around something else had happened to make things worse. She could only wonder how much worse things were going to get before they succeeded in catching or killing, preferably catching, Kieran Wright.

"Mrs Milton had her son in a booster seat in the back of the car. He's two years old and he was asleep," Reid repeated the information he had been given.

"Damn!" Martins swore in an out of character display of temper. "Tell me everything you know about the car and where it was heading." She scribbled down what she was told and then hung up.

"More trouble?" Nigel Wallis asked blandly from his position across the desk from Martins.

Martins scowled. She didn't need to hear it in the lawyer's voice, or see it in his face, neither of which gave any hint of what he was thinking, to know that Wallis was deeply interested in hearing what had happened. She was all too aware that the succession of phone calls she had received, not to mention her reaction to them, made it impossible for her to dissemble and suggest that everything was okay.

Since she couldn't do that she decided to ignore the question entirely. Wallis would have to find out what was going on the same way as everyone else, through the news.

"You're certain you have no idea where I might be able to find Mrs Skinner?" she asked as she got to her feet in readiness to leave.

Wallis answered with a brief shake of his head. "No, sorry, Elaine doesn't work as far as I'm aware, so if she isn't at home I have no idea where she might be."

"And you don't have her mobile number?"

Wallis shook his head again. "I haven't had cause to contact her often, and when I have I've always done so on the home number, which I've given you."

Martins left without another word. She was dialling the number for the first of those she needed to call so she could make arrangements to handle the situation before she reached the law firm's lobby. She needed to get an alert out for the car that Wright had stolen so it could be located, hopefully soon. She also needed to apprise the armed response team of the latest information; they would have to plan how to deal with the new development, and that was not going to be easy now that Wright had a hostage, whether he knew it or not.

18

Louisa rang the doorbell and then stepped back to look around the front of the property while she waited for a response.

From what she had learnt about the Gouldings, specifically that they were closely related to Sir Virgil Foulds, the rich and well-known businessman, she was not surprised that they lived in the largest, and what was clearly the most expensive, property in Oakhurst. Nor was she surprised that the garden at the front of the property more closely resembled a show-piece, of the sort that might be entered in a Britain-in-Bloom competition, than the kind of place a person would spend time to relax.

She was wondering what Theresa Goulding was going to be like, and how she was going to get answers to her questions — she had had no luck getting the Ryders to talk about the murder of their daughter — when she was distracted by the opening of the front door.

"Can I help you?"

"Hello." Louisa had found pictures of Theresa Goulding online while researching the family, so she knew the middle-aged woman in front of her was not the one she was there to speak to. "Is Mrs Goulding home?" she asked. The personalised number plate on the BMW in the drive suggested that Theresa Goulding was there but didn't guarantee it.

"Who can I say is asking?" Anna Becker asked in a voice that was accented with the German tones of her father.

"Louisa Orchard, I'm a freelance journalist." She held out one of the business cards she had had printed.

"Wait here."

Louisa didn't have to wait on the doorstep for long, no more than a minute passed before the housekeeper returned.

"Mrs Goulding is unavailable," Anna told the journalist. "And she is not interested in talking to the press," she added in a tone that made it clear what she thought of the media — nothing positive.

It came as no surprise to Louisa that Theresa Goulding was unavailable to talk to her, nor that she had no interest in talking to the press. It was a rare person who wanted to talk to the press after losing a loved one. Her job required that she at least make the effort to talk to the relatives of those affected by the murders that had occurred in Oakhurst however.

"If she should change her mind, I'm available to talk any time," Louisa said, not wanting to push things in case she ruined any chance she had of getting an interview in the future. "Before I go, would you ask if she knows whether Kieran Wright has been re-arrested yet."

Anna froze in the act of closing the door. She stared at Louisa for a long moment before turning away without a word, so she could head back down the passage. This time she didn't shut the door, she left it ajar, an indication of how shocked she was by what she had just heard.

Louisa watched the housekeeper through the partly open door and saw her walk straight down the passage towards the rear of the house, where she knocked on a door and then disappeared into the room beyond. She reappeared with another woman, whom Louisa guessed was Theresa Goulding, though she didn't recognise her from the pictures she had seen on the internet until she was right in front of her. The loss of her daughter had changed her dramatically.

"Mrs Goulding? Hello," Louisa said in a gentle voice. "I'm sorry to disturb you."

"You told Anna that Kieran Wright has escaped." It wasn't quite what the housekeeper had passed on from the journalist, but Theresa Goulding was clever enough to figure out what Anna had been asked meant. "When? How?" she asked, making no effort to conceal either the distress the news evoked in her, or her desperate desire for information. "Has he been caught again yet?"

"Not yet, not as far as I know," Louisa said. "As I indicated with the question I asked of your housekeeper." She paused for a moment before continuing. "If you'll let me in, Mrs Goulding, I'll tell you what I know, if you'll answer a few questions from me in return. I promise to be sensitive."

Theresa hesitated, rival thoughts warring within her. On the one hand she had no desire to speak to a journalist, any journalist, regardless of how reasonable a person she seemed. On the other, she did want to know whatever the lady on her doorstep could tell her about Kieran Wright's escape. It was inconceivable to her that whatever officer was now in charge of the Wright case — she had heard what had happened to the inspector who had been in charge of the case until that morning and now she didn't know who the senior officer was, another lack she wasn't happy about — hadn't taken the time to tell her what was going on.

The need for information won out after nearly a minute and she stepped back.

"Once again, Mrs Goulding, let me say how sorry I am to disturb you at this time," Louisa said sincerely after taking a seat in the office she was shown to. "Talking to a journalist is probably the last thing you want to be doing." Her eyes were sharp enough to catch the barely perceptible nod of Theresa Goulding's head. "And I wouldn't normally trouble you while you're still grieving, but under the circumstances I think the public has a right, even a need, to know everything there is to know about Kieran Wright and the crimes he has committed — they need to know how dangerous he is."

Theresa Goulding seemed lost in her own world. She gave no sign of hearing a word of what Louisa had said, or even of being aware that she was there. It was several moments before she reacted to Louisa.

"Yes, yes, of course, people should know what he's like," she said. "They should know what he did to my...my Rose, my little darling, and to those other girls, and the officers who tried to arrest him."

"Why don't we start with your questions, Mrs Goulding," Louisa said, figuring that she would be more amenable after getting the answers she wanted. "I don't have all the information I'm sure you want, but I'll tell you what I know." It was just as well, she thought, that she had connections in town who could keep her up to date with the situation there.

"How did he escape, and when?" Theresa wanted to know.

"I don't have the exact time, but it was somewhere around ten when he escaped," Louisa answered. "I'm not sure if you're aware, but Wright was taken from here to hospital after being arrested." A shake of the head told her that Theresa hadn't known. "According to my source, Wright was hit on the head during the arrest and was taken to the hospital to check there was no internal bleeding or brain damage..."

"Of course there's brain damage," Theresa declared forcefully. "He's deranged. Why else would he have done what he did?"

Louisa nodded. She couldn't bring herself to disagree because she thought much the same thing — nobody in their right mind would commit the crimes Kieran Wright was supposed to be guilty of. What she knew of the crimes made her think of Peter Sutcliffe, Jack the Ripper, and other killers who had committed similar crimes — the one thing they had all had in common, other than the violence of the murders they had committed, was that in one way or another they were all mentally disturbed, not that that excused what they had done.

She was sure that once Wright was caught and examined he would be found to be similarly afflicted. That made it a virtual certainty that he would end up in Broadmoor, or some other secure facility for criminals with dangerous mental health problems.

"Well Southdene hospital is where he escaped from, one of the x-ray suites to be more exact, though how he was able to do so isn't known at the moment." Louisa didn't miss the anger and distress that flickered across Theresa's face when she said that. "What I do know is that Wright killed a constable during his escape, and a civilian whose car he stole to make his getaway. I've also heard that he has since killed another couple of people, including a teenage girl of about the same age as your daughter. And just recently he stole another car." She saw no point in holding back what she knew since it was going to be on the news soon enough.

"How have the police not caught him?" Theresa wanted to know. "He's not that intelligent. I remember Rose saying how dumb he is when they split up, surely you're not telling me that an idiot like him is smarter than the police."

Louisa could only shrug. "I'm sure they're doing everything they can," she said unconvincingly. "I have tried to find out what is going on with the search for Kieran Wright, but no luck. The police aren't revealing anything."

"They might not tell you anything, but they will tell me," Theresa said with brisk confidence as she picked up the phone on the desk in front of her. "And if they won't tell me, they will tell my husband's uncle, Sir Virgil. He's very eager to be kept up to date with what is happening. He doted on Rose and won't be happy with the news you've given me, with any of what you've said."

Louisa had discovered during her research that Rose Goulding was related to Sir Virgil Foulds but hearing how close the relationship was made the prominent businessman's connection to the story more important. She put that from her mind quickly as she realised that Theresa intended calling the police in town straightaway. She didn't want to get forgotten while Theresa concentrated on her phone calls.

"Before you make that call, Mrs Goulding," she said quickly, "perhaps you could answer my questions, then I can get out of your hair and leave you to get on with whatever it is you have to do."

Theresa was tempted to ask the journalist to leave without answering any of her questions, which she was reluctant to do, but after a moment she replaced the phone. She had made an agreement to answer questions from the journalist, and if there was one thing her husband's uncle insisted on, it was that once made, an agreement should be stuck to.

"Very well, Ms Orchard, what is it you want to know?" she asked in a voice that left Louisa in no doubt how little she wanted to be questioned about what had happened to her daughter.

"Your daughter, Rose, was the second girl to go missing, wasn't she?" Louisa asked. She wanted to confirm some of the things she had heard while eavesdropping in the pub before she asked anything more substantial.

Theresa nodded but didn't say anything that might help the journalist with her information gathering.

The answer was less than she had hoped for, but Louisa didn't let that deter her. "The first girl to go missing was a Georgina Ryder," she said after consulting her notes, not that she really needed to. "And she had been missing for a week before your daughter also went missing. I assume the police did everything they could to find her during that time." As she hoped, that encouraged Theresa to give a verbal response, instead of a non-verbal one.

"They said they did." The doubt in Theresa's voice was almost overpowering. "If what I saw was everything they can do, though, I'm not surprised they had no luck finding poor Georgina. I'm surprised her parents didn't put more pressure on Inspector Stevens and his officers to get help, I would have if I had been in their position. I did when...when Rose went missing." Her voice cracked, and for half a second she appeared to be on the verge of losing control, but then she got a handle on her emotions, temporarily at least. "I would have done more, made more of an effort to get them to do more, do a better job, but my...my husband made me back off and leave them to do their job."

"What happened when Rose went missing?"

Theresa closed her eyes briefly as though the question was too painful for her to think about. She opened them again to answer. "Rose was supposed to meet her father and me at The Oaks, Sir Virgil was paying one of his regular visits, and we were all supposed to have dinner. She never turned up. I had to make excuses to Sir Virgil for her absence — I said she was ill. Sir Virgil doesn't like tardiness or broken appointments, from anyone, though he's probably more lenient with Rose than anyone else. When I got home after an uncomfortable dinner, I discovered that Rose wasn't home, and that she hadn't been since school.

"I immediately went to the police station and reported her missing, but I was told they could do nothing until she had been missing for at least a day — two days in Rose's case because of her 'reputation.'"

"Didn't it make any difference that there was already a girl missing?"

"No." Theresa shook her head as she watched the journalist scribble down what she had said. "They didn't seem to think that mattered at all. They didn't care that Rose was missing, didn't even think she was really missing. I was told that she was probably just off getting into trouble or having fun, simply because she's got into trouble before." The distress on her face deepened and her hand trembled as she reached for her cup, which she quickly put down again when she discovered that the tea it held had gone cold. "The officer I spoke to made it clear that he thought I was making a fuss about nothing."

Louisa shook her head and offered a few words of commiseration and disbelief. "You'd think they would have shown more compassion under the circumstances. Being spoken to like that would have been bad enough at the best of times, but with another girl already missing it could hardly be said you didn't have cause for concern." She had encountered that kind of attitude from police officers a time or two, so it didn't entirely surprise her, but a quiet and friendly village like Oakhurst — she assumed it was normally a quiet and friendly place — was not somewhere she would have expected to encounter it.

"Constable Black seemed more concerned with the fact that it was coming up on time for his shift to end. I got the distinct impression that he was far more interested in getting me out of the station, so he could lock up and go home, than he was in the possibility that my...my little girl was missing." Once again, she had to take a moment to compose herself. "If I believed in such a thing, I would say it was Karma that he was one of the officers Wright killed when they went to arrest him. I don't believe in it, of course, and in any case, I wouldn't have wished for anyone to die like that, gunned down while trying to do their job."

She may not have wished for it, Louisa thought, but neither was she likely to lose any sleep over it. "What did you do after that?"

Theresa didn't answer straightaway, instead she called for the housekeeper, who appeared so rapidly Louisa suspected she had been waiting outside the door, perhaps even listening at it.

"A fresh cup of tea, Anna," she said, holding out her cup and saucer. Her eyes flickered to Louisa, as though she was trying to decide whether to offer her a drink. Good manners suggested she should, but that would give the journalist time and an invitation to ask more questions of her, something she was reluctant to give her. Manners won out in the end. "And get Ms Orchard whatever she would like."

Louisa had not expected to be offered a drink, but she recovered quickly to request a black coffee with two sugars.

When Anna left to make the drinks, Theresa answered the question that had been put to her. "After reporting Rose missing I came home and told Brian, my husband, how I had been treated by Constable Black. I intended calling Inspector Stevens, or perhaps even the chief inspector in town, to report how I had been treated, and to demand that action be taken immediately to find Rose, before she suffered whatever fate had befallen

Georgina Ryder, a fate we now know. Brian talked me out of it though." Tears glistened in her eyes, though whether they were for the fate of the girl who had fallen into Kieran Wright's hands before her daughter or regret for having allowed her husband to talk her out of doing what she thought was the right thing, was uncertain. "He said we should wait until morning, in case Rose was just out with some friends, before we did anything else. You can imagine how I felt when I heard that a young girl had been found murdered."

Louisa nodded. She was not a parent, but it required little in the way of imagination to put herself in the place of one.

"When I heard that the girl who was found was Georgina, not Rose...I'm ashamed to admit it, but I was relieved."

"There's no reason for you to feel ashamed," Louisa reassured her. "I imagine anyone in your position would have felt as you did."

Theresa looked no happier for the words of comfort. "Once I got over being relieved, I realised that what had happened to Georgina might also have happened to Rose. I went to speak to Inspector Stevens to find out what was being done to find Rose, and the person who killed Georgina. Everyone I spoke to was in shock, we haven't had a murder here in about ten years, and that was nothing like what happened to Georgina."

"What happened when you spoke to the inspector?"

19

Melissa had everything she needed from Marius Kowalski soon after she began questioning him. She persisted, however, despite the annoyance the stable-hand displayed at being made to answer questions that were different only in the way they were phrased, because she had read that people who lied were often caught out by the same question being asked in a different way.

Only when she was satisfied that Kowalski's answers were staying the same, and she felt confident he was telling the truth, did she end the informal interview. Kowalski's relief was palpable as he left the booth and returned to his friends at the pool table, taking what remained of his drink with him.

Melissa paid no attention to the abrupt departure, she had better things to worry about than the irritation of a suspect in a relatively minor crime. More than she thought, she soon discovered when she left the pub and found a news crew setting up their equipment right outside.

Had she been concentrating a little more on her surroundings, rather than on what she still needed to do before she could think about clocking off for the day, she might have been able to duck away before she was seen. There was no time for her to get out of sight once she did spot the news crew. She barely had time to register their presence before a microphone was thrust in her face, while a camera was swung round to capture both her and the man who blocked her path.

"Constable Turner, as the officer who arrested Kieran Wright this morning, what do you have to say about his escape? Do you feel as though what you went through to catch the person responsible for a succession of murders," the reporter's eyes went to the dressing on Melissa's cheek and the circle of bruises around her throat, "has been betrayed by the failure of your fellow officers to keep him in custody?"

Melissa caught herself as she was about to answer him. She wanted to say that of course she didn't feel betrayed, that it was a ridiculous suggestion, but she realised it would be a bad idea for her to say anything without approval from a senior officer, doing so would put her career in jeopardy.

She felt unnatural as she forced herself to respond with a stiff 'no comment'. She had always thought it an indication that someone wasn't very bright if they could only respond to a reporter with 'no comment'. Now, though, she appreciated that it was hard to say anything else without revealing something.

Her non-committal response given, Melissa turned away from the unwanted attention of the reporter and his camera-man, so she could get on with the work she still had to do. Top of the list being to call Marius Kowalski's alibi to find out if the stable-hand had told the truth.

"How about Wright's kidnap of a baby after a narrow escape from the police, do you have any comment on that?"

"He's done what?" Melissa couldn't help herself. She wanted to ignore the journalist and get on with her work but hearing what Kieran had done made that almost impossible. She wanted to be sure she had heard him right, and if she had she wanted to know what was going on with the situation.

"Kidnapped a two-year-old boy. According to my information the boy was in the back of a car Wright stole."

"Jesus Christ!" Melissa realised straightaway that the profanity was most likely not a good thing, especially since she was being filmed. For all she knew the signal was going out live. It passed her lips before she could think about it, let alone stop it, though.

The reporter smiled a little when he heard the constable's reaction to his information, as though it was exactly what he had hoped to hear. "Has Kieran Wright lived here in Oakhurst all his life?" he asked, determined to keep Melissa talking now that he had got her started.

"Yes."

"So, you must know him, all of the Wrights, pretty well."

"I thought so."

"What sort of person is he, Kieran Wright? Did he ever give any hint that he was capable of murder, or of kidnapping children?"

Melissa knew she should ignore the questions, give the reporter nothing, and go about her business. She knew she should leave for a variety of reasons, but she couldn't seem to do so. It was as if she was rooted to the spot, and against her will she found herself answering the questions.

"He was a nice guy, nice enough anyway. I didn't know him as well as I do other people around the village, not as well as I thought I did," she admitted. "I was finishing secondary school when he started, so I didn't see much of him there. Outside of school he's spent most of his time helping his dad keep the farm running, and since he's not been in any trouble before all this, I've not had much reason to get to know him well. Mostly I know the troublemakers, and those who live or work in the heart of the village."

"So, you had no reason to suspect that he might be a danger to people before all of this started?"

Melissa shook her head. "He was a suspect after the murders began, but no, before all of this happened I wouldn't have thought him the sort of person who would do anything like this. I wouldn't have thought anyone in the village could do it. That's why Sergeant Mitchell was so quick to believe that Mr Wild was the killer."

20

Oblivious to the child in the back of the car he had stolen, Kieran was just beginning to think he could relax for a bit, that he was no longer in immediate danger. He had been driving around for about twenty minutes when he decided that, and it was at that moment that a patrol car showed up in his rear-view mirror.

He held his breath and hoped that it was nothing to worry about, and the police car would take the next turning without troubling him. He realised that was not to be the case, however, when he saw the officer behind the wheel ignore the turning as he spoke into his radio.

Kieran didn't wait to see what the officer was going to do, instead he followed his instincts and spun the wheel. First, he went to his right, thinking to speed off down the other side of the road; oncoming traffic made that impossible, however, so he quickly spun the wheel the other way to mount the pavement.

With his foot pressed down on the accelerator he sped along the pavement, scattering pedestrians, who found themselves in danger of being run down. Unfortunately, the pavement was barely wide enough to take the car, and only three out of the five people put in danger by his recklessness were able to get out of the way. Two did so by darting into the shop they were passing, and the other by diving into the road, where he would have been run down anyway were it not for the quick reactions of the driver who swerved out of the way at the last instant and crashed into a car coming the other way.

The two pedestrians that failed to get out of the way in time were an elderly man, who couldn't move quickly enough, and a young woman who found herself with nowhere to go to avoid the rapidly approaching vehicle. In the end all she could do was jump up to take the impact on her legs and try to lessen her injuries.

Kieran was aware of hitting the two, he could hardly have been ignorant of doing so when the woman rolled over the bonnet of the car and up onto the roof before falling off behind it, but he paid no mind to them, and gave no thought to the injuries they had received.

He kept going without slowing until he reached the next junction. Only then did he take advantage of a gap in the traffic, which had been brought to a halt by his actions, to return to the road.

He was half a mile down the road before he thought to check his mirrors to see if he was still being followed. He was confident that his manoeuvre had left the patrol car too far back to have a clue which direction he took when he turned off the road, but when he checked he was annoyed, and more than a little angry, to see that the car, or another one, was only a short distance behind him.

A series of abrupt turns failed to lose his pursuer and he became desperate, overtaking and cutting between cars at every opportunity, and driving at speeds that would have been dangerous if he was the only person on the road.

The danger to himself and to everyone else on the road and the pavements mattered not a jot to him. All that did was getting away from the police, which he seemed incapable of doing.

There was one thing that Kieran's crazy driving did accomplish, it woke up the child in the back of the car. He announced his presence with a loud wail as he sought his mother's reassurance that everything was alright.

The sudden noise from the back seat startled Kieran, who twisted his head quickly to see what had caused it. It proved to be a bad idea. He was halfway through a turn when his attention was dragged to the back of the car, where he was shocked to see the young boy. He had no idea how he had failed to see the boy before, either when he hijacked the car or when he looked in the rear-view mirror.

Before he could even begin to think about what he could do about the boy, he caught sight of something out the corner of his eye that whipped his head back to the road ahead.

Kieran took his foot from the accelerator and pressed down hard on the brake the instant he saw the van in front of him. At the same time, he spun the wheel in a desperate attempt to avoid a collision. He was too late. The van was too close by the time he saw it, and he was going too fast to stop quickly.

To make things worse he turned the wheel the wrong way, straightening up rather than continuing the turn he was already in the middle of, which might have saved him.

The two vehicles impacted with a noisy crunch that drew the attention of everyone within a hundred yards. Some of the witnesses hurried towards the crash, and that, combined with the sight of the police car he had been trying to elude stopping a dozen or so yards away, made him panic.

Hurriedly he tried to get the stalled engine started again. Twice, three times he turned the key in the ignition without success, and on the fourth try he gave up. He might have continued trying but in the side mirror he saw that an officer had exited the patrol car and was approaching cautiously, his extendible baton at the ready.

"Get out of the car slowly, and with your hands where I can see them."

Kieran ignored the order shouted at him by the constable, just as he ignored the increasing volume of the siren that announced the approach of a second patrol car. He was too caught up with trying to work out what he should do, how he could get away, and not just in the short term but in the long term. He needed a plan, he needed somewhere he could go where the police wouldn't find him.

First, though, he needed to put some distance between himself and those who wanted to lock him up.

A renewed bout of crying from the back seat put the idea in his mind and he twisted around to reach into the rear of the car. With hurried moves, and a complete lack of concern for whether he hurt the kid, he undid the buckle that kept the boy safe in his booster seat and pulled him out.

He held the boy tight with one hand, so he couldn't wriggle free, while with the other he threw open the door and snatched up the knife he had taken from the Skinner house.

The moment the approaching constable saw the young boy in Kieran's grasp, and the knife being held to his throat, he stopped in his tracks. That pleased Kieran, it was just what he had intended, though he didn't leave things there. His eyes darted all around, searching for any other trouble, but kept coming back to the constable as he gave a command of his own.

"Ditch the baton and the radio and back up."

Kieran watched the constable do as he was told. It took him a few moments to remove the radio, by which time the second patrol car had arrived and come to a stop behind the first. Two officers got out and began to advance slowly and cautiously until they reached their colleague and saw why he was doing nothing. They immediately stopped and stared at the murderous teen, their faces revealing their uncertainty over how they should handle the situation.

Though he was now facing three officers Kieran wasn't worried, he wouldn't have even if they had given any indication of having a plan for how to deal with him for he felt confident that he had the upper hand — so long as he had the boy he was in control. He still needed to get away, though, and with another look around he made the decision about where he was going to head for.

He couldn't have said why, the idea held no logic he could identify, but he felt sure that if he could cross the bridge, which was only about a hundred and fifty yards away, and reach the other side of the river, he would be able to get away.

Slowly, Kieran backed away from the trio of officers and began making his way down the road towards the bridge. It wasn't easy for he soon found that walking backwards, so he could keep the cops in sight, was next to impossible if he wanted to remain on his feet.

After he stumbled for the third time, and bumped into his second vehicle, he changed what he was doing. Instead of watching the cops constantly and paying only occasional attention to where he was going, he turned around, so he could see where he was going and avoid walking into anything or falling over.

Doing that meant he had to keep looking back over his shoulder to see where the cops were. He didn't want to give them the freedom to get too close, though he couldn't seem to stop them following him completely.

Every time he felt they had got too close, he stopped to make a show of the knife he had pressed to the boy's throat. He drew blood the first time, and that was enough to make the cops back off each time, though they resumed following him the moment he turned his back on them again.

Kieran would have liked to stop his pursuers permanently, but he couldn't think of any way to do so without attacking and possibly killing them, and he didn't think much of his chances against odds of three to one. It wasn't just the cops he had to think about, the driver of the van he had run into was trailing after the officers, and the look on his face suggested the beefy, tattoo-covered man would like to do significant violence to him for threatening a child — the size of the muscles on his arms indicated that he wouldn't need a baton like those carried by the three officers to inflict that violence.

In this way Kieran made it about two-thirds of the way across the bridge. He was beginning to think that he was going to make it all the way across, and that he would somehow be able to get away when he got there, when a patrol car, its lights flashing and its siren loudly proclaiming its presence, came to a skidding, sideways halt a short distance away, blocking as much of the bridge as it could.

A second patrol car joined the first, while a third, arriving almost in unison with it, blocked a portion of the bridge behind him. Within moments there was a semi-circle of police officers keeping Kieran from making any more progress towards his destination.

He reacted instantly to the situation by thrusting the boy out over the railing and yelling, "Get back, all of you. Get back or I drop 'im."

His move had the desired effect, they all retreated, expanding the semi-circle, though they continued to keep him trapped. No matter which way he looked he could see no space big enough to make him think he could escape. The only possible escape route that he could see was over the railing and into the river below. He doubted that any of the officers surrounding him would follow him into the water, for the same reason that he didn't fancy taking that way out of his predicament himself.

"We can work this out, Mr Wright," a sergeant, the most senior officer in the group, said in as calm and pacifying a voice as he could manage. "Just let the boy go, there's no need for him to get hurt."

"I said back off, get the hell away from me," Kieran snarled. "Clear away or I'll drop 'im." He made as if to let go of his burden and saw the police back off further, though still not far enough to give him a way of escaping.

"Calm down, just calm down. You don't want to hurt the boy, do you? He's just a kid, hasn't done anything to anyone, least of all you," the sergeant said, hoping that he could keep the killer talking long enough for a more senior officer to arrive and take over the situation. "Let him go and let us take you in, things will go better for you if you do. It'll be better if you give yourself up."

"Better, how in hell can things go better for me?" Kieran demanded. The muscles in his arms were beginning to feel the strain of holding the boy out over the sluggishly moving river. He wasn't all that heavy, but it did require an effort to keep hold of him. He resisted the urge to bring the boy in, though, he didn't want to do anything that might give any of the officers reason to believe that he was relenting, or that it was safe for them to make any kind of move against him. "You think I'm just gonna be allowed to walk away if I let the boy go. I'm not an idiot. If I let 'im go, they'll throw me in a hole and lose the key.

"If we still had the death penalty, I'd get it."

He had stopped moving when he was surrounded, but now he began edging towards the far end of the bridge again. He wasn't prepared to make the leap from the bridge into the water, he was sure that doing that would cause him injury, perhaps even kill him. He had, however, seen something on the river that convinced him he was going the right way, and that the river was his best means of escape. He had to hurry if he was going to take advantage of what he had seen, though.

Kieran was relieved to see the officers to his left back off and give him more space as he neared them, but no matter how much space they gave him, he knew they wouldn't stop pursuing him unless he gave them a good reason to do so.

He was about a dozen yards from the end of the bridge when he decided what the reason had to be. He had been ignoring the sergeant and his continued efforts to persuade him to release the boy whose life he threatened, but now he turned back to face him.

"You want me to let the boy go?" he asked, his eyes moving around the loose semi-circle of officers, which didn't quite trap him where he was but did limit his options. He brought the boy in, so he was no longer dangling over the river, more to give his tired arms a rest than to give the cops a reason to think he was about to give up. He kept the eight-inch long blade of the kitchen knife he had stolen pressed against the throat of his hostage, who was no longer crying and wailing, because he had no more tears to shed, and because his throat was too sore for him to make any kind of noise. "Then I'll let him go."

In a move that caught all the officers by surprise, Kieran spun back to the railing and heaved. The boy went flying out of his hands and over the railing. For a moment he seemed to hang in the air, and then he plummeted towards the river.

No sooner was the boy out of his hands than Kieran ran for the end of the bridge. He barged past the nearest of the constables, who was so surprised by what had happened that he was flat on his back, with the fleeing murderer half a dozen feet beyond him, before he had any clue what was going on.

Kieran didn't dare look back to see if anyone was chasing him. He was sure if he did he would trip or fall, and if that happened the cops would be on him before he could get back to his feet. He had the knife and the extendible baton, and he was prepared to kill to get away, but he still didn't think much of his chances if it came to a fight.

That was why, when he was brought down by a flying rugby tackle, he slashed the air wildly with the knife to drive back the constable who had crashed into him, struck him a glancing blow on the side of the head with the baton and kicked wildly to free his legs.

The moment he freed himself he scrambled to his feet, so he could continue his flight towards the end of the bridge.

In addition to the constable who had tackled him, two of the other constables were closing in on him, and their proximity lent wings to his feet, giving him the impetus to run faster than he would have been able to normally.

He grabbed the railing when he reached the end of the bridge and used it as an anchor, so he could turn more quickly without losing his footing. He then rapidly descended the stairs that led to the riverbank, almost tripping in his haste.

Startled looks from the people on the riverbank, who had been watching events on the bridge as best they could, followed Kieran as he raced along the tow path. Their shock at his antics increased when he reached a small motorboat and bent to quickly release the rope mooring it to the bank before jumping on board.

A glance at the front of the boat revealed that the key was in the ignition, which meant he didn't have to try and get it from the man in the back, and he hurried that way, so he could start the engine. Given how his luck had been going, he was surprised when the engine turned over straightaway.

He didn't waste time wondering at that change in his fortunes, instead he pushed the throttle to its stops and spun the wheel to take the small boat away from the riverbank.

Within seconds the boat was a dozen yards and more out into the river, heading upstream.

"What the hell d'you think you're doing?"

Kieran spun round to face the owner of the boat — he assumed the man in the rear was the owner — and noticed straightaway the length of pipe in his hand. He didn't allow the pipe to trouble him, though, for he still had his knife and the baton.

Three quick steps brought him within striking range of the man and Kieran immediately lunged, thinking to end matters quickly. Unfortunately, he lost his footing as the boat rocked and he tumbled to what he considered the deck, enabling his target to dodge out of the way and retaliate by swinging the pipe he held.

Kieran rolled onto his back in time to see the pipe descending towards his head. Hurriedly he twisted out of the way. The pipe thudded into the deck no more than an inch from his head, making him flinch, though that involuntary reaction to the near miss didn't stop him retaliating. A wild slashing move with the knife made the man draw back, but not quickly enough. When Kieran scrambled to his feet he saw fresh blood on the blade of his weapon, and a deep cut that bled profusely on the arm of the boat's owner.

Driven on by the sight of the blood, Kieran attacked again, determined to finish the fight quickly so he could complete his escape. He lunged, seeking to plunge the blade into his target up to the handle, and when he missed because of a last-second dodge he sliced the blade through the air, hoping to open his chest from one side to the other.

A lurch of the boat knocked him off-balance and he had to throw out a hand to keep from falling overboard. He didn't cause the damage he hoped to, but he did inflict a small injury, which was better than nothing.

He recovered from his stumble to see the owner bending to retrieve the pipe he had dropped when his arm was cut, and he immediately lashed out with a booted foot. The boot caught the man in the face, knocking him backwards, and Kieran sprang forward, so he could bury his knife in the man's stomach.

Ignoring the cry of pain from his victim, Kieran yanked the blade out, causing blood to well up from the wound, and plunged it in a second time and then a third.

After stabbing the man for a fourth time he tossed the knife aside and reached down to grab him by the front of his t-shirt and heave him up. It took a fair bit of effort, both because of the size of his victim and because he had used up all the energy he had regained from his meal and his nap, but Kieran succeeded in dragging the body to the side of the boat. Once there he rolled it overboard.

He turned away before the splash came so he could hurry over to the wheel and get control of the boat, just in time it turned out for up ahead was a narrowboat. If it had taken him just a few seconds longer to get to the wheel it would probably have been too late, as it was he only just managed to avoid a collision.

Kieran spun the wheel so sharply to get out of the path of the narrowboat that the boat he was on ended up pointing straight at the bank of the river. Hurriedly he spun the wheel back the other way, so he could avoid running aground. It took him a short while to get the boat under control because he kept over-correcting with the steering, but he got there in the end.

Once he had the boat moving in a straight line up the river against the current, and he was no longer in danger of running into either the bank or anything that happened to come down the river, he settled back to enjoy the trip.

It was a pleasant afternoon, and he didn't think there was much chance of the police finding him, so he let his worries melt away while he considered what he should do next and where he should go.

21

When she caught a glimpse of the time on the screen of her mobile, Melissa was shocked to see that she had spent half an hour answering the reporter's questions. It was a long time, even longer since she had not intended answering a single question.

She was annoyed with herself. Despite not being able to remember any of the answers she had given, she was sure what she had said would not be approved of by Inspector Martins when she heard them. Whether Martins would disapprove more of the answers themselves, or the fact that she had allowed herself to be interviewed without seeking approval from a senior officer was something she was not so sure about.

Her uncertainty and annoyance combined to put her in a state on the edge of panic as she worried that the interview she had not intended giving would cause problems for her career.

She wanted advice but could not think who to turn to for it. Her mum and gran were always good sources of advice, but on this occasion, they had no experience of the type of situation she found herself in. Her second choice would have been Sergeant Mitchell, but he was dead, followed by Inspector Stevens; he wasn't dead, but he was just as unavailable because of the heart attack he had suffered.

It wasn't until she was almost at the door of the police station that she thought of someone she could call who might be able to give her advice. She should have thought of him straightaway, but it didn't really surprise her that she hadn't, she had only known him for a short while.

"Hi, Zack, you're not busy, are you?" Melissa asked when her call was answered. Unlocking the door, she slipped inside the station and hurried over to the alarm box to turn it off.

"No, I'm just deciding what to put together for lunch," Zack said. "What's up?" The anxiety he could hear in his new friend's voice told him that something was.

"I've got a problem. I've done something I probably shouldn't have, and I'm worried it'll cause me problems with the job," Melissa admitted. "I could do with some advice on a related problem as well. Well, it's not really a problem, at least not yet, but it could become one, and it's connected to something I've already been called about, and I'm sure I'll be called about again soon." She was speaking too quickly in her haste to say everything that was on her mind and she forced herself to stop and take a breath.

"Why don't we start with what you did," Zack said. He closed the fridge and then did the same for the cupboards. He couldn't make up his mind what to have so he decided to put off having anything until his appetite was a little stronger. "If we can figure out a way to fix that problem, I'm sure everything else will look better." Leaving the kitchen, he headed down the passage to the living room, where he settled himself on the pillow that was passing for a seat. "What is it you've done you don't think you should have?"

"I gave an interview to a journalist," Melissa said after a brief pause, during which she steeled herself to hear what an idiot she had been. "I didn't intend to," she went on when Zack said nothing. "He was there with a camera crew when I came out of the pub, though, and stood right in my way, with the camera in my face. I tried to avoid him, but when he told me Kieran's now kidnapped a little kid, well, somehow I ended up answering all his questions."

Zack knew he shouldn't be, but he couldn't help being amused by the worry evident in the young constable's voice. She was so eager to be a good police officer, and so concerned that she had messed that up with what she had done. Once he had himself under control, he didn't think Melissa had heard his quick chuckle, for which he was relieved, he said, "It's never a good idea to give an interview without it being cleared through your superior first, and I'm pretty sure Inspector Martins is going to be far from happy with you for doing so." He could almost hear Melissa's heart as it sank, which wasn't what he was after. "That said, you don't work for Martins, you're not part of her department, so she can't do anything to you directly, she'd have to go to the chief inspector to try and cause trouble for you, and I don't think that's likely to get her anywhere."

"So, you don't think I need to worry about the interview?"

"Probably not as much as you clearly are. Unless you said something really stupid, you'll probably suffer nothing worse than a bit of a talking to, if that." Zack was pretty sure that if she actually worked for Martins, whom he suspected was a strict person when it came to things being done without her permission, she would suffer worse than a talking to, but she was fortunate enough not to be in that position. "What's the other problem you're worried about?"

"Well it's only a matter of time before Jack Peters calls to complain about the news people outside the pub," Melissa said. "They've set up in the car park out front and he's bound to want me to get rid of them. If I don't he's likely to do something himself, and he's never been the most diplomatic of people. Trouble is, I don't know what I can do."

"Not a lot," Zack admitted. "You can move them on from the pub car park, if the landlord asks you to, but they have the right to set themselves up on any piece of public land, so long as they are not impeding a right of way or anyone's business. The chances are the next spot they choose will be right outside the police station. You're not the first person to want to get rid of nosy reporters who're being overly inquisitive, it's more hassle than it's worth, though.

"Trust me, you're better off ignoring them as best you can, and giving the same advice to the rest of the village. Only a bigger story happening somewhere else will get reporters to leave without the answers they're after before the story goes stale."

Melissa couldn't keep her disappointment from her voice as she said, "So there's nothing I can do about them. What about the journalist that's going around talking to anyone and everyone she can find that's connected to the murders? Can I do anything about her?"

"That depends, have you had any complaints about her?" Zack made a mental note to keep an eye out for anyone who looked as though they could be a journalist. He didn't fancy being interviewed, but he was more concerned with making sure that Tara was not troubled in any way. After everything she had already been through, the last thing she needed was to be hassled by a journalist looking for a story.

"Not really complaints," Melissa said, "but John Ryder, Georgina's dad, has rung to say the journalist was there. He wouldn't let her in or talk to her, but his wife was upset. Verity's really been struggling with what happened to their daughter, and this is the last thing she needed. If the journalist's already been to see them, it's only a matter of time before she gets to the Gouldings, to my aunt and uncle, and to you."

"That thought had occurred to me," Zack said. He saw Tara glance his way from the laptop, curiosity on her face as she wondered who he was talking to and what they were talking about. He was glad that she could hear only the one side of the conversation; if she could hear what Melissa was saying he was sure she would panic and become upset. "As with the other situation, there's not a lot you can do unless someone makes a specific complaint. There isn't much you can do if someone does make a complaint either, except maybe have a word and tell her to back off. She might or might not listen to you, it depends on the type of person she is. I doubt she's going to do anything that will give you cause to arrest her.

"My advice, try not to think about her. There's nothing you can do about it, so just avoid her if you can and focus on that vandalism case you've got going."

"Thanks." Melissa regretted the slightly sarcastic tone in which she said that the moment the word escaped her lips. Zack couldn't help it if she didn't like the advice he had for her, he could only give her the best advice he had gleaned from his time as a detective inspector. "Sorry," she apologised quickly, not wanting to offend him if she could avoid it. "I guess frustration and tiredness aren't a good mix, especially when I'm worried that if she finds me I'll end up speaking again, like I did with the reporter. I didn't mean to speak then, but somehow I did."

"No need to apologise," Zack told her. "After what you've been through, a little frustration and worry are to be expected. If I think of anything you can do, I'll let you know."

"Thanks." This time Melissa spoke with genuine gratitude.

"Anything going on?" Sophie asked once Zack was off the phone, by which he knew she meant was there anything they needed to worry about.

"No, not really," Zack said. It was not that he wanted to deceive his friend, far from it, he intended telling her what was going on, just not when Tara could hear. "Melissa's just been left on her own to look after the whole village, the officers up at the farm don't count," he said quickly when he saw Sophie open her mouth. "They've got their own work to do there and can't help, so she's stuck trying to take care of everything. That includes all the people who are just being nosy and trying to find out what's going on. She doesn't want to be rude to anyone and was wondering if there was any way to get them to leave her alone."

He received a hard look from Sophie, but she said nothing, so Zack thought he might have got away with it for the time being.

22

Melissa ended the call to Zack and immediately dialled another number. She cancelled the call before it could ring, though, after changing her mind about what she was doing. She was sure that DI Martins would want to know that there were reporters and a journalist in the village but was reluctant to tell her.

If she told her she would have to admit that she had allowed herself to be interviewed. She didn't fancy being reprimanded for her lack of judgement in allowing that to happen; if it was possible she wanted to put off being reprimanded for as long as possible, preferably forever.

For a few moments she just sat there, not sure what she should do next, then it came to her. She should call Natasha Greene, as she had been intending to do before she was distracted and bamboozled by the reporter outside the pub. In just a few moments Melissa had her phone to her ear and was listening to it ring as she waited for Marius Kowalski's alibi to answer, so she could establish where the stable-hand was during the night.

The phone rang for almost a minute before it was finally answered.

"Hello, Mrs Greene, I'm Constable Turner from Oakhurst Police Station. I'm sorry to bother you, but I need to talk to you about Marius Kowalski."

"Marius Kowalski?"

Melissa was not convinced by the supposed ignorance from Greene. She wasn't sure, though, if the denial of knowledge was because Greene didn't want to talk to the police about her lover, perhaps because her husband was there, or if there was another reason.

A quick glance at the clock on the wall of the office told Melissa that it was before five, which in her opinion made it unlikely that Mr Greene was home. Since that was the case she figured there had to be some other reason why Greene didn't want to talk to the police about Marius Kowalski. Most likely she simply didn't want to admit that she was having an affair.

Melissa could understand that, but it didn't help her.

"Yes, Marius Kowalski, until recently he was a stable-hand at the Jameson Riding School," she said. "I've had to speak to Mr Kowalski about an incident that took place at the riding school overnight. He claims that the two of you are lovers, and that he couldn't have been involved in the incident because he was with you all last night." Melissa didn't miss the alarm in Natasha Greene's voice as she responded to that.

"I've no idea what you're talking about, constable, or what he's talking about. I remember him, vaguely, but I never had much to do with him. I don't know why he would have said such a thing. A lie like that could be very damaging to someone in my position, and I would appreciate it if you would warn Marius of that before he decides to go telling anyone else about us." With the barest of courtesies, Greene ended the call.

Melissa felt like swearing as she stared at the now silent phone in her hand. It was as obvious to her that Natasha Greene was lying about her and Marius being lovers as it was that she was alarmed by the phone call. Even with her limited experience she could tell that from what Greene had said, especially her use of Kowalski's first name.

Figuring that out didn't help her with what the next step in her case should be, however, since Greene had made it clear that the subject of her and Marius Kowalski was not one she wanted to talk about.

It was a couple of minutes before she decided what to do, at which time she hit the redial button.

"Mrs Greene, it's Constable Turner again. Please, don't hang up," Melissa said quickly before she could be left holding a dead phone again. "I appreciate that this is not something you want to talk about, and that you are concerned that your husband may find out about this conversation. I assure you, though, that anything you say to me will be treated as in the strictest confidence, your husband will not learn of it from me." Greene remained silent, but Melissa took the fact that she had not yet hung up as a good sign. "I have no interest in what you and Mr Kowalski have been doing, beyond the fact that he has been accused of a serious crime and he has named you as his alibi for the time of that crime."

The silence from Mrs Greene continued for almost a minute. "What has Marius been accused of?" she asked finally.

Melissa could almost picture the other woman looking around surreptitiously to make sure that no-one was listening in on her conversation. "He's been accused of causing a lot of damage to the vehicles belonging to the stables and riding school. They were all seriously vandalised last night, and because of his reaction when he was sacked the Hewitts think he could be responsible.

"Mr Kowalski claims that he was at home all last night and couldn't have had anything to do with the vandalism. He also claims that you were there with him from about eight o'clock last night until around ten o'clock this morning. If you can confirm that for me, I'll be able to forget him as a suspect and look elsewhere for the person responsible."

"And if I don't?" Greene asked.

"Then Mr Kowalski will remain a suspect and may be charged, which would see him put on trial. The result of which is that he could go to jail, for up to three years. There might even be consequences for you, if it were to be discovered that you had lied."

"What do you mean?" Greene asked sharply, alarm in her voice again, stronger than before.

Melissa had been sure she would get a reaction from Natasha Greene with that, which was why she had said it. "If Mr Kowalski is prosecuted for the vandalism, and his lawyer proves that you could have provided him with an alibi but chose not to because you didn't want your husband to find out about your affair, then you could be charged with wasting both police and the court's time. Not only that but it's more likely that your husband would find out about the affair because of that than if you simply confirm Mr Kowalski's alibi to me now.

"Of course, if you aren't having an affair with Mr Kowalski, you have nothing to worry about." She felt uncomfortable as she said that. It wasn't that she didn't believe what she was saying, she knew that if Marius Kowalski did get charged with the vandalism and was put on trial, and it was proven that Natasha Greene could have prevented it, there was every chance she would be charged. Knowing it was the truth didn't stop her feeling as though she was blackmailing Greene into putting her marriage at risk.

"Yes," Greene said after a minute that seemed to last for an hour. She wanted to lie, to deny the affair and defy Marius to prove it in court if he ever ended up there, but she knew her husband, and knew he wouldn't need proof. The suggestion that she had been having an affair would be enough for him.

"Yes what, Mrs Greene?" Melissa asked. She was sure that she knew what Natasha Greene meant by 'yes', but she needed clarification.

"Yes, I was with Marius last night," Greene said with obvious reluctance. "We've been having an affair and I spent the night with him at his place. Is that it, is that everything you need, can I go now?"

Melissa would have liked to say that that was it and she could go, unfortunately she couldn't. "I'm afraid not. I need some details from you, and at some point, I'm going to need you to come down to the station and give an official statement. I'll try not to keep you any longer than necessary." She heard the sigh of frustration from Greene but ignored it. "What time did you get to Mr Kowalski's house last night?"

"About eight. It might have been a bit after, but not much."

"What did you do?" If there was one aspect of her job that Melissa didn't like, it was this, prying into people's personal lives.

"We had dinner, watched some TV, had sex, and then went to sleep," Greene said in a rush, her words almost mixing together, so quickly was she speaking, as though by saying it rapidly she could eliminate or skip over whatever she was feeling.

"Were you there all night?"

"Yes."

"What time did you leave?"

"I thought Marius told you that, I was there until about ten this morning. My husband was away on business, and my daughter spent last night at a friend's, that's how I was able to stay at Marius', and stay so late this morning. I didn't have to make sure Vanessa was up for school."

"Is it possible that Mr Kowalski could have left the house after you went to sleep?"

"No."

Melissa was surprised by how emphatically Greene said that. "How can you be so sure?"

"Because he snores," Greene answered. "I was awake half the night listening to him. If that hadn't kept me from sleeping, his bed would have. He's got to have just about the worst bed ever, there's no way I could have slept in it. And there's no way Marius could have left without me knowing about it."

"I guess that's it then, I can scratch Marius Kowalski as a suspect. Thank you, Mrs Greene, I appreciate you taking the time to talk to me." Melissa ended the call after reminding Natasha Greene that she would need to come in at some point to make an official statement regarding what she had said.

23

Kieran had been on the river for a little over half an hour when he saw the pub.

The Angler's Haunt was built right on the bank, with a beer garden where people could sit and enjoy their drinks, while watching the flowing water and the boats that travelled up and down it. He remembered the pub, he had been there several months before as part of the birthday celebrations for one of his friends.

It was one of the few occasions when his father had allowed him to go out and have the kind of fun that was normal for a person his age. Even then he had only been allowed to go on the promise that he would be home by midnight and up in the morning to complete his chores.

In remembering the pub, Kieran also remembered that the friend whose birthday he had celebrated lived near there. It would be a risk to go to his friend, but not a great one. He didn't think Brian had ever watched or listened to the news, except by accident, which meant the chances of him knowing what was going on in Oakhurst were small.

He debated with himself for only a few moments before making his mind up, which was time enough for him to travel another couple of hundred yards upriver. More importantly, it was time enough for him to follow the river round a bend and lose sight of the pub.

He started to turn the boat, so he could head back round the bend, but quickly realised that it would not be a great idea for him to disembark at the pub's small jetty. There was too great a chance that one of the people drinking in the beer garden would have seen or heard the news and would recognise him. Now that he was away, and the police were no longer following him, he didn't want to do anything that would get him spotted again.

Instead of returning to the pub, Kieran looked up and down the river to be sure he was alone and then angled the boat towards shore. Just before he rammed the bank he spun the wheel to head back out into the middle of the river and quickly jumped off the boat.

With the gap widening between boat and shore he only just managed to cover the distance and land safely. His right foot dipped briefly into the cold water before he could scramble to the top of the bank, but other than that he was okay.

He remained there while he regained his breath, watching the boat make its unmanned and unsteady way upstream. Idly he wondered how long it would keep going before it hit something or ran into one of the banks. The way the nose was angled he thought it most likely that it would hit the far bank, but that left him curious about what would happen to it after that. It didn't really matter, he decided, so long as when the police found the boat they would be looking for him somewhere other than where he actually was.

Once he had recovered from his exertion, Kieran turned away from the river and began making his way through the trees back the way he had come towards the Angler's Haunt. He had no intention of going to the pub, though the temptation to stop off for a pint or three of cider was almost overwhelming, but he needed to get close enough to it for him to remember the route to his friend's house.

He had walked from Andrew's place to the pub on the night of his friend's birthday, so he was reasonably confident that he would remember the way back to Andrew's house once he saw something that was familiar.

24

Martins' heels thudded loudly on the bare concrete, echoing up and down the corridor, as she strode along behind the prison guard. The noise only stopped when they reached the door at the corridor's end, where it was replaced by the rattle of keys, first as the guard searched for the right one, and then as the key was inserted into the lock and turned.

The next noise to fill the silence was the protest of hinges in need of oil, followed by a heavy bang as the door crashed into a metal pole that stuck up from the floor, to which the door could be secured.

"When you're ready to leave, just bang on the door," the guard said once Martins was through, he then shut the door and locked it.

Martins glanced over her shoulder at the locked door but returned her attention to the room before her almost immediately. The visiting hall was empty but for herself, a guard on the far side of the room, and the inmate she was there to see, and she strode briskly over to the lone occupied table, paying only minimal heed to the drear room.

"Hello, Mr Wright," Martins said when she reached the table where Kieran Wright's father, who was on remand for the attempted murder of Zack Wild, waited for her, watched unceasingly by the guard. "I'm Detective Inspector Martins."

"What do you want?" Glen Wright asked in a tone that added the 'hell' without the need for him to voice it.

Martins ignored the way she was spoken to. "I've been placed in charge of the situation in Oakhurst, and I'm here to talk to you about it."

"What's happened to Harrison, I thought he was in charge."

"He's in hospital," Martins said. She had decided on her way to the prison that there was no benefit to her playing coy about why she was there or what had happened, both in the village and outside of it. "He was shot."

Wright scowled at the inspector while his fingers played with the cracked and scarred face of the table that sat between the two of them. "You'd better not be looking at me. I tried to kill Wild, I'll hold my hand up to that — it was not as if he could do otherwise since he had already confessed to the attempt on the author's life and had signed a statement to that effect — but I had nothing to do with Harrison being shot."

"I wasn't about to suggest you did, Mr Wright," Martins said. "We already know who is responsible for the attempted murder of Inspector Harrison, it's your son, Kieran."

Wright was so shocked by that declaration that it was a short while before he could say anything. "That's bollocks," he snapped when he finally found his voice. "I don't know what game you're playing, but there's no way Kieran killed that inspector. He wouldn't kill anyone."

"We have proof, we have witnesses, and we have absolutely no doubts about your son's guilt."

"If you're so bloody sure it was Kieran, why the hell are you here? Why aren't you back in Oakhurst, arresting him?"

"Because your son isn't in Oakhurst, and I need your help to try and find him."

"What makes you think I'd help you arrest my own son?"

"You want to see the person who abducted your daughter and left her for dead caught, don't you?" Martins saw the perplexed look on Glen Wright's head as he nodded and realised that he hadn't worked out what the question meant. "Well your son is the one responsible for your daughter being in the ITU."

"You're out of your mind if you think that," Wright said. He surged to his feet, but quickly returned to his seat when he saw the guard move forward out the corner of his eye. "Kieran would never hurt his sister, never! Whoever tried to kill Emily raped and murdered those other poor girls, and that wasn't Kieran, that's not the kind of person he is. I don't know how Wild's convinced you he didn't kill those girls, or how he's convinced you it was Kieran, but you're looking for the wrong person."

"We're not. I appreciate that this is hard for you to accept, Mr Wright, but I need your help, and I don't have the time to sugar-coat this news. Every moment that your son remains at large is another moment in which he could attack someone else. I need to catch your son, and the quicker the better." Martins could see that Glen Wright was still not willing to accept what he was being told so she tried again, taking a different tack. "It wasn't Mr Wild who convinced Inspector Harrison that your son is the murderer he was looking for, it was your daughter..."

"Emily, she's woken?" Wright asked, a desperate eagerness in his voice.

"Not so far as I am aware. I was referring to your other daughter, Tara. She discovered that it was her brother who was responsible for the murders, and he tried to kill her to keep her quiet. Ironically, it was the man you tried to kill, Mr Wild, who saved her. He also helped keep your son from escaping when Inspector Harrison and the officers from Oakhurst went to your farm to arrest him. That is when Kieran shot Inspector Harrison and killed two of the officers with him."

"If you're certain it was Kieran, and he's already been arrested," Wright's voice was flat and emotionless, as though what he had heard had left him numb, "what d'you need my help for? Sounds like you've already got everything sorted."

"Unfortunately, that's not the case." Martins didn't like admitting what had happened but had no choice. "Kieran escaped from custody several hours ago, and has since disappeared, though not before attacking and killing several more people. His victims now include a two-year-old boy, whom he threw into a river to distract the officers attempting to apprehend him. The incident was witnessed by more than a dozen people, so there can be no doubt about what happened.

"Thanks to the bravery of two officers, who jumped into the river after him, the boy was saved, but that does not change the fact that your son is a very dangerous individual who has killed, and is clearly prepared to kill again, in order to get away."

"What d'you expect me to do about it? I'm stuck in 'ere, and even if I wasn't there's bugger all I can do."

"Actually, that's not true, there's a couple of things you can do. First off, you can tell me everything there is to know about your son, especially anywhere you think he might go, places he knows, places he's been to, holiday destinations, anywhere you think he might go to hide." Kieran Wright did not own a passport, her team had been able to discover that, so Martins thought it unlikely that the murderous teen would attempt to get out of the country, at least in the short-term. "We also need to know about your son's friends."

"Kieran doesn't have many friends," Wright said. "At least not that I know of. I don't remember him mentioning more than a handful of names, especially since he finished school, and most of them live in the village."

"That will make things easier for us," Martins remarked. She had not expected it to turn out to be the case, but she had been a little worried that Kieran Wright would have a vast network of friends and acquaintances, all of whom would need to be checked out and spoken to in case they had been contacted by the teen or they knew of somewhere he might be. "There is one other thing I'd like of you, Mr Wright," she said, sliding her notepad and pen across the table so he could begin writing down what he knew. "I'd like you to make a public appeal and ask your son to surrender himself."

Wright looked up from the notepad. "You really think anything I say is gonna convince Kieran to just give himself up? He's got to know he's gonna be spending the rest of his life behind bars. Even I can see that he'd be an idiot to just give himself up, and if he's the one nearly killed my little girl, my Emily, I want him caught."

"No, I don't imagine it will make any difference," Martins admitted honestly. "But the effort must be made. As a result of your son's actions the armed response team is on alert, if they should be on hand when Kieran is found again he could be at risk of being shot. It's in his best interests to give himself up. If he should be shot, I want to be able to prove that I have done everything possible to resolve the situation without further loss of life."

Five minutes later Martins was on her phone, reading off the names Glen Wright had written down for her, as she followed the guard who had shown her to the visitor's hall out of the prison.

"Find out everything you can about all of them," she instructed DC Reid, "and have someone check them all out to make sure Wright isn't hiding out with one of them." She was about to hang up when she thought of something else. "Call whoever's at the Wright farm and have them check whatever computers are there. We need whatever friends Wright has on social media. It's a long shot, but he may try and get help from one of them rather than from one of the real-world friends his father knows about."

"There's a problem with that, ma'am," Reid said reluctantly. "The forensics team, and the officers that were with them, have finished at the farm and are on their way back to town. There's no-one there to check the computer."

"Call that constable in Oakhurst, Turner, then and have her check the computer."

"Yes, ma'am."

25

Melissa was studying a map on the computer, doing her best to memorise the route she would have to take to get from Oakhurst to the address she had found for Ralph Graves, when two things happened simultaneously — the phone next to the keyboard rang, and someone knocked loudly on the front door of the station.

She picked up the phone and, glad that it was portable, got to her feet so she could see who was at the door. She was tempted to just ignore the door, to not even look to see who was there, but she couldn't ignore the possibility that it was someone with a problem, rather than someone wanting to know about the morning's events.

"Oakhurst Police Station, Constable Turner, how can I help you?" she answered the phone.

The moment she left the office and started down the passage, Melissa saw that it was just as well she had not ignored the person at the door. On the doorstep was not one of the villagers but a uniformed police officer, whom she hoped was the help she had been promised.

"Constable, this is Detective Reid, from Branton."

"Hi, what can I do for you? Have you caught Kieran yet?" Melissa would have had her fingers crossed, if she hadn't needed one hand to hold the phone to her ear and the other to unlock the door. Once she had the door open she gestured for the constable to enter and follow her.

"I'm afraid not, not yet anyway," Reid said, before adding quickly, "but it's only a matter of time. That's why I'm calling, we're trying to trace all of Kieran Wright's friends, so we can check whether he's been in touch with any of them and make sure they're all aware how dangerous he is. If he does get in touch, we need them to know to tell us about it, so we can catch him. We've spoken to Wright's father and got all the names he knows, but there's a good chance that Wright has online friends his father doesn't know about. We'd like you to go out to the farm and check the computers there, find out who Wright has been in contact with online, and let me know what you find. Can you do that?"

"I'll see what I can do. I can't promise anything, though, the computer might be password-protected, in which case you'll have to get a tech expert to unlock it before you can get what you want." She was prepared to put money on that being the case. She didn't suppose that Glen Wright used whatever computers were at the farm, he was much more of a practical, hands-on person and didn't have much use for technology unless it could be used to make the process of farming easier.

She was sure, however, that Kieran and his sisters would have separate accounts, especially if they had to share a computer, and would have them password-protected so their siblings could not see their personal stuff.

"Is there anything else you need me to do?"

"Not that I know of right now," Reid said. "If we think of anything, I'll call you back."

Melissa hoped nothing else would be thought of, but if it helped to catch Kieran she was prepared to do just about anything, no matter how tired she was. She put that thinking from her mind as she slipped the phone into her pocket and turned her attention to the constable she had let in.

"Sorry about that, I'm Constable Turner, Melissa."

"Browning, Phil, hi," he returned the introduction. "I was sent out here to give you a hand, apparently you're all on your own."

"Not quite, but Constable Johnson has been detailed to guard the Wright farm, so he's not in a position to help me with anything right now."

"Okay," Browning said with a nod. "So, what's the situation here? I've heard what's been on the news, obviously, but they rarely have all the details."

"I'll make us some coffee and fill you in," Melissa said, thinking that she would have to do so quickly if she was going to get out to the Wright farm and check the computers. Why Detective Reid hadn't called Johnson and asked him to check the computers, she didn't know.

As she led the way down the passage to the small kitchen, she began filling Browning in on what had happened in the village, and what the current situation was. Even condensing things as much as she felt it was possible to do without missing out any important details, it took several minutes for her to bring him fully up to date. By the time she was done they had their coffees and were seated in the back office.

"So, there you have it," Melissa said, putting her coffee down. "That's how things stand here in Oakhurst right now." She could see on Browning's face just how relieved he was not to have been in the village that morning. She could hardly blame him for feeling that way, if she had known what was going to happen that morning she would have arranged to be somewhere else, as far away as possible.

The other thing she could see on her new colleague's face was how glad he was to be in the village then, rather than in town where he might have to face Kieran Wright, which she also couldn't blame him for.

"So, the village is grieving and trying to come to turns with one of their own turning out to be a murderer, a serial killer no less; you've got reporters and journalists trying to talk to anyone who had anything to do with what happened, and you're investigating vandalism at a local stables." Browning shook his head. "I thought villages like this were supposed to be quiet, peaceful places. Doesn't sound like things have been all that peaceful."

"Believe me, this isn't how things are here in Oakhurst normally," Melissa said. "The village is usually about as peaceful as you imagine, with only the occasional drunken bit of trouble, or a dispute between neighbours."

"Thank god for that." Browning didn't fancy having to work, even temporarily, in a troubled and trouble-filled village with little in the way of backup. "So, where do we stand on the vandalism, what have we got and where do we go next?" If there was one aspect of his new assignment that he was glad about, it was the opportunity to spread his wings a little and show that he was ready for advancement.

"Right now, we haven't got much," Melissa admitted. "I haven't long eliminated one of the two suspects I was given, unfortunately it was the one with the best motive, he has a solid alibi. If you don't mind, I'd actually like you to go back to town; the other suspect I was given lives there and we need to know where he was last night." She felt a little strange, acting like she was in charge of a fellow constable, especially when that constable was at least five years older than her. She took heart, however, from the lack of concern Browning showed for the situation. "I'd go myself, but Detective Reid just called, that's who I was on the phone with when I let you in, he wants me to take care of something here in the village."

Browning nodded. "I'll have a read of the file, so I know all the details, then head off. Have you got the address where I'm going?"

Melissa copied the address, and what few details she had for the stables' former security guard, onto a fresh page of her notepad and then tore it out. Now that she had help and she didn't have to drive all the way into town to track down Ralph Graves, a task she hadn't been looking forward to, she felt better about her situation.

MELISSA WAS ON HER way up the road to the Wright farm — she was pleased to see that the crashed vehicles from that morning had been removed, though she had no idea when it had happened for she had not seen them taken away — when she thought of something she needed to do. She slowed her pace, having chosen to walk rather than drive, and turned to walk up the path to the front door of Zack Wild's house.

As she headed up the path she noted that the living room windows were still boarded up. She wondered how long that would continue for. She would have expected Zack to organised for them to be replaced, but she supposed recent events had left him too preoccupied to take care of things.

"Hello, Melissa," Zack said when he saw who was at the door. "Are you here for any reason in particular, or have you finally got some free time?"

"No, no free time," Melissa said, with only a hint of the frustration she felt in her voice. "I'm on my way up to the farm so I can find out about Kieran's friends, a detective from town called and asked for the info. I thought I'd stop off and see if Tara would like me to get anything for her. As far as I know the forensics guys and the cops from town are finished at the farm, so there shouldn't be any problems."

"That's good of you," Zack said. Stepping back, he let Melissa in and then closed the door behind her while she made her way into the living room.

"Hi, Tara, I'm heading up to the farm to do some stuff and thought you might like some clothes, so you can get out of your uniform. You might like a few of your things as well since we don't know how long you're going to be here." Melissa turned to Zack then. "Have you heard back from Tara's aunt yet?"

"Not so far. She's at least five hours behind us, though, so I don't think we're going to hear from her yet. Maybe in a few hours."

"Will I be staying here till my aunt comes and gets me?" Tara asked in a small voice that suggested it was not something she had thought about before then but was something that she was now worried about.

"That's up to you," Zack told the young girl. "I'm happy for you to stay here until we get things sorted with your aunt, if that's what you want, but if you'd rather be somewhere else, I'm sure that can be arranged." He smiled to show that he would not be offended if she chose to be somewhere else, but he wasn't sure that Tara even noticed the gesture, let alone appreciated it.

Tara shrugged. "May as well stay here," she said with a passivity that troubled Zack.

"Well I'm happy to have you," Zack said. "It's just a shame my daughter can't come and stay for a bit. She's younger than you, but I think the company would be nice."

"Now that's decided," Melissa said, "if you tell me what you want, and where I can find it, I'll bring you your things."

"MELISSA, WHAT ARE YOU doing out here?" Constable Johnson asked when his colleague arrived at the Wrights' farmhouse.

"The detectives in town want me to check some stuff out on the family's computers, I take it you've heard Kieran's escaped."

Johnson nodded. "I'm glad I'm not involved in chasing him down. I overheard some of the Branton cops talking as they left, and he's killed a bunch more people since escaping. Catching him's going to be a nightmare."

"Too right. They'll manage it, I just hope it doesn't take them too long, and he doesn't hurt too many more people before they get him. How've things been here?" Melissa asked. Looking around the yard she saw the bloodstains that gave evidence of what had happened there that morning.

"Boring, for me at least," Johnson said. "All I'm doing is standing here, waiting to stop anyone going up to the farm, not that anyone is likely to want to. There's no point in me being here, but they've told me I have to stay here 'til that Inspector Martins says I can leave. Complete waste of time if you ask me."

"Maybe not," Melissa disagreed. "There's a journalist and some reporters in the village, and sooner or later they're going to find their way up here, so you'll most likely be busy at some point."

After chatting for a little longer with her friend and colleague, Melissa left him and started across the yard to the house. She skirted the bloodstain that showed where Sergeant Mitchell had died and pushed open the door, which had a large, ragged hole in the middle, so she could enter the house.

She didn't have to go far to find the only computer possessed by the Wright family. As Tara had told her, it sat on a small table in the far corner of the living room. The moment she got her first look at the system, Melissa was sure the next half an hour and more were going to be very frustrating for her. Even the computers at the police station were not as old as the one the Wright children had to deal with.

Her fears were realised when she saw how slowly it booted up.

After about thirty seconds she decided that waiting there for the computer to load to the desktop would drive her round the bend — the system was even slower than she had thought. Instead of staying there she decided to make better use of her time by getting together the things that Tara had asked for.

She found Tara's bedroom and located the rucksack Tara used for school. She then made her way over to the chest of drawers by the window, where she began searching for the clothes Tara wanted. The teen had not been specific, so Melissa had to use her best judgement to figure out what she was likely to need.

In addition to the clothes, Melissa filled a second bag with the other items Tara had requested: her mobile phone, mp3 player, a few CDs and books, and some DVDs, as well as a few other bits and pieces.

Melissa left the bedroom with a bag in either hand, and was about to descend the stairs so she could see if the computer had finished booting up when she thought of something else Tara was going to need — toiletries. There was a wash bag in the cupboard by the sink and she stuffed it with feminine hygiene products, which she doubted Zack had. It was only when she reached for the toothbrush that she realised she had a problem.

"Hi, Zack, sorry to bother you, again, you must think I'm a right pain in the ass by now," Melissa said when he answered his phone. "Can you ask Tara which toothbrush is hers?" It only took a few moments to get the answer she needed and then she hung up, after accepting Zack's assurances that she was not a right pain.

The computer had not reached the desktop when she returned to it, but it had reached the login screen. Clicking on the icon for Kieran's account, Melissa was pleased, but surprised, to see that there was no need for a password. Pulling out the swivel chair, which looked to be even older than the computer, she sat down and got to work, opening the web browser to check Kieran's social media.

26

It took Kieran longer than he anticipated to get to his friend's house.

Not only was The Angler's Haunt farther from the spot where he had parted company with the boat then he had thought, but he got himself turned around a couple of times. He ended up walking back the way he had come for a distance before he realised his mistake.

Finally, he reached the pub. At least he got close enough to see it through the trees, and things got easier after that. He exited the woods once he was sure there was no-one around to notice him and made for the road. From there he followed the route remembered from the one other time he had been there until he reached his friend's house.

He felt a momentary panic as he got close to his destination, brought on by the sudden thought that Andrew might be at work, or his housemate might be home. It subsided as quickly as it appeared, pushed away when his brain reminded him that his friend didn't have a job to be at, and his friend's housemate was a truck driver who was rarely at home.

His concerns were further eased when he reached the house and saw that Andrew's car, the old banger he had bought before he even passed his driving test, was parked out front.

Striding up the path he rang the bell and banged on the door the moment he reached it. He rang the bell and banged on the door a second time when there was no response after a minute. It wasn't until he had done so for a third time that he heard someone come thundering down the stairs. A few seconds later the door was snatched open.

"What?" The one-word question was snapped almost before the person opening the door could see who was on the doorstep, and the moment he did his tone changed. "Sorry, Kier, didn't know it was you, I was in the middle of something."

Kieran could easily imagine what it was his friend had been in the middle of from his sweaty appearance, and the fact that he had answered the door in just his boxers. The handbag hanging on the end of the banister also helped him to a conclusion. "Didn't mean to interrupt your fun," he apologised.

"No worries. So, what're you doing here?" Andrew Westenra asked as he stepped back to let his friend into the house. "I didn't think your dad let you off the farm till it's too late to do much of anything, let alone have any fun."

Before Kieran could respond to that there was a call from upstairs, "What's going on, Andy? Are you coming back to bed?" Kieran recognised the voice of his friend's girlfriend, whom he was none too keen on. He had never understood what his friend saw in Sandra Mullins, who had been half again as big as any of the other girls when they were at school and was now even bigger.

"I'll be right there, babe," Andrew called back. "You can tell me what's going on in a bit, Kier, make yourself at home, there's beer in the fridge." He clapped his friend on the shoulder and then hurried away up the stairs, so he could return to his girlfriend.

Once his friend was out of sight Kieran gave in to the shudder he had been suppressing at the thought of Sandra naked and in bed. As he made his way down the passage to the kitchen he hoped that Sandra was not a screamer; it was bad enough that he knew what was happening upstairs, or what would soon be happening, he didn't want to hear it going on.

Thankfully, there were no cringe-inducing sounds from upstairs by the time he made his way into the living room with a bottle of beer from the kitchen. As he settled himself on the sofa he took the extendible baton and the knife from his pockets, so he could sit without stabbing himself. He stuffed them both down the side of the cushion, where they were out of sight but within easy reach.

KIERAN HAD BEEN ALONE on the sofa for somewhere around an hour, which he filled by watching music videos, when he was finally joined by his friend and his friend's girlfriend.

Andrew sat himself at the far end of the sofa, while Sandra settled herself between the two of them. Kieran was sickened to see that she had become even fatter since he last saw her, something he would not have thought possible. She was now so large that she filled up all the space between the two men, and a little more, and Kieran could feel the heat of her body through his jeans where her leg pressed against his.

He was not sure what sickened him more, her size, or the memory that he had once thought she was cute.

When he was fourteen, and she thirteen, he had been interested in Sandra. More than interested, they had dated for a short while — dating was perhaps a stretch of a description since all they had really done was find quiet places where they could make out — and Sandra had become the first girl he saw naked.

It was the sight of her naked, overweight body that had turned him off her.

It was all he could do to keep himself from snatching up the knife from its hiding place and cutting her down to a more normal size. How he managed to restrain himself he didn't know, because the urge was almost overwhelming.

"So, Kier, you wanna tell me how come you're here?" Andrew asked after a long pull at his bottle of beer. "I can't imagine your dad just let you take time off from helping around the farm. It'd be the first time ever if he did."

"He insisted on it," Kieran said, enjoying the startled look that remark drew. He had had plenty of time to come up with a reason for him being there, and so was able to deliver his lie without it sounding false. "Ollie Ryder's after me again. If this morning's anything to go by, he wants to leave me in worse shape than he did last time." He didn't like to admit that he had almost been hospitalised by his girlfriend's cousin, he still held onto the idea that he could have beaten Oliver Ryder if the fight had not been broken up by the police, but it was a situation that Andrew would understand. "Dad decided that having me away from the farm for a couple of days while things cool down is better than having me out of action for a month or more with something broken."

"What did you do to upset Georgina this time?" Andrew didn't have to think too hard to come up with a reason why Oliver Ryder wanted to beat up his friend, he remembered from school how protective Ryder was of his cousin, and how willing he was to hurt anyone who even looked at her funny.

"Buggered if I know," Kieran said with a shrug. "We had a silly argument about something, I don't remember what, and she stormed off. Next think I know, Ollie's after my head. The moment dad heard what was going on he decided the best thing I could do is get out of the village until Georgie's calmed down."

"Which she probably already has," Andrew remarked. "That girl doesn't know how to hold a grudge."

"I know. Georgie's not the problem, she most likely forgot about the argument five minutes after it happened. It's just my bad luck she must have bumped into Ollie before she did calm down. Ollie's the problem, it'll be a couple of days at least before he cools off, no matter how many times Georgie tells him to leave me alone." Kieran shook his head, as though unable to work out how his girlfriend and her cousin could be so different. "So, is it alright if I crash here for a coupla nights?"

"Sure, no worries, 's'long as you're okay with the sofa," Andrew said without hesitation.

Kieran could see that Sandra was not happy that he was being allowed to stay there. That didn't surprise him, she had hated him ever since he rejected her after seeing her naked. She had never said as much, but he suspected that she would prefer it if he and Andrew weren't friends. He ignored her, and the dark look she threw his way, though, and concentrated on the TV, it was the only way he could keep from doing something he probably wouldn't regret, but which would cause him problems of the sort he had come to his friend's place to avoid for a while.

The three of them were on the sofa for about a quarter of an hour before the adverts came on, and the moment they did Kieran's stomach rumbled, loudly.

Before she died, his mum had always said he had a healthy appetite, his dad, on the other hand, was more inclined to say he had a bottomless pit where his stomach should be. Whatever the reason, he had always eaten more than just about anyone he knew, but today he seemed to have an even stronger appetite than usual.

An advert for diet lasagne, not a meal that would normally interest him, sparked the rumbling, which drew a laugh from Andrew.

"Sounds like you could do with something to eat," Andrew said once he stopped laughing. "How about you, Sandra, d'you want something?"

That was a stupid question, Kieran thought. If there was one person who ate more than him, it was Sandra. He was hungry most of the time, but he had never known a time when she wasn't hungry.

"I could eat," Sandra said with a nod. "Are you going to cook?"

Andrew nodded. "Not sure what, but I've got a few things in the fridge I can throw together." He got to his feet and left the room, so he could make use of the one skill he possessed, the ability to take a bunch of random ingredients and turn them into something that was more than simply edible, it was delicious.

The moment Andrew left the room, Sandra snatched up the remote control from the coffee table and began flicking through the channels. Kieran was sure she didn't actually care about finding something different to watch, she just wanted to annoy him. He was determined not to give her the satisfaction of seeing that she was succeeding though.

As best he could he ignored the TV, which was displaying an ever-changing image as Sandra moved from one channel to the next, and then on to the one after that, and focused on the bottle of beer he was sipping from.

The air of indifference he had assumed vanished in an instant when Sandra came across a channel that was showing the local news. She was flicking through the channels so rapidly she barely had a chance to see what was on the screen before the image was replaced; because of that she had moved on to the next channel before she realised what she had just seen. Hurriedly she went back.

"...should see Kieran Wright they are advised to keep their distance and call the police immediately. Under no circumstances is he to be approached, he is extremely dangerous and almost certainly armed. Once again, police are on the lookout for this man..."

"ANDY!"

Sandra's frantic shout for her boyfriend became a cry of pain as Kieran snatched up the knife from its hiding place and stabbed her in the stomach. He wrenched the blade free and was about to plunge it into the bulging belly for a second time when the thunder of footsteps in the passage announced the imminent arrival of his friend.

He immediately leapt to his feet and, with an enormous effort, heaved Sandra up. At the same time, he spun her around as though she was his dance partner, rather than his latest victim, so that by the time Andrew appeared in the doorway he had her in a tight grip, the blade of the knife pressed against her throat.

"What the hell, Kier, what're you doing?" Andrew asked, coming to an abrupt stop when he saw that his girlfriend was being threatened by his friend. It took him a moment to realise that Sandra had already been injured and was bleeding profusely from her abdomen.

His girlfriend's situation, despite the severity of it, was driven from his mind as he turned to the television, sure that he had heard the newsreader wrong.

"...to say how many people Kieran Wright has killed so far, but it is believed that the teen, who began his rampage by murdering his girlfriend, sixteen-year-old Georgina Ryder, just a week and a half ago, could have killed as many as a dozen people, most of them today, following his escape from police custody..."

"No way, this can't be true," Andrew said in a disbelieving voice. "Tell me it's not true, Kier, tell me it's not true." He didn't want to think that his friend was capable of what the news was saying he had done, but the knife Kieran was holding to Sandra's throat suggested strongly that he was. His disbelief was magnified when he saw the pictures of Kieran's alleged victims that the news was showing. He knew several of them and was horrified by the thought that his friend had killed them.

"I didn't wanna do it," Kieran said. He glanced at the TV briefly, but quickly returned his attention to Andrew, in case his friend was going to try something stupid. "But those girls were a bunch of cock-teasing bitches and they got what they deserved, and those others should have left me alone. If they had they wouldn't have got hurt."

When he was able to drag his attention away from the television, which only happened when the news story changed, Andrew stared at his girlfriend and the knife at her throat. A thin red line showed that Kieran was pressing the knife into Sandra's skin hard enough to draw blood.

"There's no need for any of this," he said, distressed by the fear he could see in Sandra's face, and concerned about how badly she was injured. He could not see the wound clearly but looking at the bloody blade in his friend's hand — he was not sure he could really call Kieran a friend anymore — he was sure it was serious. "Just let her go, we won't tell anyone you were here, will we, Sandra."

Kieran's laughter was high-pitched and humourless, and tinged with madness. As he laughed he dug the knife a little deeper into Sandra's throat so that blood didn't just show in a line below the blade, it ran down her throat to stain the neck of the t-shirt she was wearing.

"D'you think I'm an idiot?" he asked, tightening the grip he had on Sandra's shoulder as though she was going to try and get away, which was unlikely since the expression on her face suggested that she was too scared to do anything. "You think I don't know you'll call the cops the moment I'm out of here."

"We won't, I promise," Andrew said, speaking as convincingly as he was able. "You think I'd sell you out, you're a mate. Come on, let me take Sandra to hospital, she's hurt. You can do whatever you want, go wherever you want, the cops'll never know you were here, I swear. I'll even give you my car, so you can get away, and some money. I haven't got much, but I know James has some stashed in his room, and Sandra's got some in her handbag, it's yours if you'll let Sandra go and leave us alone."

Kieran thought about the offer for only a fraction of a second before he nodded, once, short and sharp. "Okay, get me the keys and the money. I'll let Sandra go when I've got them, not before. And don't even think about calling the cops."

That was exactly what he had been thinking about doing once he was out of sight of his 'friend', but Andrew quickly dropped the idea. It was clear that Kieran was crazy, but it was also evident that he wasn't a complete idiot.

Andrew was sure that if he thought for one moment that the cops had been called, Kieran wouldn't hesitate to take it out on Sandra. That was the last thing he wanted, so he resolved to do no more than he had said, get the keys to his car and whatever money he could find, and hope that Kieran would let them both go once he had what he wanted. He had his doubts about that but could not see that he could do anything else other than hope.

He returned to the living room as quickly as he could, though it still took him a couple of minutes, and was relieved to see that Sandra had suffered no more harm, though her face was a mask of pain and her eyes were red from crying — her tears had created wet trails down her cheeks.

Andrew worried about the extent of the injury to her stomach, which he was sure was the cause of most of her pain. There was nothing he could do about that, though, until he was able to get her away from Kieran, which would only happen — he hoped it would happen — when he gave his 'friend' what he had in his hands.

"Here you are, I got what you wanted." Andrew held out his hands to show the keys and money.

Kieran looked at the money for several long moments as he tried to decide if there was enough for his purposes. "Bring it over here and give it to me," he ordered finally. "Slowly. Do anything stupid and you'll both regret it." The fear in his friend's eyes told him that Andrew understood what he meant and would not do anything he wasn't told to. Confident that he would soon be out of there and on his way, even if he didn't know where to, Kieran let go of Sandra's shoulder, so he could take the keys and money, at the same time he eased the blade from her throat. That was when the unexpected happened.

The moment the knife was no longer digging into her throat, threatening to cut it at the slightest movement from either her or Kieran, Sandra threw herself backwards. The move was prompted by fear, not bravery. After what she had seen and heard on the news, she was sure that Kieran was going to kill both her and Andrew, no matter how much they cooperated.

Kieran was caught by surprise by the sudden move and the two of them fell backwards, with Sandra landing heavily on top of him. Her weight driving the air from his lungs with a sharp exclamation.

Sandra wrenched the hand holding the knife away from her throat, thankful that her injuries hadn't been added to, and struggled to her feet. She had not gone more than a couple of steps when the pain from the stab wound in her stomach was driven from her mind as the knife that had been pressed to her throat was plunged into her back. She screamed so loudly she was sure everyone in the street must have heard her.

The sequence of events was so unexpected that shock froze Andrew in place. It was only when Sandra screamed, filling the living room with her agony, that he broke the stasis.

For the briefest fraction of a second, he was torn by uncertainty over what he should do, whether he should make a run for it and try to get help or try to help his girlfriend himself. The bloody knife, which Kieran raised in readiness to use again, sent him racing from the room.

It didn't surprise Kieran that Andrew chose to bolt rather than be brave, he had been the same at school whenever someone gave him trouble, but he couldn't afford to let his friend get away. Spinning Sandra away from him so she fell into the coffee table, smashing it with her weight, he darted for the door.

He hissed in pain, sure that a rib, perhaps more than one, had been broken when Sandra fell on him, when he collided with the door frame. He didn't allow it to stop or even slow him, however, there was too much at stake.

He reached the passage in time to see Andrew fumbling with the catch on the door and lunged for him. The blade of the knife he held in his right hand, which was coated with so much blood it was almost impossible to tell that it had ever been anything other than red, led the way.

The tip of the blade penetrated Andrew's back and he arched away from it, though there was nowhere for him to go other than into the door. Kieran buried the knife up to the handle in his friend, while his left hand clamped over Andrew's mouth to keep him from crying out and alerting the neighbours to the fact that something was going on.

It was pure instinct that made him cover Andrew's mouth. If anyone was home in either of the neighbouring houses, they would already have heard the screams from Sandra, which meant it could be only a matter of time before the police were on their way, and he could not afford to hang around any longer than was absolutely necessary.

Pulling the knife from Andrew's back, Kieran dragged him away from the door and threw him down the passage. He turned back to the front door then, so he could peer through the spyhole in the door, and once he was sure there was nothing for him to worry about he left it.

His intention was to head into the living room, so he could retrieve the key to his friend's car, and the money. Before he could do that, though, he saw that Andrew was crawling towards the kitchen at the far end of the passage. Abandoning his plan, he hurried along the passage to the figure on the floor.

"This is your fault, Andy, yours and hers," Kieran snarled as he bent, his teeth gritted against the pain that made him more certain than he had been before that at least one of his ribs was broken. "If you'd just behaved yourself you could have lived," he said as if he genuinely believed that he hadn't intended killing his friend from the moment he saw the news report naming him a murderer.

Grabbing Andrew by the hair, Kieran lifted his head, exposing his neck. In one quick move he stabbed down, plunging his knife into his friend's neck at the angle where it joined the shoulder. Blood spurted, narrowly missing Kieran as it rose to paint the wall. Once, twice, three times the blood spurted, leaving long jagged red lines up the wall, before the pressure dropped and the rest of the blood seeped into the carpet.

Though he wanted to, he didn't stay there to watch Andrew die, he left his twitching body to drain the last of his blood without a witness and hurried into the living room. He could not hear any sirens approaching, but he was not so stupid as to believe that that meant he was safe.

He needed to get away from there quickly if he wanted any chance of avoiding being caught. Unfortunately, he encountered a delay, or rather a distraction, the moment he entered the living room. On the TV, seeming to fill the screen, was Melissa Turner.

As if the sight of her wasn't bad enough, the constable was being interviewed by a reporter in the car park outside of Oakhurst's pub.

"...none of us had the slightest clue of the sort of person Kieran was before all of this," she was saying, "though I'm sure we'll all be thinking back over everything we saw, heard, and knew of him, looking for any clue that might have warned us."

"Is it true that you were the first of the officers investigating the case to think that Zack Wild was not the killer you were after and you needed to be looking elsewhere."

"You fucking bitch!" Kieran shouted at the TV, as though the people on it could hear him. Rushing forward he kicked at the TV. The blow smashed the screen into a spider's web of cracks that no longer showed the object of his anger, but that didn't stop him kicking the TV a second time, sending it backwards into the wall behind it. "This is all your fault," he screamed at the no longer functioning appliance. "You're as bad as all the others, just another nosy, interfering, annoying, cock-teasing bitch! If you'd just kept your nose out, everything would have been alright. I should have killed you when I had the chance."

No sooner had he said that than he knew where it was he had to go, and what he had to do. A smile lifted the corner of his mouth, but it was not one that anyone would have wanted to see, it was a cruel smile that hinted at violence and nastiness.

27

Martins was on her way back from seeing Glen Wright when her phone rang. Her immediate thought was that something new and bad had happened.

"Martins," she said once she had turned off the main road and found a safe place to park.

"Ma'am, it's Reid."

"What's happened?" Martins was sure, from the tone of Reid's voice, that she was right, and it was bad news.

"I'm at Andrew Westenra's," Reid said. "He's one of Kieran Wright's friends, I came here to talk to him about Wright, but it seems as though Wright got here first."

Martins felt her heart sink into her stomach. "What's the address?" she asked. "I'll be there as soon as I can," she said once she had it.

It took about thirty-five minutes for Martins to reach her destination, and when she did she found that the street outside the house she was after had been closed off. Yellow tape prevented anyone who didn't have permission to be there getting within thirty feet of the house, while within the taped off area was a pair of police cars, four uniformed officers, two at each stretch of tape, and an ambulance whose lights were still revolving slowly.

The fact that the paramedics were sitting in the ambulance, doing nothing, gave Martins a pretty good idea of the situation in the house.

When she made it to the front door, which stood open with a uniformed constable to one side of it, Martins found that the situation was as bad as she could have imagined.

"Reid," she called out as she stepped over the threshold, summoning her subordinate while her eyes remained on the body further along the passage and the dark red lines staining the wall above it, lines she didn't need to be told were blood. "What's the situation?" she asked when Reid appeared in the doorway of the living room.

"Not good, not good at all," Reid said with a shake of his head. Stepping back from the doorway, he made space for Martins to enter the room. "It's impossible to say why Wright came here. He might have been looking for somewhere to lay low for a while, or he might have been after help, money or something, or it might have been something else entirely. Whatever it was, the result is clear.

"The body in the passage is that of Andrew Westenra, we found his driver's licence in a wallet upstairs and were able to identify him from that. Similarly, we id'd this lady," Reid gestured to the body on the floor of the living room amid the ruins of the coffee table, "from the driver's licence we found in the handbag on the bannister. I'm assuming she's Westenra's girlfriend, because she doesn't live here. According to her licence she lives over on St Michael's Avenue.

"Westenra was stabbed in the back, and then again in the neck. The second wound was the fatal one; I'm sure you saw the blood on the wall of the passage as you came in."

Martins nodded. "Hard to miss. What about the woman?" As hard to miss as the blood in the passage was the bloody wound in the abdomen of Sandra Mullins and the cut to her throat. "How did she die?" She supposed the stomach wound might be the cause of death, but she doubted the injury to her throat was; it had bled but appeared too superficial to have been fatal.

"Bled to death, like Westenra, though not as quickly. That's not official of course, we'll still need a post-mortem. She was stabbed twice, just like him, once in the stomach and once in the back. Westenra was already dead by the time I got here with Constable Yeardley, but Mullins was still alive, just." Reid glanced at the body, a look of regret and disappointment on his face. "We did everything we could, but she died before the ambulance got here. The paramedics did their best to revive her but no luck, they declared her dead ten minutes ago."

"I can't believe Wright managed to kill both of them without making any noise," Martins said. She looked around the living room for a moment before moving to squat at the side of Sandra Mullins' body, so she could take a closer look at the cut on her throat. "Were there any reports of trouble before you got here?"

"No, nothing." Reid shook his head. "But there's no-one home on either side to have heard anything. I assume they're at work."

"So, we don't know when this happened, or even if it definitely was Wright."

"We don't know exactly when it happened, that's true, but we can be reasonably certain it was Wright."

"How's that?" Martins asked.

"This was down the side of the sofa." Reid produced an evidence bag which held an extendible baton. "It needs to be checked for prints, of course, but we know Wright took the baton from the officer he killed at the hospital. It'd be a bit of a stretch for a baton to be here without Wright being involved in what happened."

"That's true enough," Martins admitted. "So, we can be pretty certain Wright was here, and it can't have been that long ago." She was sure it must have taken a while for Wright to get there from where he was last sighted on the river. "You said Westenra has a driver's licence, does he have a car?"

"I'll find out straightaway," Reid said, kicking himself mentally for not thinking of it himself. He took out his phone as he stepped away from his superior, so he could call the station and get the answer to the question. It took him less than a minute. "He's the registered owner of a blue Ford Escort. I've given orders for the description to go out to all patrols — it's not outside so I assume Wright's taken it."

"Seems likely," Martins said, a little annoyed that the alert had been delayed because Reid hadn't thought of something as simple as checking whether Wright could have stolen a car. "We'll just have to hope that someone sees him soon." She debated for a moment whether to have the car's description released to the public via the news stations but decided against it. She didn't want to have to worry that Wright would hear the news and ditch the car in favour of a vehicle they didn't know about. "What happened to the TV?" she asked, switching tracks, both mentally and verbally, as she sought to make sense of what had happened at the house.

"It looks like it came a cropper when Mullins was killed," Reid said, sparing the broken TV a quick glance. "Hopefully forensics will be able to tell us once they've been through the room. They should be able to give us a narrative of what happened."

Martins had her doubts, not that forensics would be able to figure out what had happened, but that the TV had been broken when Mullins was killed. She could not have said just then why she doubted that, but she did.

28

When she reached the path that led to the front door of Zack's house, Melissa found a stranger on the doorstep. Even before she heard what the lady was saying, Melissa guessed that she was the journalist she had been called about.

"...sure you won't speak to me, Mr Wild? This is a big story and getting bigger every hour if what I hear from town is true. There are already news crews here, it's only a matter of time before more arrive, and more journalists like me, and most of them won't be as considerate of the feelings of those they speak to," Louisa told the author. "They're all after this story, and they won't stop until they've got every angle of it they can from everyone even remotely involved with the murders. And you're more than just remotely connected to them if what I've heard is right."

"I don't care how many journalists or reporters come knocking," Zack told her. "They'll all get the same answer I've given you. I've got nothing to say, now or in the future."

"Do you think they'll just accept that?"

"They'll have to, it's the only response they're going to get from me, now will you please leave, or do I have to ask Constable Turner to escort you from my property?"

Louisa glanced over her shoulder, following Zack Wild's eyes, and saw the constable. "I'll go," she said without protest, accepting that to do otherwise would only make it harder to get the interview she was after. "You'll talk to one of us eventually, though, as will you, constable, and someone will talk to Tara Wright as well — I know you're looking after her. When you do, you'll realise that I'm the best choice, I'll treat you far better than any of the others will."

Zack watched the journalist until she disappeared behind the hedge that separated his front garden from the pavement. Only then did he step back from the front door, so Melissa could enter with the two bags she had brought from the farm. He closed the door the moment she was inside, in case Louisa Orchard had stopped the moment she was out of sight and was planning on running back up the to push her way inside. Not that he thought that likely.

"I take it that's the journalist I've been getting calls about," Melissa said as she carried the bags into the living room.

"I'd guess so," Zack said. "She seemed more pleasant than the average journalist, so I'd watch out if I were you." He saw the curious look Melissa threw his way. "It's easier to ignore the rude journalists than it is the ones who are pleasant and polite. If they're rude to you, you can be rude to them in return, which frequently gets rid of them, but you can't do that with the ones that are polite, not if you're a generally decent person, and they use that to get you to talk to them. That and surprise questions, as you've already learned."

Melissa flushed at the reminder of the interview she had given earlier but didn't comment; she couldn't deny that that was how she had been tricked into opening up. "So how do I deal with her the next time she finds me?" she asked. "Even if she doesn't find out where I live, which won't be difficult for her, all she's got to do is stakeout the station — I've got to go back there some time, which I'm sure she realises."

"Just refuse to speak," Zack told her. "If you can't say nothing, say 'no comment' and refer her to Inspector Martins. Whether it's her, or another journalist, they'll get the message sooner or later, especially since they'll know that as a constable there's every chance you don't know a lot and aren't allowed to speak about an active case. They'll give up on trying to talk to Tara pretty quickly for similar reasons; hassling a child for an interview would make them look bad, and without parental permission they wouldn't be able to use it anyway."

"So it's just you that really has to worry about the journalists and reporters." That didn't seem very fair to Melissa.

"Of the people here, yes," Zack said with a nod. "But I'm not the only one in the village. Anyone who's got a connection to what happened here in Oakhurst, no matter how small, is someone the journalists and reporters will want to talk to."

"What do we do about it?" Melissa couldn't think of a solution, but she hoped there was one.

"There's not a lot we can do," Zack told her, dashing her hopes. "They'll lose interest sooner or later, we can only hope it's sooner." What he didn't say was that their best hope of being forgotten by the news media was some other serious crime happening elsewhere, and he sincerely hoped that would not happen.

29

His eyes darting left and right Kieran searched the car park, both for somewhere to park — what better place, he had realised, to hide the car the police would be looking for soon, if they weren't already, than amongst hundreds of others — and for a replacement vehicle.

It would be so much better, he thought, if he could hotwire a car, but that was something he had not the first clue how to do.

He also kept an eye out for security guards, or anyone else who might observe what he was up to.

Nothing that was a cause for concern caught his eye by the time he found a vacant parking space. There were several, for the car park was far from full, but he ignored the first few he came to because they were all together, and he didn't want to leave the car noticeable by its isolation. He parked between a burgundy Vauxhall and a beige Skoda and settled down to watch for a likely target.

He had an idea of what he was after, but it was almost ten minutes before anything appeared.

No sooner had the radio announced that it was time for the five o'clock news, the day had disappeared on him in a way he would not have believed possible, then he saw what he was after. Behind him, on the other side of the double line of cars, a woman, she looked to be middle-aged, not that that mattered, stopped a trolley filled with carrier bags at the rear of a grey Ford Focus.

When he was sure that she was at her car, Kieran turned off the radio and got out, taking the still bloody knife from the pocket of the door at his side as he did so.

He left the car that used to belong to his friend unlocked, and with the keys in the ignition, as he walked away from it. He didn't know what the chances were that a car thief operated there — he had heard that car parks attached to shopping centres were prime targets — but if one did he wanted it to be as easy as possible for the car to be stolen.

Kieran's eyes searched his surroundings unhurriedly as he approached his target, the knife held out of sight at his side. He was ready to abort at the first sign of a witness, ready to simply duck away between cars and be gone before anyone could get a good look at him, but he was glad that that did not prove necessary.

The woman he had targeted remained unaware of his presence until the last moment. She was too busy moving the bags of shopping from the trolley to the boot of her car to notice him.

With a last look around he brought up the knife, so he could plunge it into the woman's back. At the same time, he clamped his free hand over her mouth to keep her from crying out and drawing attention to them.

He twisted the knife, worsening the wound he had caused, as he pulled it out and shoved his victim forward, bundling her into the boot of her own car. He was a little concerned that when he took his hand from her mouth the woman would cry out or make some other noise. He solved the problem by pushing her face into her shopping and slamming the boot so any noise she did make would be muffled.

He shoved the trolley away, tossed the last bag from it onto the back seat, and then slid behind the wheel so he could start the engine and reverse out of the parking space.

With a new vehicle, one the police didn't know about, he felt confident in succeeding with the tentative plan he had come up with. The plan was not going to get rid of the cops entirely, that was unlikely to happen unless he could somehow get abroad, but it would at least get him revenge on those responsible for his problems.

30

"There you are, Martins," Detective Chief Inspector Collins said when his subordinate entered the office. "Have you made any progress in finding your murderer yet?"

Martins could tell from the tone in which the question was asked what answer her superior wanted, unfortunately it was not the answer she was able to give. "I'm afraid not, sir," she admitted. "We're no closer to catching Kieran Wright than we have been at any point today. We've had a few close calls, but somehow this guy keeps getting away."

"How do you explain that?" Collins wanted to know. He was far from happy with the situation.

"I can't, sir," Martins said, trying not to sound as defeated as she felt. She had always prided herself on only being associated with cases that she could solve quickly, and which would help her in her rise to senior rank; the Wright case threatened to derail her career however. "There's no good reason for him to be able to keep getting away like he does. He's of no more than average intelligence, and not especially skilled at anything. As far as I can tell he just seems to be having a lot of good luck, and us a lot of bad. It's that, and the fact that he is clearly prepared to be violent at any opportunity, and he doesn't care who he hurts or kills.

"It's only a matter of time before we catch him, though."

"And in the mean time he's going to keep on killing people. How many is it he's killed now?"

Martins had to think about that for a few moments while she mentally added up the bodies that Kieran Wright was responsible for. "A dozen, sir, that we know of."

"He's killed a dozen people, most of them today." Collins wanted to throw his hands up in despair. "You do realise that that makes him one of this country's worst killers, certainly from recent years, not counting terrorists. I'm sure you can imagine what tomorrow's headlines are going to be when the press realises what he is responsible for, if they haven't already. You've had the armed response team on standby all day, how is it you haven't managed to catch him? And don't tell me luck, it shouldn't be this difficult to catch one killer, a killer we have identified, a killer who is nothing more than a teenage farmer's son."

"If we could corner him long enough for the armed response team to get there, we'd have him. The trouble is, we haven't been able to. We've got no idea where he's going, we're not sure he does either, so we can't set a trap for him, and we're restricted on what we can do. We're doing our best to head him off and surround him when we get a sighting, but that's not easy.

"The one time we were able to do that he had a hostage and was able to escape before the armed response team could get there. They were only a minute or so away when he threw the kid over the bridge and escaped."

"I was told there was more than half a dozen officers on the bridge for that incident, surely that should have been enough to stop him getting away." Collins simply could not believe that Wright had been able to escape when faced with odds of six to one. It was the incident that was causing him the most trouble, both from the media and from his superior, Superintendent Unswell.

"If it hadn't been for the boy Wright was holding hostage, I'm sure they would have been," Martins said. She had spoken to the officers who were on the bridge, and while she was frustrated that Wright had not been caught, she could hardly complain about the decisions made by them. "They couldn't ignore the threat to the kid. I don't even want to think about the kind of press we'd be looking at if they had, and they definitely couldn't ignore it when he dropped the kid into the river."

Collins scowled. "I know that, but it doesn't help us. We need to catch him, and quick. He can't hide from us forever, can he?" He was relieved to see his subordinate shake her head. "So, what are you doing to find him?"

"We're contacting all of Wright's friends and social media contacts to be sure they know he's dangerous. We have no reason to think he'll go to any more of his friends after what happened at Andrew Westenra's, but we want to be sure that if he does we'll hear about it. And we're searching for Westenra's car, which we believe Wright stole after killing his friend. On top of that I've got the tech guys monitoring all of Wright's social media accounts in case he should try and get in touch with someone that way. We're also trying to figure out what he might be intending to do.

"To be honest, I don't think he has any clue what he's going to do. If he wanted to get out of town he could have managed that already. I suspect he's afraid of going too far from anywhere that is familiar to him."

"Have you put out an alert for the vehicle you believe he's driving?"

"Yes, sir. I've made sure all patrols know what vehicle we're looking for, and they've all got orders to watch it discreetly, if they can, after reporting its location. They also have orders not to approach without backup."

"What about the media, have they been notified?"

"No, sir."

"Why not?"

"I don't want Wright to know that we know what vehicle he is using," Martins said. "If he knows we're looking for the car he took from his friend after killing him, there's a chance he'll dump the car and get another one, perhaps at the expense of someone else's life. If that happens we'll be back to square one, with no idea where he is or what vehicle he is using."

Collins thought about that for a moment before deciding that it made sense. Despite that he disagreed with the decision. "Get the car's description out to the media. I heard what you said," he told Martins, holding up a hand to forestall whatever it was she was about to say. "And you may be right, but I think it's a risk we have to take. The patrols we have out there don't cover enough of the town to be as effective as either of us would like — it's not something I'm going to go telling the media, but it's the truth, and we both know it. We need the extra eyes that telling the public will give us. It's far more likely that a civilian will see the car than one of our patrols."

"Yes, sir," Martins said reluctantly. "I'll get right on it."

31

Melissa was enjoying some down time — enjoying was perhaps not quite the right word since she was still at the station, filling out the paperwork to bring her vandalism case up to date, but it was better than how most of her day had gone — and considering calling it a day and going home when the phone rang.

A little hesitant after fielding several calls from journalists who wanted to know about recent events in the village, she answered the phone.

"Oakhurst Police Station, Constable Turner speaking, how can I help you?"

"I'd like to report a domestic disturbance."

"What sort of domestic disturbance?" she asked.

"It's my neighbours," the woman, whose voice Melissa didn't recognise, said. "There's been a lot of shouting, and what sounds like smashing plates and slamming doors."

"What's the address?" Melissa pulled a scrap of paper towards her and picked up a pen, so she could scribble down what she was told. "And what's your name?" The phone went dead in her hands at that, which didn't surprise her. It had been common when she worked in town for people reporting a domestic disturbance to not give their name or address because they didn't want to become too closely involved.

Remembering the domestic disturbances she had dealt with before, she found herself unwilling to head off to the address she had been given on her own. It was not that she was scared, she told herself quickly, just cautious, and with good reason; she had seen first-hand that the perpetrators of domestic violence were likely to lash out at anyone who annoyed or angered them, even if that person was a police officer.

Knowing that, she knew it was not a good idea for her to go and deal with the situation without help. The problem was she had no help to take; Constable Browning hadn't returned from questioning Ralph Graves about the Jameson Stables' vandalism, and Johnson was still guarding the Wright Farm. The only other option was to request help from town, and that would take at least an hour to get there, which could prove fatal for whoever was the subject of the domestic disturbance.

Half a minute or so after the end of the phone call, which was about all the time she felt she could spare for thinking, Melissa realised that there was an alternative to taking uniformed help. It was not exactly conventional, and she was far from sure that her idea would be approved of by a senior officer, but she felt as though she had little in the way of choice.

"Zack, it's Melissa, sorry to bother you, yet again," she said when her call was answered.

"That's okay, what can I do for you?" Zack didn't mind the number of calls and requests for help he had received from the young constable — he suspected another was in the offing. Given that she was working on her own, without even the benefit of a superior officer to turn to for advice, it would be unkind of him not to aid her in whatever way he could. He did hope, though, that the situation in the village would settle down soon so he could return to the peaceful lifestyle of a writer he had been trying to live before Kieran Wright turned murderer.

"I've just received a report of a domestic disturbance. It sounds like someone is having a major go at his wife or girlfriend. Would you mind going with me to check it out?" Melissa asked. "I could go on my own," she said quickly, "but I'd rather have backup, just in case there's any real trouble to worry about, and it will take too long to get any from town."

Zack barely had to think about that, though he did glance briefly at Tara and Sophie. He saw no reason why they couldn't be left so he said, "Sure, I'll be there as soon as I can. Do you want me to meet you at the address or at the station?"

"I think it'd be best if you meet me at the station, so we can go there together," Melissa said.

"Okay, I'll be right there." Hanging up, Zack turned to Sophie, who was looking at him, the expression on her face telling him that she already had some idea of what he was going to say. "That was Melissa, she needs some help with a domestic disturbance call. Will you be alright if I go out for a while?"

"Of course. What do you think's going to happen?" Sophie asked, though she didn't wait for an answer because she doubted he had a sensible one to give. "Anyone would think you're still part of the service, though. You're a civilian now, remember, it's not your job to be going out on domestic disturbance calls anymore, even if you miss it."

"If you think I miss being a detective, then you're crazy," Zack said as he grabbed his keys and wallet, the two things, along with his mobile phone, he always made sure to take with him whenever he left the house. Despite the certainty with which he spoke, he was not sure that he had convinced himself, let alone Sophie. He was happy with his new life as a writer, but whether working on a novel in his detective series or looking into an unsolved case for a true crime book, he could not deny that he missed his former job as a detective inspector. It was a job that he had left more out of practicality than desire. "I'll be back as soon as I can. If I'm lucky this won't take long."

He took his car down to the police station. It didn't save him any time over walking there, but it did save him the strain that walking would have put on his back. He had been lucky enough not to have too much trouble with the various injuries he had received during the investigation into the murders up to that morning but now, as though his body had decided to shrug off the painkillers he was taking, he could feel an ache in his back and arm and the occasional sharp twinge.

Another consideration that made him take the car rather than walk was the leaden sky overhead, and the intermittent rain that threatened to become a downpour. The weather people had been predicting a storm since morning, but the gathering clouds were the first sign that they might be right.

MELISSA WAS WAITING for Zack when he got to the station and quickly led him from his Aston Martin, which she cast admiring, jealous eyes at, to her far from exciting means of transportation. She wanted to suggest that they go to the domestic disturbance in his car, but thought better of it, doing so would be pressing her luck, especially since her only reason for even thinking of it was that she wanted to find out what it felt like to ride in such a nice car.

"I'm really sorry to get you involved in this," she said as she drove them away from the police station. "They did send me a constable to help out, but he's back in town trying to find a suspect in the vandalism case, so I'm on my own again for the time being, since Adrian still hasn't been told he can stop guarding the Wright Farm."

"Don't worry about it, I'm happy to help out, though I'm not sure your superiors will be all that pleased when they find out you've been getting help from a civilian." Zack knew what he would say if he was still an inspector and he learned that one of his officers had involved a civilian in a case without authorisation, but as both a civilian and a former inspector, he could see why Melissa had asked for his help — she had no alternative.

What had begun as just a few spots per minute became a downpour that was only a little short of torrential by the time they reached their destination, one of the better neighbourhoods outside of the village.

Reluctantly they got out of the car and darted up the path to the front door, where Melissa rang the bell, and then rang it again when they got no answer. Only when the bell had been sounded for a fourth time did they receive any indication that someone was coming to answer it; the light shining through the small coloured window at the top of the door had already told them that someone was home.

"Hello, Mrs Greene is it?" Melissa asked of the woman whose face appeared in the gap when the door was opened a crack. "I'm Constable Turner, this is Mr Wild — she was relieved when nothing was said about the fact that she was accompanied by a civilian — we've received a report of a domestic disturbance at this address, is everything alright?"

"Y-yes, everything's okay," Mrs Greene said in a voice that shook a little too much to be convincing. "Th-thanks for checking but everything's fine."

Melissa couldn't help thinking that she knew the voice and the name from somewhere. She was too concerned by what she recognised as the beginnings of a black eye to give much thought to where she knew the voice from, however. Not only had the woman's eye started to swell shut but there was bruising all around it, and marks that Melissa felt confident in identifying as defensive wounds on her hand and arm. It was clear that the domestic disturbance had gone beyond angry words and a few smashed dishes.

"Would you mind if we came in for a moment, Mrs Greene, just so we can take a look around and make sure everything is alright."

Mrs Greene looked unhappy. "There's no need," she said quickly. "Really, everything's fine, it was just a little argument. I don't know who called you, but they've wasted your time."

Melissa offered a small smile. "I'd rather be called and have my time wasted than not be called when something happens. We'll only be a few minutes, but we need to make sure everything's okay." For a moment she thought the door was going to be shut in her face, but then it was opened wide as Mrs Greene stepped back. "Thank you."

The door was shut the moment both Melissa and Zack were inside to keep out the rain, which was heavy enough that it had left them both soaked despite the relatively short time they had been on the doorstep. Mrs Greene then steered them into the living room, which Melissa noted with a tinge of jealousy was both more pleasant and more expensively furnished than where she lived.

"Who reported there was a domestic disturbance here?" Mrs Greene asked.

"I can't reveal that," Melissa said, not that she could have if she was willing to. "Who were you arguing with?" she asked as she looked around the living room for any evidence of the dispute that had been reported, evidence beyond the state of Mrs Greene's face, which she could now see included a bloody lip, making it clear that she had been hit at least twice.

Melissa found what she was looking for when she glanced through the archway that led into the dining room. She guessed that the table, a medium-sized affair made of a varnished dark wood, had been set for dinner when the argument erupted. One place-setting was still there, awaiting a meal that was most likely not going to appear, while the rest of the crockery, and some glassware, was in pieces on the floor.

"My husband," Mrs Greene said, before adding quickly. "It was nothing, though, just a disagreement. I don't even remember what it was about." She flushed, as though she realised how unconvincing her words were.

"It doesn't look like just a disagreement," Melissa said, her eyes on the remains of what she suspected had been some quite pricey china. "He hit you, didn't he."

Mrs Greene's hand went to her face, perhaps to try and conceal her injuries, which, fortunately, were relatively minor, especially when compared with those Melissa had seen recently. Her hand stopped before it got to either her lip or her eye, hesitating in mid-air for a moment like she had been struck by indecision, and then slowly lowered. The look on her face made it clear that she had realised that it was pointless for her to try and conceal what her husband had done, the damage had already been seen.

She nodded.

"He's got angry before, lots of times. It seems like he can always find a reason to get angry. It's like I can't do anything right, no matter how hard I try, but he's never hit me before." There was an air of resignation about her, but also of relief, as though she was glad to finally be able to talk about her situation. "He's normally careful to avoid having a go at me when Vanessa is around, but this time he didn't seem to care whether she saw or heard him."

"Vanessa is?"

"Our daughter."

"Where is she now?" Melissa wanted to check that she was alright and hadn't been traumatised by witnessing a violent argument between her parents. "How old is she?"

"Seventeen, and she's out," Mrs Greene said. "She went out before he hit me, she went out not long after her father started shouting at me."

"So she wasn't hurt."

Mrs Greene shook her head. "No, her father would never hurt her," she said as though she had not only just said that until today's incident her husband had never hit her.

"That's good." It was only a small comfort to Melissa that there had been only the one victim of Mr Greene's anger, but it was a comfort nonetheless. "Where's your husband now?"

"No idea. He went out after throwing the plates and hitting me," Mrs Greene said. "He didn't say where he was going, but he rarely does. He's probably gone to the golf course to have a few drinks, that's where he usually goes when he needs to calm down."

Melissa was not entirely convinced by what Mrs Greene had said, there was something about the woman's demeanour that suggested she had a better idea of where her husband was than she claimed, and it was not the golf course.

"What exactly happened tonight?" When she heard Greene's response Melissa realised with a sinking feeling that she did know her.

"He got a phone call not long after he got home from work, I don't know who it was from," Greene said, pre-empting the next possible question. "Whoever it was, they told him I was having an affair. They knew all about it. They told him who I've been seeing, they even told him I was with Marius last night. He was so angry when he got off the phone; I've never seen him so angry.

"He didn't even ask if it was true, didn't give me a chance to try and deny it, he just started calling me a slut and a whore, and anything else he could think of. Vanessa asked him what was going on and he snapped at her, that's when she went out. The moment she was gone he started throwing things. I tried to calm him down, and that's when he hit me." Tears were running down her cheeks by this point as she recounted, between sobs, what had happened. "He kept calling me names and telling me how horrible I am, and how I don't deserve everything he does for me. Then he left. I thought he was going to hit me again, he looked like he wanted to, but he just said he was going to show me what happens to people who make a fool of him and stormed out.

"Who could have told him about Marius, especially about last night? I've always been so careful."

Melissa restricted herself to shrugging, afraid that she would give herself away if she tried to respond to the question verbally.

"Are you sure your husband went to the golf course?" Zack asked, speaking for the first time since arriving at the house. Like Melissa, he suspected that Mrs Greene had not told them all she knew. "Is it possible that he has gone to find this Marius and, to quote you, 'show you what happens to people who make a fool of him'?"

"How would he know where to find him? I wouldn't tell him."

"So he asked where Marius lives."

"Maybe off whoever called him."

Zack and Melissa spoke at the same time, their words mixing.

"Do you know where this Marius lives?" Zack asked, a note of concern in his voice.

"Do you think Thomas is going to attack him?" The alarm that thought inspired got through Greene's sobbing and she stared at the two before her with wide eyes.

Zack nodded. "I think it's a possibility given what has happened here. Can you tell us where he lives, and how to get hold of him? I think we need to check on him and make sure he's alright. Will you be alright if we do that?" He didn't want to go off and leave someone who had been the victim of domestic violence on their own if she didn't feel safe, especially when her husband could return at any moment. The problem was, Melissa had no support to send to check on Marius, whose last name he didn't know, in their place.

"Yes, I'll be fine." Greene did her best to sound as though she believed what she said. "I'm sure when Thomas gets home it'll be just like every other time he's got angry about something. He'll be very sorry, and will apologise for everything, then he'll offer to take me away somewhere or buy me something to make up for it. If he's drunk, or still angry, I'll just lock the door, he can find somewhere else to sleep. I'm sure he won't have a problem managing that." She gave them the address and contact details for Marius Kowalski then.

"OKAY, WHAT'S GOING on, Melissa?" Zack asked once they were back in the car and heading down the road.

"What do you mean?"

Zack admired her attempt to sound innocent and confused, but he had seen and heard people trying to be just about everything a person could be over the years, so he was experienced in telling when a person was lying. "You know something about that domestic disturbance, what is it?"

Melissa hesitated, and then grimaced as she accepted the inevitable. "I think I'm responsible for the husband hitting her," she said.

"Why do you think that?" Zack didn't look at Melissa, he was too busy peering through the windscreen in an effort to make out the road ahead. It was a task that was made almost impossible, despite the headlights that Melissa had on high-beam, by the lashing rain that had soaked them to the skin.

The only thing that could make the evening more miserable...before he could finish that thought everything outside the car was illuminated by a bolt of lightning that reached down from the heavens. The lightning was followed a few seconds later by thunder that rumbled distantly like the stomach of some hidden giant. Zack hoped Sophie and Tara were okay, and that the boards covering his broken windows would not be affected by the storm.

"Natasha Greene is the alibi of the stable-hand I spoke to earlier about the vandalism at the Jameson Stables," Melissa told him as she too strained to see the road through the rain.

She doubted she had to worry too much about oncoming traffic, only an idiot would be out in such conditions without a very good reason, but there was still the chance that something could end up in the road. If something did and she didn't see it soon enough, she would crash, something she wanted to avoid. That was why she was creeping along at barely fifteen miles an hour.

"I called Mrs Hewitt earlier to tell her that Marius Kowalski was no longer a suspect, and to see if she had thought of anyone else who might be responsible for the vandalism. She wanted to know why he wasn't a suspect anymore and I made the mistake of telling her. I know it's not really an excuse, I messed up, but I'm so bloody knackered it's hard to think straight.

"Marius told me that Mrs Hewitt made up an excuse to sack him because he wasn't interested in her, and I think she called Mr Greene and told him about the affair because she was pissed off about it. If you're right about Mr Greene going looking for Marius so he can beat him up, that's probably what Mrs Hewitt was after, revenge against Marius for rejecting her. I guess Mrs Greene has too much on her mind with what's happened tonight to remember that I was the officer she spoke to earlier about Marius and the stables."

Zack was silent for a few moments as he watched the rain beat against the windscreen with such ferocity that it was hard for the wipers, even working at maximum speed, to keep the glass clear.

"You definitely messed up," he said finally. "There's no denying that." Out the corner of his eye he saw Melissa's face fall, it was clear that she had been hoping for some reassurance from him. "But under the circumstances, I don't think anyone can really blame you. You've had a busy week, and a hell of a last twenty-four hours, and you're working with barely any support. Mrs Greene has been hurt, and if she makes a complaint something could come of this, but she wasn't hurt badly, and I don't think anyone's going to want to punish you for this mistake after you helped to catch a serial killer this morning." He offered Melissa a small smile, which helped to alleviate the worst of her self-recriminations. "If anything does come of it, it probably won't be anything worse than an informal caution to be more careful about what you say to people, and to treat this as a lesson to learn from.

"Just be thankful that Mrs Greene wasn't hurt more seriously, and the daughter was only shouted at."

32

Paul Maitland wandered up and down the rows of cars occupying the car park attached to the large Asda situated just outside of Branton town centre.

A casual observer might not have realised what he was doing, but a security guard almost certainly would, which was why he kept an eye out for anyone in a uniform. He was a thief who made a living stealing from cars, often making as much in a week as he could from a regular, full-time job.

A blue Ford Escort caught his eye and he looked around quickly. When he was sure that he was unobserved he slipped down the side of the car, so he could look through the windows. It was the kind of vehicle with which he had had a fair amount of success in the past — he would have preferred to target more expensive cars, he could make more money, and quicker, by doing so, but they were harder to get into, and the police were more likely to pay attention to reports of BMWs and Mercedes being broken into — and he had his fingers crossed that he would be successful again as he bent to look in the back.

There was nothing of interest in the back seat, or the shelf behind it, and he couldn't see anything hidden under either the driver's seat or the passenger's. He suspected he had made a bad choice and would have to find another likely vehicle, nonetheless he moved on to check the front of the car. That was when he got a surprise.

The driver's door was unlocked. It was a little surprising, but it was not the first time he had found a car that someone had forgot to lock. The bigger surprise was seeing that the keys had been left in the ignition. That was something he had never come across before and he had to look twice to be sure he had not imagined things.

Paul had to think about his discovery for a short while before he made up his mind about what to do. He had never been a car thief, he was a thief who stole from cars; despite that he could not help thinking that he should take advantage of the opportunity that had fallen into his lap.

He may not have stolen a car before, but he knew just who he could take it to, and who would pay him as much as he could normally make in a couple of weeks for it, perhaps even more. That would enable him to put some money away for the next time luck was not on his side and give him some to treat himself with.

His decision made, he pulled open the door. He was about to slide behind the wheel, so he could take the car when he found himself on the receiving end of another surprise, this one far less pleasant.

"Hey, what d'you think you're doing?"

Paul straightened up quickly and looked around to see where the shout had come from. He did not, even for a moment, consider that he was not the target of it, he knew instinctively that he was. A security guard, middle-aged and overweight, like the majority of those employed by the security firm Asda used, was a short distance away and striding towards him, an accusatory look on his face.

The moment he saw that Paul slammed the car door and took off in the opposite direction. He skipped between cars until he got to the next row and could move more freely. He picked up his pace then until he was running towards the nearest exit, confident that he could easily get away from the guard, who could only manage a pace that at best merited the description lumbering.

Despite being certain that he could get away without any difficulty, he kept one eye over his shoulder. It was because of that that he failed to see the shopping trolley being pushed by a young mum, who was trying to control both it and her toddling son, until it was too late to avoid it.

Paul crashed into the trolley, knocking it over and sending both himself and the contents flying. He landed heavily on the concrete and lay there for a few seconds with the breath knocked out of him. He scrambled to his feet quickly once he recovered and set off again, leaving the guard to check on the woman whose shopping he had just spilled.

In barely sixty seconds he was out of the car park and heading down the road.

33

Melissa felt a moment of panic as she put her foot on the brake and the car began to aquaplane. There was so much water on the ground that she didn't think she was going to be able to control her car before it crashed into the pub.

She wouldn't have minded the loss of control so much if she had been driving fast, but by the time she put her foot on the brake in the car park she was doing less than ten miles an hour.

"Just as well your brakes are in good shape," Zack said in a surprisingly calm voice when the car came to a stop no more than three feet from the pub's entrance.

"Remind me to get them checked," Melissa said. "I think I'd like them in a little better shape than that." She remained where she was, clutching the steering wheel, until her heart stopped pounding quite so forcefully. She threw open the door at her side then and stepped out into the lashing rain.

Had she been dry she would have cursed at suddenly finding herself drenched, but she was still soaked from the short time she had spent in the rain at the Greene house. As a consequence, the downpour had no effect on her, other than to make her move cautiously towards the door of the pub out of fear that she would fall over.

Wet through, Melissa was sure she was going to catch pneumonia, which was the last thing she needed just then, but there was nothing she could do about it until she finished her day's work and could get home, strip off, and step into a steaming hot shower.

It must be worse for Zack, she realised. Tired though she might be, she was at least basically healthy, her unofficial partner was still recovering from a sprained ankle, a nasty knife wound to his arm and, worst of all, being shot with a shotgun. He should not have been out of hospital, in her opinion, let alone walking around, but she had forgotten about that when she asked him to accompany her. Now that she remembered, she felt guilty for doing so.

She was tempted to tell him to go home, that she would finish up, but though she didn't know him as well as she would like, she was certain that he would refuse and insist on sticking with her.

Zack got to the pub's door ahead of Melissa, so he held it open for her and then let it swing shut behind him. Immediately the voice of the storm, the howling of the wind and the thunder which rumbled overhead several times a minute, was cut in half.

The remaining noise might have been drowned had there been any noise in the pub, but it was only half full — Zack was sure that a lot of the villagers who would normally have been there for a drink and some socialising were being kept away by the weather — and the majority of those that were there were quiet, their attention on a table near the bar.

"Looks like you've got everything under control, Jack," Melissa said to the landlord as she approached the table over which he stood guard, and around which were sat two men, one of whom she recognised as Marius Kowalski.

She guessed that the second man, who was staring at Kowalski with hatred on his face, was Thomas Greene. She also guessed that the golf club that lay on the table between the two men was the method by which he had chosen to show Kowalski how he felt about the affair with his wife.

"What happened?" she asked. Though she could guess, she needed to be certain before she could take any action.

"I don't know how it started," Jack Peters said. "I was behind the bar and didn't see. I didn't even see this guy come in." He indicated Thomas Greene, who continued to glare at Kowalski, without giving any indication that he was aware there was anyone around him. "Suddenly there was a lot of shouting from over by the pool table, name calling, that kind of thing, followed by a yell of pain. That must have come from him." He nodded towards Kowalski.

"You're not bloody kidding," Marius said through gritted teeth as the landlord nodded in his direction.

Melissa saw that Marius' arm, where he was rubbing it, was bruised and swollen, indicating that he had been hit at least once with the golf club. She wondered if the arm had been broken.

"Can you tell me what happened, Mr Kowalski?" she asked, taking a seat at the table between the two men. She didn't like that the entire pub, it seemed like, was watching her and the table; she would have preferred at least a little privacy, but could not think of a way to change the situation without leaving the pub.

Marius shrugged. "I was in the back, having a drink with a couple of mates and playing pool, when he appeared and started yelling, called me an 'asshole' and a 'sonofabitch' and just about every other name under the sun. Not that it was easy to make out what he was saying — I've heard drunks that're easier to understand. I couldn't even be sure who he was having a go at, me or one of my mates, or if he'd got the wrong group entirely.

"I tried calming him down, so I could find out what was going on and what he wanted, that's when he hit me. He pulled that club from behind his back and started swinging like he's playing baseball or something. Smashed me in the arm with it twice and was aiming for my head when Pawel got it away from him."

Melissa assumed that Pawel was one of Marius' friends, but it didn't really matter so she didn't ask, instead she focused on what did. "Do you know why he attacked you?"

"No." Marius shook his head. "I don't even know who he is."

"I'm the guy whose wife you've been screwing," Thomas Greene shouted angrily. Surging to his feet, he made to snatch up the golf club, so he could recommence his attack. Before he could do so, however, he was forced back into his chair by the burly landlord, who had assumed a position directly behind him. "I would have thought you'd have found out what I looked like in case you bumped into me. I know all about your affair with my slut of a wife, I even know you were with her last night. When I'm done with you you're not going to be screwing anyone for a long time, maybe not ever."

"I'd keep quiet and avoid making threats, if I were you, Mr Greene," Melissa told him. "You're in enough trouble as it is. I've got you on assault; with all the witnesses here, there's no chance of you getting off on that, and I've got you on domestic abuse. I'm confident your wife will testify against you."

"What's happened? What's he done to Natasha?" Marius asked in a sharp, worried voice.

"He hit her," Melissa said. She continued quickly when she saw Marius' cheeks flush with anger. "It's okay, she's not seriously hurt, but the courts are now taking domestic abuse very seriously." She made a mental note to get photographs of Natasha Greene's injuries before the bruises faded and the defensive wounds healed. "Mr Greene," she returned her attention to him, "I am arresting you on suspicion of domestic abuse and assault..." She read him his rights. "Will you come quietly, or will it be necessary for me to handcuff you?"

34

Martins stalked through the rain to where DC Reid waited for her. To say that she was unhappy was an understatement. The rain, which was all but torrential, had soaked her to the skin within seconds of her getting out of the car, but she had been unhappy before then.

She was not surprised that Kieran Wright had abandoned the car he stole from his murdered friend, she had expected that. It didn't make her feel any better about the situation to have predicted it, though, since she now had to try and work out if Wright was on foot or if he had stolen another vehicle.

"What do we know?" she asked briskly once she reached Reid and the car. There was a security guard behind and to one side of Reid and Martins, between blinks that worked to keep her eyes clear of the rain, looked him over briefly before turning her attention back to Reid.

"Not much," Reid admitted, as unhappy as his superior. "The car was discovered by accident; we've got no idea right now when it was parked here, we can't even be certain it was left here by Wright, we're waiting for forensics to check the car over. It seems likely it was him, though, the car was left unlocked and with the keys in the ignition.

"Most likely he didn't care what happened to the car after he dumped it."

"Maybe he was hoping it would be stolen, so we'd have a harder time finding it and getting back on his trail," Martins said. It was a smart move from someone she did not think of as smart, and she wondered what else the teen killer was going to do to stay a step, or even two or three, ahead of them. It would be helpful, she thought, if they had the slightest clue where Wright was going, but she doubted the teen knew himself, which made things more difficult.

"It nearly was."

"What?" Martins looked past Reid to the security guard, bewildered by the sudden comment from him.

"It nearly was stolen," the guard said, stepping forward so he could be heard more easily over the rain and the wind, and the distant thunder, all of which combined to make conversation difficult. "If I'd come this way a minute later, the car would've been gone."

"What do you me..." Martins was cut off by an especially strong gust of wind that sucked the air from her lungs. Once she got her breath back she said loudly, "Let's get out of this so we can talk. Leave someone here to keep an eye on the car," she directed Reid.

She was still soaked, and uncomfortable because of that, but she felt a lot better once she was inside the supermarket and out of the wind, which was more annoying than the rain.

"What do you mean the car was almost stolen?" she asked when she, Reid and the still unnamed security guard were all together and off to one side of the entrance area of the supermarket, where they could talk without being either overheard or disturbed.

"I was doing my rounds when I saw someone acting suspiciously."

"Who?"

The guard, whom Reid suddenly realised he had not introduced, an error he quickly corrected, shrugged. "I don't know his name," he said. "But I've seen him around from time to time. I'm sure he's a thief and he steals from cars, we've had reports of cars being broken into and things taken, but I've never actually caught him in the act. He was at the car you're interested in when I challenged him. He took off straight away. I gave chase, but he got away."

Looking at the guard, Martins was not surprised to hear that he had failed to catch the suspected thief. She was sure it had been a long time since he had caught anyone who could move quicker than a snail.

From the pocket of her soaked jacket she took out the printout she had been carrying all afternoon. The printout was as wet as she was, and the paper started to tear when she unfolded it, but the image was okay, just about. "Is this the person you saw?"

"No." Luke Catchpole said with a shake of his head. "That's the kid who's been on the news today, that murderer you're looking for. I'd have recognised him if that was who I saw, and I'd've called you guys straight off. No way I'd've chased after him. Kid I saw was probably 'bout the same age, though. I can give you a description if you want it."

"Maybe in a minute," Martins said. She didn't care about a petty thief who stole from cars in a supermarket car park, her interest was in whatever information Catchpole could provide that might help them to find Kieran Wright. "Do you know when the car we're interested in was left here?"

"Not a clue. I'd have to check the security tapes to try and figure that out, sorry."

Martins was not surprised by that, but the expectation of the answer did not diminish her disappointment. "Get someone on that," she directed Reid. "I want to know when the car was left here, and if Wright left on foot or in another car, and what time. If he left in another car, I want to know the make, model, colour and licence number, and I want an alert put out for it, and officers at the address of the owner in case Wright decides to hide out there. When you've done that I want every CCTV camera within a mile checked — I don't care how many officers it takes, Wright has got to show up on those cameras, and we should be able to track him through them." There were not nearly enough CCTV cameras around town for her liking, but she was sure that whether on foot or in another stolen vehicle Kieran Wright had to be findable on them. The only question was how long it would take to find him.

Once Reid had taken on board all the instructions and had gone off to find the security office, which he had been given directions to, Martins turned her attention back to Catchpole. "What did you do after you failed to catch the guy trying to steal from the car? How did you know the car was stolen?"

Catchpole didn't like being told he had failed, but he could hardly deny that that was what had happened, so he ignored it. "I came back to the car, so I could check it out, that's when I discovered it was unlocked and the keys had been left in the ignition. I called through to control, so they could put a call out over the tannoy for the owner. Obviously, they never showed up. They tried several times, but no-one came to say it was their car, so control called you guys to try and find the owner. The moment your guys heard the licence number they told us the car was stolen and we needed to keep an eye on it until someone got here."

"Is there anything else you can tell me?" Martins asked, sure what the answer was going to be before she heard it.

Catchpole shook his head. "Nope. Sorry I can't help you catch this kid. From what they've been saying on the news he's a nasty piece of work."

Martins had to agree with that. It was a far gentler description for the teen than she had heard from others, but it was on the right lines.

35

Melissa was halfway to town with Zack and her prisoner, Thomas Greene, when they were almost run off the road. She was driving as carefully as her reflexes would allow, but that didn't matter when the other car came haring around the bend far faster than it was safe to be driving in such conditions. She had some warning that there was a vehicle approaching, for the glow from its headlights was visible through the rain and the gloom even before it reached the bend. The glow only told her that there was another vehicle out there, though, not that it was going so fast, nor that it was being driven by a maniac.

When the headlights swept around the bend the intensity of them dazzled Melissa, making her blink rapidly. As she blinked she got a fleeting impression of a looming mass that was far closer than her brain said it should be. She reacted instinctively by spinning the wheel and standing on the brake.

Her reactions were not quick enough. A crunching sound, which was closely followed by the squealing sound of metal scraping against metal, made Melissa cringe. She felt a stab of panic as the car rocked, and for a moment she thought it was going to roll, a concern that was not helped when the wheels on the passenger side left the road and struck the rough ground that separated the road from the trees.

A sigh of relief escaped her when the car came to a stop, still upright, and was followed by a muttered prayer of thanks when she peered out the windscreen through the rain and saw that they had stopped short of running into the thick trunk of a yew tree by less than a foot.

Glad that they were safe, Melissa turned her attention from what was ahead of her to what was behind. All she could see of the car that had struck her was the dim glow of its rear lights, though, and they quickly disappeared as it continued down the road to the village.

She could not imagine who would be driving so recklessly in those conditions. It beggared belief that anyone would put their life, not to mention the lives of their passengers, if they had any, and other road users at risk by driving in such a way.

She wanted to give chase, so she could arrest the driver, but abandoned the idea as soon as it popped into her head. She would have to drive as recklessly as the guy — she assumed it was a guy — who had hit her just to catch up, which would be dangerous enough if she was on her own. She certainly couldn't do it while accompanied by two civilians, one of whom was in handcuffs and being taken into custody.

Another thing that kept her from giving chase was the need to assess the damage to her car and get it back on the road. She hoped she was going to be able to manage that, because if she couldn't they were likely to have a long wait for a tow truck, assuming one would come out before the weather eased.

"Are you both okay?" Melissa asked of her passengers once she had brought her racing thoughts back to where they needed to be. She could feel her heart thumping so forcefully against her ribcage she thought it was going to beat its way out of her chest; it was slowing gradually, though, so she ignored it.

"I'm good," Zack said, glad that he had not been on the side of the car that was hit, though that did mean he had had a better look at the tree they nearly hit than he would have liked.

In the back seat, Thomas Greene nodded. "Who the hell was that?" he asked in a voice that reflected how shook up he was by the incident.

"No idea," Melissa admitted. She was glad that none of them had been hurt, and just as glad that Greene had calmed down, he had been angry and almost raging in the back seat when they left the pub. "I barely had time to be sure it was a car, no way in hell I could see who was behind the wheel. I'm not sure I'd have been able to do so even if it wasn't pissing down, he, I assume it was a he, was gone too quickly. I couldn't even tell you the colour of the car, let alone the make or model. How about you, Zack?"

Zack could only shake his head. "Sorry, I didn't see any more than you did. Those high-beams were just too bright, and the car was gone before I recovered. I think it was a dark colour, but I can't be certain. I just hope he — I'm assuming, same as you," he said when Melissa directed a querying look at him. "I just hope he gets wherever he's going without running into anyone else. The next person might not be as lucky as we were." He didn't like to think how bad things would have gone for them if they had been on the bend, rather than approaching it, when the car hit them.

"Yeah. I don't suppose there's any point in me trying to track them down; without any clue what sort of car it was, let alone who was behind the wheel, catching them will be an absolute sod. Do you think I'll be able to claim for the damage from the service?" Melissa asked hopefully of the former detective inspector as she removed her seatbelt and threw open the door next to her, so she could check how bad the damage was. She had her fingers crossed that it would not prove too serious; with both the station's patrol cars out of action, she needed her car to do her job.

"I don't see why not," Zack said. Under the circumstances he thought Melissa had a better than evens chance of being reimbursed for whatever damage her car had suffered, but it was likely to be quite some time before she saw the money, and some penny-pinching finance officer was bound to try and find some way of avoiding paying the bill.

While the rain beat down on her head and shoulders, and the wind tried to blow her off her feet, Melissa played the beam from the torch Zack had taken from the glove compartment along the side of the car. Dismayed, she took in the missing wing mirror and the damage to the front wing, driver's door and rear driver's side door.

It could have been worse, a lot worse, but that didn't make her feel any better about the hundreds of pounds of damage that she could see.

With an unhappy sigh, she turned off the torch and got back behind the wheel, so she could try and return the car to the road. Thankfully, the two driver's side wheels were still on the road, and the passenger side wheels did not seem too deeply mired in the mud, so she felt reasonably confident that she could get back under way without having to call for help.

36

Kieran swore, and jerked the steering wheel first one way and then the other, as he fought to avoid the oncoming car that appeared out of the rain and the darkness and keep the car he had stolen on the road.

Somehow, he managed to avoid crashing, though he knew that both cars had been damaged during the collision. The damage didn't bother him. He didn't care one bit about the other car, and the only concern he had for his own was how the damage affected the car's ability to be driven. Fortunately, his car continued to drive without any problems.

It was neither the collision nor the damage that had caused him to swear, it was his recognition of the driver of the other car as Constable Turner. He was heading back to Oakhurst because he wanted to revenge himself on those he blamed for his current situation, yet the chief among them, Melissa Turner, was heading away from the village.

He was tempted to turn back so he could chase Melissa down and put an end to her, he could then carry on to the village to take care of his other targets: Zack Wild, who had interfered where he had no business and helped to arrest him, and his sisters, both of whom had put him on the path to being arrested by nosing around in things that had nothing to do with them.

Kieran decided against turning around to chase down Melissa Turner. In the time it took for him to consider doing so he was a quarter of a mile, perhaps more, further down the road and the other car was no longer visible, not even its lights. On top of that he was sure that Melissa had not been alone in the car, and though he wasn't afraid of anyone, the presence of others with his target complicated things more than he liked, especially since his only weapon was a knife.

Fortunately, he had a plan for getting himself a better weapon. He wanted a shotgun, so he could kill anyone he wanted without needing to get up close and personal, and he knew just where he could get one without too much difficulty. His plan meant stopping before the village, but that was not really a problem, the lack of visibility caused by the weather was, however.

Visibility was so bad that he was on top of the turning he needed to take before he saw it. He slammed on the brakes, and then had to fight to control the car as it went into a skid. It took him more than a hundred yards to stop the car, and once he had, somehow doing so without crashing or even leaving the road, he backed up to take the dirt track that led into the trees from the road.

As impatient as he was, Kieran knew there was no way he could avoid a crash if he tried to drive fast down the path he was on. It was even darker there than it was on the road with the rain hammering down — his headlights barely penetrated the gloom — and there was simply no way he could avoid hitting a tree if he tried to drive at more than the five miles an hour he was going at.

Even driving slowly, he could not entirely avoid the trees that grew close to, but somehow had not invaded, the seldom used and ancient path, which ended after about a mile and a half at a clearing.

When he was a kid, before she died, Kieran's mum had told him how the Romans had occupied the area on which Oakhurst now sat, and that before the Romans there was an ancient settlement with shrines precious to the druids who controlled the area. The clearing he was now in was supposed to be one of those shrines; the presence of a metre-high white rock, carved with symbols that were still just visible, suggested the clearing really had been a druid holy place two thousand years ago.

That was not why he was there, though. He had been interested in the history of the area when he was a kid, an interest encouraged by his mum, and by the occasional Roman coin or artefact that was found by one of the farmers whose lands surrounded Oakhurst. Now, though, his only interest in the clearing was in the fact that it marked the starting point of his quest for revenge, for a reckoning of recent events.

It was quest he felt was blessed, not by God, whom he had never really believed in, but perhaps by the older gods who had ruled the area long ago, which would explain the storm. Without the storm it would be difficult to get his revenge, he would be too easily seen by anyone who was looking, but with the storm he could sneak up on anyone and everyone.

Stopping the car once he was in the clearing — he did not skid this time, both because of his slow speed and because the mud grabbed at the wheels and made it difficult to keep the car moving at all — Kieran threw open the door and got out. He promptly slipped over and landed on his face, getting a mouthful of mud, which he spat out disgustedly as he struggled to his feet.

The still open door of the car provided a handy climbing frame, without it he would have ended up back on his face at least a couple of times. Once he made it to his feet he clung to the car door for a few moments while he steadied himself.

When he felt confident, he left the car and, with slow and careful steps, headed for the small pool in front of the sacred rock, whose purpose he couldn't begin to guess at. He made it without falling over, a minor miracle, and began searching for the reason he was there, the stream that led away from the pool.

It was more difficult to find than usual because of all the rain, which had swelled the pool to double its normal size, swamping the area. Once he found the stream's starting point, though, it was easy to follow the flowing water through the trees.

From his childhood explorations, not that he had been able to do too much exploring once he was old enough to be judged of use around the farm, Kieran knew that the stream meandered through the trees until it joined the river. From the river it was a fairly easy walk to his first destination, the Wilcox farm, and that was why he had gone to the shrine.

There were plenty of other places along the river where he could have dumped the car and saved himself the walk through the trees. He didn't know if the car had been reported stolen, however, and the clearing guaranteed it wouldn't be found, and no-one would know that he had returned to the village.

It would have been much simpler, he realised as he trudged through the woods, each step a trial because the mud sucked at his boots and threatened to glue him to the spot, if he had thought of returning to the village that afternoon when he had the boat. In the boat he could have simply followed the river all the way back to Oakhurst; it would have required a lot less hassle and aggravation, not to mention risk.

Another thought that occurred to him during his fight with the mud, which was more energy-sapping than anything else he had done that day, was that he could have driven straight to the Wilcox farm, without the need to go through his current ordeal.

He dismissed that notion as soon as it occurred to him. The storm might be the worse he had seen or experienced in at least three years, but that did not mean everyone in the village would be indoors. There was a chance, slim perhaps but still there, that someone might be out and about, and that they would see him as he drove through the village to the Wilcox farm, which was the only way to get there. That was a chance he was not prepared to take.

All day he had been forced to run and react because of bad luck or a lack of caution. Now he was determined to think things through and only act after he had done so.

Once he had the revenge he was there for, he intended spending some time thinking about what he was going to do for the rest of his life. It had to be possible to evade the police and find somewhere to settle down with a new name, somewhere he could make a living. Oliver Ryder and his friends were able to get by without jobs, so he must be able to do the same. After all, Kieran reasoned, they were not all that bright, and he was at least as smart as them.

ABOUT AN HOUR AND A half after he left the car at the shrine, Kieran reached the Wilcox farm, where he crouched by the side of the chicken coop. Straining his eyes, he peered through the darkness and the rain to try and make out the house.

He was still trying to see the house well enough to figure out the situation, and decide what to do, when lightning split the sky almost right in front of him. At the same time thunder rumbled overhead; the storm that had followed him ever since he left town was now on top of him.

The combination of sound and noise was enough to startle Kieran, and he stumbled from his crouched position into the chicken coop next to him. The chickens had already been unsettled by the weather and now they kicked up a fuss, angry at being disturbed more than they already had been.

37

Donald Wilcox was on his feet and at the window the moment he heard the din being made by the chickens, or at least as soon after as his arthritic knees would permit.

"What's the matter with you?" Julie Wilcox asked of her husband, surprised by the suddenness with which he had moved. The pain in his joints made it rare for him to move with anything resembling speed.

"The chickens, something's spooked them."

"It's just the storm, They're always like this."

Donald spared his wife the briefest of glances before turning his attention back to the yard, which was being lit by the lightning that flashed across the sky several times a minute. "They're not normally this bad," he said, leaning forward until his forehead was almost touching the glass as he searched the yard for anything that was out of place.

"The storm's worse than usual, that's all it is," Julie said complacently, barely lifting her eyes from the TV, on which she was watching a rerun of 'Allo 'Allo, a comedy that never failed to at least make her smile.

"Something's out there," Donald said, as though he hadn't heard his wife, "or someone."

Scowling, Julie set down her knitting and pushed herself up from the sofa, so she could join her husband at the window.

She stared out into the yard for almost a minute but could see nothing out of place. Finally, she said, "You're imagining things. There's nothing out there but the storm, and that's enough to rattle anything or anyone. I hate to think of the damage we're going to have to clean up when it's over."

"I'm not imagining anything, there's someone out there," Donald insisted, not happy that his wife didn't believe him, though he knew he should be used to that since disbelief was the reaction he almost always got from her. It didn't matter what he said, she never took his word for anything. "There, by the chicken coop." He pointed as lightning brightened the sky again.

KIERAN CRINGED AS EVENING became day for a moment. He had not worried about the lightning before, but now that he could see that the Wilcoxes had pulled back the curtain and were looking out the living room window, he worried that he might be seen.

He tightened his grip on the knife he held and ran through his options — he didn't have many — while he tried to decide what to do. He kept as still as he could in the hope that he wouldn't be seen, and that the Wilcoxes would conclude that the storm was the reason for the fuss the chickens were making, at which point they would relax and go back to whatever it was they had been doing.

He was thinking that the best thing he could do was wait until Donald and Julie went to bed. Being old, and farmers, he suspected they would not stay up late, so he wouldn't have to hang around for too much longer; it was already past eight, and if they were anything like his father they would head up to bed at about nine. That plan went out the window when Donald disappeared from the window and then appeared at the front door a few moments later, armed with the shotgun Kieran had come to steal.

"WHAT DO YOU THINK YOU'RE doing, you old fool?" Julie demanded of her husband as he collected his shotgun from the cabinet in the corner of the living room and checked that it was loaded.

"What do you think I'm doing? I'm going to go out there and deal with whoever it is messing with our chickens," Donald told his wife. Satisfied that both barrels of his gun were loaded, he snapped the breech shut and made for the front door.

"You're crazy," Julie told him. She tried to grab his arm to keep him from going out into the downpour, but he just shrugged her off. "If there is someone out there they've got to be crazy, so they're not going to be scared off by an old man, even one with a shotgun, and if there isn't someone out there, you're going to catch pneumonia for no reason. Let me call the station, have someone from there come out and check around. If there is a prowler out there, let them deal with him, it's what they're paid for."

"I've never needed anyone to help me protect this place before, and I'm not about to fall into that habit now." His face set, Donald pulled open the door and walked out into the storm.

Julie made a face at her husband's back, annoyed by his stubbornness, but made no further attempt to stop him. Instead she closed the door and left it on the latch, so Donald could get back in once he was done checking the yard, she then returned to the living room to call the police station. She was not convinced that there was anything or anyone out there, but she thought it best to have the police come out and check, just in case Donald was right. He was too old to be getting into anything with a prowler, even if he did have his shotgun.

KIERAN SWORE AS DONALD stepped out into the yard and made a beeline for the chicken coop. There was no way he could avoid being seen, which left him wondering how he was going to keep from getting shot and get the shotgun away from the elderly farmer.

For a moment he was tempted to run away and find somewhere else to get a gun, but that would be cowardly, and he refused to think of himself as a coward. There was no way he was going to back away from someone he was sure was old enough to collect a pension.

Staying where he was he crouched as low as possible in the 'shelter' of the coop in the hope that the lightning, which had been coming every fifteen to twenty seconds, would hold off. That did not happen, but it did do him the courtesy of waiting until Donald Wilcox was almost on top of him before lighting up the sky again.

With Donald only half a dozen steps away, Kieran used the illumination to his advantage. He leapt to his feet, springing forward as he did so to close the gap between them before the shotgun could be brought to bear on him.

"You!" Donald recoiled in shock and horror when he saw who it was that had startled his chickens and brought him out of the house. The intensity of the rain had made it almost impossible for him to see through his glasses, which was why he had got so close to the coop without seeing anything. Before he could recover, let alone do anything about the sudden presence that loomed before him, like shoot the teen murderer he had thought was locked up, he felt a sharp pain in his stomach.

He cried out, though the noise was drowned by a fresh rumble of thunder, and looked down, his hand going to his stomach, where he saw he had been stabbed. He started to collapse. His legs buckled under him and he felt himself fall to the ground.

He tried to stand but his muscles would not obey. The only ones that would were those that gave him control over the shotgun, and even then, he struggled to get it to do what he wanted. The gun was too heavy for him to control with only one hand, and he could not seem to loosen the grip he had on the hand grasping the knife buried in his stomach.

Kieran reacted the moment he saw the barrel of the shotgun waver and start to move towards him. He grabbed the muzzle with his free hand, so he could keep it away from him. At the same time, he twisted the knife and pulled it free, so he could stab Duncan a second time. He wanted to finish the old farmer off quickly, so he could deal with his wife.

Before he could deliver the second, and he hoped fatal, injury he was forced to snatch his hand away from the shotgun as Donald's finger twitched on the trigger, firing the weapon.

Instinctively Kieran lashed out, knocking the weapon away with his arm so that if it was fired again the blast would be directed anywhere but at him. Behind him, he could hear the chickens squawking and flapping their wings and making as much noise as it was possible for a dozen poultry to make. At the same time, he struck with the knife, slashing downward.

He caught Donald across the face, opening his cheek from his eye to his jaw. It was a nasty injury, but not a fatal one, and Kieran was forced to follow Donald to the ground, so he could attack again, this time stabbing him in the chest — he thought he had got him in the heart but wasn't sure. What he was sure of was that if Donald Wilcox was not dead he soon would be from loss of blood, and that was good enough for him.

Pushing himself up from the ground he wrenched the knife free from Donald's chest and made a half-hearted attempt to wipe the blade clean on his jumper. He then bent to pull the shotgun from Donald's hand. It had only been fired once, but he still cracked the breech to make sure he had a usable shell as he headed across the yard to the house.

He pushed the door open when he got there, pleased but not surprised to find that it had been left on the latch. In two steps he reached the living room doorway, where he saw Julie Wilcox, her hand on the phone that sat on a small table next to the sofa. He reacted immediately, afraid that she was about to call the cops, or alert someone else to the fact that he was there.

38

Melissa was looking forward, longingly, to an end to her day. She was only about ten minutes outside of Oakhurst, having dropped Thomas Greene off at the main station in Branton, when the phone in her pocket began ringing.

She started to take her hand off the wheel, so she could get the phone out, but quickly thought better of it. As confident as she was in her ability to control the car, and as carefully as she was driving, she couldn't help remembering the sudden appearance of the car that had hit her on the way out of the village. If another car were to appear, it was doubtful that she would be able to avoid a collision with only one hand on the wheel.

"Would you mind?" she asked of Zack, who had been staring out the window next to him, as she lifted her hip in a clear invitation.

"Sure," Zack said once he realised what it was Melissa wanted of him. He leant over to slip his hand into the proffered pocket in search of the ringing phone. He found it easily enough and pulled it out. "Hello, Constable Turner's phone."

"It's a Mrs Wilcox," he told Melissa when the caller had finished speaking and he had worked out what she was saying, which was not easy because of how fast the words were coming. "She says her husband went out to check for a prowler and she thinks there was a shot. She'd like you to take a look around and make sure everything's alright."

"A prowler, in this weather." Melissa gave the rain an extra hard stare. "They'd have to be crazy." Though not as strong as it had been even half an hour ago, the storm was still a powerful display from nature, and the rain continued to beat down with enough force to hurt anyone with sensitive skin caught out in it. "Do you mind?" she asked Zack, sure that by now he must be wishing he had never met her, let alone agreed to help her out.

Zack shook his head. "No problem. It's probably nothing, her husband's probably just been spooked by the storm, but it's better to be safe than sorry." He lifted the phone again. "We'll be there as soon as we can, Mrs Wilcox." He could hear the relief in her voice as she thanked him.

ZACK GOT OUT AND HURRIED through the mud to the gate of the yard in front of the Wilcoxes farmhouse. He swung it open and quickly moved out of the way to let Melissa drive through while he shut it behind her.

He left the gate and started across the yard in time to see Melissa slowly turn the car around. He was also in time to see the headlights pick out first the chicken coop, with its unsettled occupants, and then the body that lay on the ground a short distance from it. He swore. After this morning he had thought he had seen his last body, outside of a film or television series.

Hurrying over to the body, Zack waved for Melissa to stay in the car for a moment while he checked things out. He dropped to his knees in the mud next to the body and reached out a hand to check for a pulse. He stopped himself when he saw the cut across the face and the dark stains on the jumper, one over the stomach and the other over the chest. Combined with the lack of respiration, they convinced him that he would be wasting his time.

Instead of putting his fingers to the throat of the elderly farmer, he took hold of the bottom of his jumper, so he could lift it up and take a quick look at the wounds. He did so not out of any kind of morbid interest in seeing the injuries, but out of the curiosity that stemmed from being a former detective, and from being an investigator who sometimes looked into unsolved crimes.

"He's dead, isn't he."

The question, which was all but shouted to be sure it was heard above the wind and the rain, made Zack jump, even though he knew who had voiced it. It was the suddenness of it, when he had indicated that Melissa should not join him straightaway that caused his reaction. His heart thudded in his chest a few times before slowing back to a normal rhythm as he turned his head to look up at Melissa, who had managed to step up to his shoulder without him hearing her.

He nodded. "That isn't what troubles me, though," he said, wishing he didn't have to make an already difficult day more so. "This gentleman, whom I assume is Mr Wilcox, was murdered, he was stabbed twice from what I can see, though there may be other injuries — I don't want to move him to check since it's clear he's dead, and I don't want to disturb any evidence. What really troubles me, though, is that Mrs Wilcox was clear that her husband took his shotgun with him when he went to check the yard, yet, as you can see, there's no sign of it."

"You're saying we're dealing with a murderer who's just upgraded his weapon from a knife to a shotgun." Melissa could not have looked less happy about the situation. "Do you think it could be Kieran?" she asked. Her eyes searched the barely-lit yard for any sign that they were not alone. Just the thought that there might be someone out there with Donald Wilcox's shotgun, whether it was Kieran Wright or someone else, was enough to send a shiver of apprehension dancing up and down her spine. "They haven't caught him yet, at least they haven't told us they have."

"That's a possibility," Zack admitted. "I don't know the guy well enough to say what the chances are of him coming back to the village, though I've got to say, if he has even half a brain he'll be trying to put as much distance between himself and Oakhurst as possible. Of course, it could just as easily be someone else."

That was not a thought that comforted Melissa, not that she liked the thought that Kieran Wright could have returned to the village and got his hands on a shotgun any better. Unsurprisingly, she could not think of a single positive thing she could take away from the murder of Donald Wilcox.

She remembered Julie Wilcox then and stood up, the farmer's wife had slipped her mind in the discovery of her husband's body. A sick sense of anticipation clutched at her as she started towards the farmhouse, the front door of which, ominously, stood open. If Julie was alright, Melissa was sure she would have appeared in the doorway after hearing the car pull into the yard, which she should have been able to hear despite the weather. At the least she would have given some sign of still being alive.

Zack left the body and hurried after Melissa the moment he saw where she was heading. He said nothing because he knew that as a police officer Melissa had to do what she was, and that if he were in her position he would do the same. The house had to be checked, both to make sure that Julie Wilcox was alright, which he doubted, and to see if Donald Wilcox's killer was still around.

They were at the door, and about to cross the threshold, when Zack caught Melissa's shoulder and forced her to slow down. "Careful," he cautioned in a soft voice. Though he supposed there was no reason to be quiet, if the killer was still at the farm, hiding out or perhaps waiting in ambush, there was every chance he or she already knew they were there.

Melissa nodded. She stepped over the threshold and approached the living room doorway, doing so one cautious pace at a time, her senses alert for danger. As she did she took her extendible baton from its holster and opened it to its full length with a flick of her wrist.

She was ready to use the baton at the first sign of trouble, but that went out the window the moment she entered the living room and saw the body of Julie Wilcox slumped over the arm of the sofa. The sight of Julie Wilcox's face, not that there was much of a face left, was enough to sicken Melissa, who had to turn away and take deep breaths to fight back the urge to throw up.

Zack was more used to death, and even murder, in all its various guises, but he still found what had been done to the farmer's wife a hard thing to stomach. As far as he could see, Julie Wilcox had suffered only the one injury, but he could not deny that that injury was an horrific one.

"What the hell happened to her?" Melissa asked once she had her stomach under control, and she no longer felt as though she was going to spoil the Wilcoxes' carpet.

"At a guess, I'd say she was shot in the face with her husband's shotgun," Zack said, sure that Melissa would come to the same conclusion he had when she was thinking more clearly. "The big question is, 'why?'. Did whoever did this come here simply to kill them, to rob the place, or did they have something else in mind." Not knowing the Wilcoxes, it was hard for him to make any guesses about the motive of their killer, though that did not stop him looking around and making a few assumptions based on what he could see. "You stay here," he told Melissa, lapsing automatically into the tone of command he had used when an inspector. "Call Martins and tell her what's happened, and make sure she knows we've got an armed killer somewhere in the village, and that we're going to need an armed response team. I'll check the house, make sure it's clear."

"I can't let you do that," Melissa protested. "You're a civilian. I shouldn't have brought you here, I certainly can't let you go off and check the rest of the house, especially not on your own. What if the killer's still here? You're not armed with anything, you've got no way of defending yourself, especially against someone we're sure has a shotgun. If anything happens to you, I'll be responsible." She regretted saying that the moment the words were out; her primary concern was not that she would be responsible if something happened to Zack, it was that something might happen to Zack, which would be bad enough if he was a fellow officer, and a whole lot worse since he was a civilian.

"I'll be fine," Zack assured her. "The killer's gone. He, or she, has probably been gone since just after Mrs Wilcox's phone call. If they were still here, they could easily have killed us already. I'll be right back." He gave her no more time to debate his decision, he simply turned and left the room.

39

Kieran stepped out of the Wilcoxes' Land Rover — after killing the elderly couple, it had made sense to take their vehicle, so he could get to the centre of the village without having to trudge several miles through the storm — and glanced around, blinking rapidly to clear his eyes of the rain.

With the weather as bad as it was he didn't expect to see anyone out and about, and he didn't. The street was empty. He was glad about that since it meant there was no-one to see him, and his return to the village was a secret — he thought Julie had been about to make a call, rather than just finishing one, when he found her in the living room with her hand on the phone.

Grabbing Donald Wilcox's shotgun and the knife from where they lay on the passenger seat, he slammed the driver's door shut with an elbow and nudged open the gate of the house he had stopped at with his foot.

He jabbed at the bell with the point of his knife the moment he reached the door.

There was someone home, he knew that because light was shining through a chink in the curtains that had been pulled across the living room windows, but it was a minute before the door swung open.

He was disappointed to see that it was not Melissa who stood in the doorway, mouth agape and eyes wide with fear as she stared at the weapons he held, it was her housemate, Polly Evans. He supposed he should have realised that Melissa might not be back from town yet, but he had thought enough time had passed for her to have returned.

Stepping forward, he entered the house as Polly backed away. It amused him that though her eyes switched constantly from the shotgun in his right hand to the knife in his left, they lingered on the bloody blade. He had no idea why the knife scared her more than the gun, but neither did he care. All that mattered was that she was scared, he liked it when he could see fear in a person's eyes, and that she had not made a noise.

"Stay there," he instructed once Polly had gone far enough that he was able to hook the front door shut with his heel, which he did without looking. The door banged shut, making more noise than he really wanted it to, but he doubted it mattered — with the storm still raging, he doubted there was any chance of the neighbours hearing anything of what happened. He even thought it possible that he could fire the shotgun without it being heard, but he didn't want to take a chance on that if he could avoid it.

"Where's Melissa?" he asked. He assumed she wasn't home, otherwise she would have come to the door, or at least called out to see who was at the door. "I said, where's Melissa?" he repeated the question when Polly didn't respond. "Answer me!" he snapped.

He pressed the point of his knife to her cheek, hard enough to draw blood. He didn't want to hurt her, not much, not then, but he did want to encourage her to talk. The reaction he got was not the one he was after, though. Instead of answering his question, she trembled so violently he thought she was going to fall over, and then she wet herself. The crotch of her jeans darkened and became damp and a few moments later a trickle of pee ran out from the leg to stain the carpet at her feet.

Kieran's disgust at Polly's reaction showed on his face as he quickly moved back out of the way, so he could avoid getting any pee on his feet.

"You disgusting bitch!" Kieran had to force himself not to look away. He could not believe what Polly had just done. None of the other people he had confronted or attacked, not even Daisy Hawkins, who had been only fourteen, had reacted in such a way.

He had been toying with the idea, more than just toying with it really, of getting her to strip off so he could have some fun, kind of a warm-up before the main event — the main event of course being the punishment of Melissa, which he intended making last for a while.

Now that he had seen her reaction to a simple prick of the cheek, though, he had absolutely no desire to pleasure himself with her.

He raised the shotgun, using the hand with the knife to steady the barrel, as he mentally switched from plan A: questioning Polly and then using her for his pleasure before killing her, to plan B: simply killing her. His finger was tightening on the first trigger when he thought better of using the shotgun as a murder weapon. There was no point in him taking a risk on the blast being heard and his presence discovered, not when there was a better way.

"Get on your knees," he ordered, dipping the shotgun's muzzle momentarily to reinforce his command.

"Please," Polly whimpered. "Don't kill me. I'll do anything you want, anything." Her hands, which shook so badly she could have been mistaken for someone with a medical condition, went to the front of her blouse and she began fumbling with the buttons there.

Kieran knocked her hands away with the shotgun as he said, "Don't waste your time. If you think I'd do anything with someone who pisses their pants like a baby..." He didn't finish that sentence, instead he gestured with the gun for her to get down. "Get on the floor, put your face in the carpet. Do as I tell you," he snapped when she didn't move. "Do it and I'll make it quick. If I have to tell you again I'll make you suffer."

From somewhere Polly found the courage she had so far failed to show, or perhaps it was simply that her fear had reached the level at which she thought her situation could not get any worse. Whichever it was, instead of obeying the instructions she had been given, she turned and sprang for the stairs. Where she intended going was unclear for there was no escape to be found on the first floor of the house.

Without hesitation, Kieran dropped the gun and swapped the knife from his left hand to his right as he gave chase. It was not much of a chase, he caught up to Polly before she could make it to the fourth step and grabbing her arm he spun her around. She lashed out with a foot, but he dodged it easily.

Before she could recover, or make any further attempt to get away, he pulled her towards him by her leg and buried the knife in her chest. The knife plunged into her heart and he felt its final beat vibrate along the length of the blade.

He was disappointed to see the light and the life fade from her eyes. He had wanted to take his time and punish her for not doing as he ordered, he could not do that now.

Slowly, he unsheathed the knife from her breast and wiped the blade on her blouse; there was still blood on it, but it was old, from his previous victims. Once he had done that he descended the few stairs he had climbed and retrieved the shotgun. He then made a quick search of the house, which he soon discovered was empty save for himself and the body on the stairs. Of Melissa there was no sign.

Despite the length of time it had taken for him to get there after the near collision, he realised that Melissa must either still be in town or on her way back. Either way, he was sure that when she got back she would go first to the police station, if she wasn't already there, because she would only have gone to town in this weather for something work-related.

Leaving the body of her housemate on the stairs for Melissa to find, should she come home before he caught up with her, Kieran went around the house and turned off those lights that were still on. He didn't want to spoil the surprise for whoever discovered it, whether it was Melissa or someone else.

He returned to the storm then, which was no longer as furious as it had been when he killed Donald Wilcox. He hoped its fury would not abate entirely before he finished what he had come back to the village to do; if that were to happen he would be vulnerable.

He had his three targets in mind and was confident of finding them all before the night was over. Flitting around the edges of his brain, though, was the idea of killing everyone and burning the village to the ground. That would teach them all, all those people who thought he was nothing, who figured he would not even have got a job working for his father if he wasn't all but free labour.

He was especially keen on the idea of burning his family's farm, showing his father exactly what he thought of it and of him. For years he had been belittled, talked down to or ignored by his father, who never bothered to hide the fact that he considered him cheap labour, and good for little else, and barely that, while doting on Emily and Tara.

Except for one or two rare occasions, he had never been allowed to live the life he wanted, to do what he wanted, he always had to put the farm and the family first.

Warmed by visions of flames consuming his family's farm, and the rest of the village, Kieran headed down the road to the police station.

40

Zack was back in the living room a couple of minutes after leaving it, having finished his check of the house.

"The house is clear, there's no-one here but us," he told Melissa once she finished on the phone with Martins. "There's no sign of anything being taken either, other than the shotgun."

Although she looked relieved that there was no-one hiding in the house, waiting to kill them, Melissa didn't look any happier about the situation, nor did she show any sign of understanding it better.

"If nothing's been taken, apart from the shotgun, what was the point of this?" she wanted to know. "Was it just to kill Donald and Julie, to get the gun, or something else?"

Zack could only shrug. "I don't know them, so I can't say, not for sure. I'm not convinced the goal was to kill them, though."

"Why do you say that?"

"It's doubtful that anyone would have come out here in this weather to rob the place, especially since there's no sign of anything but the shotgun being taken. Likewise, I can't see anyone coming out here just to kill them. Only someone desperate is going to be out in this weather, and I can't see anyone being desperate enough to kill two old people that they would come out in a storm to do it.

"Kieran Wright, on the other hand, he's already out in this weather, and he's desperate, we know that, so I can easily imagine him coming here to get a better weapon than the knife he had. With a shotgun his chances of getting away are a lot better." Zack didn't like to think of the teen serial killer getting his hands on a shotgun, after what he had done with one that morning, but it was the only explanation that made sense to him.

"I don't like what you're saying," Melissa said unhappily as she fiddled with her phone. "I can't disagree with it right now, though I'd like to, especially after what Inspector Martins told me, but I don't like it." Melissa gave a shudder, as if to illustrate how she felt, and looked hurriedly around the room, her eyes darting everywhere as though she expected the murderous teen to suddenly spring out from behind the sofa or something. "Wright stole a car from the car park of an Asda in town several hours ago. Once they discovered what he had done they were able to track him through a bunch of CCTV cameras until he got to an area where there aren't any cameras. That area is not far from the road that leads from town to here, and the timing means he could well have been the one who side-swiped us."

Now it was Zack's turn to look less than happy. "I can't imagine he's come back to the village just to get a gun."

"Why else would he have come back here? As you said, with a shotgun his chances of getting away are better, so I can understand him coming back to somewhere he knows he can get a gun, but I can't imagine him having any other reason for coming back here. Surely coming back makes it harder for him to get away; he should be putting distance between himself and here if he wants to escape."

"Revenge," Zack answered her.

"Against who?" The moment she asked the question, Melissa realised that the answer was obvious. "Against me, you mean?"

"And against me, I helped stop him getting away, and he's not likely to be happy about that." Zack's face fell as a thought occurred to him. "He might also have it in for Tara; if she hadn't found that phone this morning, you might not have had a clue that he was the killer, not me. He might even decide not to go after us, if he is out for revenge, but to go after our friends and family instead." His hand was already in his pocket and he quickly pulled it and his phone out. "Is your mum still at your nan's?" he asked as he called Sophie.

Melissa nodded, even though he didn't explain why he had asked.

"Sophie, I need you and Tara to go next door, get Melissa's mum and gran, and go down to the pub." The urgency in Zack's voice kept Sophie from questioning his instructions. "I need you to do it right now, and I need you to stay there until I tell you otherwise. Keep a sharp lookout on your way there, and don't stop for anything."

"You really think he might try and kill Tara, or my mum or gran?" Melissa asked, trying, and failing, to keep the fear she felt from her voice.

"I don't know," Zack admitted. "I don't know Kieran Wright well enough to say what he will or won't do. I can't even say for sure that he's back in the village and looking for revenge, though from what you and Inspector Martins said, it seems a strong possibility. After everything he's done so far, though, I don't think it's worth taking a risk on being wrong. Better to be safe than sorry.

"Did the inspector say anything else other than that Kieran was heading this way when he was last seen on CCTV?"

"Not much. She said we should go to the station, or somewhere else safe, and wait, she's had an armed response team on standby for most of the day, and they'll be on their way here as soon as." Melissa was glad of that, but she was aware of how long it was likely to take for them to get to Oakhurst from town, and that was if there were no problems on the way.

She had been surprised to make it all the way into town, and back to Oakhurst, without encountering a single uprooted tree or fallen branch. That was unusual, especially given the ferocity of the storm.

"When they get here they'll start working on a plan for figuring out where Kieran, or whoever did this, is. Rather them than me, I say." Hunting down a killer who was known to be armed was not something that appealed to her in the slightest, which was why she had never considered applying for, let alone joining, the armed response team.

"Before we go we should find something to cover the body outside with," Zack suggested. "It's probably a waste of time, but you'll want to try and preserve as much evidence as possible." He didn't think there was any probably about it, it would be a waste of time to cover the body, by now the rain would have taken care of whatever evidence might be around, but the attempt had to be made.

A DOZEN QUESTIONS, if not more, danced around Sophie's mind as she lowered her phone following Zack's call. She could not ask them, though, because Zack was gone, and because his instructions were urgent and left no time for questions. They barely left her time to realise that whatever her friend had gone off to help Constable Turner with must involve danger to her, to Tara, and to Melissa's mother and grandmother.

Just the possibility of that was enough to get her moving quickly.

"Tara." Sophie had to call the teen three times before she got her attention. "I need you to get something on your feet, Zack wants us to go to the pub."

"Is everything alright?" Tara asked worriedly, taking her cue from the expression on Sophie's face and the tone of her voice. Abandoning the laptop she had spent almost the entire day messing about on, she got to her feet, so she could stand in front of the woman she had only met that morning.

"I don't know," Melissa said honestly. She couldn't see the point in trying to reassure Tara that everything was okay when she had no idea, and she doubted it was true. "All I know is that Zack wants us at the pub. I'm sure he'll tell us what's going on when we see him."

Tara hesitated for a moment longer, but then she remembered that hesitating had nearly cost her her life that morning. She hurried from the room, so she could grab her trainers.

Tara made no comment as she watched Sophie peer through the spyhole in the door, and then stand on tiptoes to look out through the semi-circle of coloured glass at the top, as though she expected to discover a masked madman waiting outside for them.

The main reason she said nothing was that she was scared. Sophie's actions made her think they were in danger, and that reminded her uncomfortably of the events of that morning when her brother had tried to kill her, using his Land Rover as a weapon. She felt herself tremble, only a little at first, but her tremors quickly became stronger, and she had to fight the urge to retreat to the living room, and the cushion where she had been safe for most of the day, lost in the world of the internet.

"Okay, let's go." Sophie pulled open the door with one hand, while with the other she took Tara's, so she could keep her close.

That was when she discovered how afraid the young teen was. "It's okay," she reassured Tara. "Whatever's going on, we'll find out soon enough, in the meantime, we'll go to the pub and have something to drink. There's no need to worry."

It took her a few moments, but she got Tara moving. With the passage light off and the front door closed, she gave it a quick shove to make sure it was secure, Sophie hurried through the rain to her car.

"HELLO." IF SHE WAS surprised to find a strange woman on the doorstep during the middle of a storm, Hazel Turner didn't show it. Melissa's mother acted as though it was the most natural thing in the world.

"Hi, I'm Sophie, a friend of Zack's from next door," Sophie spoke quickly, with an eye over her shoulder on the car to be sure Tara remained alright. "I know this is going to sound really strange, but Zack wants me to take you and Melissa's grandmother — she could see her in the living room doorway — down to the pub."

"Is everything okay?" Constance asked, moving to stand at her daughter's elbow so she could see Sophie, whom she had met the other day, better.

"I don't know." She could see no reason to make the situation worse by guessing at what was going on, nor did she want to suggest that everything was okay and there was nothing to worry about. "All I know is that Zack went off to help Melissa with something several hours ago, I don't know what, and then a few minutes ago he called to say he needs me to take Tara Wright to the pub and keep her there until he's able to get there to tell me what's going on. He asked me to take the two of you to the pub as well. I hope there's nothing to worry about, but I've learnt that when Zack tells me to do something like this, it's best to do it and find out the reasons why later."

Melissa's mother was uncertain about following instructions from someone she didn't know, relayed by someone else she didn't know. That was clear from the look on her face, which suggested she was on the verge of refusing to go with Sophie and shutting the door in her face. Before she could do that, however, her own mother settled the matter.

"We'll be right with you," Constance turned away from the door with the intention of returning to the living room and replacing her slippers with more appropriate footwear. She stopped when she caught the look her daughter directed her way. "I may not know Zack Wild all that well, but I trust him, and if he says we should go to the pub, then that's where I'm going. He's with Melissa, so I assume that she wants us to do as he's told his friend."

"If that's what Mel wants, why hasn't she called to tell us, rather than letting us hear about it from someone I've never even heard of before, let alone met?"

"Perhaps she can't get to the phone," Constance suggested. "I wish it were otherwise, but Melissa is all but on her own at the moment, which is most likely why she felt it necessary to ask Mr Wild for help. Who knows how many things she could be trying to get done, especially with this storm. If it makes you feel any better," she said, clearly unhappy with her daughter's reluctance to do as had been requested of them, "Mr Wild is a famous writer, and a former detective inspector."

"How is that supposed to make me feel any better? Until this morning he was also suspected of multiple counts of murder, that's hardly going to make me trust him."

Sophie's face darkened as she prepared to defend her friend, whom she was keen to get away from the village as soon as she could, so he wouldn't have to continue dealing with the small-minded and prejudiced thinking that had led to his becoming a suspect in the murders in the first place. Constance stepped in before Sophie could say anything, though.

"Mr Wild was a suspect because of Lewis, and you know how he is, or was. I'm going to the pub with Sophie, if you want to stay here, that's up to you, but I would rather you come with me."

Annoyed, but unwilling to go against her mother, Hazel Turner surrendered. "Fine, I'll go to the pub, but I don't like doing this on the word of someone I've never met."

41

Kieran found the police station in darkness when he got there. There was no sign that anyone had been there in the last few hours, or that anyone, especially the object of his interest, was due there any time soon. That left him wondering what to do, whether he should stay there, go back to Melissa's house and wait for her there, or go looking for one of his other targets.

He thought about it for a few moments and decided to give it a bit of time there. Since he was sure she had gone to town for something work-related, he felt it likely that Melissa would come to the station upon her return from town before going home. With that in mind, he left the front doors of the station and went looking for a good spot to hide, somewhere that would let him see both the car park at the side of the station and the steps at the front, so he wouldn't miss the constable if she did go there.

When he walked round the side of the station to cross the car park to the bushes that bordered it and saw Zack Wild's Aston Martin, he realised he had almost certainly made the right choice.

He had not seen the person in the passenger seat of Melissa's car when he side-swiped it, but now he realised it must have been the author. That meant the old gods who had sent the storm to conceal him were further blessing his mission of revenge, and there was a good chance he would be able to get two of his targets without any extra work. If he was really lucky, he would be able to get his sister's location from Melissa before he killed her, and that would make things a lot easier for him.

Once he found a likely spot, which didn't take him long, he wriggled and squeezed his way between the two bushes he had picked, ignoring the many scratches he received in the process. He settled down then to wait, confident that no-one could see him; he doubted he could have said that if it hadn't been for the storm, but the weather and the time of day combined to make him all but invisible from more than four feet.

Patience was not a trait he possessed in abundance, and Kieran soon found himself fiddling with both the shotgun and the knife as he fought the urge to leave the bushes and go looking for the constable and the author who topped his list of targets, or perhaps his sister.

Truth be told, he wasn't really fussed who he found, he just wanted to kill someone.

When all of this started, killing had been the last thing on his mind. It had just kind of happened with Georgina, while with Rose it had been a matter of preservation. He had known from the first moment he went after her, spurred on by his anger and his lust, that he couldn't let her live. If he had she would have gone straight to the police.

After that, and especially today, he had found himself enjoying the act of killing more and more. He kept denying it, but deep down he knew that he found killing someone, especially when he did so with his knife or his hands, as much of a rush as sex.

Just the thought of killing Melissa, Zack Wild, and his sister was enough to send a rush of anticipation through him. He wondered how they would react when they realised they were about to die — would they be scared, would they try to run, or would they fight for their lives. He hoped they would be scared, that was what he liked best. He hadn't liked how Polly responded to the fear he had inspired in her, the memory of her wetting herself was enough to disgust him all over again, but the level of fear she had shown was better than he had got from anyone else.

42

Sophie looked around the moment she entered the pub but could see no sign of Zack, not that she really expected to. She was sure he was still with Melissa, assisting the constable with whatever situation had caused her to ask for help.

Whatever he was doing, she hoped he would get there soon and explain what was going on. No matter how bad the situation was, she doubted it could be as bad as the scenarios her mind was conjuring up, and at least she knew she would be able to figure out a way to deal with it once she knew what it was.

"If you want to find a table, I'll get us some drinks," she said, glad that she knew where Zack kept his backup credit card, the one he didn't carry with him in case he lost his wallet, or it was stolen, and glad also that she knew his pin number. It wasn't that she was unwilling to spend her own money on the drinks, but she was close to the limit on her credit card, and in her overdraft on her debit card — both situations would be fixed once she got paid, but that was not for another week and a half — and she didn't want to have either card rejected, which would be embarrassing.

"Thank you," Hazel said with an effort at graciousness as she accepted the Bacardi and coke she had asked for, though she could not entirely conceal the fact that she was still not happy to be there. "Did your friend say when he and Mel will get here to tell us what's going on?"

Sophie shook her head. "I imagine it depends on how long it takes them to finish what they're doing, and I've got no idea what that is," she said before the question could be asked. "Here you go, Tara, a coke for you, and a G and T for you, Constance." She put the drinks in front of the teen and Melissa's grandmother and sat down with her own, a Bacardi and coke, like Hazel, though in her case it was a double. "I didn't know if any of you fancy a nibble, but just in case..." Reaching into her pockets she produced a couple of bags of salted peanuts, a similar number of dry roasted nuts, and two bags of cheese and onion crisps.

"How are you doing?" Constance asked of Tara after a short period of awkward silence had settled over the table. "It's not been a good day for you, has it?"

Tara shook her head between sips of coke. She felt a little better than when she left Zack's house, a little less scared, but she was still worried; she had no idea why they had been told to go to the pub and could only think that there must be some kind of trouble, which had her thinking about her brother, and his attempt to kill her that morning.

"I'm fine," she said, though the shiver she couldn't entirely control suggested otherwise. She didn't know why she felt cold, she was wet from the rain, but the pub was more than warm enough to compensate for that. Nor did she know why she kept looking around at everyone, except that she couldn't help wondering about them, wondering what was behind their smiles, and what they really thought and did when they were on their own — she had known many of them for most of her life, so she should know what they were like, but she had known her brother for all her life, and it had transpired that she didn't know him at all.

"I'm sure everything will be okay," Constance said. She had never experienced shock herself, never in her life had she been through anything traumatic enough to result in it, but that didn't mean she was incapable of recognising when someone was afflicted with it. "And I'm sure Zack and Sophie will take good care of you until something more permanent can be sorted out."

43

Martins listened to the phone ring and ring and ring. With each ring she felt her concerns grow; in her mind there were only two possible reasons for Constable Turner not to answer her phone: the first reason was that the storm kept her phone from working properly, she doubted that possibility because if that were the case her own phone most likely wouldn't be working either, and the second was that Turner had found the person responsible for the murders she had reported, and was incapable of answering her phone as a result.

Martins didn't know if it was Kieran Wright that she and the armed response team were on their way to Oakhurst to search for, or if it was some other killer, though she thought the latter unlikely. What was certain was that they were after someone who had got their hands on a gun, which meant he or she had to be found quickly.

She hoped it was Kieran Wright, because if it wasn't then they were going to be looking for an unknown killer, while a teen serial killer was given an opportunity to disappear.

When the phone stopped ringing and switched over to Melissa's answer-phone, Martins ended the call and immediately dialled the constable's number again. While she listened to it ring she willed the distance between them and the village to disappear, so she could find out what was going on and resolve the situation.

MELISSA'S PHONE STOPPED ringing just before she came to a complete halt alongside Zack's Aston Martin in the car park at the side of the station. It began again before she could turn off the engine, let alone remove her seatbelt or get out of the car.

Hurriedly she reached a hand into her pocket, while with the other she released the seatbelt and threw open the door at her side.

"Constable Turner," she answered the phone. Nudging the door shut with her elbow she made for the rear of the station and the door there, Zack on her heels. "Hello, ma'am," she said when her caller identified herself. "Sorry I didn't get to the phone before, I was parking."

"It doesn't matter," Martins said dismissively. Now that she had heard the constable's voice she felt a weight lift from her shoulders; Turner was not dead, nor did she sound as though she was injured, which was good news, though it did suggest that she had not encountered the killer, and therefore most likely didn't know where he, or she, was. "Where are you now?"

"At the station," Melissa said. "I've just got here with Zack Wild, I'm on my way inside."

"Okay, stay there, and keep the doors locked until we get there, just in case it is Wright," Martins instructed. "If it is him, he's almost certainly back there for a reason, and that reason could well be to get you." She wished she knew the teen well enough to be able to figure out what he might be thinking or planning, but she didn't have the benefit of even a single conversation with him to help. "We're about twenty minutes away, so we'll be there soon."

"I'll keep an eye out for you, ma'am."

KIERAN WAITED UNTIL he saw both Melissa and Zack head away from him towards the rear of the station to leave his hiding place. The bushes on either side of him caught at his clothes as he pulled himself free of them, but he gave no thought to any damage that might have been done, either to his clothes or to him. The only thing that mattered was getting to his targets before they got inside and made things more difficult for him.

He darted across the car park as quickly as he could without breaking into a full run, switching his weapons over so he was carrying his shotgun in his left hand, while the knife was in his right and ready to be used, as he did so. It seemed to him that his footsteps were as loud as the passage of a whole herd of elephants, and he was convinced that the clatter made when the knife hit the shotgun was loud enough to have been heard by everyone in the pub next door. Neither the constable nor the former detective gave any indication that they had heard him, however.

Kieran reached the back door to the station on the heels of Zack Wild. Since he had no plans for the author beyond seeing him dead, he didn't hesitate to plunge the knife into his back. He twisted the knife nastily as he shoved Zack ahead of him into the station; the moment he was inside he slammed the door behind him.

"No, ma'am, I've been trying to think where..." The sudden and unexpected cry of pain from Zack made Melissa cut herself off mid-sentence and spin round so she could see what was going on. "Kieran," she breathed. A detached part of her brain noted with amazement that although there was surprise in her voice, there was no fear, neither a crack nor a tremble, despite the wild and erratic way her heart was beating.

The same detached part of her also took in the knife that protruded from Zack's back as he lay on the floor. She wanted to go to him and check whether he was still alive, but the shotgun in Kieran's hands told her not to.

"What was that, constable?" Martins asked, pressing the phone more tightly to her ear, as though that would help her to hear better. She thought she knew what Melissa had said, which was why she was encouraging DC Reid, who was behind the wheel, to drive faster, not that that was easy with the armed response team's van ahead of them, but she couldn't be certain.

"What are you doing here, Kieran?" Melissa asked in a louder than usual voice to try and ensure the inspector heard her, in the hope that she would figure out what the situation was. "I'd have thought you'd be miles away by now, you've had enough time to put a good bit of distance between yourself and here. From what I've heard, though, you haven't made it any further than the far side of town. Why's that?"

Mindful of how far away Martins had said she was, Melissa sought to keep the murderous teen distracted long enough to let her, and the armed response team she was bringing, get there.

"That's down to you, this pain in the ass," Kieran kicked Zack as he stepped over his body and deliberately trod on his fingers, "who I thought was going to take the blame for everything I've done. He would have if it wasn't for you, and my nosy bitch of a sister. Where is she by the way?" he asked as he advanced on the constable.

"She's at the pub," Melissa told him. She wasn't certain that Tara was there yet, but if she wasn't, she would be soon, and Melissa took comfort from knowing that the girl was safe from her brother, no matter what happened next.

'Keep him talking, we'll be there soon.'

She heard Martins' instructions in her ear and knew that she was aware of the situation. That wasn't going to help Zack, but it might help her, if she was lucky.

Kieran swore. There was no way he could get at his sister if she was at the pub, surrounded by however many people were taking shelter there from the storm. Even with a pump-action shotgun, rather than a double-barrelled one, he would have a hard time dealing with the situation. To get his sister he would have to fire-bomb the place, and he didn't have the materials to make even the crudest of Molotov cocktails.

It angered him to think that after coming all the way back to the village, he would only be able to get two of the three targets he had come for. There would be another time, however, he was sure of that, after all, the fates clearly favoured him, why else would they have sent the storm to conceal his movements.

"I'll just have to settle for you, and him." He jerked his head towards the body of Zack Wild as he made his way down the passage towards Melissa. "Now back up and drop the phone."

He had missed that she had a phone to her ear before, and for a moment he worried about who she was on the phone with. His worry disappeared quickly, though, for he was confident that he could be finished and gone before anyone could get there. Even if he couldn't, he was armed, and it was doubtful anyone who came to Melissa's rescue would be.

"I said drop the phone," he snarled when Melissa didn't follow his orders quickly enough.

"Okay." Melissa lowered the phone from her ear and dropped her hand to her side, only then did she release the phone, when it had the least distance to travel to hit the floor and was less likely to break. "There you go, I've got rid of the phone. What else do you want of me?"

"I want you to back up," Kieran told her. "I'll tell you when to stop. And keep your hands where I can see them." He was sure that Melissa didn't have a gun, he doubted there was a handgun to be found anywhere in the village, but he wasn't about to take a chance on being wrong. "That's good, now keep going," he said when she began retreating up the short passage as directed.

For every step backwards she took, he took one forwards, so the distance between them remained the same, though he did allow himself a brief pause, so he could stamp on the phone and destroy it.

44

"Get a move on," Martins all but yelled into her radio at the driver of the van carrying the armed response team.

She wasn't sure what had happened exactly, but she had heard Melissa being told to drop the phone, and that worried her, especially now that the phone line had gone dead. She had no way of knowing what was going on at the station, and consequently no way of knowing if the constable was still alive.

Of equal concern was the fate of Zack Wild. Melissa had said the former detective inspector was with her, but there had been no mention of him beyond that, and she had not heard him speak, which left Martins worried that Wild was already dead.

While the two-vehicle convoy, which hardly warranted the word, raced through the darkness and the rain on its way to a confrontation with a killer, Martins dialled Melissa's number. She did so repeatedly. Each time it switched over to the answer-phone, she cancelled the call and redialled.

She hoped that if she could speak to Wright, she could keep him from killing Melissa for long enough for the armed response team to get there and figure out a way to resolve the situation. Time and again, though, all she got was the answer phone, leaving her to wonder if Wright was ignoring the phone, or if it was ringing at all — she guessed at the latter.

"THAT'S FAR ENOUGH," Kieran said once Melissa reached the open space at the end of the passage, off which was the station's two cells on one side and the small kitchen on the other. "Now strip."

Melissa knew she should have expected the order after what he had done to Georgina, Rose and Daisy. He clearly enjoyed killing, but first and foremost he was a rapist, and so was bound to want to have some 'fun' with her since she was reasonably attractive. It still came as a bit of a shock, however, and she hesitated, reluctant to give him what he wanted.

"I said strip!"

The words were almost drowned by the blast from the shotgun as Kieran fired it into the wall behind her. Melissa didn't need to hear them to know what he had said, though, for the anger, which made his eyes bulge, and which suffused his face with red, told her all too clearly what he was trying to convey.

Despite that she was still slow to obey him, and she did so only after he spoke again. Even then it wasn't his words that made her reach for the zip on her jacket, it was the movement she saw in the passage behind him.

"I've got another barrel, and plenty more shells," Kieran warned Melissa. "If you don't start doing what I tell you, the next shot's gonna do some damage."

ZACK FORCED HIMSELF not to react as he was kicked, and his hand trod on. That wasn't too difficult for the pain radiating from where he had been stabbed — he could feel that the knife had been left in him, but he thought that might actually be a good thing since it was most likely keeping him from losing a lot of blood — masked the pain from those more minor injuries.

Harder to conceal was the fact that he was still breathing, albeit as shallowly as he could to limit the movement of his body and keep Kieran Wright from realising that he was still alive. He was sure that if the teen did realise that he was not yet dead, he would quickly rectify the situation.

Fortunately, Kieran seemed more interested in dealing with Melissa than in ensuring the body on the floor of the passage was not feigning death, which meant that Zack, badly injured though he was, remained alive.

Once Kieran had gone past him Zack opened his eyes, so he could find out what was going on. What he could hear was not enough to help him figure out where Melissa and the killer were.

When he saw that they were both at the far end of the passage, and at least a dozen feet away, he knew that he was going to have to move if he wanted to stand any chance of helping Melissa. The problem was that his legs didn't seem to want to work. Though he tried, he couldn't get to his feet, leaving him with no choice but to crawl.

It was slow, and difficult, but bit by bit Zack pulled himself towards the teen, whom he hoped would remain ignorant until he was close enough to try and help Melissa. He also hoped that Kieran wouldn't jump the gun and kill Melissa out of hand. From what he could hear, he didn't think that was going to happen, not that he thought what Kieran had in mind was any better than him killing Melissa.

MELISSA COULD NOT BELIEVE that Zack was still alive, she was sure the knife in his back had killed him. Seeing him crawling slowly towards Kieran was so startling that she nearly called out.

She quickly stopped herself. She didn't want to let on to Kieran what was going on behind him and give him a chance to finish Zack off, though she worried that she might have inadvertently given something away through the expression on her face.

To her relief, Kieran either missed the significance of the look on her face, or her expression hadn't changed as much as she thought. Either way, he showed no sign of being aware of anything other than what was in front of him.

Determined to keep Kieran oblivious to Zack for as long as possible, and preferably until it was too late for him to stop whatever the author was going to do, Melissa began to strip. She did so as slowly as she thought she could get away with. First, she slipped out of her jacket, which she kicked away when it hit the floor, so she wouldn't be in danger of tripping over it if she had to move quickly. After that she unbuttoned her blouse, one button at a time, before untucking it and slipping it off her shoulders.

Kieran's eyes lit up as her bra was first exposed, and then revealed fully, and Melissa couldn't help wondering what it was that excited him so much: the mere sight of a pair of breasts, albeit ones that were still hidden by an uninteresting bra; the fact that she was revealing herself willingly, or at least more willingly than Georgina, Rose, or Daisy had; or the size of her chest. She had no illusions about her breasts, they were average in size, no more than that, but average for a woman in her early to mid-twenties who had left puberty behind was still bigger than what Kieran's previous victims had had to show.

Whatever the reason for Kieran's excitement, Melissa decided that the best way to maintain it was to expose her top half completely and give him something to feast his eyes on.

Exposing herself to a murderous rapist was not something she wanted to do, but if it kept her alive long enough for Martins and the armed response team to get there, she was prepared to do it.

ZACK DRAGGED HIMSELF closer to the shotgun-wielding teen while he was engrossed with Melissa, who had slipped the first strap of her bra off her shoulder.

He paused for a moment to regain his breath, he didn't think it had ever taken him so much energy to travel such a short distance, and then he pushed himself up in preparation for making a move. That was far from easy because the moment he manoeuvred himself into more of an upright position, the pain from the stab wound in his back magnified by a factor of about five. It was so extreme that it was all he could do to keep himself from blacking out. Being shot had hurt less, which he wouldn't have thought possible.

Reaching up with both hands, he simultaneously grabbed the back of Kieran's trousers, so he could yank him down, and hit him in the back of the knee. The result was that Kieran fell backwards to land on top of him, which Zack hadn't anticipated, and which he could have done without.

What he had anticipated, hoped for, and was pleased to see, was that the muzzle of the shotgun in Kieran's hands flew upwards to point at the ceiling. Zack had hoped also that Kieran's finger would jerk on the trigger, safely discharging the weapon's second barrel where it would do no harm, except to the building.

He made no attempt to restrain the cry that erupted out of him when the weight of Kieran's body knocked him backwards and the handle of the knife hit the floor, driving the blade further into him. His scream echoed off the walls of the passage while he fought a losing battle with unconsciousness and his blood spilled onto the floor, creating a puddle beneath his body.

45

Kieran was so stunned that Zack Wild was still alive, when he had been sure he was dead, that for several long seconds he simply lay on top of him. He didn't recover until he felt Zack shift under him; it was an involuntary movement brought on by a spasm of pain, but he didn't know that.

Unsure what the man beneath him was doing, and keen to finish him off quickly so he could get back to what he was doing, Kieran elbowed Zack in the face, and then pushed himself up so he could hit him again with more force.

Three more times he hit him, twice in the stomach, and again in the face, rocking Zack's head back as he tried to lift it, so it struck the floor. When he saw that the author was still, Kieran started to his feet to give himself space to use the shotgun he had picked up again.

His lips curled into a smile that was anything but pleasant when he saw that Zack's eyes were open and he was aware of what was going on.

He wished he could have his sisters there as well. He wondered if before they died, and he intended killing them both for sticking their noses in where they didn't belong and causing him so much trouble, they would show any gratitude for him not taking them as he had Georgina, Rose and Daisy, and as he was going to take Melissa.

His finger was curling around the trigger when he caught sight of movement out the corner of his eye. Automatically he turned towards it. He wasn't quick enough, however. The barrel of the shotgun, which was turning with him, stopped suddenly as it was grabbed by Melissa, and he found himself in a wrestling match for the weapon.

MELISSA WAS ABOUT TO finish removing her bra, having taken as long about it as she could, when she saw Kieran fall backwards and the shotgun tilt away from her towards the ceiling.

For a second, she remained where she was, amazed by what had happened. She would not have thought it possible that after being stabbed, and crawling the length of the passage, Zack still had the strength to tackle Kieran.

When she realised that Zack was not moving after being landed on, she hurried forward to help him.

Her bra had fallen away by the time she reached Kieran, who was now on his feet, but Melissa paid no attention to that as she grabbed the double-barrel of the shotgun to keep the twin muzzles away from her. Despite what Kieran so clearly wanted to do to her, she doubted he would hesitate to pull the trigger if he got the chance.

Using both hands Melissa twisted the barrel, first one way and then the other, as she wrestled with Kieran for control of the weapon. It was a fight she didn't really expect to win, Kieran had the advantage of being bigger, stronger, and having a better grip. As with her stripping, though, every second that she was able to keep him from doing something fatal to either her or Zack was another second in which Martins and help could arrive.

She tried to gain an advantage by putting a knee into Kieran's groin, an attack that had mixed results. She was thrown off-balance for a moment by her move, but Kieran's eyes went wide, and he let out a howl of pain as he took his left hand from the gun.

For the first time Melissa had an advantage and she pressed it, forcing Kieran backwards so he would trip over Zack, whom she hoped was still alive. The paleness of his face had her worried on that score. At the same time that she forced Kieran onto the back foot, she wrenched and twisted at the shotgun and struggled to keep his fingers away from the trigger.

It was hard to tell which of them was more surprised when the shotgun went off with a blast that filled the passage with noise. Pain was mixed with surprise for them both as they slumped on top of Zack, still clutching the shotgun.

The three of them made a jumbled heap of limbs, under which was a rapidly growing puddle of blood.

46

Martins had her seatbelt off and the door at her side open before the car had come to a stop outside of Oakhurst's police station. The moment the car ceased moving she was out and heading for the double doors at the top of the steps. She was stopped before she could get there, though.

"You'd better let us check the place out first, ma'am," Sergeant Ince, who was in charge of the armed response team, said, putting an arm out to keep the inspector from getting too close to the building.

His team were already out of their van and taking up positions that would allow them to cover as much of the building as possible and assess the situation inside.

The first part was easy since the building was separate from those that surrounded it, and the land on which it sat gave full access to every corner. The fact that there were only two access points, the double doors at the front and the single door at the back, also helped.

Assessing the situation within the building was not as easy. The double doors at the front were glass, and provided good visibility of the reception area, but the back door was solid wood, and there were no windows along either side, meaning they could see nothing of the building's interior beyond the reception.

"What's the situation?" Martins asked after five minutes, during which Sergeant Ince and his team moved about a lot, without seeming to accomplish much.

"We've got nothing at the front," Ince reported. "Nothing on visuals, standard or infra-red, and nothing on the mikes either. Mind you, it doesn't mean much that we're getting nothing on the mikes," he admitted. "All this wind and rain is playing hell with them. With all this background, it's doubtful we'd pick up a conversation at normal levels unless someone is right on top of the mikes."

"What about at the back?"

"They're still getting set up there, it'll be another minute or so, but the mikes are just as useless there." The frustration he felt at his equipment being defeated by the weather was clear on Ince's face. "We're trying to scan the building with the infra-red camera, but I can't guarantee we'll see anything. We may have to go in blind."

Martins didn't have to ask to know that that was a possibility Ince didn't like, nor did she have to ask why — going in blind increased the chances of things ending badly. After the way the hunt for Kieran Wright had gone throughout the day, Martins wanted as clean an end to the situation as possible. If it was at all possible to avoid going in blind and chancing a disaster, she was determined to do so.

"I'll try calling, see if I can stir some kind of a response," Martins said. Taking out her mobile, she sheltered in the back of the armed response team's van as she dialled the number for Constable Turner's mobile phone.

As before, it went straight to the answer phone, which Martins took to mean the phone had either been turned off or smashed — she feared the worst. After trying three times, without getting anything other than the answer-phone, she tried the number for the station. She fancied she could hear the phone ring in the station, even over the wind and the rain, but still got no answer, and after almost a minute she found herself back at Melissa's answer-phone message after the call was diverted to the duty officer.

Martins tried the number she found for Zack Wild then. That number rang and rang without being answered, but before it could switch over to the answer-phone she abandoned the call, her attention having been attracted by Sergeant Ince.

"What is it?"

"We've got something, ma'am," Ince said. Turning the laptop he was at so Martins could see the screen, he pointed to what the tiny camera inserted under the door at the rear of the police station had picked up — a jumble of limbs. "Two, maybe three people, hard to make out. Infra-red's picking up some heat, but I can't be sure if they're alive or if it's just residual. Do we go in?"

"Yes," Martins said without hesitation. With bodies on the ground, possibly dead, there was no choice but for them to go in and find out what the situation was. She hoped that if anyone in the station was dead, it was only Kieran Wright, and not either Constable Turner or Zack Wild.

"Okay, give us a few to get set up." Ince pushed the laptop away and climbed down from the van, lifting his radio as he did so. "Breach in thirty, go in front and back, thirty on my mark, mark."

From the shelter of the van, Martins watched as the armed response team made hurried, final preparations. After about thirty seconds there came a bang and a flash of light as the double doors blew inwards, the glass gone. A second, muted bang came from the rear of the building, indicating that the door there had suffered a similar fate.

Before either the light or the noise had faded away, Sergeant Ince and the three officers with him, all of them armed with MP5 sub-machine guns, were through the doorway and in the station. Martins wanted to follow them, but she knew better than to enter the building until it had been declared safe.

"All clear, ma'am, you can come in."

The call came less than two minutes after the team entered the building. Martins wasn't sure if that was good or bad. The lack of gunfire left her equally unsure; it could mean Wright wasn't there, in which case the hunt for him would continue, or that they had captured the murderer without the need for gunfire. She suspected that if that was the case Sergeant Ince would have reported that they had their target in custody.

Wondering was not going to bring her any closer to knowing what the situation was, only getting in there and seeing for herself would, so she left the van and hurried up the steps into the building.

She strode quickly through the broken security door and down the passage in search of Sergeant Ince and his team. It didn't take her long to find them, they were gathered in the open area at the end of the passage between the cells and the kitchenette. Most of them were staying out of the way, but Sergeant Ince and one of his officers were on their knees by the far passage.

"What's the situation?" Martins asked. Approaching the two officers, she moved around them until she could see what had their attention, which she was unsurprised to see was the jumble of bodies she had seen on the spy cam.

"Not good," Sergeant Ince said without taking his eyes off the bodies before him. "Appears to be all three of them: Kieran Wright, Constable Turner and Zack Wild. Wright's a goner." There was no trace of concern in his voice as he said that. "Looks like he took a shotgun blast to the groin, long enough ago that he's bled out. I don't think there's anything we could have done for him if we were on the spot when he was shot. I'm not even sure there's anything a full surgical team could have done."

Martins felt no sympathy for the killer. As far as she was concerned, Wright had reaped a richly deserved reward for everything he had done, and she was sure the public would feel the same when they heard what had happened. She quickly pushed Wright from her thoughts, since there was nothing she could do for him, and turned her attention to the other two who made up the bundle of bodies on the floor.

"What's the situation with Constable Turner and Mr Wild?" She couldn't see either of them well enough to gauge how badly hurt they were, the size of the pool of blood under them had her concerned, though. Even assuming Wright had bled out completely, the pool seemed too large for either Turner or Wild, if not both, to be without serious injury.

"Constable Turner has a pulse, it's strong enough to suggest she's not in immediate danger, and she doesn't appear to be bleeding. It's hard to be certain, though, she could have internal injuries." Looking up at Martins, he said, "I'm reluctant to move her in case she does have internal injuries and it makes them worse, but if we don't, I can't check on Mr Wild, and given how white he is, I'd say his condition's the worse of the two."

Martins thought about it for less than half a second before coming to a decision with the rapidity that had helped her to acquire her nickname 'The Rocket'. "Move her, but be careful. I'll get an ambulance on its way." Straightening up, she moved away to make her call, glad that the storm was not affecting the signal on her mobile phone. She hoped the air ambulance would be able to make it through the storm, she wasn't sure Zack Wild would last if he had to wait for a regular ambulance to make the hour-long drive from town, and then the equally lengthy drive to the hospital.

LOOSE ENDS

1

Harry Benson woke with a start. Sitting bolt upright in bed, his eyes darted around the dark bedroom for some clue to what had woken him.

When the sound of breaking glass reached him, he realised what it was that had disturbed his sleep. Worried that someone was breaking into the surgery downstairs, he threw back the covers and got to his feet.

He was about to head out of the room when common sense overtook him. Turning back to the bed he shook his wife awake, which took some time as she was blessed with the ability to sleep through virtually anything.

"Honey, I think someone's trying to break into the surgery, call the station and see if someone can come out." A nod of his wife's head, and a weary wave of one hand, was all the acknowledgement he got, but he accepted it.

On his way out of the bedroom he glanced at the clock. It was gone five a.m., which meant he wasn't losing much sleep, for which he was grateful, but it did raise the question of who was breaking into his surgery at that time. His surgery had been broken into a few times over the years, generally by people wanting the drugs he kept locked up, and in his experience, thieves weren't usually up at five in the morning, there was too much chance of someone being around to see them.

As stealthily as he could, he made his way downstairs. He didn't want to disturb whoever had broken in, he wanted to catch them in the act. Catching them might deter the next person who thought of trying to get a quick fix or of making some money from his surgery.

From the failure of his burglar alarm to go off he assumed the thief, or thieves, was more professional than those he had been troubled by in the past. It was only when he reached the bottom of the stairs that he realised his mistake; all the noise he could hear was coming from outside, rather than in his surgery, which explained why his alarm hadn't gone off.

Curious to know what was going on, but no longer as concerned, Harry made his way outside. It didn't take him long to realise that the noise, which sounded suspiciously like breaking glass, was coming from the side of the house, where his car was parked.

Worried, he hurried along the path, shivering slightly in the cool, early morning air. The clouds that remained of the previous evening's storm blocked the rising sun, making it colder than it should have been.

"Hey! What do you think you're doing?" Harry called out when he rounded the corner of the house and saw the figure — he couldn't see the figure's face, it was shadowed by the hood of the jacket they were wearing, he couldn't even tell if it was male or female — beating enthusiastically on his car.

At the sound of his voice, the figure stopped mid-swing and whipped around to look in his direction. The moment they saw him, the figure dropped what they were beating on the car with and took off, sprinting up the drive and out into the road.

Though the figure passed within half a dozen feet of him, Harry was so startled by the sudden flight that it wasn't until they were out of the drive that he was able to collect himself and give chase.

The figure had gone no more than half a dozen yards when they stumbled.

Harry knew what had happened, he'd done it often enough himself; they had caught their foot in the pothole he had written to the local council about on several occasions.

Despite the limp caused by the stumble, the figure continued to outpace him and, reluctantly, Harry was forced to abandon the chase as it became clear that he wasn't going to catch them.

2

Melissa saw Kieran's whole body flinch as the shotgun went off in their hands. His mouth gaped wide, but his cry of pain was drowned by the noise of the weapon. So too was her own cry, caused by the butt of the shotgun as the recoil slammed it into her stomach, driving the air from her lungs and doubling her up.

As she collapsed on top of Kieran and Zack, who seemed unaware of what had happened, Melissa saw the mess that had been made of Kieran's groin by the shotgun blast. She didn't know if he was dead, but she couldn't help feeling a sense of satisfaction that, alive or not, he would never again be able to hurt anyone the way he had hurt Georgina, Rose and Daisy, and the other girls he had attacked.

HOW MANY TIMES SHE had re-lived the moment when she shot Kieran Wright dead, Melissa didn't know. She was glad when the ringing of her phone disturbed her sleep, though, she didn't want to go through it again.

While she struggled to open her eyes — they felt as though they were glued shut — she reached out to grope on the bedside table for her phone. The muscles of her stomach protested painfully at the movement, but she gritted her teeth and did her best to ignore it.

"Constable Turner, what's up?" she asked tiredly when she found the phone and brought it to her ear. She wasn't sure what the time was, but based on how tired she felt, she was sure she had only got a couple of hours of sleep. It had been past three when she got back from the hospital in town and made it into bed, and since she couldn't hear either her grandmother or her mother moving around she knew it had to be before six.

"Melissa, it's Kate Benson," the vet's wife said in a voice that was as sleep-filled as Melissa's. "Harry thinks someone is trying to break into the surgery. I know you've been through a lot over the last day or so, but can you come over. If someone is trying to steal from the surgery, Harry's likely to get himself hurt."

Though every nerve in her body screamed for her to say no, Melissa couldn't bring herself to. "Sure, I'll be over as soon as I can."

Ending the call, she threw back the covers and got out of bed. Her body protested every movement, voicing its dissent noisily from every abused muscle she possessed. Ruthlessly she pushed aside her body's complaints.

It wasn't until she crossed to where her clothes were piled on the chair in the corner of the room that she realised the problem she had. Her uniform was stained with blood, both Kieran's and Zack's, it was also still damp after the soaking she had endured during the previous evening's storm. She had little choice about wearing it, though, since she had no spare clothes at her grandmother's.

MELISSA FELT A SHIVER of apprehension run through her as she pushed open the front door of the house she shared. She vividly remembered the scene that had welcomed her when she got back from the hospital after being attacked by Kieran. She would never forget the sight of her housemate, Polly, dead, her blood covering the walls of the passage and staining the carpet beneath her.

The discovery of her housemate's body was why she had slept at her grandmother's.

With an effort, she pushed aside her recollections, she had a job to do and she wasn't going to get it done by standing in the doorway.

She entered the house and, being careful not to step in the patch of carpet stained by Polly's blood, crossed to the stairs so she could head up to her bedroom. She felt uncomfortable in the house for the first time, and she hurried to strip off her stained uniform, have a wash, and then dress in a clean uniform so she could leave.

On her way out of the house she downed two of the painkillers she had grabbed while in the bathroom. She hoped they would take effect soon because just breathing was painful.

ONLY WHEN SHE PULLED up at the vet's did it occur to Melissa that she didn't need to be there. She was not the only police officer left in Oakhurst, there was Constable Johnson. If she had thought to change the phone at the station so it diverted to her colleague, who was uninjured, she would not have got the call and would still be asleep.

She thought briefly of calling Adrian, so he could take over from her, but that seemed pointless. In the time it would take for him to get there she could probably deal with whatever the problem was, even taking her injuries into account.

It had been overcast when she woke, but the clouds were clearing as Melissa got out of her car. It wasn't going to be a perfect day, the weather on the radio had indicated more rain was due; nonetheless it was almost certain that today was going to be better than yesterday. It was hard to imagine how it could be as bad.

Pushing aside thoughts of the weather, Melissa made for the door to the surgery, which opened just before she reached it.

"Morning, Harry," she said tiredly.

"Morning, Melissa," Harry returned the greeting, sounding far more awake than the constable. "Things aren't quite as Kate told you when she called," he said, stepping aside so Melissa could enter. "Our early morning visitor wasn't after the surgery's drugs, they didn't even break into the surgery."

"So, what did they want?" Melissa asked, looking around. She could see no sign of damage or a break-in.

"My car, apparently," Harry said. "Whoever it was, they did a number on my car. They beat the hell out of it with an iron bar. They smashed all the windows, slashed the tyres and sprayed graffiti on it."

"I take it that's the iron bar they used," Melissa said when they reached the kitchen and she saw the bar on the table.

Harry nodded. "I found it after they ran off. They must have dropped it when I chased them."

Not at all sure what she was doing, Melissa carefully picked the bar up, so she could examine it. "Nothing special about it is there," she observed. "Unless they can get some fingerprints off it in town, I don't think it's going to be much use in helping me find the person who messed up your car. I don't suppose by some miracle you have any idea who might be responsible."

"No," Harry said with an unhappy shake of his head. "I wish I did. I can't even give you a very good description of them; they were covered in one of those hooded jumper things."

"Whatever you can give me will help," Melissa told him. Setting the iron bar back on the table, she took a seat and pulled out her notepad and pen.

Harry didn't say anything straight away, instead he pulled out a chair and settled himself across the table from Melissa. "There was only one of them," he began, "and they were short, no more than five-three I'd say. They had a slight build as well. From their size they could have been a kid, but I can't imagine a kid doing the kind of damage they did to my car."

"You'd be surprised what kids will do now," Melissa remarked. "Can you tell me anything else about them? Maybe what were they wearing?"

Harry had to think for a moment before answering. "Tracksuit trousers, dark ones, grey I think, and a hooded pullover, like I told you; that was dark as well, blue or maybe black. Oh, and they have a limp."

"A limp?"

"Yes, their right leg. They caught their foot in that pothole outside and stumbled. They must have twisted their ankle or something because after that they were limping." Harry shook his head. "Even with a limp they were too quick for me to catch."

"I wouldn't beat yourself up too much about that. If they were willing to take an iron bar to your car, who knows what they'd have been willing to do to you if you had caught up to them." The vet wasn't an old man, but neither was he young, and Melissa didn't like to think of what could have happened to him, especially after all the violence she had witnessed and endured recently. "Can you think of anything else?"

"No, nothing comes to mind."

"In that case I'd better take a look at the damage." Melissa put away her notepad and got to her feet, so she could follow the vet as he led the way outside and round to the side of the house, where his car was.

"Bloody hell." The profanity escaped her the moment she saw the car. "Whoever it was, they really did a number on it, didn't they," she remarked as she slowly circled the vehicle, taking in the damage, which was on a par with that done to the vehicles at the Jameson Stables. She wondered if there was a connection between the two events, and when she saw the red lettering that stood out against the beige paint of the car she realised it was a strong possibility. "Can you think of any reason why someone would want to write that? Has anyone called you a murderer recently."

She had known Harry Benson for a long time and wouldn't previously have thought him capable of anything more serious than the occasional curse. Recent events, though, had made her realise how wrong she could be about someone, no matter how long she had known them.

"No," Harry said with a shake of his head. "I don't think I've ever been called a murderer in my life, and I can't think why anyone would want to call me one now."

"Do you have anything to do with the Jameson Stables?"

"Of course," Harry said. "I handle all the veterinary needs of the stables, either myself or John. One or other of us is out there at least once a fortnight, why?" He couldn't keep how perplexed he was from his voice.

"You've heard what was done to the stables' vehicles? Well the damage to your car is pretty similar to what was done to them, even down to the red paint used to graffiti it," Melissa told him. "Can you think why someone would target both you and the Hewitts?"

"No, I can't think why anyone would call the Hewitts murderers, any more than why they would call me one."

"In the case of the stables the vehicles were spray-painted with the word 'liar'. Are you sure you can't think why someone would want to call one or both of the Hewitts liars, and you a murderer?"

Harry shook his head. "I'm afraid not. I'm sure whoever has done it has a good reason, but I can't imagine what that might be. I hope you find them soon, before anyone else has their car damaged and defaced."

Melissa looked at the vet for several long moments, not sure how he could be so calm when he had already told her he was annoyed enough at the time to give chase to the vandal. Finally, she gave up trying to figure it out. He had always been one of the most good-natured and kindly people in the village. Combined with his concern for animals, that had resulted in him being given the nickname 'St Francis of Oakhurst'.

"I certainly intend catching them, whoever they are, before they can damage any more vehicles," Melissa said determinedly, though privately she had to admit that she didn't have the first clue how she was going to manage it, since she had no idea who was responsible. One of the suspects she had been given for the vandalism at the stables had turned out to have a cast-iron alibi, while the other was still being investigated, as far as she knew, but she couldn't imagine why the sacked security guard would have a problem with the vet.

Thinking of Marius Kowalski, her suspect with an alibi, reminded her that she needed to speak to Catherine Hewitt. She didn't know if she could charge Catherine with anything if she was the one who had called Thomas Greene with the details of his wife's affair, but she could at least make her aware of the result of her phone call and warn her against doing anything similar in the future.

"I'm going to have to come back in a bit," she said, turning away from the car. "When I've had a chance to collect the camera from the station, so I can take pictures of the damage. I'll also need to take a statement from you at some point."

As she stepped away from the vehicle, Melissa felt her foot connect with something, something which skittered away with a metallic scraping sound. Looking down she saw that she had kicked a can of spray paint, which she hadn't noticed while circling the car. She hurriedly darted forward to stop the can with a foot before it could disappear under the bush it was heading towards.

"Have you got a plastic bag in the house, or perhaps in the surgery?" she asked, bending to get a closer look at the can, though she was careful not to touch it and disturb any fingerprints that might be on it.

"I'll have a look. I'm sure there must be something suitable around."

"Thanks."

3

Z ack struggled to sit up straighter when he saw Melissa in the doorway of his hospital room. It was a difficult and painful manoeuvre for him, even with help from Sophie; the injuries he had received last night, combined with those he was still recovering from following the attempts on his life, made every movement a source of pain.

"Morning," he said as Melissa moved into the room. "I didn't expect to see you this morning. To be honest, I didn't even know for sure that you were alive."

Hearing that, Melissa glanced over at Sophie, a questioning look on her face.

"He hasn't long woken, I haven't had a chance to tell him what happened after he lost consciousness. I don't even know most of it myself," Sophie admitted. The first she had known that there was anything wrong last evening was when she tried calling Zack to find out how much longer he was going to be. His failure to answer the phone had told her that something was wrong, but not what; she had only learned that when the hospital called her as Zack's next of kin.

"I'm not sure I do either," Melissa said as she grabbed the empty chair in the corner of the room and moved it closer to the bed. "So much happened yesterday, it's hard to believe it all happened in such a short time."

"Tell me about it. It always seems to me as if nothing happens for ages," Zack remarked, "and then it all does at once. Anyway, since I'm sure you know more about what happened yesterday than either Sophie or me, why don't you fill us in."

"Sure." Melissa fidgeted on the seat until she got herself comfortable. "I hope you don't mind if I just give you the highlights, though, I can't stay long."

Zack nodded.

It didn't take Melissa long to bring Zack up to date on what had happened that he didn't know about. She had no sooner finished when her phone rang, forestalling Zack, whom she could see was about to say or ask something.

"Constable Turner," she answered the call, hoping it didn't signal more trouble back in Oakhurst. She doubted it. Before coming to town, she had switched the station's phone system so that any calls would be diverted to Constable Johnson and not to her. If any fresh trouble had occurred, she shouldn't be getting called about it. "How can I help?"

"Constable, this is Doctor Monroe, I'm trying to reach Inspector Harrison, is he there?"

It was a moment before Melissa recognised the name of the doctor who was looking after Emily Wright. "I'm afraid he isn't," She told him, uttering a silent prayer that the worst hadn't happened, and that Kieran hadn't claimed one more victim after his death.

"Do you know where he is?" Doctor Monroe asked. "I've tried calling both he and Sergeant Mitchell, but I haven't been able to reach either of them."

Melissa was silent for a moment. "Sergeant Mitchell is dead, he was killed yesterday morning, and Inspector Harrison is in hospital. Is there something I can help you with?"

"I'm sorry to hear that." Surprise filled the doctor's voice. "I assume you know who is now in charge of the case, so perhaps you could tell them that Emily Wright has woken. She wants to speak to Sergeant Mitchell, though clearly that isn't possible, so whoever is in charge will perhaps do. She says she has important information.

"I don't think it wise for her to exert herself, but she is insistent."

"I think I know what she wants to say," Melissa said. "If she's insisting, though, it might do her good to get it off her chest. I'm already in the hospital, visiting a friend, so I'll come up and see her. If what she needs to say is something the inspector needs to know, then I'll get her over here to speak to her." She finished the call as quickly as she could without being rude. "I'll be back as soon as I can," she told Zack and Sophie. "Emily's woken, she wants to speak to an officer."

"I'm pleased to hear it," Zack said, genuinely relieved that the teen had woken.

WHEN SHE REACHED THE ITU room where Emily had lain in a coma since being discovered, Melissa saw that the teen's eyes were closed. Her immediate thought was that Emily had fallen back into her coma, and she had missed her chance to talk to her. Emily's eyes popped open as she moved further into the room, though.

"Hi, Melissa," Emily greeted her weakly.

"Emily," Melissa returned the greeting. "How are you feeling?"

"Crap, like I must look. Where's Sergeant Mitchell?" Emily asked. "I need to tell him, I know who attacked me and killed Georgina and Rose."

"The sergeant isn't around," Melissa told her, wishing she had someone more senior with her. "A lot's happened since you were attacked, there's an inspector in charge of the case now. I'm sure she'll be in just as soon as I have a chance to let her know you're awake." A look from the doctor who was hovering at the side of Emily's bed warned her not to say too much just then. Since the doctor didn't know everything that had happened, she assumed it was because Emily hadn't long woken and shouldn't be overtaxed. "Don't worry, we know who is responsible for the attacks."

"You do?" Emily's voice rose in surprise and she tried to sit up, only to be stopped by the doctor's hand on her shoulder. "How did you find out it was Kieran? Have you caught him? Has he hurt anyone else?" The questions tumbled from her lips, dying off as her voice cracked.

Despite the situation, Melissa couldn't help smiling at the teen's earnest eagerness for news. "I don't think now is the time to tell you everything that's happened since you were attacked," she said, mindful of the cautionary look on the doctor's face. "You haven't long woken, and I'm sure it would be better for you to rest than to worry about what's been happening while you were out of it. All you need to know right now is that we know it's Kieran and he's been stopped. Everything else can wait until you're better."

Reluctantly, and only after a look at the doctor, Emily nodded her agreement. "Will my family be coming in to see me?"

"I'm sure they'll be in when they can," Melissa said evasively after a brief hesitation. "In the meantime, I need to get back to work, I've got a vandal to catch." She saw that Emily was going to say something else, probably ask a question about her injuries based on the way the teen's eyes lingered on them, but Melissa left quickly to avoid having to come up with an answer that wouldn't sound like an evasion.

ZACK SEARCHED MELISSA'S face for some clue to how she had found Emily when she returned to his room.

"You'll be pleased to hear that Emily seems as though she's going to be alright," Melissa said. "It's probably going to be a while before she's fully recovered, but she was making sense, which is a good sign."

"That's good to hear. After all the tragedies, it's good to know something positive has happened."

Melissa nodded. "Definitely. I'm sure Tara will be relieved to hear that her sister is going to be alright, I'll bring her in later. I don't fancy being the one to tell Emily what's happened, but I suppose I'd better at some point, before Tara blurts it out by accident."

"That would probably be for the best," Zack said. "If she isn't told gently, it could be too much of a shock for her to handle."

"Before I leave again — I only popped back to let you know the situation with Emily — I'd like a little advice, if you don't mind."

"No problem, what's up?"

"I told you about the vandalism at the Jameson Stables, didn't I? Their vehicles were smashed up and had the word 'liar' spray-painted on them." Zack nodded. "Well there's been a second incident, this time at the vet's. Harry Benson's car was smashed up first thing this morning; this time, though, the word sprayed on it was 'murderer'. I'm at a loss," Melissa admitted. "The two incidents are obviously the work of the same person, they're too similar not to be, but I've got no idea who could be responsible, or why. Harry chased the person who smashed up his car, but couldn't catch them, and he was only able to give me a rough, and pretty useless, description."

"The graffiti has to be your clue to the vandal," Zack said after a few moments of thought. "Whoever is responsible, they clearly consider one or both of the Hewitts a liar, and Mr Benson a murderer."

"I know Marius Kowalski, the stable-hand who was sacked by the stables, thinks Catherine Hewitt is a liar. I haven't had anything to do with the studio or its owners in a long time, so I couldn't say what sort of people they are. Harry Benson, though, I've known him pretty much my whole life, and I can't imagine for one second that he could kill anyone, no matter what provocation he was given."

"Everyone is capable of murder, it's just a matter of finding the right trigger; recent events should have shown you that. That said, for the purposes of your investigation, it doesn't really matter if he is capable of murder, only that someone thinks him capable. And that someone obviously believes that the Hewitts are involved with whatever murder they think has been committed.

"I take it Mr Benson looks after the horses at the stables."

Melissa nodded. "He doesn't have a clue why he and the Hewitts have been targeted, though. His relationship with the stables, apparently, is no different to his relationship with the farms in the area."

"Has he had cause to put down any of the horses at the stables recently?"

"No idea."

"I'd ask if I were you. People get very emotional when it comes to animals, sometimes more so than when it comes to people," Zack explained. "If one of the horses at the stables has been put down recently then someone may have been upset by it, and they may well blame the Hewitts and Mr Benson for it. Mr Benson being the one bearing the brunt of the blame because he was the one who actually put the horse down."

"You think that could be the reason for the vandalism?" Melissa asked.

Zack shrugged, something he immediately regretted doing. "It's a theory, nothing more. If there is any more vandalism in the village, you'll know it was most likely wrong. It's somewhere for you to start, though."

Once she had all the advice Zack could give her, Melissa took her leave. As keen as she was to get on and solve the vandalism, she couldn't help wondering if she was going to be allowed to. She didn't know the exact procedure following such an event, but she was sure there was going to be an investigation into the death of Kieran Wright, and it was possible that while the investigation went on she would be suspended.

"YOU NEVER TOLD ME," Zack said after Melissa had left, "what you did with Tara."

"It's okay, she's alright, perfectly safe," Sophie told him. "When the hospital called to tell me where you were, I asked Melissa's grandmother to look after her until I got back, once I got over the shock of hearing that you were back in hospital that is. If I'd known becoming your emergency contact was going to involve so much work, I'd never have agreed to it." She grinned when Zack poked his tongue out at her.

"I hope her aunt calls soon," Zack said. "The situation was far from ideal before last night, now it's pretty well screwed up."

"That's one way of putting it," Sophie said with a short, humourless laugh. "Saying that, I'd better get back to your place. Thanks to you being in here I've got to babysit Tara, wait for her aunt to call, deal with the window people who are supposed to be coming today, and god knows what else."

4

The moment she returned to Oakhurst Melissa went to the vets, where she was almost knocked off her feet the moment she opened the door.

Her stomach muscles protested loudly as she grabbed at the door to keep from being mown down by the large dog that made a break for fresh air. The sudden burst of pain reminded her how long it had been since she took any painkillers, and she couldn't help wishing that she had some on her to take the edge off her stomach's complaints.

"Sorry about that," Mrs Underhill apologised as she struggled to get her pet under control. "He's always the same when I bring him here. I don't know why, but Bruiser's terrified of the vet."

"That's okay. Calm down, Bruiser." She attempted to settle the excited Labrador and untangle herself from his lead, which had become wrapped around her leg.

"Bruiser, behave," Mrs Underhill said sharply, reaching out to smack her dog smartly on the nose. He subsided immediately, as he had been trained to do.

Melissa was relieved when she finally got herself free and was able to make it to the reception desk. "Hi, Kate, is Harry in?" she asked.

"Hello, Melissa," Kate Benson greeted her with a smile. "Sorry for overreacting this morning, blame Harry for waking me up like that."

"That's okay," Melissa reassured her. "Is he in? I need to ask him a few questions about this morning's vandalism."

"He's with a patient at the moment, I'll buzz through and let him know you're here."

"Kate said you have some questions for me about this morning," Harry said when he finished with his latest patient, a brightly coloured Macaw, and Melissa entered his surgery.

"Yes. I want to know if you've put down any horses from the Jameson Stables recently."

"No. Do you think that's what the vandalism is about, a horse from the stables?"

"It might be. Are you sure you haven't had to put down any of the stables' horses recently?"

"Positive. I can't speak for John, though."

"What do you mean?"

"I mean John might have had to put one down. If he did, he didn't tell me, but unless there were complications, I can't think why he would have."

"Is he around, I'd better ask him if you're not sure."

Harry grimaced. "He's on holiday. I can have Kate check his records if you like, but you'll probably get an answer quicker by asking the Hewitts."

"I'll do that, thanks."

"You're welcome. Out of curiosity, why do you think a destroyed horse might have something to do with my car being vandalised?" Harry couldn't see the connection.

"It's just a theory, but I'm wondering if someone might be upset about one of the horses from the stables being put down. You haven't put any down, but if John has then your car might have been the unfortunate victim of their anger." Melissa thought it best not to mention that the idea wasn't hers. "As I said, it's only a theory. It might turn out that I'm completely wrong."

MELISSA KNOCKED FOR a second time, and then moved to peer through the window in the office of the Jameson Stables.

"They're not in there."

Melissa spun round and found herself looking at a young man of about eighteen. She guessed from his appearance that he was one of the stable-hands. "Do you know where they are?"

"Yeah. Catherine's giving a lesson down at the South paddock, and Mr Hewitt is at the stables. Would you like me to show you the way?"

"Please." She didn't really need a guide, she had been there before, and she could see the stables from where she was, but Melissa figured the stable-hand would follow her anyway, so she might as well have him with her.

A few of the horses in the stables poked their heads curiously over the doors of their stalls as the pair passed. Melissa paid them little attention, though, for she was focused on finding Miles Hewitt, whom she could see no sign of. It wasn't until she was led through the doors at the far end of the stables that she found him; he was in the yard outside examining a horse.

"Mr Hewitt," the stable-hand called out. "You've got a visitor."

Miles Hewitt glanced up briefly, and then returned his attention to the horse. "She's a beautiful animal, isn't she," he said. "We've moving into training racehorses, and this is our first." He turned away from the horse then and focused on

Melissa. "So, constable, have you got any news on the vandal who messed up our vehicles?"

"I'm afraid not, though I do have a possible lead," Melissa said. "Have you had to have any horses put down recently?"

Bemused by the question, it was a few moments before Hewitt responded. "Yes, I have," he said finally. "I had to have a mare, Meadow, put down last week. I don't see what that could have to do with the vandalism, though."

"It's just a theory," Melissa told him. "Has anyone been overly upset about the horse being put down? Maybe they've said or done something that might suggest they blame you and are angry enough to vandalise your vehicles and Harry Benson's car in revenge?"

"Harry Benson's car?" Hewitt's bewilderment increased. "What are you talking about? Harry's car wasn't attacked, it was only the stables' vehicles."

"Yesterday it was the stables' vehicles," Melissa said. "Harry Benson got paid a visit first thing this morning. His car was smashed up, and 'murderer' spray-painted over it. The theory I'm working on is that someone is upset about one of your horses being put down — you've just confirmed that that happened — and has decided to take it out on the stables and on Harry."

"But Harry had nothing to do with the mare that was put down, it was John Daws that dealt with her."

"John doesn't live at the vet's, though, and whoever is responsible for the vandalism might not realise that it wasn't Harry who destroyed the horse. It could simply be a case of Harry's car suffering because it was the only one at the surgery when the vandal went there. I found a can of spray paint and an iron bar at Harry's this morning, they're being checked by the lab in town, so they might be able to tell me something, but if you know of anyone who might be upset over the death of the mare, it could save some time."

"There's Sam Glover."

The answer came not from Miles Hewitt but from the stable-hand who had led her there, and Melissa turned quickly towards him. "Sam Glover? Who's he, and why would he be so pissed off over the death of a horse?"

"Not he, she," the stable-hand corrected her. "Sam's a she, she rides here."

"Was Meadow her horse?"

"Not officially," Hewitt took over. "She didn't own Meadow, but she had been riding her for the past year. Meadow was ill, and Sam had to give up riding her, but she still came over every day to look after her, until last week that is. I don't know where Sam's been, if she's just given up, but I haven't seen her around here for over a week now. Unfortunately, Meadow took a turn for the worse, and the decision was made to put her down."

"What happened after that?" Melissa asked.

"Nothing as far as I'm aware. I couldn't even tell you if Sam is aware that Meadow was put down."

"She knows," Robbie, the stable-hand, put in.

Melissa turned her attention back to him. "You're sure about that?"

Robbie nodded. "She was here the other day. I think she's been on holiday or something, that's why she hasn't been around, but she was here the other day, that's when she found out about Meadow. I know because she got pretty angry about it. I was out here, and I could hear her at the far end of the stables. She called Mr Hewitt a liar, said he'd told her Meadow was going to be alright."

"Why didn't you tell me about this yourself, Mr Hewitt?" Melissa asked.

Hewitt looked from Melissa to his stable-hand, his expression blank. "This is the first I'm hearing about it. If I had known about this I would, of course, have told you. As I said, I haven't seen Sam Glover in over a week. To the best of my knowledge she hadn't been here in that time."

"So, this Sam Glover is upset about the death of a horse here at the stables, and has been heard to call you a liar, Mr Hewitt. It follows that she would also be upset with Harry Benson, or at least with the vet surgery, over the destruction of the horse. She definitely sounds like someone I should be speaking to. Do you know where I can find her?"

"Her address should be in the records," Hewitt said, "it shouldn't take long to find."

5

After leaving the stables, Melissa decided to pick up Johnson before going to speak to Sam Glover about the vandalism. Given the damage that had been done to the studios' vehicles, and to Harry Benson's car, she thought it best to have support, just in case the teen was the vandal, and she wasn't prepared to simply give herself up. First, though, she had a detour to make.

"Hi, gran," she said when the door opened. "How's things?"

"Everything is okay here," Constance told her granddaughter. "How are you? You went out very early this morning, is everything alright?" Stepping back, she made room for Melissa to enter and then closed the door behind her.

"Somebody smashed up Harry Benson's car and I had to go and check it out. It looks like the same person who smashed up the vehicles at the Jameson Stables."

"Why couldn't Adrian, or someone from town, have dealt with it?" Constance asked as the two of them entered the living room. "After last night you deserve some time off. Besides, you're injured, you shouldn't really be out of bed, let alone working."

"I forgot to change the phone at work," Melissa said. "So I got the call. I guess I could have called Adrian and had him go out to Harry's, but I didn't think about it until I was there, and, anyway, I was the one who dealt with the vandalism at the stables yesterday. With a bit of luck, I'll be finished with this case soon, then I can take some time off and rest." She looked forward to doing that with an eagerness she hadn't felt for anything in a while. "Hi, Tara," she said to the young girl on the sofa.

"Hi," Tara returned the greeting, her voice hollow, without looking up from Zack Wild's laptop, which continued to distract her from recent events. It was needed now even more than it had been yesterday. Kieran might have tried to kill her, on top of being a rapist and a serial killer, but he was still her brother, and she was sad that he was dead. "How's Zack? Is he okay? Sophie said she was going to call and let me know, but she hasn't."

"She's probably forgotten. Zack's okay, or as okay as he can be under the circumstances. He'll be fine," Melissa reassured Tara. "It might be a while before he's out of the hospital, but he'll make a full recovery. There's someone else who will make a recovery, your sister." She saw the surprise and relief on Tara's face and went on quickly. "It's going to be a while before she's out of hospital as well, but she woke up this morning and was speaking, so she should be okay, in time.

"I'll take you in to see her later, if you want, I'm sure she'd like that."

"Okay, thanks." Tara brightened briefly, but almost immediately sank back into the gloom that surrounded her. "Is dad going to be home soon?"

Melissa wasn't sure how to respond to that. "I don't know," she admitted after a few moments. "As far as I know he is still being kept on remand, but I'll make some calls and see what I can find out. Have you heard from your aunt yet?" she asked, changing the subject.

"Yes," Hazel said. "She called an hour ago, after getting in touch through Facebook."

"What did she say? What did you tell her?" Melissa asked of her mum.

"I told her everything," Hazel said. "I thought it best that she knows the full situation. I didn't think it would help to conceal anything."

"Is she coming over?"

Hazel nodded. "She said she would be here as soon as she could but couldn't say when that would be because she had to make some arrangements."

"Will I have to go and live with her and Uncle Henry in Canada?" Tara asked, looking up from the laptop for the first time. Her expression gave no hint as to whether that possibility was something she was okay with or not.

"I don't know, it's something your aunt and your father will have to discuss. It may even be that social services has a say in the matter. I just don't know what the procedure is in a situation like this. How would you feel if you do have to go to Canada with your aunt?"

"I don't know." Tara shrugged.

Melissa chatted with her family, and with Tara, for a little longer and then said goodbye so she could get on with, hopefully, finishing up the vandalism case.

6

With Johnson a step behind her, Melissa walked up the path to the front door of the address she had been given for Sam Glover. She rang the bell the moment she got to the door, and then stepped back to look around for any sign that someone was home. There was a car in the drive and she took that as a good sign.

"Hi, is something the matter?" The man who answered the door looked worried by the presence of two uniformed police officers on his doorstep.

"Mr Glover?" Melissa asked.

"Yes. Can I help you?"

"Hello, Mr Glover, I'm Constable Turner, and this is Constable Johnson, we'd like to speak to your daughter, Samantha, is she home?"

Looking even more worried, Mr Glover nodded. "What do you want to talk to her about? Has something happened, is she in trouble?" Before either officer could respond he turned away from the door and called out. "Sam."

"What?" A return shout came from upstairs.

"Get down here."

"Why?"

"There's someone here to see you," Vernon Glover shouted up to his daughter.

"Who?" Footsteps signalled the approach of the teen.

"Get down here and you'll find out."

Both Melissa and Adrian heard the teen's sigh of frustration over the sound of her footsteps as she descended the stairs. The footsteps stopped when the teen was halfway down the stairs, the point at which she could see the two police officers waiting for her by the front door. She turned, as if to hurry back up the stairs, but then stopped and slowly continued her descent.

"You're here to arrest me, aren't you," she said when she reached the foot of the stairs.

"What would we arrest you for, Miss Glover?" Johnson asked.

"What's going on?" Vernon Glover wanted to know, looking in concern from his daughter to the constable.

"For smashing up Mr Benson's car, and the cars at the stables," Sam said, her gaze fixed on the floor at the feet of the two constables, though a couple of times her eyes flickered to her father, who was too stunned by his daughter's admission to say anything.

"I think we should go into the living room and talk," Melissa said.

Vernon Glover led the way into the living room, though he didn't sit, instead he paced up and down. "What the hell is going on? What have you done?" he demanded, stopping in front of his daughter and fixing her with an angry stare when she sat on the sofa.

"I...I." Sam's voice faltered in the face of her father's obvious anger.

"You said you smashed up Mr Benson's car, whoever he is, and the cars at the stables," Glover said. "Is that true?"

Sam nodded glumly, keeping her eyes averted from her father.

"Why?"

Since she wanted to know as well, Melissa had no problem letting Mr Glover question his daughter.

It was several long moments before Sam could bring herself to answer her father's question. "They...they killed Meadow," she said finally, the words coming with difficulty.

"Meadow?" Glover looked bewildered. "That horse you're always talking about?"

For a second time, Sam nodded. "They told me she was going to be alright. They promised," she said angrily. "But the moment I couldn't go to the stables to look after her they killed her."

"So you vandalised their vehicles?" her father asked.

"They deserved it," Sam said angrily. "They lied to me, and they killed Meadow."

"Except it wasn't Harry Benson who put Meadow down," Melissa said.

"What?" Sam looked round her father at the constable.

"It wasn't Harry Benson who put Meadow down, it was John Daws, so you vandalised the wrong car this morning. As I understand it, there was some hope that Meadow would recover from her illness, unfortunately, she took a turn for the worse last week. An effort was apparently made to let you know the situation, but they weren't able to get hold of you."

"We were away on holiday last week, abroad," Glover said.

"That's unfortunate," Melissa remarked. "As I said, they tried to get hold of you, but when they couldn't, and it became clear that Meadow wasn't going to recover, Mr Hewitt and Mr Daws agreed that putting her down was the kindest thing they could do."

A tear glistened in the corner of Sam's eyes. "What's going to happen to me?"

"You should have thought of that before you decided to go off and vandalise people's vehicles," her father told her harshly. "It's bad enough that you decided to do something so foolish, but to do it over a horse." His disgust was evident in both his face and his voice. "So, what is going to happen to her?"

"That's a little uncertain at the moment, Mr Glover," Melissa said. "Sam will have to accompany us to the station, so we can take her statement and she can be bailed, you'll have to come with us for that, but beyond that it will depend on the Hewitts and Mr Benson. I've known Harry Benson a long time, and I think he can be persuaded to let you off with a caution in exchange for community service, and perhaps paying for the repairs to his car. I can't speak for what the Hewitts will do, however. I'll do my best to persuade them to take a reasonable line, under the circumstances, but I can't guarantee anything."

Melissa was relieved when both Sam and Vernon Glover agreed to come to the station without any problems. It meant a bit more work for her, taking Sam Glover's statement and arranging for her to be bailed, which might even require a trip to Branton, but at least she would soon be able to take a break and begin the process of recuperating from her injuries.

She couldn't remember the last time she had looked forward to a period of time off with such eagerness.

Don't miss out!

Visit the website below and you can sign up to receive emails whenever Alex R Carver publishes a new book. There's no charge and no obligation.

https://books2read.com/r/B-A-BNVD-NQGU

BOOKS 2 READ

Connecting independent readers to independent writers.

Did you love *The Oakhurst Murders Duology*? Then you should read *Inspector Stone Mysteries Volume 1 (Books 1-3)* by Alex R Carver!

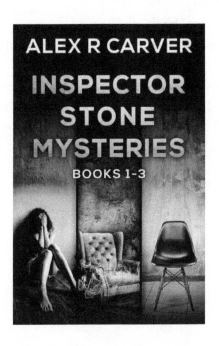

Volume 1 of the Inspector Stone Mysteries, containing books 1-3

Where There's a Will (Book 1)

The kidnapping of a child on the way home from school is every parents worst nightmare, for the Keatings it's no nightmare, it's a reality.

A reality made worse when it is suspected the Russian Mafia is behind the kidnapping to force Owen Keating to sell his business.

Are the rumours true, or is there something else going on?

An Eye For An Eye (Book 2)

A sudden surge in murders across Branton leaves Nathan Stone wondering if the town has gone made, or if they could all be the work of one man. If so who is it, and why is he killing such a diverse group of people.

A Perfect Pose (Book 3)

The murder of a teen model draws Nathan Stone back to work after the tragic events of An Eye For An Eye.

When rumours surface of abuse at the studio where Ellen Powers worked, Nathan must investigate whether that is why she was murdered, or if her death is connected to her pregnancy.

Read more at https://alexrcarver.wordpress.com/.

Also by Alex R Carver

Cas Dragunov
An Unwanted Inheritance

Inspector Stone Mysteries
Where There's a Will
An Eye For An Eye
A Perfect Pose
Into The Fire
A Stone's Throw

The Oakhurst Murders
Written In Blood
Poetic Justice

Standalone
Exposed
Inspector Stone Mysteries Volume 1 (Books 1-3)
The Oakhurst Murders Duology

Watch for more at https://alexrcarver.wordpress.com/.

About the Author

After working in the clerical, warehouse and retail industries over the years, without gaining much satisfaction, Alex quit to follow his dream and become a full-time writer. Where There's A Will is the first book in the Inspector Stone Mysteries series, with more books in the series to come, as well as titles in other genres in the pipeline. His dream is to one day earn enough to travel, with a return to Egypt to visit the parts he missed before, and Macchu Picchu, top of his wishlist of destinations. When not writing, he is either playing a game or being distracted by Molly the Yorkie, who is greedy for both attention and whatever food is to be found.

You can find out more about Alex R Carver at the following links

https://twitter.com/arcarver87
https://alexrcarver.wordpress.com/
https://medium.com/@arcarver87

https://www.facebook.com/
Alex-R-Carver-1794038897591918/
Read more at https://alexrcarver.wordpress.com/.

CPSIA information can be obtained
at www.ICGtesting.com
Printed in the USA
BVHW071611200120
569971BV00004B/679